The Eighth Scroll

DR. LAURENCE B. BROWN

THE EIGHTH SCROLL

2007

The Eighth Scroll

Throughout the history of humankind,
There have always been kings.
But there has only ever been *one* King of kings,
And this book is dedicated to Him.

PROLOGUE

Qumran, on the Dead Sea, 68 CE

When death approaches, your life will play before your eyes. The elder who told Jacob this, years before, now lay crumpled in a bloody heap before him, nestled in ringlets of his own intestines and oozing the stink of disembowelment. Jacob tore his gaze from the twitching corpse, locked eyes with the Roman legionnaire who lifted his weapon from the lifeless body, and froze when the legionnaire raised his gore-streaked sword for the stroke that would sever Jacob's neck.

As though with a mind already detached, as though time itself paused to honor him with one last memory, Jacob recalled not his whole life, but only the last hour: He had been hunched over in the bowl of his cave, working frantically to hide the Essenes' library of scrolls.

One glance out the mouth of the cave at the darkening sky, mirrored in the vast expanse of the Dead Sea below, told him he had run out of time. *Why did I ever join the sect of Essene Jews? If they knew my Christian beliefs, they would banish me forever.* The instant he conceived the thought, his mind conjured up memories of slashing swords, screams, and bodies tumbling to the dust in pieces. "That's why I joined," he said to himself. "For protection." For a moment he reflected how, thirty years ago, the Romans had hunted down the disciples of Jesus, the Christ. Now, two years into the Jewish Rebellion, the Romans hunted down *all* Jews, excepting his own sect of Essene Jews.

But every Essene knew their scant protection could end at any instant, and Jacob couldn't banish from his fears the tales of wild beasts tearing Christians to pieces in the Roman Coliseum, which Emperor Nero had kept lit at night with human candles.

"Martyrs," he muttered, but found little consolation in the word.

Jacob snatched up the most precious of all the scrolls. The parchment whispered against his fingers as he swiftly rolled it. Despite his reverence for this scripture, his hands shook and he splattered hot wax as he dripped it from his candle to seal the free edge of the scroll. He forced himself to draw deep breaths of the musty cave air until his hands steadied, and then stamped the puddles of fast-cooling wax with the Roman captain's signet ring. Then he applied a linen wrap and sealed the free edge of the wrap as well.

He shoved the scroll into an exquisite limestone jar, but then froze. Gently, he placed the jar on the floor of the cave, grabbed handfuls of his shoulder-length hair close to his scalp with both hands, and rocked himself until he felt his nerves still. "Calm down," he told himself. "Just calm down." Slower now, Jacob removed the scroll from the jar, checked it for damage, and gently slid it back into the jar. Then he fitted the lid with a sandy rasp, picked up his sputtering candle, and poured a ribbon of molten liquid into the seam. After he sealed the jar closed, but before the wax had a chance to cool, his Essene brothers arrived. Jacob jumped up and wrestled three earthenware jars, each half the height of a man and filled with scrolls, to the cave entrance. He stumbled in his haste and nearly dropped one jar. The rough pottery slipped in his fingers, but he caught it in time; it bumped the floor of the cave but didn't break. The brothers heaved the jars into their arms, cast Jacob a worried glance, and then hurried off to hide the jars in distant caves.

Jacob returned to the cubit-long limestone jar, sized for a single scroll, and applied the captain's ring to the cooling wax around the lid. Why *had* the captain ordered him to hide the scrolls? Jacob had heard the rumors, of course. Roman legionnaires with

Jewish sensitivities, or "Christian—Jewish" in everything but name. Romans who tormented the followers of Jesus, the Christ, by day, and then prayed for forgiveness to the God Jesus had spoken of at night. He had heard such men existed, but had never met one. Until the captain of the legionnaires.

Jacob buried the limestone jar in the mountain of parchment sheets stacked in the center of the cavern. He said a quick prayer, sweat streaming from beneath his arms as he raised his quivering hands to the heavens, and then bolted from the cave.

The barren Judean desert seemed drawn closer to the heavens by the crimson ceiling of sunset, but Jacob had no time to enjoy the view. With practiced speed he picked his way across the ridge of land that led to the complex, passing groups of legionnaires as they lounged on the terrace, their weapons ever near at hand. He feigned calm when he visited the captain in his quarters, but once he had returned the captain's signet ring he rushed toward the dining hall's welcoming glow and the voices of his milling brethren, his fears flailing about in his mind.

By the doorway and to the right, the captain had instructed.

Why? Jacob wondered, even as he entered the dining hall and sat as bidden.

That *why* haunted him during the conversation and dinner that followed. Midway through the meal, and fighting the quivering weakness in his legs, he made to stand when the doorway filled with the bulk of a legionnaire, his sword naked in his hand.

Like shadows in an unfocused nightmare, Jacob could barely make out the mass of forms behind the soldier. He cast a glance at the only other exit. It, too, was filled with a clot of legionnaires. He scanned the room to find his brothers frozen, their food and drink suspended midway to their mouths.

The Roman captain shouldered his way into the chamber and shouted, "Stay sitting!"

The words caught a few brothers as they rose, and they lowered back to their seats while the captain repeated his command, this time more gently, as if to reassure a child.

A child about to be slaughtered, Jacob realized.

The captain let his eyes rest on Jacob a split-second longer than on the others. Then he said, "I have been ordered to kill anyone here who refuses to swear loyalty to the Roman Empire."

So that's it. That's why the captain wanted the scrolls hidden.

"Until now your protector, Agrippa II, has never demanded an oath of allegiance," the captain continued. "That has changed. With the rebellion of your people, an oath is demanded."

"Our hands are empty and you know it," one of the Essenes said. "We have no weapons. How are we a threat to you?"

"My orders are absolute," the captain replied. "You swear allegiance, or die. Who is first?"

One of the brethren stood and strode toward the captain, a short, squat man of timid demeanor Jacob knew but slightly. The lead soldier stepped between the two and met the Essene's chest with the tip of his sword. Unshaken, the Essene said, "We swear devotion to One, and to One alone," and then looked past the soldier and locked eyes with the captain. "And the One to Whom we swear devotion is the One Who made us, and the One Who made *you*, and the One to Whom we shall *all* return."

Another step closer, and the Essene forced the soldier to retract his arm into a fully cocked position, resting its tip against the brother's chest.

"The same One Who will judge all of us, and assign the righteous to Paradise, and the sinful to hellfire," the brother continued. "To this One, The All-Mighty, we swear allegiance, and to Him alone."

For a moment, Jacob felt the brother's words fill the chamber and bolster the faith of the believers. But then the soldier drove his sword home.

The blade exploded a foot out the man's back. The soldier gave the sword a sharp quarter-turn, then wrenched it back out with a sucking sound and a gush of blood.

The squat man, bent forward by the blow, abruptly straightened and turned around to face his brothers. Triumph on his face, he pointed to the heavens.

The second thrust drove the sword in the man's back and out the front. He staggered forward and looked down, and blinked as he watched the blade retract through his chest. Then he dropped to his knees, coughed up a great gout of blood, fell sideways into the lap of a brother and died, a smile on his bloodied lips.

The captain stepped to the side, and Jacob watched as soldiers surged from the darkened doorway like emissaries from hell. The air filled with shouts of testimony from the faithful, grunts and curses from the soldiers, and the wet, *chunking* sound of metal meeting flesh. Swords swept in great arcs, blades plunged into bodies, and battle-axes cleaved the air and buried their blades in flesh and bone. An occasional groan escaped the dying, but never a scream or sob, and not one oath of allegiance to the Romans.

Jacob found himself on his hands and knees, sheltered between the wall and the legs of the captain. The soldiers were crazed, the chamber poorly lit, and the legionnaires flowed through the doorway, straight past him, with nary a glance backward. Jacob's favored elder fell to his knees nearly in front of him, groaning incoherently as he scrabbled to scoop up the guts that spilled from his slit-open belly. The Roman who stood over the elder beheaded him with a swipe of his sword, kicked the corpse to the floor, and then knelt beside it and hacked at the headless torso. Horrified, Jacob nestled closer to the wall.

The legionnaire pulled his sword from the elder's body, turned and latched eyes with Jacob. Standing, he lifted his blood-streaked sword and stepped into striking range.

When death approaches, your life will play before your eyes.

Jacob's mind snapped back when the captain whirled, jerked Jacob to his feet and pinned him against the cold stone wall, waving the solder away.

To Jacob, the captain whispered harshly, "Do you swear allegiance to the One True God, to The Almighty? Answer quick and answer loud."

"I—I swear allegiance!" Jacob shouted as his eyes danced across the insanity and gore, paralyzed by the ghastly vision.

The captain whispered, "Say it again, but louder. Do you swear allegiance to the One True God?"

Jacob jerked his eyes back to the captain's face, a grim, taut mask with eyes that betrayed only the barest twinkle. He gasped a breath in two quick stutters and yelled, "*I swear allegiance, I swear allegiance!*"

Soldiers turned from their kills and snickered, unaware of the props behind the play. The closest legionnaire lowered his sword, spat into the dirt floor and turned away in disgust.

"This one bears true allegiance!" the captain yelled to them. "Let no one harm him, for he is under my protection!" He turned back to Jacob and whispered, "Peace be with you, my friend. Pray for me." Then he swung Jacob around like a puppet and shoved him through the doorway.

Straight into the arms of a waiting legionnaire.

And at that moment, Jacob knew death. The certainty of it cast a blanket of calm over him and he closed his eyes in prayer.

"Hey, enough of that," the legionnaire said with a grim chuckle. "Look where that got your friends."

Jacob froze, disbelieving, but the legionnaire grabbed his arm and led him out of the complex. At first his legs faltered, but the legionnaire steadied him as though guiding a man feeble with fever. At the outer wall, the Roman belted something around his waist and whispered, "Food and currency." Jacob's fear-weakened legs nearly buckled when the legionnaire draped a full water-skin over his shoulders, but he straightened immediately when he felt a ring slipped onto his finger.

"Captain changed his mind," the soldier said. "He said you'll need this more than he. Now listen carefully. If anyone stops you, show him the ring. That will guarantee you safe passage. Next, use your water sparingly. It must last until you find safety. You can't go to Jerusalem. That would be suicide. So take the trade route opposite. And stay away from here until this is over. And Jacob? May God be with you."

Jacob swallowed hard with a throat sucked dry by fear. So it was true. There *were* friends, albeit the most hypocritical kind, in the ranks of the Romans.

But there was no time for talk, and the legionnaire gave him a push-start backward into the darkness and drew his sword. Jacob stood numbly and watched, helpless as a lamb before the slaughter, but the soldier only winked, turned, and disappeared back into the complex.

For a moment, Jacob stood rooted to the spot, but then the demons of his fears spun him around and chased him into the night.

* * *

Following the massacre, the legionnaires looted the complex, seeking the treasure of the Essenes. They found nothing, and so set their sights on the northern caves. The main body of soldiers arrived in darkness as the first of their ranks emerged from a cave with torch in one hand and sheets of parchment in the other.

"Nothing but skins wasted with writing," he shouted, then flung the documents back in the hole and spat after them.

"Bring them out and burn them!" a voice from the pack called.

"Don't waste your energy," the soldier replied. "Oy, your head's not made for anything but chipping ax blades."

With that, he drew back his arm and took aim for the opening with his torch. Before he could throw, a rock fell from above and exploded the torch in his hand, showering those nearby with flaming cinders. In the stunned silence that followed, a second rock fell and hammered the baked soil at the foot of the lone soldier. His comrades reflexively held their torches away from their bodies or dropped them, so as not to make a target. A few ran to the mountain face for cover, others scattered away.

But the lone soldier stood fast, head cocked to one side, illuminated by the ring of dropped torches. The splintered remnants of his own torch dangled in his hand. A frozen target in a circle of light, he appeared to be listening, or perhaps tempting the unseen enemy.

Nothing happened.

"A rockfall, that's all," one said from the darkness.

Cautiously, the legionnaires returned. They found the lone soldier's head was not cocked to one side, as they had supposed. Rather, his skull was crushed and his face was sheared off to the bone, streaming blood and gore.

Still standing, the corpse voided its bladder and bowels with a wet gurgle.

"The stew of death," one said darkly.

A light gust of wind nudged the standing corpse. It tilted first a degree, then two, then ten, and accelerated to land full and hard like a felled tree.

As the dust settled, three soldiers silently lined up in front of the cave to avenge the death of their comrade. As if on cue, all three whirled and drew back their torches to cast.

For the two on the sides, falling rocks exploded their skulls and took their heads off at their necks. The soldier in the middle spun from one horror to the other, then turned to run. A huge boulder, larger than a team of horses could pull, fell seemingly from nowhere and pounded him into the ground, leaving nothing but a bloody splatter and a single mangled arm protruding from beneath its massive bulk.

Those who escaped flew across the terrace as if chased by the vengeful ghosts of those they had killed. Those who sought the shelter of the mountain soon realized their mistake, for first one, then another, then six or seven shouted of the terror that beset them there. When they ran, they shook scorpions from their feet and ankles, and trailed serpents that flailed like ribbons in a high wind. They died as they ran, and dove to the ground as if to tackle their escaping souls.

Few of the soldiers ventured out of the complex after that, and none slept.

At first light, two skeptics sought their fortunes in the caves to the southwest, but never returned. Others approached the northern caves to verify what witnesses already knew. No rock had ever fallen with such explosive force, and no machine of war could have budged, much less heaved, such a monstrosity of a boulder.

Thus the caves were sealed, not by an avalanche but by the legend of a curse, the fear of which held generations at bay. And in time the caves were forgotten, in much the same way the mind rejects memories too fearful to hold.

* * *

Nineteen hundred years later, any memory or legend of what we now call the Dead Sea Scrolls had died with their keepers, the Essene Jews. Even those closest to the cliff dwellings, such as Ahmed, didn't know their history. A simple Bedouin child of nine years, Ahmed had survived both the Judean desert and World War II, which ended just the previous year. He knew no playground other than the dusty terrace at Qumran, no body of water other than the Dead Sea, no life other than of deprivation.

Yet he was, at this instant, learning of miracles.

The elderly she-goat's udder bobbled against his little fist while he milked jet after jet into his steel bowl, gasping with each squeeze of his fingers. Three times he filled his vessel, and three times he poured the warm milk down the neck of his *laban*-skin. Better acquainted with hunger pangs than the satisfaction of eating his fill, such abundance was beyond Ahmed's power to comprehend.

Just this morning, Father had told him to slaughter this goat, for meat that was sorely needed by their family. Yet Ahmed had tarried. Hours later, when the goat went missing, he knew he was in for a beating, for goats that old never return. Whether she wandered off to the seclusion animals seek when dying or was taken by predators as ravenous as his family, she was gone.

Yet at day's end, when a lone goat crossed the terrace with the springy step of youth and rejoined the flock, he recognized the aged, sun-bleached face. But she pranced on legs that barely held her the day before, with taut udders where withered bags had hung useless since the last full moon.

The days that followed were no less remarkable. Fresh milk and *laban*, the thin yogurt of the Bedouins, filled the family's stomachs as never in memory. Such was the abundance, the family considered it a duty to share. And so it was that bread was broken and *laban* poured with their fellow Bedouins for the first time since the end of the War.

The bounty and celebration lasted until the next half-moon, when the animal began to tire and her udders became dry as dust once more. Again, Ahmed's father commanded the goat's slaughter. And again Ahmed disobeyed, but this time not from laziness. The next day, when he watched the goat leave the flock and totter off toward the cliffs, gratitude compelled him to let her go. Thanks to her, he had slept more nights on a full stomach in one month than in the rest of his nine years combined.

With the close of day, however, the goat once again pranced into the flock, unbalanced by the weight of her distended udders. Ahmed laughed aloud in amazement. The cycle renewed, he protected his blessing closer than the rest of his flock altogether. When she began to decline again, a full month later, he watched her with the eyes of an eagle. The morning she departed the flock in the direction of the cliffs, he followed, determined to discover the source of her rejuvenation.

CHAPTER 1

Ocean City, Maryland

Three in the morning? Who the h——?

The phone rang again, and this time the harsh jangle grabbed his legs by the ankles and flung them over the side of the bed. Dr. Gerald Hansen lifted the bedside phone's receiver and held it over the cradle. The ring silenced, he was about to replace it when he remembered someone might actually be on the other end. He raised it to his ear and croaked, "Hello?"

"Greetings, old boy. How are things in your corner of the world?"

Frank Tones. Who else could be so rude?

"Asleep, Frank," he mumbled. "That's how things are. And if I had my way, I'd snooze through the rest of 1987."

"Smashing, smashing. Sooo, seen any good movies lately?"

"Uh, Frank, you never go to the movies. Matter of fact, you never go anywhere unless there's a dig. You on one now?" He raked the bedside table with splayed fingers to find his reading glasses. Wearing them made him think more clearly, and he needed that right now. Frank's surprise wake-up calls had a history of firing the afterburners on his own career.

"Right you are, old boy," Frank chirped. "I say, fancy a little jaunt, do you?"

Gerald yawned as he slid the glasses up his nose. "Hey, Frank, uh, any idea what time it is stateside, *old chap?*"

"Sure I do." Frank dropped the phony British accent. Both Harvard men, Frank constantly teased Gerald for having slipped the

Harvard chain and gone off to teach at Oxford. "Seven-hour difference? I figure that puts it at three AM your time. Why do'you ask?"

Sighing, Gerald scrubbed his scalp through his graying sleep-tufted hair, an old trick for keeping himself awake. "Oh, no real reason. Just wondering if this could've waited five hours."

"Ha, ha. No, not possible, old chum. That would put the kibosh on my high tea. Couldn't have that, now, could we dear boy? But I say, if you prefer to snatch a couple winks, we'll talk later. After I speak with Crawley, perhaps?"

Gerald laughed at the standing-but-empty threat. Crawley, while his staunchest academic enemy, was hated by nobody more than Frank Tones. "Sure, do that," he said. "Talk to Crawley. Yeah, help the guy out. I hear he's behind on his mortgage and Cindy's *still* nagging him for a bigger house."

"Music to my ears! I thank God for all the sorrow that insufferable twit took off my shoulders when he lifted *that* chick from my nest."

"But we hate him anyway, don't we?"

"You hold him down and I'll stomp on him." The accent disappeared again, but not Frank's ire. "But now I've got what I need to dropkick that chunky coprolite into oblivion. After this, he'll need a job as waiter to attend our award ceremonies."

Gerald conjured an image of Crawley's fat face sculpted from a chunky lump of fossilized feces. "*Now* I'm awake. So where are you, and what've you got?"

"Nubia, still sifting the sands of time, trying to pinpoint when Christianity bitch-slapped the Cult of Isis into oblivion. I'm on Rybkoski's dig, and I've found something *veeery* interesting."

Gerald stopped scratching and went silent. Nothing was "interesting" to know-it-all Frank. Nothing. He'd never seen Frank, an archaeological guru if ever there was one, impressed or otherwise caught off-guard by any find. His genius and raging ego simply didn't permit it.

Mind racing with thoughts of Rybkoski's dig/Nubia/ Christianity versus the Cult of Isis, he cleared his throat and asked, "Okay, Frank, what's up? Give."

"Oh, what, you interested? Gee, come to think of it, Gerry, it *is* early on your side of things. Tell you what … get your beauty rest, we'll talk later."

"We'll talk now, or I'll be on the first plane out there."

"Funny you mention that. I've already booked your flight. Oh, and Gerry … come on the QT. And I do mean quiet. Hush-hush, mum's the word, very red-ribbon, eyes only. And PS, I'm dead serious. Don't tell *anybody*."

Frank's sudden guarded tone forced the smile from Gerald's face. "You still haven't answered my question. What's up?"

"When I see you. For now, I'll just say there's more at stake than our careers."

Gerald paused to remember other digs he'd attended where things had gone wrong. "You're not, ah, putting us in harm's way, are you, Frank?"

"Ger, it's not our lives I fear for. It's our *souls*."

* * *

"So where are we going *this* time?" Michael asked while he gazed out the car window on their way out of Ocean Beach. "To meet Dr. Tones, I got that part. But where?"

Gerald, distracted by Frank's weird behavior on the phone, didn't process it as a question, but as an addition to the guilt he lived with. Michael had grown up around archeological digs. Susan, may she rest in peace, had demanded partnership in his work as well as in the raising of their only child. And since Michael was happier homeschooled than stuck in a classroom, the three of them had returned to the field as a family. Until …

Now, with Michael on the steep slope to maturity at fifteen, Gerald felt his son needed more stability. That was one reason he'd tried to stick to teaching rather than fieldwork.

I'm sorry I never gave you a proper home, he wanted to tell him, but they'd had that discussion many times before, and Michael's reply was as predictable as it was transparent. *That's all right, Dad,* he'd say. *You tried.*

Tried. And I did tr—

"Earth to Dad. Hello? I asked where we're going."

"Sorry," Gerald said, jerking out of his reverie. "Okay, I'll give you another hint. Somewhere between Egypt and Upper Sudan."

Michael laughed. "There's *nothing* between Egypt and Sudan. No. Wait a minute. Trick question. An ancient civilization, I bet. Nubia?"

"Bingo. Funny how Frank always catches us on vacation, isn't it?"

"Yeah. Hilarious."

Michael's sarcasm bit, and Gerald was about to bite back when he caught himself. "You've got to roll with me on this, son. It's just you and me now, so where I go, you go too."

He checked his rearview mirror as they cleared the last stoplight and slipped onto the freeway. Although he now taught the academic year at Oxford, Gerald always took Michael back to their vacation home on summer break. With its three-mile beach and boardwalk, Ocean City and a growing boy seemed a perfect match. But now the resort was growing small in his rearview mirror. *Small, crowded, and noisy.* He pushed back a groan and started counting down to their scheduled departure.

* * *

Two connecting flights and the better part of a day later, they were over Egypt.

Despite connections in London and Cairo, Frank hadn't scheduled a layover, which reflected either urgency, careless planning, or a deliberate lack of consideration. Knowing Frank, Gerald realized he couldn't eliminate any of the possibilities.

Michael's face shone with the refreshment of sleep, but at fifty-three, Gerald's tolerance for travel had slipped down the sharp, serrated edge of middle age, and with it his ability to sleep on planes. Nonetheless, he insisted on maintaining their stampeding packs.

As a boy, he had loved Jack London's books, especially the so-called Klondike stories, where he'd been entranced to learn that most newcomers to the Alaskan wilderness weren't prospectors. Instead, they occupied the towns and trading posts, awaiting news of a successful strike. When it came, they literally dropped everything, shouldered their prepared stampeding packs and rushed to the site to stake a claim. From that memory, Gerald had conceived the Hansen Stampeding Packs.

Now, yawning, he stood from his aisle seat, wrestled his pack from the overhead bin and raided it for his inflatable pillow. As he retook his seat, he leaned across Michael, looked out the window and grunted. "The Aswan Dam and Lake Nasser," he muttered. "Worst archaeological disaster of the century. The largest manmade lake in the world, and it floods some of the most precious archeological real estate in the world."

"Dr. Tones *is* a bit mental, isn't he?" Michael asked. He'd heard the complaint before.

Gerald grinned at him. "Just a bit. You keep jumping subjects like that, I might think you are too."

"Seriously, Dad. Why do you hang around him? You don't even work for the same university. And he's unstable. Maybe even dangerous."

"Maybe. But mental imbalance is often the price tag of genius. Anyway, Frank's a miracle worker at excavations. Digs like he has a witching-stick for pay dirt. Me, I'm better at the write-up. And, I've got, ah, better academic connections. Besides, since we don't work at the same university, we don't threaten each other's position. It's a comfortable partnership. We're more successful together than either of us would be alone."

"All the same, if he backslaps me again, I'll bury him in his own dig."

"If he slaps you again, I'll Bruce Lee him before you do."

Michael cocked his head and grinned. "Uh, no offense, Dad, but you're not exactly the kick-ass type."

An intrusive toddler peeked between the seats in front of them. Gerald tried a peek-a-boo, and got a blank stare for a response. "Maybe not," he sighed, "but I wasn't there. He does it in front of me, we'll gang up on him. Anyway, I want to see what you can do with all those martial arts you've been studying."

Michael gave him a satisfied smirk. "Me too."

Gerald tried a couple of funny faces on the kid, but got the same blank stare. He dug in his pocket, retrieved his keys and jingled them in the toddler's face. Nothing.

Thinking, *Fine, you asked for it,* he dipped his fingers into Michael's water glass and gently flicked a sprinkle through the seats. The space cleared to the tune of a delightfully outraged bellow.

Gerald leaned back, smiling, then flexed his shoulders and wormed himself into his seat.

Michael probed him with disapproving eyes. "You ever do that to me?"

"Only when you refused to share your toys."

"With whom? I'm an only child."

"With me, of course." He flashed a grin, donned his blackout shades and positioned his pillow, let out a lung-collapsing sigh, closed his eyes and sank into the quiet of his soul ... just when the flight attendant announced preparations for landing, and would everybody please return their tray tables and seatbacks to their full and upright positions?

"Payback," Michael muttered.

* * *

Gerald led Michael off the plane with the deep relief he only felt when he flew and, more to the point, *landed* in a plane operated by a third-world airline.

His relief didn't last. If the plane didn't kill him, the taxi ride to the hotel almost certainly would. After the third wild swerve at tachometer-twitching speed, Michael gripped his seat and said, "Couldn't Dr. Tones have picked us up?"

"He's busy at the dig," Gerald managed through gritted teeth.

"Great. But why aren't we staying there? Not that I'm disappointed."

"No room there. That's why he's putting us up at the hotel."

Gerald called to the Sudanese taxi driver's broad back, "Hey, can you slow down a little?"

"No English," the driver said in Arabic, his eyes dancing between the road and his rearview mirror.

Gerald noticed the chain of green prayer beads triple-looped around the man's wrist and repeated his request in Arabic.

"No Arabic!" the man replied in English. His eyes on the rearview mirror were now near panic.

Gerald exchanged mystified looks with Michael, and they both swiveled their heads to the rear window ... just as the cab dove into another dip in the irregular dirt road and lunged out the other side, catching air with two wheels. Even so, Gerald thought he'd made out another car far behind, buried in their dust-trail. Two more lurching backward glances left him one-hundred-percent sure and seventy percent nauseated. And worried. The second car was dancing as wildly as the one they were in. Frank's parting words flashed through his mind: *Ger, it's not our lives I fear for. It's our souls.*

"Hey, are we being followed?" he asked in Arabic.

"He friend. We racing," the driver said through tight lips. With a spin of the steering wheel, he swung the cab into the city of Wadi Halfa, then wove through the web of streets and alleys with as much familiarity as a rat running a much-trod maze for its dinner.

* * *

Gerald didn't make it inside the hotel before weak knees and nausea forced him to the well-worn steps at its entrance. To distract himself from his roiling gut, he ordered his eyes to open and surveyed his surroundings. During their memorable taxi-ride, the entire city looked as though its buildings had been randomly deposited on the flat, barren plain, like dollops of cookie dough dropped onto a flour-dusted baking sheet. It was the same here, with buildings thrown together with mud-brick and corrugated iron. He could only see one electric and one telephone line, and both ran to the hotel. And yet, though impoverished beyond belief, the people walking by nonetheless appeared content.

Willing his stomach to settle, he looked around, but couldn't see the car that had been following them.

"Uh, Dad, you sure we're in the right place?"

Michael stood by their stampeding packs and scanned the misshapen two-story building behind them, horror on his face.

Gerald could only nod his head. In America, this neighborhood wouldn't even qualify for ghetto status. But this ramshackle hotel was the mid-twentieth-century Sudanese equivalent of the Ritz. "You were expecting a Hyatt, maybe?" he managed.

"No, just a hotel."

"It *is* a hotel."

"How can you tell?"

Gerald jerked a thumb over his shoulder at a rough-edged cardboard sign he'd seen before collapsing, nailed above the door and handwritten with a marking pen. "Sign says so. Trust Frank to book the best for us."

"Told you he was mental. I'll check it out, okay?"

Gerald waved him inside and scanned the, well, what could he call it but a street? In this place, streets existed in the sense that deer trails exist, this one with buses, cars and donkey-drawn carts, all following in the dirt tracks of those before them.

Michael returned, stood beside him, and followed his gaze into the car-trail some might call a street. "Report?" Gerald asked without looking up.

"I'm getting why we couldn't find it in the travel guide. On a scale of zero to five stars? This one would earn a black hole."

"Rooms?"

"Spartan. Dust everywhere."

"Phones?"

"One. In the lobby."

"TV? Arcade games?" He tilted his head up to where Michael stood.

Michael sniffed dramatically and wiped a nonexistent tear from his cheek. "TV? *Dragon's Lair* and *Tron*? In my dreams."

Gerald pulled himself to his feet and placed a hand on Michael's shoulder. "You might have difficulty finding your amusements, but from what I see, the locals have difficulty finding food. Let's go."

* * *

Across the street and two houses down, a powerfully built man trained an eye through a frayed curtain. The window was streaked with ridges, whorls and grimy inclusions that spoke of the shoddiest manufacture. However, it proved clear enough to serve his purpose.

When his targets entered the hotel, the man turned from the window to see a bedroll, a teapot and cup, and a pile of empty gunnysacks by the door. Otherwise, the space was bare to its naked mud-brick walls. Except for the source of the pungent smoke fogging his vision now.

He strode through the grayish vapor to the corner, where the Sudanese taxi driver sat, back to the wall and legs splayed on the dirt floor, eyes glazed over from the hashish. Despite the native's lassitude, he pulled greedily on the hose of a filthy two-foot-tall water pipe. The sight reminded the burly man of how a baby nurses from its mother, even when satiated, milk-drunk and half-asleep. The smoke stung his eyes, and the constant bubbling of the native's inhalations reminded him of a fish tank's aerator.

"I told you to tape their conversation," the man said while he pocketed a miniature recorder. He raised his other hand and ran it through the tight curls of his black hair. "How'd you expect them to talk with you driving like a lunatic?"

The driver tilted the water pipe's brass mouthpiece from his lips. "I tell you. Car follow me. I see car follow, I drive crazy, try to lose him."

The burly man had seen the vehicle swerving away when the taxi driver slammed on his brakes at the hotel. *How did the Vatican learn about this so fast?* he wondered.

He replayed the car's appearance in his mind, placed it with what this fool had just told him, and decided there was no other possibility. Working for Mossad, he could blend in anywhere.

Anywhere in the world, there were Jews willing to fight for the Zionist cause. It was just the opposite with the Italian Mafia. The moment they stepped out of their territory, they stood out like … well, like Italians in Sudan.

Keeping his eyes on the driver, the man said, "So, not only did you *not* lose the car that was following you, but you got nothing on tape. What the hell do you think I'm paying you for?"

"I try," the driver said with a shrug, and returned to his brass nipple.

"Okay. But tomorrow, try better." *You idiot.* He turned and walked toward the door, not for a moment intending to leave.

"You pay today, I try tomorrow."

The burly man stopped, his hand frozen on the door's rough rope handle. After a moment, he dropped his hand from the rope, nodded to himself, turned and strode back to the corner. "You're greedy."

"You no pay, I no taxi."

The man pulled a folded envelope from his back pocket and tapped it hesitantly against the palm of his other hand. Then he dropped it to the dirt floor, just beyond the native's outstretched legs. As he had expected, the driver hitched himself up to a sitting position and bent forward to take the envelope. The water pipe's mouthpiece never left his lips until, without a word, the big man dropped to one knee and put his entire weight behind an openhanded chop to the back of the driver's neck. The blow's force bowled the driver over, his flailing legs toppling the water pipe as he fell. Red-hot coals and smoldering hashish flew from the burn-bowl and scattered in the dirt.

The man took a moment to survey the scene, then rolled the unconscious Sudanese onto his side. Then he pulled a handkerchief from his back pocket and shook two brown-paper sachets the size of sugar packets from its folds, dropped them to the dirt floor and rolled the body back to cover them.

He retrieved his envelope, stood and stowed it in his pocket, and in the same motion withdrew a knife. The folding knife was locally made and beautifully crafted, purchased that morning as a souvenir for his nephew.

Bending down and opening the knife in one smooth move, he yanked the turban from the driver's head and bundled it around his knife-hand. One quick motion slit the driver's throat. He watched with fascination as blood spurted, first in strong jets the tempo of a heartbeat, then in weak but rapid pulses that signaled loss of blood pressure and a heart fighting to compensate. The flow spread to the native's waist, where it sizzled one of the hot coals scattered from the water pipe. The stench of scalded blood filled the room, but the burly man stayed where he was, drawing deep breaths of the fumes while an intoxicated smile tightened his lips.

He held the turban over the Sudanese driver's neck until his death-throes ceased, for he knew a single reflexive spasm could spray enough blood to mark him as the murderer. He waited two minutes, and then stuffed the wound with the blood-soaked turban. Straightening, he cleaned and pocketed the knife, thinking his nephew would someday prize it for its gruesome history. Then he retrieved the driver's death warrant.

After the driver had left for the airport to pick up the Hansens, as a standard precaution, he'd searched the room and found the two pages stashed between the gunnysacks. The first page contained notes in Arabic that described the burly man's appearance, and the dates and service he had contracted with the driver. On the second, more damning page, the native had sketched a remarkable likeness of the big man's meaty face. With the exception of police artists, he'd never seen such an accurate portrait drawn from memory. Why the driver had done it, he didn't know. Perhaps for blackmail later. What he did know was that he couldn't allow any man with bad intent and such accurate artistry to live.

Yet it was the notes that interested him most. He still smiled at the driver's description of him as "a bear of a man in his early twenties." When he first read the notes, however, the next line had caught him off-guard. The Sudanese had correctly judged him either Syrian or Jewish by appearance, but most definitely Israeli by accent.

Thinking, *Huh, I've got to work on my accent,* he sat down with his back blocking the door, to await nightfall and his partner's signal that it was safe to leave the house.

CHAPTER 2

Gerald watched Michael kick the dust outside their hotel while the pastel palette of an African sunset invaded the heavens. He couldn't help but wonder when, exactly, Michael had grown up. Well-muscled but not overbuilt, relaxed but surprisingly fast in his reflexes thanks to his passion for martial arts, his son had matured into the trim teenaged athlete he'd never been. *From Susan's side,* he thought with a pang. *Her eyes, too. Intelligent. Aware. The same eager, open face—*

"Dr. Tones isn't coming to meet us?" Michael asked suddenly, and looked up to catch him staring. "What?"

"Oh, nothing," Gerald said quickly and looked down the street. "Frank said he'll see us at the dig. That must be the transport."

He pointed as a Land Cruiser that had just turned a corner glided toward them, so heavily dusted, its true color was obscured. Not until the driver opened his door did the doorjamb reveal that the paint was white, not brown.

The driver's turban was dusty, too, and wound in the strangely disordered bundle peculiar to the Sudanese. "I am Mahmood," he said, then ushered them into the backseat with a broad smile and the words, "You are welcome."

"Uh, wait a minute," Michael said while Mahmood walked around to the driver's side. "He said 'You're welcome' before I said 'Thank you.' What's up with that?"

Gerald grinned. "It's a little different in Africa. Here, hosts greet their guests by bidding them welcome *first*."

"So, in other words, he welcomes me to his car and I'm supposed to say 'Thank you'?" Michael said.

"That's right," Gerald whispered while Mahmood took his seat and fired the ignition, then pulled away from the hotel, accelerating slowly to allow the children on the rear-mounted spare tire to jump off safely. Then he turned partway in his seat, fixed Michael with a warm gaze and broad smile, and repeated, "Welcome, welcome, you are welcome."

"Uh, Thank you," Michael said.

"You're welcome," Mahmood replied, drawing a chuckle from Gerald.

They drove south, skirting the edge of Lake Nasser for the first half of the trip, hugging the east bank of the Nile on the second.

"Where's the dig?" Michael asked.

"Between the third and fourth cataract of the Nile."

"Dad, if you're testing me, I know what that means."

"Just checking. So?"

"*Sooo*, assuming we're talking rivers and not eyes, a cataract is a large waterfall or rapids."

"A gold star for you, me boy. Now, 'campanile.'"

"A bell tower."

"Catachresis."

"Catachresis, catachresis," Michael said, and tapped his temple.

"Don't tell me I've stumped the amazing Michael Hansen, Walking Encyclopedia."

"No, no, just give me a minute." Michael closed his eyes, drifted off and seemed to wriggle through a rent in the dimensions of consciousness. "Let's see ... casuist, cat, catabolism, catachresis. Here it is. Catachresis: incorrect use of words."

"Which dictionary is that, Michael?"

"Oxford. Merriam-Webster's offers either 'use of the wrong word for the context,' or 'use of a forced and especially paradoxical figure of speech.'"

"That's a rare ability you've got," Gerald said, shaking his head in wonder. "Be thankful for it."

Michael shrugged. "Sure. But I'll be even more thankful when I can figure out how to cash in on it."

Chuckling, Gerald slapped his shoulder gently. "That's my capitalistic boy."

* * *

Whatever Frank was hinting at in his phone call, the camp's appearance yielded no clues to Gerald. They arrived as darkness overtook twilight, pushing the last deep-blue fringe to the horizon, where one more shove would put it over the edge. Light spilled from many of the trailers' windows, pooling on the ground at irregular intervals in the main section of the encampment. Nothing out of place there. Nonetheless, he could only vaguely make out the extensive but shallow pit that was the unlit dig. He could see a maze of stone walls, but it was too dark to see any detail.

Disconcerting, he thought as the vehicle bumped and dipped past.

"Hey, Dad, if they found something important, shouldn't the site be lit?"

"Definitely. Wonder why it isn't."

Mahmood parked next to the dining trailer, and Gerald was first to the stairs. The screen door sprang open as he reached for the handle. Framed in the backlit doorway were tanned legs in khaki shorts, an oversized bush shirt and photographer's vest topped off by a wild mane of shoulder-length hair. The handlebar moustache and wayward beard encircling sun-reddened eyes threw him at first, but there was no mistaking the crooked twice-broken nose.

"An aging hippie dressed as a field photographer," he said. "Frank Tones in the flesh."

"Heard the car," Frank said, and then stepped close and lowered his voice. "We'll eat dinner for appearances, and then slip off to my trailer to talk. Just follow my lead."

"Nice to see you, too, Frank."

"Swallow the sentiment," Frank said with a smile. Then, voice even lower, he added, "When you see what I found, you won't care about social niceties."

Frank turned to reenter the trailer, but immediately spun around again. "Oh, and don't mind Trevor. He's only along for the ride. He knows nothing."

"Trevor? My *boss* Trevor? What's he doing here from Oxford?"

Without answering, Frank took another spin and disappeared through the doorway.

Gerald caught the door, turned to Michael and shrugged both shoulders.

"You tackle him, I'll tie him up and beat it out of him," Michael said.

"You'd like that."

"We'd *both* like that." Michael wasn't smiling.

Now when exactly did you figure that *out?* Gerald wondered, but said nothing, just stepped inside and was immediately seduced by the mingled aromas of a busy kitchen. He checked the serving counter, found it empty, and looked around the room. Frank was at the far end of the long table set down the length of the space, and sure enough, Dr. Trevor Mardle, chairman of the Department of Anthropology and Archaeology at Oxford, was seated opposite. Instantly recognizable, Mardle's ruddy complexion, soft features and kind eyes accented the frailness of his slight, sixty-plus frame and even slighter amount of gray hair. The adjacent chairs were empty, which left the pair conspicuously isolated from the other workers, students and the odd professor clustered at the other end of the table.

"Hey, Dad," Michael whispered while they walked toward Frank and Mardle, "notice how everybody stays an arm's length from Dr. Tones? Dr. Mardle's the only one offering him a clear shot."

"Michael," Gerald growled from the corner of his mouth, and then smiled and greeted Mardle when his boss got up from his seat. While they shook hands, he felt Mardle's eyes openly search his face. *He's as surprised to see me here as I am to see him. Didn't Frank tell him I was coming? What's going* on.?

As if reading his mind, Mardle said, "Guess you didn't have a better way to spend your summer either. When I heard Frank was doing salvage archaeology in Nubia, I saw a chance to keep my hand in the field during the day," he paused to smile at Frank, "and cross swords with a barely adequate opponent at night."

"'Barely adequate,' ha!" Frank said as he draped one arm over the back of his chair. "Keep that up and we'll *see* who throws the board tomorrow night!"

Gerald knew Mardle and Frank not as chess masters, but chess fiends. Both regularly conducted multiple simultaneous matches at local chess clubs, and rarely lost a board. Over the years, the tally of their wins still added up to a draw. And although few could follow the finer points of their games, Gerald had attended just to witness their fiery banter.

But he'd never seen them together on a dig. Not even once.

He took a seat beside Mardle, looked across the table at Frank and asked, "So what have you found? Another Temple of Amon?"

"If only," Frank said with a sigh. "Actually, this is a residential complex. Ordinarily, we could take our time. But, we can't. More dams are planned. Not of the Nile, of course, but of tributaries. That makes our time here tight. Extremely tight. We fully expect this area to be underwater in a few years."

Michael had given up looking for a food server and moved to stand beside Gerald's chair. "Salvage archaeology? Like a rush job?"

Frank looked up at Michael with sober appraisal. "You raising this kid in an altered timeframe, Gerry? He looks more twenties than teens. Talks older too. Bet I could still take him, though."

He spoke to Gerald, but his eyes never left Michael's. Gerald felt tension build in his chest, like angina. When Frank harassed his son before, Michael was a kid lacking confidence, still in the grief-throes of losing his mother. That was before the martial arts classes. Now, he'd seen Michael spar in competition, and realized anyone bullying his son would need major medical insurance and a prayer.

Even so, the last thing he wanted in front of his boss was a confrontation. He struggled to think how to defuse the situation until Frank, in a masterful tension-breaker, winked at Michael and continued.

"Salvage archaeology is like scooping M&M's ice cream with a backhoe. You're liable to shatter the chocolate nibbles. But we're racing against time, so all we can do is plow through looking for the big stuff, like mosaics and statues. In the process we're bound to compromise some of the smaller stuff and—"

"And the scientific process," Mardle said with a sigh. "If we had our way, this would never happen. But bigger interests prevail, and given the pressure of time, we can either excavate one site with care or several in haste."

"You can't finish the work underwater?" Michael asked. "After they fill in the lake?"

Mardle shook his head. "Too difficult, risky and expensive, with far too low a return."

"So what's special about this site?" Gerald asked, hoping for a hint.

Mardle locked eyes with Frank.

"Not nearly as special as we'd hoped for," Frank said quickly, and the shadow that crossed his face was so slight and fast, Gerald was certain the others didn't see it.

"If nothing interesting shows up, we might abandon it soon," Frank continued. "We have other leads, and Rybkoski's already left to arrange permits. He's got the funding for the moment, and I'm tagging along until my grant's approved."

Gerald realized he'd hit a dead end, at least for now. And when Frank had said he was keeping Trevor Mardle in the dark, he'd apparently meant it. He considered another attempt, but Mardle looked up and said, "Ah, the food arrives at last. You two grab your meals while I have a word with Frank in private."

Gerald followed Mardle's gaze and saw that a line had formed at the serving counter. "Get you anything, Trevor, Frank?" he said as he stood.

"We'll be along in a moment." Mardle's eyes were back on Frank.

Gerald patted Michael on the back, and they sauntered over to join the line.

"Looks like we came on the right night," Gerald said as he picked up a steaming bowl of groundnut stew. He paused to inhale the vapors and felt every nerve in his nose tingle from the aromatic spices. While he waited to fill his tray from the other stations, he put the stew to the test. The peanuts melted in his mouth and the chicken meat fell off the bone.

"Peanut stew," Michael said. "You gotta wonder how many asthmatics this would kill back home."

"Might be a death worth having," Gerald moaned, spooned another sample and closed his eyes as his taste buds took over his senses.

By the time he returned to the table, fatigue had taken second place to his appetite, and he couldn't wait to dig in. But as he placed his tray beside Mardle, he glanced across the table and found a storm rolling on Frank's face. *A volcano, more like it. Those cheeks look ready to explode.* His eyes darted from Frank to Mardle, who sat with his elbows propped on the table, head bowed into his hands, his demeanor unreadable.

He felt Michael come up behind him, and watched from the corner of his eye as his son quietly placed his tray on the table and took one step back.

Mardle slowly raised his head, met Frank's frenzied eyes across the narrow table, and said, "Check."

Frank slammed both fists on the table, setting the trays and dishes dancing. The room went silent as he jumped to his feet, spun around and gave them his back.

Gerald sputtered, "Frank, what's—?"

"Tomorrow!" Frank commanded without turning.

Yeesh, what kind of a lead is that for me to follow? Gerald thought, recalling Frank's instructions outside the trailer. "Frank," he said, "we dropped everything and came running from the other side of the world at *your* request. Now what's going on?"

"*Tomorrow!*" Frank yelled as he raised his fists and shook them.

Gerald addressed his friend's back in as soothing a voice as his own fury could manage. "Hey, you know what they say, old chap. How do you know we'll all still *be* here tomorrow?"

Frank spun around to face him, punched both fists onto the tabletop, leaned over them menacingly and said, "Tomorrow! You got that? We'll do this *tomorrow*. How do I know we'll all be here tomorrow? Because I'm the god of archaeology, that's how. I'm the god of archaeology, you got that?"

"*Aothu Billah!*"

Gerald turned and found Mahmood seated to one side, his food untouched, his broad smile gone, replaced by a downcast face. The Sudanese shook his head rhythmically, as if swaying to an ill wind.

"*Pfft,*" Frank said in Mahmood's direction, and then turned on all of them and blurted, "The god of archaeology. Got it? And you're my subjects!"

And with that, he spun on his heel and stormed from the room, slamming the door behind him. As he stomped down the stairs, Gerald felt the floor of the trailer shake like the aftershock of an earthquake.

"Well, Dad," Michael said after a long moment, "you *did* tell me he's conceited."

"Yeah. But I've never seen it rise to *that* level."

"Then again," Mardle said, "you've never played chess with him."

After Mardle got his own meal, they turned their uneasy attention to the food, and Gerald asked, "Okay, what was *that* all about?"

"Something personal between us," Mardle said, keeping his eyes on his tray. "I had no idea he'd go off like that but, well, you know Frank."

Gerald nodded and forced a grin. "Yeah, we know Frank all right. So, Michael, where would you place Frank on the scale of T-shirt to straitjacket?"

Michael lowered his spoon, swallowed and said, "Padded room, five-point restraints and a bite block. Minimum."

CHAPTER 3

After dinner, the three of them stepped outside to gaze at the star-studded dome overhead. Silence was seasoned with the occasional cricket's chirp and the distant call of a mournful river bird. Despite his fatigue, Gerald stopped to savor the mild breeze that tempered the evening's heat. But then he realized the darkness before him was moving. As his eyes adjusted, he could make out animal forms of considerable size slinking between the camp trailers.

Michael saw them too, and whispered, "Uh, Dad?" His whisper became a shout at the sound of a massive shotgun blast, quickly followed by two more. Gerald and Mardle practically had to pick him up from the ground.

"What ... What was *that?*" he asked when he regained his footing.

"Sorry," Mardle said. "The wild dogs are drawn by the smell of food. Every now and then, the sentries fire shotguns to scare them away."

A few passing staff, anonymous in the dark, drew close, either out of curiosity or to offer reassurance.

Michael looked at Mardle, eyes wide. "What, they kill them?"

"No, no, my boy. As I said, they only frighten them off. We have a curfew here, so everyone's in their trailers by midnight. After that, the guns stop so we can sleep. Those bold enough to venture out after that? Well, they're—"

"On their own," Gerald finished.

The night was shattered by another blast, and Michael flinched.

"Afraid of guns, are you, Michael?" Mardle asked.

"Not if it's my finger on the trigger," he said. This time, his voice didn't waver.

Mardle nodded, shook hands with both of them, and turned to go back inside.

And the strangers in the shadows dispersed.

* * *

By the time they entered the SUV for the rough ride back to the hotel, Mahmood's smile had returned.

"So," Michael asked, "we heading back to the States, or sticking around waiting for Frank to up his lithium prescription?"

"Don't know," Gerald answered, looking thoughtful. "Mongo only pawn in game of rife."

Michael rolled his eyes. "No, really, Dad."

Gerald thought of Frank's blurted promise. "Let's see what happens tomorrow."

Michael clenched his hands in his lap and watched the last of the trailers jiggle past as they bounced over the rocky terrain, then let his eyes linger on the darkened excavation site. "Dad, I've got a bad feeling about this. We're talking about Dr. Maximum Madness in an unlit dig where they regularly try to shoot out the stars. Whatever Frank found, how good can it be?"

"If it looks like a waste of time, we'll bag it and go home. Shouldn't cost us more than a day to find out."

"Well," Michael said, "whatever he found, I hope he didn't steal it."

"Hey!"

"That's the real reason he calls you in on his finds, isn't it? You said so yourself. After that scandal, no academic journal in the world will publish his work, unless it's under someone else's name as first author."

Gerald went silent a moment, then said quietly, "Don't be too hard on the guy. You have no idea how tempting it can be to pocket something for your own collection."

"You never did."

Gerald cleared his throat.

"Dad?"

"Well, nothing as valuable as a pharaoh's necklace."

"Daaad!"

"Look, Mikey, everybody does it. Maybe you start with some dirt or a few stones, just to remember the dig by. But sooner or later, something that nobody'll miss catches your eye."

Michael leaned his head against the back of the seat. "I can't *believe* this. After all these years of drumming honesty into me, I discover my father's an international antiquities thief." He leaned forward and raised his voice. "Hey, Mahmood, there a car phone in here? I need to call Interpol."

Mahmood glanced at him with a quizzical expression, and Michael sat back. "Just kidding. Never mind."

After a moment, Gerald said in a low voice, "Remember the Phoenician vase?"

"The one Mom loved so much?" Michael's eyes riveted on him in the dim light. "Did she know it was stolen?"

Gerald sighed. "Such an ugly word. I like to think of it as being on permanent, inter-collection loan. For display purposes only. But to answer your question, no. Can you imagine your mother having known about that?"

"No way. If I'd taken a breath of someone else's air, she would've squeezed it out of me. So ... the Phoenician vase? No biggie. Dime a dozen. What else?"

"The little scarab you used to play with—"

"Dad, get to the big things. Any mummies hidden in the basement?"

"Just the vase and the scarab, actually."

"Dad, that's *nothing* stuff. On a scale of Aztec gold to petrified boogers, that's—"

"You don't need to rank this, Mikey. I *know* it's small stuff. I'm only saying I understand Frank's temptation."

Michael leaned back again, but now his face held the smile Gerald had hoped for.

"Huh. My father the grave robber. Can't wait to tell my children. Know what they'll say? 'Grandpa's going to hell.'"

"Keep talking like that, Mikey, and I'll consider myself already there."

Five minutes later, Michael said, "Hey, Dad, you know what Dr. Mardle told me his name means? It's an old Suffolk word that means 'pond.' It gained the double meaning of pond *and* 'conversation' because people used to congregate by the ponds to chat. Pretty mental picture, huh?"

Gerald failed to answer. Michael nudged him gently, got a soft snore in response, realized his father had surrendered to fatigue, so turned his attention to the front seat.

"Mahmood, why did you say *Aothu Billah* back there? Why did you 'seek refuge with Allah' when Dr. Tones made that comment about being—?"

"When he called himself a god, he denied the supremacy and Oneness of our Creator, and that is disbelief," Mahmood said. "And I seek refuge in my God *and* in your God from disbelief."

"Whoa. Your God I understand, but what do you mean, *my* God?" Michael asked. "You worship Allah, and I, well, I believe in God, but I don't follow any organized religion."

Mahmood smiled over his shoulder, a flash of white teeth in a pitch-black face. Michael sensed more to the smile than courtesy.

"My friend," Mahmood said as he returned his eyes to the road, "there are many people of many religions worshiping many gods in many ways. But know this: by whatever name you know Him, there is only one God. And the one true God is the God of you, of me, and of all humankind, whether they know it or not, whether they recognize Him or not, and whether they worship Him as He commands to be worshipped or not."

Michael glanced at his sleeping father beside him and realized he was on his own. "The Hindus, Buddhists, Jews and Christians would disagree," he said. "They would say they worship a different God."

"Two would be right, and two wrong."

"Huh?"

Mahmood braked hard and threw the vehicle into a sideways skid that left them stopped in a cloud of boiling dust. At first, Michael thought he must have offended the man, but then the dust cleared and he gasped at the dark mountain of a buffalo staring at him through the side window. Gerald snorted out of sleep, pushed off from where he'd been thrown against Michael, glanced at the beast with no more interest than if it had been a bedside alarm clock, then leaned back into his corner to fall instantly asleep.

Michael sputtered, "Gee, Mahmood, you almost killed one of *their* gods."

"That is the point," Mahmood replied while he straightened the vehicle and steered around the beast. "The Hindus and Buddhists would be right, because they worship a god or gods that don't exist. The Jews and Christians would be wrong because, like Muslims, they worship the Creator. The difference is not that we worship a different God, but that we understand Him differently. And as I said, there is only one God, and He is the God of you, of me, and of all humankind, whether they know it or not, whether they recognize and worship Him or not, and whether they are correct in their understanding of Him or not."

Another quick glance over his shoulder, another flash of white, and Michael reflexively returned the smile. They drove the rest of the way back to the hotel in silence.

* * *

The large, muscular man waited outside Frank's trailer, on its blind side, listening to the quiet humming of the air conditioner. Twenty minutes after the lights inside flickered out, the man motioned to his short, wiry companion. Together, they donned gasmasks, and then the bigger man sprayed an odorless aerosol into the air conditioner's intake. They waited five minutes, tuned their high-tech flashlights to the dimmest possible illumination, and entered the trailer.

The bigger man prodded Frank's prone form on the bed, gave a satisfied nod to find him unmoving and staring straight up. The moment the intruder moved into Frank's line of sight, Frank's chest heaved, as if to scream, but all that came out was a gurgle. With a muttered "Showtime," the big man motioned his partner to pin Frank's arms while he straddled his chest. He snapped open a sheet of clear plastic in front of Frank's eyes and then, chuckling, leisurely lowered it to cover his nose and mouth.

The moment the plastic touched Frank's face, he gurgled again and his eyelids widened. The big man snatched the plastic back and leaned close. "Hey, doc," he whispered, "who's your buddy? Who's your pal?"

Frank answered with a gurgle and a tortured hiss.

"Get it over with," the smaller man said.

Scowling at his partner, the big man stretched the plastic over Frank's face and leaned into it. "You take all the fun out of it, you know."

Frank was only able to put up the weakest of fights. In less than a minute, the killer felt Frank still completely. Five minutes later, his companion checked the pupils and found them dilated in brain death. Another two minutes, and Frank's pulse stopped.

The big man kept the plastic on Frank's face for another three minutes while his companion slipped away and fussed with a hardened leather glove and a writhing canvas bag. Eventually, he extracted a cobra from the bag and pinched its jaws open.

"After tonight," the wiry man said while his partner dismounted from Frank's motionless body, "you can call me The Snake."

"Nope," the other replied while he stretched his muscle-bound arms and chest. "From now on, I'm Big Bear and you're Little Bear."

The cobra wrapped itself around the smaller man's arm and whipped its tail wildly, but he listened raptly while his partner related the Sudanese taxi driver's description of him. When he finished speaking, despite the gasmask he still wore, the big man could read the smile in the smaller man's eyes.

"Big Bear," the smaller assassin muttered as he stepped up to the corpse. "Big Bear. Hm. That's okay, but I've got a better one." Without another word, he stabbed the cobra's fangs into Frank's neck.

CHAPTER 4

The Sudanese followed the etiquette of his religion, which taught him to return later when a door is not answered after the third gentle knock. He returned every hour to repeat the effort, but didn't manage to rouse Gerald and Michael until his fourth attempt, well after noon.

After they had demolished the heaped platter of Arabic bread, *falafel* pillows, olives and white cheese sent to their room, Gerald entered the lobby in khaki safari clothes, followed by Michael decked out in Ralph Lauren. Together, they fortified themselves with the national beverage, strong tea sweetened to a grain of sugar less than syrup. With caffeine and blood sugar flirting lethal levels, they revisited the ritual of being bid welcome to the SUV that would take them to the dig site. As Mahmood pulled out, he nosed the vehicle in the direction of a small crowd that filled the opposite side of the street, next to a parked ambulance and police car.

"What's that about?" Michael asked.

"Drugs," Mahmood replied.

Michael eyed the ambulance. "An overdose?"

"Murder, I'm afraid. While I was, ah, awaiting your awakening, the police told me they found heroin packets under the man's body. The thieves must have missed them." Mahmood tooted his horn and waved to his friends as they gave way and allowed him to ease the SUV past the scene.

Michael and Gerald peered out the window as two attendants carried a sheet-bundled body from the house to the back of the ambulance. "How was he killed?" Michael asked.

"Knife."

Michael glanced at Gerald, then back at the hotel. "Wow. Talk about hitting close to home."

"Not your lifestyle, not your risk," Mahmood said with finality.

As Mahmood spoke, the attendants hoisted the stretcher to the height of the ambulance. Gerald watched an ebony hand fall free from the sheet, a chain of thick green prayer beads looped thrice about the corpse's wrist.

The airport taxi driver?

He glanced at Michael, was relieved to see him distracted by chatting with Mahmood. "Getting late," he said quickly. "What time is it, Michael?"

Michael looked at his watch. "Two o'clock."

While the body disappeared into the ambulance, Gerald said, "Nearly wake-up time in the States. Slow start."

Mahmood cleared his throat and began to accelerate away from the crowd. "I don't like to tell you this, but there has also been a tragedy at the site. Dr. Tones was found dead this morning."

"*What?*"

The word left Gerald's lips without his being aware of it. Michael simply stared open-mouthed at Mahmood, who went on uninterrupted.

"Dr. Mardle wanted to tell you himself, but said he couldn't leave the site. So he asked me to deliver the news on his behalf. To that, I add my condolences."

Gerald's world phase-shifted, now showing as if through a camera's lens. Sound was polarized, his vision bleached to black and white. A hundred yards to the right, a flock of egrets took flight from the bank of the Nile, and he could hear the flap of their wings as if he were impossibly in their midst. The entire scene beat to the pace of his pulse in his ears, and that's what brought him back.

That's my heartbeat, he realized. *I'm still alive. But Frank isn't.* How did it happen? *I said, how did it happen? ANSWER ME, I WANT TO KNOW WHAT HAPPENED!*

Then he realized he hadn't opened his mouth to let the words out. But by then, Michael had asked the question for him.

"He died in his sleep," Mahmood said. "The team nurse thinks it was a heart attack."

"You're ... sure he's dead?" Gerald heard himself ask, as if he were two people, one hearing the other speak and thinking, *What a stupid question!*

Mahmood glanced over his shoulder, his brow furrowed. His eyes tacked between Gerald and the road for two beats, and then he spoke cautiously, as if afraid he might swamp the lines to Gerald's mental switchboard. "Well, he's not alive anymore, so yes, we're pretty sure he is dead."

"That's all, nothing else?" Michael said.

"No. There is one more thing."

"And what's that?"

"From Allah do we come, and to Allah do we return."

* * *

They drove into a quiet camp, and saw only a scant few staff working the dig. In the dining trailer, some socialized in subdued voices; others, Gerald assumed, were off on their own.

He followed Mahmood to Frank's trailer and met Trevor Mardle en route. His boss' eyes were puffy and red, and Gerald read in his face an emotional depth he knew was absent from his own. Frank, as inflammatory as his personality was, had meant much more to Trevor than to him. To Gerald, Frank had been a colleague, co-investigator and partner in academia, good for a few laughs, exotic anecdotes and career-boosting invitations. To Trevor Mardle, Frank Tones had been one thing more: a true friend.

"I didn't realize I would take this so hard," Mardle said. "The way we always went after each other at chess matches, you'd think he was my enemy. He was anything but. A good man, a ... a great academic ..."

Sensing an impending breakdown, Gerald took him by the elbow and pulled him alongside as he resumed walking toward Frank's trailer. After a moment he said, "Mahmood told us Frank had a heart attack—"

"Snakebite."

Gerald stopped in his tracks.

"There are punctures near the base of his skull," Mardle said, and tapped the back of his neck with two crooked fingers by way of example.

"I ... don't understand. How does a snake bite a fully grown man on the neck?"

"He was asleep in bed." Mardle choked on a breath, coughed and looked away, teary-eyed.

Gerald searched his mind for a connection, but couldn't find it. He managed a lame-sounding "Oh?"

"Here's his trailer," Mardle said, bowing his head and shuffling his steps in the dust. But then he raised his head, squared his shoulders and said, "I ... Rybkoski's away getting the dig permits, and his second-in-command is devastated. I haven't been inside yet. I suppose I should at least take a look."

"You don't have to." Gerald laid a hand on the frail man's shoulder and looked him in the eye. "Surely someone else can—"

"I'll just be a minute." He forced an inhalation through flared nostrils. "Come with me if you like."

He turned, but only got two steps before Gerald said, "Wait. Did they find the snake?"

Mardle half-turned and nodded. "Under the bathroom sink. Locals tell me it's common. Had I known that, I think I'd be digging nothing more than my garden this summer." A moment later, he was at the door to Frank's trailer.

Gerald watched the door swing shut as Michael stepped up beside him. A quick glance showed that the boy's face was pale. "How're you handling this?" he said.

"Not bad. Just wish I could've shaken the snake's hand and bought him a rat milkshake."

"Michael ..."

"Sorry, Dad. It just leaves me cold. You might feel the same, if it had been you he knocked to the floor."

Gerald nodded. "Well, I'm going to join Trevor. Let's meet back at the dining trailer."

"Mind if I tag along?" Before Gerald could answer he quickly added, "It's not like it's the first dead body I've seen."

How right you are, Gerald thought, though he didn't think it likely Michael was thinking of his mother. No, he was thinking of the others. Most Westerners never see a corpse, but he and Michael had seen, well, a lot. It came with working and living in third-world countries, where death is open and frequently violent. Neither was Michael ignorant of the dangers in this part of the world. He knew better than most Westerners who might think, say, that swimming with hippos in Africa is like swimming with dolphins in the Florida Keys. It isn't. Hippos have three things dolphins don't: territories, tempers and tusks. Hippos clock more human kills in Africa than all other animals combined. And two of those kills, Michael had actually witnessed.

Gerald glanced at the trailer, then back at his son. "Okay. Let's go."

Upon entering, he was immediately struck by the disorganization. Frank, for all his faults, had been a neat freak. To judge from the tracks on the carpet and the general disarray, a considerable number of people had trooped through the trailer. There was no police presence yet either. In Sudan, that was hardly unusual. Given the dig's remote location and the evidence of a natural death, the police would have to be fetched, and even then might procrastinate for days. If they came at all.

The team nurse sat on the floor, reading from Frank's library. He turned out to be a male archaeology student who had opted for a career change after a stint as an army medic. His wrinkled clothes, bronzed body and sandy-blond hair made him look more like a beach bum than a grad student. He looked up as they came in and gave a nod of recognition.

"Yeah, hi," Gerald said. There were tight-lipped smiles all around between the nurse, Gerald and Michael, and Mardle, who now stood near the closed bathroom. Gerald supposed it gave them an excuse not to look at the body in the bed.

The toilet flushed, and someone he didn't recognize came out of the bathroom. Mardle took his place.

Gerald didn't need to look at Frank. The place was as sweltering as a sauna, and the smell of cooked death told him everything he needed to know. But he looked anyway. Frank lay on his back in his underwear, his head turned to one side, facing him. A rope of drool trailed from the corner of his mouth to the pillow, where it spread out in a dollar-sized stain. His face was chalk-pale, but otherwise appeared to be Frank at sleep.

"Love his choice of boxers. Don't you?" Michael said in a low voice while he stepped past Gerald and approached Frank's corpse. "Clothes to die in."

Gerald took a second look, and couldn't believe he'd overlooked the smiley-face print on Frank's shorts. Fighting a grin, he turned back to the nurse and said, "Uh, Matthew, isn't it?"

"Mark, but that's okay, Dr. Hansen. We're all stunned."

He wanted to joke, *Fine, but where are Luke and John?* But good taste prevailed. *Turn it off, Gerald, turn it off. Get serious and deal with reality.* "Who found him and when?"

"One of his students, this morning. Dr. Tones didn't show for his seven o'clock breakfast, which he never missed. Not ever. His senior grad student got worried, decided to check on him and ... found him."

Gerald glanced at his watch. "It's been seven to eight hours, then. Is the generator working?" Another stupid question. He could hear the diesel-powered site generator chugging away. A deaf person probably could feel the vibration through the floorboards.

"Uh, sure it's working. You can hear it from here," Mark said with a quizzical look, his face projecting the unspoken question, *This your first time on a dig, Dr. Hansen?*

"Ah, yes ... right," Gerald said with a glance around the tiny room. "So, shouldn't we turn on the air conditioning? It's like an oven in here." *And Dr. Tones is the main course. Stick a fork in and see if he's done. Stop, stop, stop that! Concentrate!*

Mark shrugged. "Tried that. It popped."

"Sorry?"

"When I got here, the sun was beginning to do its job, so I switched the a/c on. Something popped. It hasn't worked since."

"Fuse?"

"Nope. Circuit breakers in this trailer. No problem."

"No, I meant an internal fuse. Is there a fuse in the unit?"

Mark cupped his chin in one hand, and stroked his lower lip with two fingers. "No idea. But there was a major spark inside the unit when it blew."

Okay, not a fuse. "And you've been here ever since?" Mark's shirt was soaked through, but Gerald couldn't imagine anyone could endure the heat for long. And the smell of death was overwhelming.

There was another flush in the bathroom, followed by the sound of water running.

"You mean, have I been here all morning?" Mark said. "Gosh, no. Who could stand that?" He glanced at Frank's body, then back at Gerald. "I'm only borrowing a book. My trailer's across the way."

"Borrowing a book? You're joking, right?"

Mark shrugged. "Got to do something while waiting for the cops. It could be all day, if today at all."

Heck, why not, Gerald thought. He gestured to the corpse and asked, "So, don't you think we should do something to preserve the body?"

"We thought of that," Mardle said as he kicked the bathroom door closed behind him. He dripped water from his face and hands as he spoke, and cast his eyes around for a towel. Not finding one, he dried his hands daintily on the window curtain. "We considered moving him to the storage trailer, but we're afraid to do anything until the police give their approval. Our electrician did his best, but tells us a beetle shorted the circuit, and he doesn't have the parts to fix it."

Michael turned from Frank's body and said, "Dad, didn't you say—?"

"In a minute, son. So we're just going to let him putrefy?"

"Um, Dad ..."

"Let me finish, Michael."

"What do you suggest?" Mark asked. "If the police order an investigation and we've already moved the body, there'll be hell to pay. Are *you* willing to assume responsibility?"

Gerald knew Mark was right, and his tolerances were already breaking down. He couldn't bring himself to look at Frank, the heat was oppressive, the smell worse, and he needed to get out of there. "Let's take this outside," he said.

* * *

"What kind of snake was it?" Michael asked from the window seat in Mark's trailer, where they'd ended up. As he spoke, he glanced outside and watched Gerald and Dr. Mardle chatting beside Frank's trailer.

"Cobra, I'm told," Mark replied, his voice muffled as he pulled his sweat-soaked shirt over his head. He threw it into a corner and reached into an overflowing laundry bin for a replacement.

"You didn't see it?"

"Huh? The snake? Not in one piece I didn't." He pulled a dust-mottled polo shirt from the bin, which for all appearances had been powder blue before having gone twelve rounds with a pair of red socks in the wash. He sniffed it, and threw that one into the corner as well. "One of the Sudanese workers took a shovel and played that snake like a xylophone. When he was done, it looked like it had been passed through a shredder." While he spoke, he sniffed another shirt from the bin, wrinkled his nose and put it back. Then he retrieved the mottled polo from the corner, shook it out and put it on. "Whatever it was, I hope I never see one alive."

"Well, cobras aren't the only things out here that can kill," Michael said while he scanned the trailer, thinking he'd never seen a place this messy unless it had been burglarized.

"Sure. There are scorpions." Mark grinned. "Or maybe you have something else in mind."

Yeah, I do, Michael thought. *Something a lot smaller than a scorpion. But I'm sure not gonna tell you.* What he said was, "Just thinking, that's all." And the vortex of his thoughts dragged him inexorably down to a tight, dark place he didn't want to go: another dig, with another corpse, and a younger him crying inconsolably over his mother, beating her lifeless chest and clutching her clothes until his father coaxed him away.

CHAPTER 5

A single policeman arrived in late afternoon, dressed in self-importance and the ubiquitous olive-green uniform that, in Sudan, could signify anything from security guard to soldier. As Gerald had predicted, the man had to be fetched in the team transport. The price of gasoline was too high, the police budget too low, and the few police cars that were running couldn't be spared for a death in a remote field that fell in the official category of "bury 'em where they die."

Gerald led the policeman to the door of the trailer where the man sniffed, peered inside, and concluded his investigation without even entering. After ordering Frank's body moved to the chilled storage trailer, he sat down in the weakened rays of a sun on final approach to the horizon to write out the death certificate.

Gerald watched the man scratch his cheap ballpoint pen on his clipboard and realized, as he had many times before, that Africa was a country where death was common and devoid of significance. For that matter, full-scale genocide would go overlooked, if not for the watchful eye of outside news agencies and the UN. In Africa, life was simply that cheap.

By the time Frank's body was moved, the team electrician returned from town with parts for the air conditioner. With the corpse gone, the windows open and the repaired unit on full blast, Gerald, Michael and Dr. Mardle entered and found the smell cleared and the trailer habitable again. Together, they collected Frank's personal effects under the policeman's watchful eye. Gerald wondered what would happen if he told the man that anything worth stealing would've been in his pocket hours ago, had he wanted it. But a glance at the man's emotionless ebony face told him such a statement could cost him a most intimate and unpleasant body search. So he said nothing while he and Mardle filled a manila envelope with Frank's smaller possessions, taken from the pockets of his clothing and from his bedside table.

"Anything on his body, Trevor?" Gerald asked. "Jewelry or anything?"

Mardle looked at him, shamefaced. "I ... I didn't think to look."

"I'll take care of it," Gerald volunteered. "You and Michael finish up here."

Mardle looked relieved, and dropped the last of Frank's valuables into the manila envelope and handed it to him. "I need to take a walk and clear my head. And thanks. I can handle sorting his things, but as far as searching his body, my apologies. I just ... can't."

"Not a problem." Gerald offered a somber smile and stepped outside, headed in the direction of the refrigerated storage trailer, but he stopped and turned at Mardle's call. Mardle was locking the trailer door.

"In case you decide to stay tonight," Mardle said, tossing him the key. "I'm sorry, but it's the only empty we have. If you prefer the hotel, I understand. But it's late, and traveling these roads is treacherous at night. So, distasteful though it may be, think about it."

Gerald watched him turn and trudge off in the direction of the dig. He weighed the manila envelope in his hand, exchanged looks with Michael, then took him by the arm and followed the policeman in the direction of the storage trailer.

After a few steps, Michael kicked a stone from his path and said, "Dad, I thought you said Dr. Tones wasn't married."

"Divorced. Ten years ago. It wasn't just bitter, it was caustic."

"And with his innate warmth and polished interpersonal skills, what a surprise that is, huh?"

Gerald drew his lips together wide and tight, raised his brow as high as it would go. "Indeed. What a surprise."

"He never remarried?"

"Not that I'm aware of. Why?"

"Well, it might be nothing, but he had a wedding band on his finger. Kind of funky-looking. But then again, pretty much all of him was funky, wasn't it? Anyway, that's what I tried to tell you earlier."

Gerald nodded. "I'll check on that." He left Michael outside and entered the storage trailer behind the stone-faced policeman.

* * *

Mahmood and several other workers had placed Frank's body on a folding table that was surrounded by boxes and covered crates. The only items Gerald found on Frank's person were the gaudy-print shorts, a cheap Casio watch, and what Michael had noticed: a primitive-looking wedding ring.

Frank's fists were clenched tight in rigor mortis, and although Gerald tried, he couldn't remove the band. Eventually he realized he'd have to be satisfied with an inspection. A quick visual brought a low whistle from his lips and a muttered, "Not like any wedding band *I've* ever seen."

The ring was iron, stained by what could be untold centuries of dry oxidation. Not the kind of wet oxidation known as rust, with its leprous flaking and surface pitting, but the smooth darkening and discoloration that formed in the absence of humidity which, once developed, was permanent.

The policeman had quickly lost interest and wandered over to survey the boxes of supplies with open interest. Gerald wasn't surprised. After all, the only items of value on Frank were the watch, a ring that couldn't be removed, and underwear nobody in their right mind would *want* to remove. Or touch.

Working unobserved, he tried once more to extract the ring, and discovered that although he couldn't remove it, it was loose enough to rotate on Frank's finger. *Yeah, that's gonna do a lot of good. Way to go, Sherlock. Another mystery solved and, and what the ...?*

Now he could see where the band widened to the ring's face, which had been trapped in the cold, curled fist. Suddenly excited, he glanced up and found the policeman dreamily inspecting cases of condensed milk.

Quickly, he returned to his task and forced a gold ring-face from between the tightly flexed fingers. Unmistakably a treasure of antiquity, the raised symbols of the gold oval shone with the whisper of greatness that, since the dawn of their profession, had drawn people like Frank and him to explore the mysteries of the past. *This is* veeery *interesting,* he thought. As the words crossed his mind, he smiled, for he recognized the echo of the same words that had brought him running to this side of the earth.

Almost immediately after he sensed the importance of his find, he realized he could do nothing about it. He took a quick mental snapshot and turned the ring-face back into Frank's fist, then tossed the watch into the manila envelope and turned to leave.

"*La,*" the policeman said in Arabic.

Gerald stopped in mid-step and turned. *No? Why 'no'?*

The policeman gestured to the envelope, and then to the table.

You've got to be kidding. He tried to argue, but after three passes down the path of reason, realized his words would've made more impression on the walls.

"*Malesh. Bukra, inshallah,*" the policeman said, and stabbed his finger toward the table repeatedly.

The three most common words in the Arabic-speaking world, Gerald reflected while he placed the bulging envelope on the table next to the body. "*Malesh.*" It's okay. "*Bukra.*" Tomorrow. And "*inshallah.*" If Allah wills.

Tomorrow. That's what Frank said. And look where it got him.

Once outside, the policeman locked the door and pocketed the key, then turned toward his waiting transport. Gerald took a path opposite, his mind still spinning with what he'd seen. As he strolled toward the dining trailer, he spotted a familiar form hunched at the edge of a pile of rubble.

"What'ya got there, Mikey?" he called out.

"Death match," Michael replied. "*Ateuches sacar* versus Godzilla!"

Gerald hurried over to find a desert scorpion battling a huge scarab beetle. The contest of strength and flailing legs reminded him of a sumo-wrestling match, only one of the wrestlers was armed with a hypodermic needle.

When the scorpion eventually gained a claw-hold and sank its stinger, the scarab shivered and curled up its legs in a climactic death.

"And the winner and still champion ..." Michael said as he slapped a flat rock in the rhythm of a drum roll, *"Godzilla!"*

He sat down in the dirt and leaned against a slab of rubble to watch the lethal victor drag off its supper. "Now *this* is where we're supposed to be, huh, Dad? Forget that virtual reality stuff, this is life real-time."

When Gerald didn't reply, he looked up and said, "Hey, Dad ... Dad? You look like you've seen a ... Hey, Dad, what *did* you see?"

Gerald glanced down and saw Michael studying his face in the last of the sun's light. *Sh ...* what was it Susan had taught Michael to say? *Shugar.* Sugar with a "Sh." *Shugar, is it that obvious?*

"Dad, I've seen that look before. What happened?" Michael stood, but now his voice held alarm.

What, now you're a mind reader? "No ghosts, son, just an old friend dead," Gerald replied, and thought, *Man, I've got to get this under control.*

"Un-huh," Michael said. "Well, when you feel like talking about it, let me know."

Gerald started walking again, and Michael fell in beside him. "Um, look Mikey, I think we'll stay a couple days, check out the dig, and head back to the States when all the loose ends are tied up, okay?"

"Fine with me, dad of dads. Actually, Nintendo deficit aside, this feels more like home than Ocean City ever does. Of course, I might not go to the bathroom for a few days, and you can take bottom bunk from now on. But other than that, it's pretty blue."

"Blue?"

"Yeah." Michael picked up a stone and tossed it wide of his target, an empty soda can lying by the side of the path. "You know, in Arabic everybody asks '*Esh laon-ik.*' They mean 'How are you?' but the literal translation is 'What color are you?' So, I'm thinking blue."

"What, depressed?" Gerald asked as they arrived at the steps of the dining trailer. He laid his hand on the railing and cocked his head.

"No, cool. Like, I'm cool. Or beautiful. Think about it. Have you ever seen anything blue that was ugly? It's the most beautiful color in the world. If it wasn't, God wouldn't have made the sky blue. Also, it's the color of extremes. Glacier ice and the tip of a welding flame are both blue. Sooo, I'm blue. Like 'hot as the brightest blue star, cool as a glacier, feeling smooth and beautiful as a clear morning sky.' Whatcha think?"

As he finished speaking, the first shotgun blast of the night shocked him into a sudden crouch.

Gerald chuckled as Michael regained his composure, then took the first two stairs in one step and called back over his shoulder, "What do I think? I think you sound stoned out of your mind. Furthermore, you just 'blue' your cool."

Michael winced. "Yep, it's gonna be a long flight home."

* * *

Rather than risk the drive to the hotel, Gerald decided to occupy Frank's trailer as Mardle had suggested. At his insistence, the workers had dug up a fresh mattress to replace the one on Frank's bed, and he and Michael headed there after dinner, when he could comb through Frank's belongings at a more leisurely pace. Following the Muslim evening prayer, Mahmood stopped by and flooded the doorway with white: flowing white *thobe* from neck to ankles, white teeth, white turban. Gerald wondered how he kept it all blazing white. *He* had gotten dusty without even leaving Frank's trailer.

"Evening, Mahmood," Michael said. "Oh, hey, wait!" Then he

took a step back and motioned with a sweep of his arm. "Mahmood, you are welcome."

The native said nothing, but looking at his broad smile, Gerald recalled Rudyard Kipling's short story, "How the Rhinoceros Got His Skin," in which the Parsee "smiled one smile that ran all round his face two times." Then he returned to the bookshelves while Michael took a break with Mahmood, who set about brewing the predictable pot of tea as only a Sudanese can.

"*Esh laon-ik,* Michael?" Mahmood asked.

"He's blue," Gerald murmured, his face buried in a book.

Michael looked at him, then Mahmood, and laughed. When Mahmood glanced in confusion between the two, he said, "Just a joke between me and Dad. I'm fine, Mahmood. How are you?"

Instead of answering, Mahmood sat across from Michael at the tiny dining table. Then he said, "All day long, I've been thinking about Dr. Tones' last words. When he called himself a god. You see, it doesn't pay to challenge the supremacy of our Creator."

Michael rolled his eyes. "He was only joking."

"Obviously. But some things you don't joke about. Like the fact that you're a pedophile."

Michael spewed his tea in a fine mist. "Wh ... *What?*"

"You see, you don't like to hear it, even in jest, and even though you know it's not true. Some people would fight over those words. Can you not imagine the Almighty to defend His honor with equal or greater zeal?"

Gerald stepped to the table, accepted a cup of tea with the hand not holding the book, and said, "Mahmood, how well did you know Dr. Tones?"

"I ran his errands from time to time, and drove him around as needed."

"So who would know what he was working on?"

"Everyone. He worked at excavating the barrows during the day and humiliating Dr. Mardle at night. He only succeeded at the first."

"Barrows?" Michael asked. "The ancient burial mounds?"

"Hmm. The same." Mahmood stood to refresh their cups.

"What period was he excavating?" Gerald asked.

"A bit of everything, I think. He was interested in the period predating Christianity in Nubia. Anything preceding the middle of the sixth century. But as you know, finding the portion of a graveyard that corresponds to a particular period can be challenging."

Seeing Gerald's surprise, he smiled. "No, I'm not an archaeologist. Chemist by education. Yet I make a better living driving for the Westerners than as a chemist amongst my own. I've been doing this for years. You pick up on things after a while."

"What's the difficulty with dating the barrows?" Michael asked.

Gerald snapped his book shut and sat down. "Here, graves are frequently dug one upon another. When the preceding occupant has decomposed, fresh corpses are placed in the old graves. So graves of differing dates can be layered and intermixed. Makes finding those of a certain period more like a game of *Battleship*. All you can do is take educated guesses and work your way around until you get a hit."

"I don't know if this will help," Mahmood said, "but last week, Dr. Tones found something that excited him very much. But what it was, nobody knows."

Gerald looked at him, one eyebrow arched. Mahmood made a dismissive gesture with his free hand and said, "Well, perhaps one of his students or Dr. Mardle knows. But other than they, no one."

After a few more sips of tea, Mahmood took permission to leave, as per local custom. But when he opened the door, Gerald stood. "Mahmood, do you notice anything unusual in Frank's death?"

The native stopped and turned around, but only partway. "Anything as in any *one* thing, or any number of things?"

Gerald shrugged.

"Yes, there is a great deal that is unusual, to be sure."

"Like?"

"Like? Well, like the cobra bite. Cobra bites swell to the size of a fist."

* * *

That night, Gerald expected a fitful sleep, crowded with visions of serpents and death. Instead, he suffered a fitful sleep crowded with questions about Frank's ring, questions only another inspection, without the suspicious eyes of a policeman upon him, could hope to answer. Eventually he gave up trying and got up to review Frank's excavation notes, which thankfully, the policeman hadn't seen.

Sometime after sunrise, he heard Michael rousing from a sleep so deep it verged on coma. By then, Frank's notes had revealed the importance of his find, and its danger. The seed of suspicion planted by Mahmood's comment had blossomed into conviction: Frank's death could very well have been murder. Even more disturbing, Gerald realized he'd inadvertently fallen into the same precarious position, possibly jeopardizing his only child as well.

So what on earth do I do next?

* * *

When the policeman returned at midmorning, he stepped out of the team transport without urgency or enthusiasm. Gerald grabbed a blue-plastic water bottle and went with him. He was surprised to find Dr. Mardle waiting by the storage trailer, standing next to one of his grad students, a puffy-eyed, sunburned but still-anemic-looking redhead named Terry Falson.

After exchanging pleasantries, Mardle said, "Terry here has had a rough night. He thought as much of Frank as I did. So he wanted to see him one last time."

Gerald tried to hide his annoyance. The policeman was trouble enough, but with the addition of the pasty-faced grad student, the difficulty in securing what he'd come for would double. "Uh, look, I understand. But do you really think this is the right time?"

But the grad student insisted despite all objections, and followed the policeman and him into the trailer. Mardle predictably turned away at the door and shuffled off, head down.

Gerald held in a relieved sigh when he found everything as he had left it. Despite the storage trailer's locked door, he'd been haunted by the thought that Frank's body might be robbed of its treasure. That the ring was still there told him that, most likely, nobody else knew its true value. Or perhaps even of its existence. Unless the supposedly grieving redhead sniffing back tears beside him was an exception.

The body had relaxed from the rigor mortis, as he'd expected. He knew rigor mortis subsides within forty-eight to seventy-two hours, under normal circumstances. But higher temperatures accelerate the process, and the baking Frank's corpse had received the previous day had done precisely that.

The moment he looked at the body, Gerald realized the heat had done something else as well. Bacterial growth increases with higher temperature, putting a dead body on the fast track to putrefaction— unpleasant, gas-generating, pus-producing putrefaction. But that wasn't all. During life, body defenses protect against the harmful effects of gastric acid and enzymes. At death, the body's natural defenses break down, at which point gastric acid and digestive enzymes attack the very tissues they occupy. Between the bacterial putrefaction and self-digestion, the contents of the gastrointestinal tract turn to goo.

It was a hint of this goo on the lips of Frank's corpse that gave Gerald inspiration.

The grad student stood on the other side of the corpse now, head bowed, one hand covering his mouth. *What is he doing here?* Gerald wondered. *The man said he wanted to see Frank. So, fine. Here he is. Now go away.*

Nothing doing. Terry Falson, for whatever reason, stayed stuck to the table as if duty bound to remain.

The policeman took up his post perusing the various foodstuffs, and it was only then that Gerald realized that although the a/c was running full blast, it was still hot inside the trailer. He looked around and discovered two of the windows wide open, with only mosquito netting as barrier. He groaned, but then felt a shiver of dread, for he was certain they'd left the windows closed and locked.

But he didn't want to, couldn't speculate on that now. *Just get this done.*

He glanced across the table; Terry had turned a mild shade of green. *Good. Let's see how you handle* this, *young man.*

"With those windows open, we have to be sure nothing's missing," he said, picking up the manila envelope. He could have poured its contents onto the table, for there was plenty of room, but he dumped them onto Frank's chest instead. Hiding his glee, he recruited Terry's help in methodically repacking the envelope, which meant the student had to fish a number of items from the nest of chest-hairs above the v-neck of Frank's T-shirt. Terry's greenish hue deepened.

Time for the coup de grace.

"My, look at his face," he said, and sighed. "Doesn't he look peaceful, Terry?"

In fact, Frank's face was horribly contorted, as though from an unseen torture. Gerald leaned over the corpse and rested a hand on the bloated abdomen. Just as Terry forced his gaze upon the pasty dead face, Gerald gave a push. A great glob of frothy goo burst from the dead lips with a gurgle and loud burp. As each bubble puffed up and popped, an appalling stench erupted from their core.

Terry reeled to one side and buckled at the waist, as if struck by a physical blow. With one down and retching, Gerald noted that the policeman had taken a sudden and intense interest in the sacks of flour. He grabbed the water bottle he'd brought and quickly squirted soapy water over Frank's swollen finger, wrestled the ring free and held it aloft between thumb and forefinger, carefully shielding the ring's face from view. The policeman acknowledged it with quick glances, swallowing hard. Terry's only response was a moan.

He dropped the ring into the envelope, announced, "That's it, then," gave the flap a couple of quick licks and sealed it.

* * *

Once outside, the air-gulping grad student's red hair looked even redder, for his naturally pale face had turned the color of chalk. Mardle dismissed him, and Gerald watched him go.

"What do you think," Mardle asked, and put out his hand for

the envelope. "Shall I take a chance with registered mail, or wait until someone can hand-carry it to the States?"

"You mean," Gerald said, "like someone who might leave in a day or two, and who'll pass through Washington, DC, on the way to Maryland?"

Mardle looked at Gerald as if he'd just woken up, and then dropped his hand to his side. "Sorry, Ger, I'm not at my best. We only see each other at Oxford, so I've come to think of you as one of us. Would it be too much of a bother?"

Gerald gave a shrug he hoped appeared casual. "I'm flying to Dulles International anyway, so I'll be in their neighborhood. No problem."

"Settled, then. But for the sake of appearances, let's make this official. Here, got a pen?"

Uh-oh, Gerald thought, *sure didn't see that coming.*

Yet if he tried to put Mardle off, Mardle would want to know why. Gerald handed over a pen, and Mardle took the manila envelope and signed his name across the sealed flap, then returned the pen and envelope and gestured for him to follow suit.

Shugar. Just … shugar!

* * *

Two hours later, Big Bear and Little Bear sat and argued over their new monikers in a ramshackle café in the heart of Wadi Halfa.

"Sounds too much like Goldilocks," the smaller man said.

"No, that was Papa Bear and Baby Bear."

"Either way. I like my suggestion better."

His hulking partner scratched the two days of shadow on his chin. "You know, it's growing on me. I especially like the image of us outwitting the park ranger. Ha, ha."

"So?"

"So have it your way, Boo-Boo," the big man said.

"T'anks, Yogi," Boo-Boo said with a nasal twang.

The satellite phone on the table between them rang. Boo-Boo answered, and after a moment clicked off.

"Well?" Yogi asked. "What's our man at the dig got to say?"

Boo-Boo sipped his coffee, took a final drag on his cigarette and stubbed it out on the battle-scarred tabletop. "He says the Hansens seem clueless. Thinks they're out of the loop."

"Which means?" Yogi leaned forward and crossed his arms on the table.

"Which means we're the only ones with the map to the treasure." Boo-Boo sighed. "We've just got to find it before anyone else does."

"So we don't get to kill them?"

"Boss says no need."

"Dang." Yogi pulled a wicked-looking gravity knife from his pocket, snapped it open with a flick of his wrist and idly dug at the tabletop. "Just when I was beginning to enjoy myself."

CHAPTER 6

After two days of dotting t's and crossing i's, which pretty much summarized Gerald's opinion of governmental efficiency in Sudan, he and Michael were ready to leave. An autopsy had proven pointless, thanks to the advanced state of decay combined with the pathologist's inclination to support police conclusions. Whatever the cause of Frank's death, on paper it was snakebite.

With his body having lost its battle against decay in the first twelve hours, shipping him home wasn't a reasonable option. Gerald considered making the effort, but swiftly realized Frank's corpse fell into the same category as the nine-hundred-plus who committed suicide at the People's Temple in Guyana: within days, the equatorial heat had cooked the bodies. By the time the cleanup crews arrived, the corpses had decayed so much, they fell apart in their hands.

He called and received permission from Frank's daughters to bury him locally, after Terry Falson's mercifully brief graveside memorial of what "Dr. Tones" had meant to the field of archeology. Trevor Mardle's eulogy was even shorter, but far more personal. Gerald wasn't sorry to depart the dig for the hotel, but he felt as though he carried an elephant on his shoulders.

Halfway to the hotel, he asked Mahmood to pull over and, once stopped, pushed Michael out the passenger-side door and followed.

"Listen," he said while he led Michael away from the car, "I have a problem."

Michael draped an arm over Gerald's shoulders. "Dad, don't be embarrassed. Happens to every guy sooner or later. Plus, you've been under a lot of stress and, let's face it, you're not getting any younger."

Gerald laughed at his first comic relief in days. "No, it's—"

"Well, if it's not that, then add bran to your breakfast, increase your fruits and fiber, avoid chocolate and coffee, and in a few days you'll be right as rain."

By then, they'd walked a distance Gerald judged as safe. "Okay, this is good, son," he said, and stopped. "I want us to look relaxed and natural. But I took you out of the car because I need to tell you something where I can be sure nobody else can hear ...."

A few hours later, he felt his life was on rewind. In a corner of the world only minimally touched by technology, the day of their departure looked no different from the day of their arrival. They hoisted their Hansen Stampeding Packs, bade farewell to Mahmood and stepped from the hot, dusty land into the hot, musty terminal.

"What's in the boxes?" Gerald asked as they approached the departure gate.

Michael turned the two boxes over in his hands, as if seeing them for the first time. "Don't know. Mahmood said one's from him, and the other's from Sudan. But he didn't say which is which."

"We have a few minutes. Open them and see."

Michael weighed them in his hand, but then stowed them in his bag. "Think I'll wait. Anticipation's half the fun, don't you think?"

No way did he think that. And neither did his son. Of that, Gerald was certain. But he was equally certain Michael had a good reason, so he let it go, instead reaching for and gently ruffling Michael's hair, which was particularly scruffy today, flying every which way in fronds like the head of a palm tree after a lightning strike. "So what's with the hair?" he said.

"New fashion," Michael replied. "Had a shower at the hotel and took a nap with it wet. This is how it turned out. Whatcha think?"

"Looks like a bird made a nest with strips from a Picasso."

"Which means ..."

"That I don't like it."

"On the other hand, think it might attract a bird?"

Gerald smiled, bowed his head and shook it slowly. "Only if it's desperate for a home."

"Home," Michael said. "*I'm* desperate for home."

Ah. Finally, the truth comes out, Gerald thought. "Well, with Frank Tones gone, maybe we can finish our summer vacation uninterrupted."

* * *

The hop to Cairo was uneventful, unlike the connecting flight to London. British Air meant better meals, safer planes, and check-in lines that actually moved. It also meant heightened security. Minutes after they arrived at the ticket counter in Cairo, Gerald found himself in pole position when a space at the counter cleared.

"Hey, Dad," Michael said as he shouldered his pack, "want that ring back? Bear with me, 'cause I'm about to pull a Frank Tones fit."

"*Next!*"

Michael grinned, bounced his eyebrows with mischief, and led his bewildered father to the counter.

He was coarse and off-putting from the start. He didn't overload the circuits of the ticket agent's sensitivities, but from the woman's face, he definitely strained their tolerance.

Gerald was mystified. He'd always considered himself a man of manners, and now wondered where his son's had gone. Ruse or not, he'd just about had enough when the ticket agent launched into her barrage of questions.

"Did you pack your bags yourself?"

Gerald said, "Yes," but Michael only grunted.

"And have they been in your possession since you packed them?"

Gerald's "yes" was rudely shoved aside by Michael's "Why do *you* care?"

The agent's voice adopted a chill that could have frayed the tips of her hair, and she spoke through clenched teeth, "Have your bags … been unattended … at any point … in time … since you packed them?"

Gerald gave Michael a protracted "cool it" look and said, "No." Michael shrugged and kissed the air in the direction of the by-now flummoxed agent.

The woman shook her head, as if convinced this would be the generation that brings ruin to Planet Earth. "Are you carrying anything you didn't pack yourselves?"

Gerald opened his mouth to speak, but was abruptly interrupted by Michael's "Sure, what of it?"

The agent snapped to attention as a new day dawned in her eyes. "Excuse me, was that a yes?"

Michael fluttered his eyelashes at her. "Gee, I don't know, I have trouble figuring out such complexities of syntax. Of *course* it was a yes! Here, give me some paper, sweetheart. I'll spell it out for you in nice, big, block letters!"

To complete the insult, he whipped a pen from his pocket and held out a hand for a sheet of paper.

"Right," the agent said, suddenly charged and cheerful. She motioned to a colleague and said with ill-disguised satisfaction, "Now, if you'll follow this nice gentleman, he'll take care of you from here."

Gerald didn't know where the "nice gentleman" materialized from, but he finally realized what was going on as Michael followed the man away from the counter. Turning to apologize, he said, "Look, I'm sorry, you have to excuse my son, he's—"

"No, I don't," the agent shot back.

"Excuse me?"

"I don't have to excuse your son. But now you'll have to excuse *me*. Next!"

"Look, this isn't normal for him. I don't know why he—"

"Well, that's perfectly *won*derful," she mewed, the purr of a cat sizing up a scratching post. "But tell you what … when I go to bed tonight I'm going to count my blessings, and high on that list is the fact that I don't have to see him again. Now, if you'll excuse me, I have to put a smile on my face for the gentleman behind you." She looked over his shoulder, said "Sir?" and motioned for him to leave.

"Um, right. Sorry," he muttered, and moved aside, "I'll just—"

The next customer stepped up to the counter, and the agent's expression transformed from Freon-frigid to generic welcome.

Gerald shook his head, turned and strode in the direction Michael had gone.

* * *

"You can't open that, you Nazi fascist whore! That's private property!"

It was a bad dream, but one Gerald had begun to fathom. And then the security guard slit open the envelope, dumped the contents on the table and started to sort through them, his steely gaze more on Michael than on the items themselves. Now the table was littered with coins, documents and pens, a wallet and passport, a watch, compass, compact camera, travel alarm, and an assortment of other oddments.

"You put those back," Michael yelled. "I know my rights! If anything's missing I'll sue. Now put those back!"

Undeterred, the guard stepped back, faked a yawn and then checked his watch. "Oh, I don't know. Looks about time for tea. Can't be missing that, now can we?"

Michael gave his hardest stare, huffed and puffed and, turning his back on the officer, stepped up to the table and repacked the envelope himself. When he finished, his shoulders slumped and he stood quietly, for all appearances deflated. "Look," he said, his back still to the guard, his voice sad, shuddering and low. "I'm sorry. We just buried an old friend, and these ... these are his things. We signed across the envelope flap so his family could see that nobody tampered with his personal stuff. I just can't go home with it sliced open like this."

There was a tense pause, then the officer sparked to life. "Oh, that's what this is all about, is it? But it's no excuse, you know. You're going to have to learn to control your temper, even when the chips are down."

Michael feigned despondency, allowing his silence to grow heavy before he continued with a convincing emotional cracking in his voice. "Yeah, you're right, but it's been tough. Again, I'm sorry." He half-turned, and flicked the cut edge of the envelope with his finger. "Guess we can't do anything about this anyway."

For a moment, neither moved. Gerald watched on the sidelines, dumbstruck.

And then the man said, "Humph. Well, that's all right then. Apology accepted." He peered at Michael's downcast face. "Right. We'll slap on some security tape, I'll sign and stamp it, and nobody will be able to complain." Thirty seconds later, he handed the envelope to Michael and said, "Here you go. Not quite as good as new, but at least it's official."

* * *

"Hey, Mr. Hollywood," Gerald said as he followed Michael to the gate, "thought you didn't like jewelry."

"What, you mean this old thing?" Michael said over his shoulder, holding up his hand and wiggling Frank Tones' ring on his finger.

CHAPTER 7

Why the chocolate bars?" Gerald asked as they neared the boarding gate.

"The foil is radiopaque."

"Now how did you know that?"

"Remember the two-pound Cadbury's you gave me for my birthday last year?"

"Who can forget?" Gerald handed their boarding passes to the gate attendant. "You left it in the car when we got to DC, it melted and we had to throw it away. *Two pounds* of Cadbury's. I almost cried."

"Yeah, that's the one," Michael said while they strolled the walkway to the plane. "It blacked out the x-ray monitor at security. When my bag went through there was this solid black rectangle, so I had to take it out of the bag and repeat the screening."

"So you folded Frank's envelope over a couple chocolate bars to bring it to security's attention?" Gerald said thoughtfully. "Pretty smart. Mikey, you have criminal potential. I may have to keep an eye on you."

"Don't think you have anything to worry about on that account, Dad. But as for the Cadbury bar ..."

"Yes?"

Michael pretended to stick two fingers down his throat, then said, "I didn't leave it to melt by accident."

* * *

Two hours and three home study modules later, Michael stretched in his seat and then nudged Gerald. "Movie any good?"

"The usual gratuitous sex and violence. You'd think they'd clean up the airplane versions. There are kids watching, after all."

"And dads," Michael said, smiling.

"Yes, well ... harrumph. Quite right, junior. I say, need any help with that optical physics, old chum?"

Michael laughed. "Now you sound like Dr. Tones."

That brought a pause. Michael broke it. "Dad, what are you going to tell his daughters?"

Another pause. This time, Gerald ended it. "They already know the cobra story. Guess I'll leave it at that. I figure they're better off that way."

"You raised me to be honest."

"Look who's talking. Who lied about the envelope?"

Michael popped a peanut into his mouth and started shelling a replacement. "Um, well, not me."

"Excuse me? What was that about something you hadn't packed yourself? Isn't that how that little play got started?"

"Yep, that's the short and the short of it." Michael popped another peanut into his mouth and offered one to Gerald. "But I didn't lie."

Slowly, very slowly, it dawned on him. "Don't tell me ... the gift from Mahmood?"

"Yup," Michael said with a crunch. "Mahmood told me that after the people, the best thing in Sudan is the peanuts."

He groaned. "So *that* was the package we didn't pack ourselves. As I said, Mikey, I'm going to have to keep an eye on you."

"So, about Dr. Tones' daughters ..."

Gerald nodded toward their dozing seatmate. "We'll talk later, God willing."

"That's what Arabs say, Christians and Muslims alike. 'God willing.'"

"True." Gerald shifted in his seat and craned his neck in search of a flight attendant. "Where'd you learn that? From Mahmood?"

"Nope." Michael leaned over and pushed Gerald's call button, then sat back. His face took on a dream-like quality, and Gerald realized his son's conscious mind had slipped its moorings and was now leafing through the pages of his mental library.

"Let's see," Michael said. "Ah, here it is. *Encyclopaedia Britannica*. Under 'Allah.' 'Allah is the standard Arabic word for "God" and is used by Arab Christians as well as by Muslims.' Also under 'Allah,' *The New International Dictionary of the Christian Church* states, 'The name is used also by modern Arab Christians who say concerning future contingencies: *In sha' Allah.* Or, in other words, 'God willing.'"

"*The New International …?*" Gerald said.

"Zondervan Publishing, 1978, page twenty-seven."

Michael spoke in the zombie-like monotone that always bugged Gerald. He snapped his fingers in front of Michael's face. "Michael? Back with me?"

Michael blinked twice and life returned to his face, "I never left you."

"I beg to differ. You scare me sometimes."

"Well, you always told me a quote is worthless without reference to its source."

"True, but sometimes you take it too far. Now, what's in the second package?"

Michael weighed the box in his hand. "Don't know. Actually, I'm afraid to look."

"Why's that?"

"Could be a Cadbury's."

* * *

Frank Tones' family had almost as many personalities as Frank had shown in the years Gerald had known him. When he and Michael arrived at the family's DC home, Frank's ex-wife, Cindy, greeted them briefly and then escaped through an obstacle course of packing boxes to the kitchen, as if running just from the memory of Frank. Her new husband, Dr. Crawley, could be heard bumbling about upstairs, but he didn't expend any effort to come down and exchange greetings. The older of Frank's two daughters sat at one end of the living room sofa and cried. The younger, a college freshman home for the summer to help with the move to a new house, was the only one who seemed composed. Rachael accepted their condolences politely, and poured the contents of the envelope onto the coffee table. While her older sister blubbered beside her, Rachael quietly sorted through her father's effects.

"Something's missing," she said.

Gerald's heart jumped.

"Of course, it wouldn't have fit in that envelope," Rachael continued. "But Dad's chess set ... did you see it?"

Gerald silently released a held breath. "Well, yes, but we gave that to Dr. Mardle. It was your sister's suggestion."

"Oh." Rachael turned the pocket camera over in her hands. "You didn't find any film?"

Gerald hadn't thought about that, but she was right. A camera but no film. Strange.

"No film in the camera, either," she said as she offered it for inspection.

Gerald took it and peered through the empty indicator window. *Now why didn't I think of that?*

"Guess we won't have any use for these ...."

He looked up and found Rachael wearing her father's reading glasses. The frames were askew, and when she removed them, she identified a badly bent temple-piece as the cause.

"Oh, sorry, that must have happened in transit," he apologized, perplexed.

She sat back and motioned to the pile. "Is there anything you'd like? To remember him by? We need to keep his papers. Other than those, help yourself."

His conscience reminded him of the ring. He took a battered fountain pen, content with the conviction that, unbeknownst to her, she had cleared his guilty conscience. "Thanks," he said in a low voice.

Beside him, Michael said, "Good choice, Dad," and gave Rachael a smile. Watching, Gerald thought, *Well, well, well.* He wondered how long it would take for Michael to casually mention they ought to invite Rachael for a visit to their house in Maryland.

Small talk and lunch followed, interrupted by an occasional outbreak of sobs from the older sister. Dr. Crawley joined them midway through the meal, offering Gerald little more than a grunt by way of greeting. He tried to appear somber, failed, and settled for silence instead. Gerald was glad when Crawley finished his sandwich and excused himself, leaving Rachael to buffer her sister's sobs with reminiscences about Frank. But Gerald noticed that even Rachael's kind words seemed to conceal long-held bitterness.

An hour later, Gerald guided Michael to the door while promising to keep in touch. And judging from the looks he'd seen exchanged between Rachael and his son, he was sure they would.

* * *

"Report," the radio crackled.

"Leaving now."

"Details?"

"Nothing noteworthy. Following. Monitoring audio."

And the inconspicuous Honda, the clone of thousands in the DC area, pulled out half a block behind the Hansens' Ford Taurus.

CHAPTER 8

That went well, don't you think?" Michael asked, sounding too casual to be casual.

"Better in some ways than others, wouldn't you say?" Gerald replied as he dialed a left turn with the steering wheel.

"You thinking of anything specific?"

"Why, whatever do you mean, my teenage prodigy?"

"Dad, do you realize you're answering all my questions with a question?"

"Am I?"

Once they were on the freeway, Michael said, "We've got a three-hour drive home. So what'll it be, religion or politics?"

"How about weather?"

"Fine. How's this: 'weather' or not the girls believed you, what do you think really happened to Dr. Tones?"

Gerald sighed. "What would you have said if I'd chosen religion instead of weather?"

Michael pulled sunglasses from the glove compartment and replied, "For the love of God, we've got to figure out what really happened to Dr. Tones!"

"Politics?"

"I hate politics."

"Me, too."

"That leaves us nothing to talk about but Frank Tones."

* * *

Four cars back, a bland, indistinct man dressed in blue-collar casual—jeans and two layers of patterned T-shirts—nudged the driver, a broad-chested, bull-necked blond stuffed into a blazer and tie. Despite his professional attire, Bull Neck's appearance and demeanor made him better suited to a job as a health club trainer than a CIA field operative. His forehead sloped, and his eyes recessed beneath the prominent brow, giving him the look of a college football jock who had difficulty maintaining passing grades.

"Okay," Blue Collar said to Bull Neck, "we know where they're going, and this is a conversation we don't want to miss. Drop back and let the alternate take over visual."

The Honda slowed and fell back, and an equally inconspicuous Toyota slipped into its place.

* * *

"All I know is that it doesn't make sense," Gerald said. He set the cruise control and stretched his legs beyond the pedals. "In fact, there are so many pieces missing, I can't begin to guess at the big picture."

Michael toyed with the ring on his finger. A perfect oval, its distinctive face contained three symbols. A rolled scroll and a broken sword each formed one arm of a V. The mouth of the V was filled with a wedge of sun, and slivers of gold radiated outward from the edge of its dome. Earlier, Gerald had said it looked like an ice cream cone. "An ancient, two-thousand-year-old, solid gold ice cream cone."

"Dad, let's go over the details. You start, and I'll make a list."

Gerald flexed his neck with a creak and a pop, gave his gray hair a brisk wake-up scrub. "Okay, let's start with Dr. Mardle. With his reputation, he should be on the biggest digs in the world. What's he doing on a dig so unsuccessful that the primary, Dr. Rybkoski, is shutting it down to move elsewhere?"

Michael nodded. "And if the dig was a failure, what did Dr. Tones find that got him all excited?"

"This." Gerald extended his hand from the armrest and tapped the ring on Michael's finger. "Definitely this."

A quarter of a mile back, the two men glanced at one another and asked, "What's 'this'?"

"Let's do our list first. We can come back to *this* later," Michael said, raising his ring hand, unaware of the Honda's driver banging *his* hand against the steering wheel and screaming, "What is *this*?"

"All right. Let's start with the obvious," Gerald said. "Why did Frank die in bed?"

"Um, he got bit by a cobra?"

"That's the party line, sure. Do you believe it?"

"Nope."

"Neither do I. He should've lived long enough to have gotten out of bed, at the very least. And Mahmood said there was no swelling from the bite. So the question is, could someone have arranged the snakebite *after* death to cover a murder?"

"Pretty speculative, Dad."

"*Very* speculative. But we've seen snakebites before. The swelling and bruising is virtually instantaneous. Tissue necrosis follows quickly. He had none of that. And by the way he was laying on the bed, he didn't struggle, didn't even try to get up."

"Maybe the venom hit the bloodstream too fast. It was a neck bite, after all."

"I could be wrong, Mikey, but I don't think it happens that fast. That cobra strike-slash-instant death scenario is pure Hollywood. Okay, next point: the air conditioning—"

"Wait a minute. What kind of cobra was this? Because the venom of the Egyptian cobra contains an analgesic peptide."

Gerald sighed. "I'm getting tired of asking this, Mikey, but how do you know *that*?"

"Cut it out, Dad. That was the kind of cobra Cleopatra allegedly used to kill herself, and they say that because of the analgesic effect, she died a painless death. A stupid, pointless death, but *painless*."

Gerald clucked reproachfully. "And she spoke so well of you."

"One more thing. The Egyptian cobra isn't aggressive. It bites only when threatened. Unless Dr. Tones rolled over it while he was sleeping, it should've left him alone."

"Uh, right. Hey, Mikey, do me a favor. Play dumb once in a while. Allow good old Dad to feel like the intelligent one for a change, okay? Now, how many nights did we sleep without air conditioning?"

"None."

"Exactly. Frank was found in his underwear, so the night must've been hot. We know that feeling. We stayed in his trailer after the air conditioner was replaced, and when we switched it off, even at night, the heat became unbearable. But Frank slept with the a/c off? Not likely."

"So what's your point? Why would anyone care whether the a/c was on or off?"

"Seriously, or playing dumb for dear old Dad?" Gerald took a break to check his mirrors and shift in his seat. "No matter. Answer your own question. When they turned the a/c on after they found his body, a bug shorted it. Now, how likely is that? As a result, Frank cooked all day. When he was moved to the cold storage trailer, I found the a/c fighting against open windows the next day. The windows won."

Michael frowned. "Someone *wanted* his body to decompose? To ruin the chance of an accurate autopsy?"

Gerald shrugged. "It's too much to be coincidence."

"Hmm. Next?"

"Right. What's next is what Rachael noticed ... oh, you do remember Rachael, don't you Michael? The younger, prettier one? The one who served you tea while I, your father, served myself?" Satisfied to see his son blush and look away, he continued, "Rachael noticed that Frank's camera had no film. Oh, and his reading glasses. The frame was bent. They were unusable. Now, how did that happen?"

"In our bags or ... in a struggle?"

"Who knows?" But I bunked with Frank on a lot of digs, and I can tell you he always fell asleep reading."

"Okay, maybe he rolled over on them while sleeping."

"Sure. Of course. He rolled one way, mashed his glasses, then rolled the other way and squashed the snake. Happens all the time. Not."

"So, adding all this up, we've got—"

"Zip," they said simultaneously.

"Which brings us back to this." Gerald pointed to the ring.

"FINALLY!" Blue Collar shouted a quarter mile back, "the 'this'!"

"But first, your old dad needs coffee. Let's take a break."

"NOOOOO," Bull Neck exploded, his outburst swept away in the slipstream of traffic.

* * *

The convenience store was unusually crowded. The only empty seats were at the end of the row of tables, next to the refrigerated display cases at the back. Bikers and construction workers filled the rest. Gerald casually wondered what an anthropologist might make of this cross-section of society a million years from now, were they to be instantly buried in volcanic ash and preserved, frozen with their drinks and donuts in hand.

"Let me see if I understand this correctly," Michael said, keeping his voice low. "According to what you read in Dr. Tones' excavation notes, he found a clay jar in one of the graves, sealed with palm fiber and pitch. There was a papyrus scroll inside. An unusually well-preserved scroll, written in ancient Hebrew and imprinted with the face of the ring, *and* the ring itself."

"Correct. Now, adjacent graves were radiocarbon-dated to the end of the first century CE. Early results on that grave weren't in yet, but Frank expected it to be the same. Which would make that jar from the first century too."

Michael nodded. "Oh, man. Time of Christ. Very significant. So, what we really want to know is what the scroll says."

"Correct-a-mundo."

"So?"

"Yes?" Hiding his grin, Gerald nonchalantly stirred a fifth sugar packet into his coffee.

"So what *DID IT SAY*?"

"Oh, nothing. Just, well, you don't really care—"

"Dad."

"Tell you what, read it yourself. Frank's assistant let me take photos of it before we left. We'll get 'em developed as soon as we get home. Come on, let's go."

"I'm gonna grab an apple on the way out."

As Michael dashed off to join the line at the counter, Gerald stood to leave and casually glanced around the store. His gaze fell upon a nondescript customer dawdling in a nearby aisle, flipping through a magazine. The customer immediately turned and bent over to replace the magazine, then stooped to browse the lower rack. Gerald shrugged. "An apple?" he called after Michael. "Thought you said it was me who needed to increase the fruits and fiber." Then he headed for the door.

* * *

"Catch anything?" Bull Neck asked.

Blue Collar fastened his seatbelt, sucked his teeth and looked critically at the mini-directional microphone pinched between his fingertips. "Yeah, one very important thing."

"What's that?"

"I heard the kid say, quote, 'did it say.' Everything else was garbage."

"Rats. This James Bond stuff never works."

"Never. Remind me to complain to Q."

And they pulled into traffic to follow.

* * *

"So, what we've got," Michael said between bites of his apple, "is a first-century grave and a scroll."

"And that," Gerald said, and pointed.

"And this," Michael said, toying with the ring.

"That! This!" Blue Collar seethed through gritted teeth. "Tell you what. Why don't you pull alongside and I'll ask them, real nice, what the heck they're talking about."

"Oh, and there's one more thing we've got," Gerald added. "We've got a dead Frank Tones. So *somebody* thinks this is worth killing for. If, that is, he really was killed."

"Which we think he was," Michael said as he nibbled the apple core.

"Which we think he was," Gerald agreed.

"Which he most *definitely* was," Bull Neck said with a chuckle.

A long pause later, Michael said, "You think we have anything to worry about, Dad? Like ... are *we* in any danger?"

"Not anymore," Gerald answered. "Sudan had me worried. That's why I didn't mention any of this until we got out of there and stateside."

Michael looked around for a trash bag, then held up the apple core. "Dad, what should I do with this?"

"The 'this?'" Blue Collar said, and then addressed the receiver, "Ah ... may I suggest the glove compartment?"

"Your choice, Mikey. Hold it till we get home, eat it, or toss it into the woods."

"WHAAAAT?" Blue Collar's eyes bugged as he yelled.

"Eat it? Blech!" Michael said. "Think I'll just hold it. Can you imagine the irony? We're worried about getting murdered, and we get arrested for littering instead."

"Oh, I wouldn't worry about that," Gerald said. "After all, it came from the earth, it can return to the earth. Here, I'll pull over. You can step out and chuck it."

"Drop back!" Blue Collar yelled. "DROP BACK!"

"Can't, too close, he'll see me." In the same breath, Bull Neck ordered the swing car, already behind them, to hang back and observe. Slowing imperceptibly, he passed the Hansen's Ford as it pulled over onto the shoulder. "Mark that spot," he ordered the swing car. "Then call clean-up, top priority. And one of you stays there until they arrive."

"*What're we looking for?*" the swing car's driver asked.

"Whatever the kid drops. We don't know what it is, but it's important. Tell them to bag everything that doesn't belong. And I mean *everything.*"

"Uh, look ... where they stopped? Looks like a garbage dump. Not only that, but the kid didn't drop it, he threw it."

"Your tax dollars at work ... I meant *everything.*"

"Got it. Hey, they're pulling out."

The Honda picked up speed from the slow lane when the Ford passed, and after a few minutes, a lone man in the swing car pulled into position and the Honda dropped back out of visual.

"Time to celebrate," Blue Collar said, and reached into the food bag. "What'll you have?"

"Good luck makes me hungry. Gimme a sandwich and an apple."

* * *

"Dad, I need to see that scroll. Now."

Gerald thought a moment, then shrugged. "We'll pull over for a photo stop."

"Sounds good. So, what do you think of Georgetown?"

"The university? Expensive."

"Think your only son's worth it?"

"By the time you're a freshman, Rachael will be a junior." Gerald turned to him and winked. "That *is* why, isn't it?"

"Yeah. But hey, did you see the way she looked at me?"

"Yup. And how *you* looked at *her.*"

"Told ya the hair might work."

Gerald shot a sidelong glance at his son's tufted hair, then into his eyes, found the look reflected back at him, and both laughed.

Ten minutes later, the men in the Honda sat parked at a strip mall, watching as Gerald and Michael walked into the Photos in an Hour Shop.

"Mission impossible," Blue Collar said to his partner. The primary close-observation operative, Blue Collar, wore his own hair in a butterfly cut, which allowed him to part it on the right, left, down the middle, or comb it straight back. Also designed for quick change, his shirt was a reversible T-shirt, both sides distinctive not only in color, but in pattern and designer emblem. Underneath, as backup, his undershirt was similarly distinctive. The one he wore this day sported the business end of a loaded revolver with the words, "Go Ahead, Punk, Make My Day" divided above and below the gun. Nobody who saw it would forget. More important, nobody who saw it would be likely to notice the face above it.

In addition to variations in clothing, Blue Collar possessed a wide variety of visual distracters: bold earrings, owl-eyed glasses, artificial facial moles and other assorted goodies designed to draw a person's attention away from his unalterable, though bland, facial features.

"Mission impossible," Blue Collar repeated to Bull Neck. "They're the only customers there. Even with all my goodies, if I follow them, they'll notice me. Remember me."

"So?" Bull Neck asked.

"So we wait. Anyway, we know what's on those photos. Why risk being spotted?"

CHAPTER 9

Fifty minutes later, the Honda was back on the road, the receiver crackling.

"Dad, listen to this. It begins like one of those Old Testament 'begat' lists. Jacob the son of Menan, the son of Eleazar, the son of so-and-so, the son of so-and-so, yada yada yada. Okay. Then Jacob identifies himself as an Israelite, a member of the Covenant of God and one of the Sons of Light ..."

A pause, then the father's voice: *"Go on, I'm listening."*

"Yeah, hang on a sec. Let me finish this ..."

"No way. The kid can read that stuff?" Blue Collar said. "Kids his age in my neighborhood can't even read a stop sign."

"Yeah, maybe," Bull Neck replied. "But the kids in your neighborhood aren't in danger of being killed."

"What, you kidding? They're offing each other every day."

"I mean by *us.*"

Blue Collar glanced at his partner's Neanderthal forehead, then lowered his gaze to his lap. "Karl, you're new at this, so let me give you a tip. Blow that Rambo stuff out your ears and just try to be a good person. These first few months will lay the foundation of your career. If you show too much interest in torture and killing, they'll find a channel for your energies, all right, but you'll lose your soul. On the other hand, if you come off like the good guy, and by that I mean you show honesty and ethics, they'll assign you to clean jobs. Not as exciting, but you'll go home every night and be able to look yourself in the mirror. So just put the bad stuff out of your mind. That's not what we're here for."

"Tim, in this line of work," Karl said with a wink, "we never know *what* we might be told to do. That's what I love about this job."

Tim turned in his seat and faced Karl with the one expression no man ever read from his face and forgot. "Like I said, you're new, and it's my job to break you in. But let me make something clear. If anyone wants to hurt that kid, they'll have to kill me first."

Karl's face stilled. "Even if we get orders from Central?"

Tim glanced out the window on Karl's side, then turned back into his seat. "What I'm saying is, the order has to come from a lot higher than Central to override the commandment not to kill. You think I'd ever kill someone who doesn't deserve it? If they don't deserve it, I'll die defending them and go to my grave happy, knowing I did the right thing."

"You're compromised," Karl said. He looked forward, his knuckles white on the steering wheel.

"And you're crazy."

"You know I'll have to report this."

"Report what you want. The day you realize you're gonna have to answer for what you do in this life, you'll understand there are limits a *man* doesn't cross."

"Dad," the receiver crackled, *"this guy was an Essene!"*

Karl opened his mouth, but closed it when Tim said, "Shh!"

"An Essene." the father's voice came through. *"Imagine that. An Essene in Nubia. Read on."*

"Let's see ... 'the wilderness retreat by the Salt Sea,' which I take to mean the Dead Sea. 'The Jewish revolt.' That's gotta refer to the Jewish rebellion of 66–70 CE. The occupation of the complex by Roman forces. The slaughter of the Essenes ... and that's it. Nothing to connect what Frank found to any of it. Where's the rest?"

"That's what I want to know."

"Me, too," Tim said, half a mile back. He glanced at Karl. "Exciting, huh?"

But Karl stared straight ahead, his upper lip curled at one corner of his mouth.

"Let me see if I understand this correctly," Michael said. "Dr. Tones' graduate student, that guy named Robert, said the end of the scroll was accidentally cut off and *lost?* Exactly how did that happen?

They unrolled the scroll, accidentally chopped off the last part of it, and then re-rolled what was left?"

Gerald drummed his fingers on the steering wheel. "Not like that. Jacob's scroll was only a single page rolled *widthwise*, not lengthwise. Imagine taking a piece of paper and rolling it widthwise, and then cutting off the bottom. The end would be lost, right? Well, that's what happened to Jacob's scroll." He paused to lower his window a crack. "Accidents like that do happen in salvage archaeology. It's like Frank said about scooping ice cream with a backhoe. Stuff gets broken. And broken off. Anyway, Robert said they rechecked the gravesite with sifters, but didn't find anything."

"So what does *he* think happened?"

"Don't know. Maybe a shovel cut the scroll during the digging, and the bottom got tossed into the rubble. Maybe it was carried off by the wind or by a wild animal."

Michael removed his sunglasses, slapped the temples closed and tossed them onto the dashboard. "That is *so* lame."

"Yeah, I know."

"In addition to which, it doesn't explain—"

"The scroll jar, I know." Gerald's face shadowed with disgust. "Robert fed me that line, and I looked from his face to the scroll, then at the *intact* scroll jar. When I looked back at him, he'd turned white as a sheet. Never seen a man that scared. Like he was about to scream, 'Don't ask!' So I didn't. But I knew he was lying, and he knew I knew."

They drove the rest of the trip home in silence. So did Tim and Karl.

CHAPTER 10

A week later, Gerald stood at the stove in his pajamas, making breakfast. He poured pancake batter and reflected how, twenty years before, Ocean City had seemed the perfect place to buy a house. A direct flight from England to Washington DC landed a three-hour drive from the resort city. The perfect place to vacation and plan for retirement.

That dream had died with Susan.

Shortly thereafter, the once-placid city had exploded with cluster bombs of yuppies. Hotels, restaurants, bars, timeshares and amusement centers multiplied as if breeding. This summer, he'd returned from Oxford to find a miniature golf and video arcade complex flanking one side of his property, and his latest homecoming gift, a restaurant under noisy construction, on the other.

He flipped a pancake and watched it fluff up and bubble, and wondered how long he could hold out. Perhaps someday a band of marauding real estate developers would stone him unconscious with colored golf balls. Then they'd beat him to death with cheap putters and drag his corpse through the streets behind a go-kart as a warning to any others who opposed progress.

"Shall I fry some bacon with this?" He turned to Michael, who sat at the kitchen counter flipping through an encyclopedia-sized tome as though browsing a magazine. But Gerald knew better.

Michael wrinkled his nose. "Forbidden, Dad."

"What subject is that?"

"Religion."

Gerald learned not to ask for book titles; they changed too quickly. Michael had a slow start in childhood due to a multilingual exposure, but rapidly developed fluency in multiple languages, both spoken and written, contemporary and archaic. Unlike other children, he never read a favorite book twice. Never had to.

He and Susan had quickly realized their son was gifted with true photographic memory, with a reading speed limited only by how fast he could flip the pages. It was different for books he read for pleasure, though; Michael could no more race through a novel and enjoy it than he could fast-forward through a movie and appreciate the acting.

He stacked the pancakes onto a plate, poured two more into the pan with a sizzle, then said, "Well, when you work past Judaism and into Christianity, you can start eating bacon again."

"Dream on, Dad." Michael reached the end of his book and flipped it closed, then looked up with a grin. "Jesus was a Jew, and taught Old Testament law. They even called him 'Rabbi.' In Matthew 5:17-18, Jesus said he didn't come to change the law, but to fulfill it. Couple years later, Paul came along and said the law had changed. So which was it? Jesus said he didn't come to change the law, Paul said the law has changed. Who's a person to believe?"

Gerald slid the platter onto the counter between them, sat down and said. "Okay, no bacon."

Michael pushed his book to one side and replaced it with another.

"What's that?" Gerald reached over and tilted the cover in his direction. "Didn't you read a Bible just last week?"

"Two. Those were numbers six and seven. This is number eight. Pancakes are burning."

Gerald jumped to the stove and flipped the darkly browned cakes. "You can keep all those versions straight in your head?"

"Sure." Michael looked thoughtful. "I just don't understand … if the Bible's the word of God, why are there so many versions?"

"It's just different wording. The meaning's the same." He stood sentry over the stove, his spatula at the ready.

"Not true." Michael started flipping pages and spoke absentmindedly as he read. "Ask anybody about the Trinity, and they'll quote the First Epistle of John, verses 5:7-8, in the King James Version. You know, the one that reads, 'For there are three who bear witness in heaven: the Father, the Word, and the Holy Spirit; and these three are one.' But the Revised Standard Version, the New American Standard Bible, the New International Version, The Jerusalem Bible *and* others either significantly altered or outright rejected that verse."

Gerald finished the pancakes, turned the stove off and rejoined him at the counter. "And why's that?"

Michael gestured frustration with one hand and flipped a page with the other. "According to The New Scofield Reference Bible and The Interpreter's Bible, that verse lacks manuscript authority. In fact, not only does it *not* exist in *any* of the ancient Greek manuscripts, but it was first quoted by Priscillian, the Spanish heretic, in the *fourth century*. A scribe wrote it into the margin of one of the New Testament manuscripts. One of the early copiers liked it, so he added it to the text. So basically, the words of a heretic came to be accepted as the words of God. Some Bibles kept it, maybe as a play to the orthodox believers, I dunno. Others are faithful to the scriptures and modern scholarship and reject it. Point is, no, not all Bibles read the same."

"You don't like archaeology, do you?" Gerald asked, and leaned onto an elbow.

Michael looked up from his Bible, his face glowing. "I do like archaeology. Really, I do. But I *love* religion. Archaeology fills the gaps in history. But religion answers the big questions."

"Such as?"

"Such as, 'Who made us?' and ...." He started to bother a pancake with his fork.

"And?"

"And ..." He raised his head and looked Gerald straight in the eyes. "And, 'What's the purpose of life?'"

"Ah." At once Susan's face leapt into view, and Gerald understood. "Your mother would be proud of you."

"And you?"

Gerald smiled and patted his hand. "I'm already proud. But your mom was the religious one in the family."

Michael smiled and bent his head to his pancake, and Gerald somehow knew their minds' eyes had focused on the same memory.

Susan's final illness had rendered her incoherent and delirious, and the fever had blinded her. But in her last moments, she opened her eyes and reached her hand to Gerald's face. *"I'm alive,"* she had said.

Gerald had cupped her burning face in his hands while tears flooded his face. "Yes, you're still alive," he'd said.

"No, not *still*," she had replied. "I *was* dead. *Now* I'm alive."

He'd thought she was hallucinating, and reached for the pitcher of ice water to refresh the compress on her forehead. But then she laid a hand on his arm and said, "Life is death, and death is life. I was dead, and now I'm alive."

Then she had closed her eyes, and her shivering stilled as her face relaxed, as though in sleep, and the most peaceful smile he'd ever seen stretched across her face. And that's when Michael had thrown himself on his dead mother and fought, fruitlessly, to bring her back.

Enough of that. He pinched his fingers into his eyes to squeeze the image away. "Mikey, you need a break from the library. You're wearing a rut in the sidewalk from our door to theirs."

Michael finished a pancake, fished another from the platter, and looked askance at him. "You prepared to finance a minor in video technology?"

He winced at the reference to the new video arcade next door. "Sure. Might even join you for a game. Anything over there I'd like?"

"Definitely." Michael smiled. *"Dig Dug."*

"Uh, you're joking."

"Nope. Just your speed. The player digs channels to subterranean air pockets, shoots monsters with a pneumatic gun, and inflates them till they pop."

"Hmm. I can think of a few people I'd like to do that to."

"Like Dr. Crawley? Dr. Chunky Coprolite?"

Laughing, Gerald slapped his napkin on the counter and got up to clear the dishes. "Nope, he *married* his punishment. Tell you what, maybe I'll join you after I check the mail."

* * *

"Check the mail? What's he talking about? You covered the mail, didn't you?"

Karl hitched his tie to his thick neck, wriggled his chin as if trying to crawl out of his collar and flexed his prominent brows. "I did. No box registered in either of their names at the post office, or any of the local mailbox rental places. And everything that comes to his home is screened."

"What about his wife?"

"Died three years ago."

Tim threw up his hands. "Idiot! Maybe they took out a box in her name before she died, and he kept renewing it because he works overseas. If he gets the wrong kind of mail *now*, it could be the death of both of them!"

Twenty minutes later, their radio squawked, *"He's on the move."*

* * *

Gerald drove to the local Mail Boxes Etc. and picked up the bank statement and telephone bill he expected, a package claim slip he didn't, and a renewal invoice for the mailbox rental. Seeing Susan's name on the invoice always brought a bittersweet pang, but he'd never changed it. *Why?* he wondered. *Because seeing mail in her name keeps her memory alive?*

As with previous years, he decided not to think about it. Instead, he closed the box and traded the claim slip at the counter for a small box plastered with a great number of colorful stamps. And a return address. In Sudan.

He opened the package in the car and drove straight to a photo developer, where he took advantage of the one-hour processing and duplicate prints special. From there he visited the bank.

Back home, he pulled into the garage, put the car in park, and was about to turn off the ignition when he noticed that, according to his radar detector, he was about to get pulled over for speeding.

He tapped the detector, picked it up and shook it, and then leaned back in his seat and stared at the full row of red warning lights.

* * *

"Uh-oh." Tim shook his head while he examined the wrapper he'd pulled from the garbage bin outside the photo shop.

"Do we get to kill somebody?" Karl asked. "Do we, do we?"

Tim turned to reply and noticed for the first time how his partner's bull neck flowed into his head without narrowing. *I was wrong*, he thought. *He's not a Neanderthal. He's a brontosaurus. The guy's a flipping brontosaurus.*

"Absolutely," he replied with a tight smile. "Namely, the idiot who allowed this package to get through."

The radio squawked again, and a voice from the electrician's van down the street from Gerald's house said, *"Hey, there they are again."*

"'They'? Who are 'they'?" Tim asked.

"Same spooks we saw yesterday *and* the day before. You know, the same guys we saw at Dulles Airport. One guy's a mountain, the other disappears when he turns sideways. Remember?"

Tim sighed. "Great. We're watching the Hansens, they're watching the Hansens, and we don't even know who '*they*' are."

"Unless," Karl said, "'*they*' are actually watching us."

"Man," Tim sighed, "I'm too old for this."

"Nah." Karl reached under his blazer and checked the gun in his shoulder holster. "Not too old. Just too caring. And that, my friend, will get you killed."

CHAPTER 11

"Dad, this is dynamite!" Michael sat at the dining room table and poured over the photos Gerald had just handed him. "No. More like a bomb. An atom bomb!"

"Depleted." Gerald stood behind him and placed both hands on his shoulders.

"Huh?" Michael turned from the photos and searched his face.

"More like depleted uranium. Worthless. Of greater harm than benefit."

"But this is priceless!"

"Listen, Mikey, what does the scroll say?"

Michael turned back to the photos, which when pieced together showed all of Jacob's scroll, beginning to end. Gerald watched, remembering the first time Michael translated a scroll by himself. At the age of eight. Raised in digs in Israel and the Middle East, in rooms wallpapered with photos of scrolls and scroll fragments, Gerald and Susan had been crouched on the floor one evening, struggling over a particular passage, when eight-year-old Michael asked for a bedtime story. Gerald had replied, "Okay, sport, soon as I'm through with this translation."

But Michael had gone to bed on promises too many times. So, instead of going back to bed, he'd looked over their shoulders and read the passage fluently. Gerald remembered being dumbstruck. Susan had swayed back from her crouch, a stray strand of auburn hair draped over her right eye, one hand resting on the floor to steady her, the other pressed flat to her chest, her wide eyes staring at her grinning son.

Later, they wondered why they'd been so surprised. Michael had grown up with the scrolls, and had absorbed and deciphered the ancient Hebrew and Aramaic as only a child can. To him, he simply did what was needed to hurry his father up so he'd read him a story. Even so, to Gerald, it was a miracle that Michael could read the scrolls as easily as he read his Dr. Seuss. So who was Gerald to argue with miracles?

"Okay, here we go," Michael said, pulling him from the memory. "The beginning, we already know. After that, Jacob describes having hidden a scroll he refers to as 'The good message,' which we would understand to mean 'the gospel' of 'a Teacher of Righteousness.' He goes on to describe——"

"Of *the* Teacher of Righteousness," Gerald corrected from over his shoulder.

"Uh, no, Dad, look." Michael placed his finger on one photo. "There's no definite article. It's *a* Teacher of Righteousness. *Anyhoo,* Jacob describes the slaughter of the Essenes and his escape to Nubia, but how he was, ah, overcome with sickness and unable to return."

Gerald lifted his hands from Michael's shoulders and took a seat next to him. "Okay. What else?"

"Well, as you know, Jacob links the wax seal on *this* scroll with that to be found on the hidden gospel," Michael said, peering at the photographs while he spoke. "Next, he describes where he hid it ...."

A moment later he looked up, eyes thoughtful. "Now that I think about it, his description of the hiding place sounds like one of the caves at Qumran. You know, the ones on the Dead Sea?"

Gerald grinned. "Yeah, I'm a little familiar. How do you think I keep you in books and video game tokens?"

With a chuckle, Michael ran his fingers through his unruly hair, then returned to the photographs. "And this is something I'm still trying to figure out. Jacob concludes by warning against the deceptions of someone he called the 'Wicked Priest.' That's the same person he also identifies as the, uh, 'The Man of the Lie.' Whoa. Them's fightin' words! Even worse, he claims this Wicked Priest dude misled the masses from the teachings of the Teacher of

Righteousness. Lastly, he advises of … hang on a sec … he advises of 'the one who teaches righteousness in the end of days.'"

He looked up and grinned. "It's like he's talking about a future prophet. A future *final* prophet. Like I said, dynamite stuff."

"And like *I* said, depleted uranium. Look, the caves at Qumran have been fully excavated. So this, this …" Gerald paused and waved both hands in the air, "this 'Gospel of the Teacher of Righteousness' is gone."

"Destroyed?" Michael looked up from the photographs and slid back in his chair.

"Or hidden by those who don't want the world to see it."

"Or it's still undiscovered?"

"Impossible." Gerald shook his head sadly. "Impossible. Those caves have been gone over with hundreds, no, *thousands* of fine-toothed combs."

"Impossible? That doesn't sound like my father speak—"

"Impossible." Gerald leaned over the table and shook his head. "Michael, I know Qumran like the back of my hand. Some caves were lost to erosion and collapse, sure. But those that survived were fully excavated. Fully. Either the scroll dropped into the Dead Sea with the collapse of a cliff, or someone already has it. Either way, it just isn't there."

Michael stared at the photos in silence. "Well, I guess these photos are worthless anyway without the original and complete scroll to back 'em up."

"Actually, they're worthless even *with* Jacob's scroll."

Michael looked up and fixed incredulous eyes on his father … who quickly raised a finger to his lips and said, "This is going nowhere. Tell you what. Why don't you go play some games and unwind? Maybe we'll go out to dinner later, how's that?"

He opened his wallet, thinned it by a couple bills, and slid them over the table. Then he repeated the "silence" gesture.

Michael pocketed the money and stood to leave. "Well, Dad, it hasn't all been for a loss. We learned something, didn't we?"

"And that would be?"

"That I can be bought." And he forced a laugh.

* * *

"Pop any monsters lately?"

Michael abandoned the video game controls and turned to see Gerald beside him. "Boy, am I glad to see you!"

"What, out of tokens?"

"No, out of my mind. Let's take a walk." He grabbed Gerald by the elbow and tried to turn him toward the exit.

Gerald didn't move. "Nooo, this is fine. Let's talk here."

"Dad, a person can *talk* here, but a person can't *hear* here." Michael laughed, but even that barely rose above the din from the machines that packed the video arcade.

"Yeah, well, that's exactly what we need right now." Gerald looked around, then asked, his voice low in Michael's ear, "Do you know what frequency's used for police radar?"

"Huh? Is this a trick question?"

"No, seriously."

"Seriously, I don't."

"Neither do I. But I do know it's in the noncommercial range, which means it's reserved for police and military. And this morning my radar detector lit up in the garage."

"So?"

"So ..." Gerald ran a tremulous hand through unruly gray hair and looked down at the floor. "So I strolled through the house with the detector on battery power, and it lit up everywhere I walked."

A long moment passed before the recognition in his son's eyes changed, first to fear, and then to false lightness.

"Hey, Dad, don't sweat it. We're in this together, okay?"

"Mikey ... Frank was murdered. So was the taxi driver who drove us to the hotel from the airport. *That's* who was killed across from our hotel. I didn't mention it at the time. Didn't want to upset you. But his hand fell out from under the sheet while he was being loaded into the ambulance. And I recognized his prayer beads. I thought we left all that when we left Sudan, but now our house is bugged. I'm certain of it."

Michael's eyes flew open. "The taxi driver?"

Gerald nodded. "That drug-related murder story Mahmood told us? I bought it. Remember the guys who followed us on that crazy ride from the airport? I figured they killed him for his drugs. Now I'm thinking they were following *us,* not him. They killed him, then they killed Frank."

"We don't know Frank was murdered, Dad."

"He was murdered. I'm sure of it. And now our house is bugged."

Michael shook his head, cast a glance at the ceiling and exhaled a long breath through pursed lips. He looked back at Gerald, forced a smile. "Bathrooms, too?"

Gerald shook his head and grinned. "No. Clear."

"Whew. Imagine having *those* tapes played back to your grandchildren. But maybe it's electrical interference or something. It *could* be something else, couldn't it?"

"When I tripped the main circuit breaker, nothing changed."

"There goes the electrical interference theory." Michael scratched his temple. "But if the house is bugged, wouldn't the bugs switch off with the electricity?"

Gerald thought a moment. "Only if hardwired."

"So in other words, we could be next in the Dead Archaeologists Club." Michael sighed. "No biggie, Dad. We've faced worse. So what about the car?"

Gerald took him by the arm and walked him down the aisle of arcade games. "Let's assume it's bugged as well. Obviously not with transmitters that would excite a radar detector, but still bugged."

"Dad, what's going *on* here?"

Gerald sat on a stool set before a *Pac-Mania* game and shook his head. "Here's my theory. Somebody's willing to kill to keep the Gospel of the Teacher of Righteousness from being found. Look, when we came home from Sudan, we didn't know the gospel existed, but now we do. And somebody … somebody who knows our connection with Frank Tones … that somebody's watching to see what we know, or what we'll do. There's no other explanation."

"So that's why we're talking here," Michael said as he leaned against a machine. "Microphone or no microphone, nobody could hear us with all this noise."

"Seemed a reasonable precaution."

"But Dad, if you knew this before, why did we read the photos in the house?"

Gerald stood and led him in another stroll down the row of machines. "I thought if I told you about bugs and bogeymen, you might not speak naturally, so I just steered the conversation. You know, convince them we know nothing and wouldn't pursue it even if we did."

"Ah. Which explains why you shut me up with your ..." Michael repeated Gerald's finger-to-lips silencing gesture. "But why let them hear us talking about Frank's photos in the first place?"

"Had to. When I picked them up, I didn't know we were being monitored. Didn't find out until I pulled into the garage. I threw the wrapping paper into the trash outside the photo shop, complete with Frank's return address and customs form declaring, guess what? That's right: *a roll of film*."

"Oops."

"Yeah. Big oops." Gerald hung his head and stopped walking. "But when the radar detector went haywire, then I realized we were being watched, and they must know about the roll of film. So I had to explain it away while we were talking. But then I made that comment about the photos being worthless, even *with* Jacob's scroll. Maybe if whoever's watching us believes we think that, we'll be okay."

"*If* they believed you," Michael muttered. "Frank was killed over Jacob's scroll, so it must be worth something." Fighting a shiver, he turned to the *Double Dragon* game next to Gerald. "If we want to look casual, we should play something." He plugged in a token. "So, if they believe us, we're fine. What about the ring?"

"Okay, I'll tell you, but you've got to ask this and some other questions once we're back in the house, and then play along. Remember, we're only safe if they believe we're not a threat, so we've got to convince them of that. Now, about the ring ...."

As Gerald finished, a booming voice overrode the noise of the machines. He turned to find a huge, barrel-chested drunk blocking the passage of a remarkably *un*remarkable man dressed in jeans and a "Go Ahead, Punk, Make My Day" T-shirt. The drunk poked a finger at the revolver on the man's shirt and said, "Go ahead, *punk*, make my *dinner*! Ah ha ha ha ha … I kill me. Or how about this? Go ahead, *punk*, make my *bed!* Come on, buddy, put an edge on it; everybody knows 'make my day.' Me, *I* want someone to make my dinner and bed! Ah ha ha ha!"

Gerald rolled his eyes, grabbed Michael's arm and led him away.

* * *

Later that night, as the lights switched off in the house, Michael's voice came over the receiver in the electrician's van half a block away. *"You know, Dad, the drunk had a point. You're pretty good with dinner, but I'd like to have someone make my bed."*

Karl looked across his greasy take-out at Tim. "Seasoned field agent, huh? You're supposed to break *me* in, huh? Well, you got yourself spotted, and the only words you got on tape are the drunk's! Impressive work, Mr. Seasoned Professional."

Tim shrugged, glanced at his watch, and mentally shot his Neanderthal partner with his own gun. How, he wondered as he scarfed down his cold beef lo mein, could the CIA be so desperate as to have promoted this moron from the classroom to the field?

* * *

The next day, Tim sat in the electrician's van, surrounded by monitoring equipment. Using a cosmetics mirror, he donned his facial accessories.

"They're entering the video arcade," the man at the rear window said.

"I should go," Karl mumbled around a mouthful of doughnut.

"My case," Tim said.

"They spotted you yesterday."

"So? They see me again, they'll think I'm one of the regulars."

"Your funeral." Karl finished the doughnut, licked his fingers and then wiped them on his wool slacks.

For the umpteenth time, Tim shook his head in dismay. Then he slipped from the van.

Karl waited until Tim disappeared into the video arcade. Then he threw off his blazer and tie, unhitched his shoulder holster, and followed.

* * *

While Michael tapped buttons and toggled the joystick, he asked, "What now, Dad?"

"Well, I'm hoping that after our conversation at home last night, they'll go away."

"Shame we can't know what they're thinking."

"Maybe we can." Gerald stepped up closer and outlined his plan.

After that, Michael challenged him to a few games, and even let him win a couple.

"If you like that one, you'll love this," the man next to them said to Michael, and gestured to a shooting game featuring a graveyard of ghouls as targets.

"Thanks. Maybe later." Michael glanced across the man's hairy mole and gold hoop earring.

"Aw, come on. Guns are nothin' to be afraid of, if it's your finger on the trigger."

Michael looked up to meet the man's gaze, and was surprised to find kindness there. "Those are—" His voice caught, and he cleared his throat and tried again. "Those are *my* words."

"I know."

"You've been following us since Sudan?"

"An associate had an eye on you there. Look, relax. I'm here to help you, not hurt you."

Michael felt his father edge up beside him. The machines continued to blast their bells and whistles, but for Michael, the room had fallen silent. "My father's friend died over there," he said.

"And I don't want to see the same happen to you."

"Why?"

The stranger shrugged. "Human decency. Golden Rule and all that happy stuff. Anyway, spooks aren't all bad. Some of us are good guys."

"Dr. Hansen," the man said to Gerald, and acknowledged him with a nod. Gerald hesitated, then politely extended his hand. The stranger didn't. Instead, Tim canted his head and cast his eyes downward at his right hand. Both Hansens followed his gaze to the tiny directional microphone pinched between his thumb and forefinger, held directly in front of the game's speaker, which was cycling an electronic come-on. "Sorry," Tim said, "but if I move my hand, its friend comes along for the ride."

"I thought you guys wore your microphones on the left," Gerald said.

"Quick observation. You have history with us, Dr. Hansen?"

"Saw it in a movie once."

Tim nodded. "On the non-dominant side, actually. I'm a lefty."

"You're not supposed to talk to us," Gerald said, more a statement than a question. He glanced again at the microphone.

"It'd cost me my job, sir."

"You say you want to help us. But it's your boss who calls the shots, right?"

Tim nodded slowly.

"So if your boss tells you to kill us ..."

"That wouldn't happen."

"You making the decisions?"

Tim lowered his gaze and slowly shook his head.

"Okay then," Gerald said. "So what're you going to do if your boss orders us dead?"

"Look, right now we're watching over you. Running protection, so to speak. You want this to go away, you let this gospel go. We're monitoring another surveillance team that might have a more unhealthy interest. I think if you drop it, they'll leave you alone. But if you go chasing after this thing ..."

"You FBI or CIA?"

Tim sighed at Gerald's question. "Look, just drop it. It's not the gospel at stake, it's your lives. If you so much as think about going after that gospel, they'll kill you twice, just to be sure."

Gerald looked down at his feet, then back up again. "Consider it dropped."

"Good. Because I was afraid what you said at home last night was just for the ears against the walls. I need you to drop this for real, and forever. *You* need to drop it for real and forever."

Michael leaned against a video machine, felt its reassuring solidity on his lower back. "So you're the ones who bugged our house."

Tim shrugged his shoulders and smiled almost sheepishly. "The way these things go, probably some are ours, some theirs. But I had an edge. I heard enough of your conversation in here yesterday to understand your plan."

"Just heard? Couldn't record it?" Gerald asked with raised eyebrows.

"Yeah, well," Tim gestured to his right hand, "microphone too close to a speaker."

"Ah." Gerald studied the stranger's face for a moment. "Aren't you afraid the others might be watching us now?"

Tim smiled. "No. They're temporarily detained."

"How's that? Or shouldn't I ask?"

"No, nothing like that." Tim scratched behind his left ear and scrunched an eye closed. "Had a couple friends on the force call a couple of their friends. We had the police pick them up this morning for loitering. Spy games. And they know it. Gets them off the street for a couple hours. Plus, every once in a while we like to remind 'em who's in charge."

Gerald shifted on his feet and looked around the room. Michael asked, "How can we thank you? For warning us, I mean."

"Leave this Easter egg hunt and go back to your normal lives. Be fruitful and multiply. Overdose on amusement parks, eat unhealthy food. Do all the happy stuff."

Tim spoke cheerfully, but then saw the question in Michael's eyes. "Look, I had a similar assignment years ago. I lost them. The review board cleared me, said nobody could've seen it coming. But the memory wakes me up at night. Maybe after this conversation, I'll sleep better."

"That's not all of it," Gerald said. Once again, it wasn't a question.

"You're right. I could say that I, like you, have a son. And that's true too. But that's not all of it either. It's just that, like I said, not all spooks are bad. You just have to know which ones are on your side. Okay, I hate long goodbyes. Goodbye, and God bless."

And with that, the man with the hairy mole and gold hoop earring turned and headed for the door.

* * *

"Anything?" Karl asked as Tim reentered the van. He was putting the final cinch on his tie as he spoke.

"Zilch."

"Zilch?"

"Yeah, it's a word. It means nothing, *nada,* bupkes."

Karl sighed. "I was watching, Tim. That was a long talk you had with them just to come up with *zilch.*"

Their eyes met, but Tim said nothing. Karl turned away with a nervous sniff. "I had to keep an eye on you. Like I said, you're compromised."

"And like I said, you're crazy."

"Maybe so, but I've got to write this up."

"Un-huh."

"And call in a report directly."

"Un-huh."

"Of course, you'll be off the case, and lucky to keep your job."

"Un-huh."

"Hope you're satisfied. Whatever it was, it must've meant a lot to you."

Tim sat down with a sigh, looked his partner full in his Neanderthal face, and said, "You'll never know."

* * *

"Mikey, you're right," Gerald said as they left the arcade moments later. "*Dig Dug is* like archaeology. Only without the heatstroke."

"I'm surprised you liked that game."

"Why's that?"

"Because it's more salvage than science, isn't it?"

Gerald laughed, draped his arm over Michael's shoulders, and steered him toward the house. "At least with *Dig Dug* we only lose a couple quarters. Lately, we've stood to lose a great deal more."

CHAPTER 12

Heard they made you," Harold Spencer growled. Affectionately nicknamed "Bulldog" to his face, the deputy director of the CIA was known as "Kibbles" behind his back, for he had a face made for dog food commercials. The two men who sat facing his desk remained silent, though Agent Timothy Snide thought he heard a smug grunt of satisfaction from the Neanderthal sitting to his left. Nevertheless, they waited until Spencer glanced up from the report in his hands and focused bloodshot eyes and lethal sarcasm on Tim.

"So, how'd that happen? Not even your wife recognizes you."

"She never sees me, sir. I'm rarely home," Tim said.

"Lucky woman. Now, how did it happen?"

"I'm sure it's all in there, sir." Tim motioned to the folder on Spencer's desk, then cast a withering glance at his bull-necked partner. "Karl seems pretty thorough ... at everything but the job."

"Well, let's see now ..." Bulldog Spencer flipped the report's pages with feigned interest. "Oh, yes, here it is. 'Walked up and talked to targets.' Introduced yourself, actually. Well, yes, that would do it. Yup, that puts a stamp and seal on it. So much for the covert aspect of the operation."

As Karl adjusted his tie and shifted in his chair, an irrepressible smile sneaked into the corners of his mouth. Tim caught that smile and wanted to slap it off with a two-by-four.

"Sir," Tim said, "we all know where this is headed. If you want my resignation, just say so."

"Oh, how nice and self-righteous of you. A resignation! But you know, Agent Snide—and by the way, is that a real name? 'Snide'? Are you sneering at me now, Agent Snide?"

"It's a real name, sir," Tim said.

"As I live and breathe. So, Agent Snide, about that resignation. You see, a resignation makes it much easier to find a new job. No, some people need to be fired, and others shot." Spencer looked down at the file on his desk and shook his head. "The idiot that paired the two of you? He mixed gold with garbage."

Spencer flipped the file closed, sat back and nodded to his assistant, who stood behind the seated duo. The assistant handed an envelope to each agent.

"That's what you've got coming," Spencer said, and raised both hands to point at the two agents.

Tim didn't bother. He watched his partner's face light up as Karl fished a check from his envelope, and knew everything he needed to know.

"Sir, thank you, sir," Karl said.

"Oh, don't thank me," Spencer replied. "That's not a bonus. That's severance pay. Fresh out of training, and already trying to bury your partner? Excuse me if I don't get up to spit in your face."

Tim watched dumbfounded while Spencer's assistant pinned Karl in his seat with a strong hand on his shoulder and stripped him of his gun. Then, in a move a pro wrestler could be proud of, he lifted Karl from his chair and walked him, spluttering, out of the room.

Thirty seconds passed, during which Spencer drummed his fingers on the file in front of him. Tim looked at the envelope in his hands as if trying to recognize it. Slowly, he ripped the end off and slid out a note that contained three words: *Check Your Six.*

"Ever hear how Baron von Richthofen, better known as the Red Baron, was killed?"

Tim looked up at Spencer's question. "Um, shot down, sir?"

Spencer laughed. "Pretty fair guess. Eighty planes to his record by the age of twenty-five. Imagine. The most famous ace in history, and how did he die? He was so focused on a kill that a Canadian pilot flew up his tail and fired a volley up his ... what's a polite term? Up his fuselage. The most famous flying ace in history, shot down and killed because he forgot the very first rule of aerial combat: Check your six."

Tim opened his palms with a gesture that registered something between surprise and *So?*

"What does that have to do with you? You were so focused on your objective, you didn't realize we had surveillance on *you*. When your partner reported you were compromised, we placed both of you under observation. The belt pack for your handheld microphone? We had your partner switch it overnight. The replacement had an internal mike pointed straight up at your face. Very high-tech. Your earphone was switched for a two-way function. Even higher-tech.

"Bottom line? I heard everything you said. Twice. And let me tell you, that was beautiful. I mean, we're going to script that and teach it. Or rather, you're going to teach it. As of today, I'm promoting and transferring you to training. Don't even *think* of saying no. It's a plum job, more money, regular hours. Over time, your wife and kids might even begin to recognize you." Spencer narrowed one eye, looked closely at Tim and then shrugged. "Then again, might not. Either way, good job and congratulations, Agent Snide. Dismissed."

Tim stood to leave in a body that no longer felt like his. "Thank you, sir."

"Oh, and Agent Snide ... When an agent goes against policy, one of three things happens." Spencer scratched out something on a sheet of paper and then balled it up. "Those who blossom with insight and promise get promoted, but those who bring risk and exposure get fired."

"You said one of *three* things happens."

"Ah, yes." Spencer stood from his desk and lifted a rectangular register hinged on the wall. "Well, option number three depends," he paused to chuck the wad of paper into the underlying opening, "on how badly a person screws up."

Both men watched the brief yellow flash as the paper combusted in the incinerator within.

"I see, sir."

"I put you in the first group, Snide. If you want to stay there, never forget rule number one. Check your six."

* * *

A week later, Michael followed Gerald into the house after a long weekend away. Together, they found a number of their carefully placed tell-tales disturbed. Both the back door and one of the windows opening onto the backyard had been opened. Otherwise, the house appeared unchanged. Even the photographs, complete with negatives, were spread on the dining room table as they'd been left. Most significantly, the radar detector drew a blank in every room.

Fifteen minutes later, Gerald hovered over Michael's shoulder, watching him fight to destroy the Death Star of the evil Empire. "Well," he said, "either all the batteries miraculously died at the same time, or everybody believed our cock-and-bull story."

Michael nodded between rapid-fire thumb-clicks. "I'm glad nobody stole the photos and trashed the house to make it look like a robbery."

"For our safety," Gerald said, "we had to give them that option. But even if they had taken the photos, we'd still have the duplicate prints I left in the safe deposit box at the bank." Michael's ship exploded before his eyes, followed by an onscreen invitation to play again. "But they left the photos alone, so I expect they'll leave us alone as well."

"Dad," Michael said as they walked toward the door, "I think it's time to move."

"Why? Bad memories?"

"Well, that too," he replied with a grimace. Then he swept an arm over the room of screaming, beeping machines. "Also getting tired of the neighbors."

"Don't think you'll miss all this?"

"I'll never miss anything as much as I miss Mom." He punched through the exit door and Gerald followed out into the sunshine and salty air.

"I was thinking," Michael said. "We could save time and hassle if we lived closer to the airport. You know. The Library of Congress a Metro stop away. The Smithsonian in our backyard."

"I see. Somewhere like ...?"

"Oh, I don't know. What do you think of Georgetown?" Michael said with a sheepish grin.

Gerald pursed his lips in mock thought. "Ah, *Raaachael*. Oh, I mean *Georrrgetown*. Now why didn't *I* think of that?"

"Gee, I don't know. Maybe because you're old enough to be her father?"

CHAPTER 13

Fifteen years ago. Fifteen years ago, but it seems like yesterday. The sound of drumming fingers lingered in Michael's mind while the last sip of strong tea faded from his tongue, remembering how calm his father had seemed under the pressure of the circumstances.

Now, Michael sat in his Harvard office, one hand on the phone in its cradle, the other still and silent, where moments before it had drummed his desktop. Thirty years old as of last week, he'd chased the Gospel of the Teacher for fifteen years, but had never stepped past the doorway of his imagination.

And now, Rachael was going after it for real. Just like his father, right up to the moment the second heart attack took him.

He leaned back in his office chair and pulled both hands into his lap, glanced over the latest in his series of articles on religious misdirection, the ones he'd been polishing when she called.

"Michael," she'd said, "I need to see you."

"Rachael, where are you?"

"Here in Boston. I'm going after Dad's killers. When can we meet?"

He sat and considered how he had rocketed to fame as one of the most popular yet controversial theologians of his time. His theories, considered seditious by many, prompted everything from job offers and book deals to death threats. But now he looked out a window streaked by the slush that is Boston in November, and counted the dead.

The Sudanese taxi driver was number one, Frank Tones number two. Michael had no proof, but he believed his father had been number three. They'd rarely spoken of it, but he knew Gerald deeply regretted abandoning the hunt for Frank's murderer and the Gospel of the Teacher. His first coronary seemed to stop his longing for good. Yet, once Michael was safely away at Harvard, Gerald resurrected the search. Zero leads and a second heart attack later, he lay recovering in the hospital.

The third day of Gerald's convalescence, Michael checked in at the nurses' station for a visit. When he looked to the end of the hallway, he saw a slight man in a white lab coat slip out of his father's room, glance in both directions, then turn away from Michael and stride down the hall. By the time Michael took a hesitant step forward, the man reached the opposite end and slid around the corner with a single sidestep. Michael sprinted the corridor, but by the time he reached the end, the man had disappeared. He heard a beeping and turned back to see a nurse rushing into Gerald's room. The moment he heard the code blue announced over the hospital speakers, he knew his father was dead.

Autopsy noted a startling electrolyte imbalance, but otherwise was unremarkable. Michael never told anyone what he'd seen, for he hadn't seen much beyond the man's narrow back and spindly shoulders. Yet since then, he'd prayed for the day justice could be brought to the spider's web of intrigue that bound his life.

That was 1998. His father, the third possible death related to the scroll.

And now, four years later, Rachael wants to try for the honor of being number four.

He stood and grabbed his coat and scarf from the wall hooks.

* * *

"Chocolate Rocks," she said with a laugh. "Brings back memories."

"Yeah, well, chocolate *does* rock!"

"Especially Cadbury's."

"Let's not start *that* again." He opened the door and held it for her. "You didn't come all the way from DC to renew an old argument."

He'd found her waiting impatiently outside the local café that was once their favorite hangout. Far from the skeletal waif he had envisioned, she looked flushed with good health and moved with the grace of a woman who spent equal time in the gym and in high heels.

"Brrrr," she said with a shiver as she entered the café. "Michael, why *did* we break up?"

"We were killing each other."

"Oh yeah. That. All the same, biggest mistake of your life."

"How's your ex?" he asked. "Any plans on getting back together?"

She grinned. "We didn't bury that marriage. We cremated it. But I'm open to offers."

He laughed while he glanced at the "leaf" menu of tea offerings, hung high on the wall behind the counter. Rachael stepped up beside him and perused the neighboring "bean" menu.

"Remember when you could buy a plain cup of coffee?" she asked. "Now, if you don't add flavored syrup, steamed milk, froth, shaved chocolate or powdered cinnamon, and order by the most ridiculous names, you're a rube."

"There's a solution to that."

She turned her head away from the menu to look at him. "Hmm?"

"Tea."

She groaned while glancing up at the leaf menu. "Black, green, herbal, citrus or spice? Caffeinated or decaf? Single or double bag? Milk, lemon or sweetener? And if sweetener, sugar, aspartame or honey?"

"Stop. Let's put this to a test. Loser buys." He led her to the counter. "Tea, please."

"One tea." The clerk looked past him to Rachael. "And you, Miss?"

"Coffee, please."

"Any preference?"

"Just a regular coffee."

"Colombian, Cuban, Kenyan, Kona, Sumatra, Blue Mountain—"

"Just a regular."

The clerk eyed her for a full three seconds. "Colombian okay?"

"Fine," Rachael said.

"Would you like flavoring in that?"

"I think you won," Rachael muttered to Michael. Then, to the clerk, "No, a plain Colombian coffee would be fine, thank you."

"Right. So-Slow Sloth, Chattering Chipmunk or Wired Weasel?"

Rachael's face went blank for a moment. Then she turned to Michael and asked, "This is still Planet Earth, right?" She turned back to the clerk. "Are those the sizes?"

"Caffeine levels. Decaf, regular, or strong."

"Oh. I'll have a Chattering Chipmunk."

"Tiny Taster, Boston Commons, Mucho Macho or Bladder-Buster?" The girl swept her hand over an array of cup sizes.

"Boston Commons," Rachael replied.

"Okay, that's a medium then," the girl said, and Rachael rolled her eyes. "Do you want to Taz that?"

"Oh for Pete's sake," Rachael said. *"What?"*

"Want to Taz that? You know, add a shot of espresso?"

"Yeesh," Rachael said, "I think ordering online might be easier."

They chose desserts, Rachael paid, and Michael carried their numbered flag to an empty table to await delivery.

Michael sat first, and watched while she wriggled out of her long winter coat. Underneath, she wore a sleeveless pantdress that accentuated shoulders and arms sculpted more for bulk than beauty. Michael wrinkled his nose, but recovered before she could catch his expression of distaste. *Dead subject*, he reminded himself. *Be nice.*

"Sleeveless, Rachael?" he said. "No wonder you're cold. What're you benching now?"

"My weight." She draped her coat over the back of a chair and sat.

"Wow. Two hundred pounds is pretty good for a girl," he said with a straight face.

"One-twenty, you bonehead. And benching one-twenty is pretty good for *anybody* my age. What about *you?*"

"I curl cans of soda. But I'm working up to a six-pack."

She leaned her chin onto her fist. "So who's the girl?"

And that's why we broke up, he thought.

"But seriously, how many black belts do you have now?"

"I was at a tournament recently."

"Yeah?"

"Yeah. Know what? A white belt won the self-defense against weapons category. All these classroom-trained black belts, and this little street-fighter white belt beat them all. Belts and ability don't always go hand-in-hand."

He went quiet and fixed her with a steady gaze. She reached across the table, laid her fingers on his left temple, and probed the invisible crease where a blow had split the underlying muscle. "How're the headaches?"

"Haven't had one for years."

She lowered her hand and ran her fingers over the faint Y-shaped scar at the angle of his left jaw. "Mikey," she said, her voice uncharacteristically soft, "we got off easy. And don't feel bad. You never had a chance."

As she spoke, his memory drifted back eight years to a humid summer evening. Nondescript forms faded in and out of the fog, the smell of steamed city danker than a wet ferret. His world had exploded in a burst of light, and something tripped the switch to his spinal cord. By the time he realized he'd been struck from behind he was on the ground, only his mind and vision functioning. One assailant pulled him into a darkened alley. A second dragged Rachael from behind, one hand clamped over her mouth. Michael's assailant looked to be in his thirties, with a face like a head of cauliflower. Rachael's teenaged captor was painted with acne.

Cauliflower dumped Michael onto the ground, kicked him savagely in the face, and then turned his back on him. Still numb from the first blow, Michael could only watch.

When Cauliflower reached for Rachael's blouse, she drove a spiked heel into her teenaged captor's foot. As he loosened his grip upon her she wrenched her arms free and grabbed for Cauliflower's crotch. He lowered his hands reflexively, and she drove a quiver of polished fingernails into his eyes. The man buckled and stepped back, and she reached over her right shoulder with both hands and grabbed her captor by his hair. In one fluid motion she knelt, hunched her back, and threw him over her shoulder. The kid landed in a roll, and tried to roll out and back to his feet. But his acne-filled face warped into terror as Rachael, still holding his hair, wrenched his head back with the muffled snap of rotten kindling. The next second she rose with a broken brick from the rubble of the alley and bricked Cauliflower's groin, then his face as he dropped his hands from his bloody sockets, and then, using both hands, the back of his head as he crumpled forward. With the dull *chunk* of a hammer on wet plaster, his skull caved.

Pulling for breath, she dropped the blood-covered brick, hauled Michael to his feet, draped one of his arms over her shoulder and walked him out of the alley, a linebacker helping an injured teammate off the field.

"Hey, don't go all flashback on me."

Michael blinked, and the background of Rachael's face faded from the alley to the coffee shop. The jangle of discordant conversations swept away the grunts of battle, and the mingled aromas of brews and pastries flushed the fetid smell of the alley from his nose.

She withdrew her hand from his face and crossed her arms on the table. "We survived, okay?"

"Did we?" he asked. "I never saw anything so vicious. Martial arts teach restraint. If I had done what you did, I'd have nightmares till the day I die."

"I sleep like a baby."

"You must have some of your father in you." He shook his head and gave her a weak grin.

She leaned into the table and pointed a sharpened fingernail at him. "Don't go silly on me. It doesn't become you. And that was mean. I'm nothing like Dad, and you know it. I just believe in … self-defense."

"No regrets?"

She leaned back into her seat and folded her arms on her chest. "The first couple months? I thought every knock on the door was the police coming for me." She gave him a snuffling laugh. "Now, it wouldn't matter if they did. But no. No regrets. The things that died that night had it coming."

Things? That's one way to deal with it, he thought. *Think of those two thugs as a couple of cockroaches.*

Or was she referring to the aftermath of that night? Their relationship wouldn't have survived much longer anyway. He'd figured that much out, though it had taken years. Rachael had endured her parents' divorce and all the squabbles that followed. No wonder she'd grown up obsessed with self-dependency. By the time they started dating in their teens, she was devoted to weightlifting and boxing. But Michael had a jumpstart in martial arts. Partnered with someone she couldn't dominate physically or mentally, he'd found her more inclined to sparring than affection. After years of breaking up and getting back together again, when she killed the two muggers, that reversed her hold on their relationship. It had fallen apart as a result.

"How's your mother?" he asked.

"Remarried."

"Again?"

"A dentist. Enough archaeologist husbands. Happier this time. I think."

"Your sister?"

"Artists don't marry. They stay single by choice and moan about it."

He laid his hands on the table. "Okay, so what's this about, quote, going after your father's killers?"

A tattooed, facially pierced *something*, more abstract-art project than waitress, drew up to their table and unloaded their orders from her tray. "One Chattering Chipmunk, Boston Commons Colombian for the lady, and your usual, Dr. Hansen."

Rachael dragged her eyes away from the steel-studded waitress, cocked her thumb and sighted her index finger between Michael's eyes. "Your *usual*? Michael, you cheated!"

"Hometown advantage. Now, you were saying?"

The waitress turned and rattled away, the chains strung between one eyebrow and an ear swinging. Rachael shook her head and paused to test-sip her coffee. By the time she lowered the cup, her expression was serious. "Last week, I attended a lecture on conflicting archaeological evidence about the origin of Christianity in Egypt. That, as you know, was one of Dad's interests."

"Not yours? Shocking."

"Yeah, right. I only went because the guest speaker had been on Rybkoski's dig with Dad. I woke from the lecture in time to catch him leaving. Nice guy. Took him to dinner, he wouldn't let me pay. Anyway, he told me that, like you, he had always suspected murder."

He toyed with his dessert. "Rachael, we've talked about this. It's a dead, dead end. And you don't want to go there. Let it go."

"How many times do I have to tell you? I'm dying, Michael. What part of that don't you understand?"

"Rachael, I ..." He bowed his head. "I ..."

"Nice hair, huh?" She bounced her hair in her hand. "It's a wig, Michael. Very expensive, very realistic, very not-me. After the chemo failed, the doctors offered an experimental regimen—"

"You told me." He fingered his teacup with one hand and motioned to her coffee with the other.

She shook her head. "An experimental regimen that might save me, but more likely would kill me." Her words were cold, as if she were delivering a lecture. "I decided not to spend the rest of my life throwing up tube feedings for a single-digit chance of a cure."

"You told me." He arm-wrestled the urge to dash his cup against the wall, and slowly lowered it to the table.

"I opted out." She test-sipped her coffee, chugged it as if it were water, and then settled the empty cup in its saucer with a hollow clatter. "From now, I've got three months. The doctors said so, and I believe them. So what do I have to lose? And why do you keep saying 'You told me' like I'm boring the socks off you?"

"Why?" He pushed away from the table, crossed his legs and turned his side to her. "You know Kübler-Ross' stages of death? Denial, anger, bargaining, et cetera? I've never gotten past denial."

She shrugged. "I hit despair two months ago. And I realized I'd never see acceptance unless I did this. It's my parting shot, Michael."

He tilted his head and looked her in the eye. "You've got to fight this. Who knows? Maybe—"

She tapped her spoon against the table and stared him into silence. "I'm dying, Michael. How I spend my last couple months is up to me, okay? Now, you gonna tell me what I need to know, or do I have to beat it out of you?" She held his gaze for a long moment, then flashed her special smile. He was beaten, and they both knew it.

He hitched himself back to face the table and pushed his chocolate-pecan torte away with a sigh. "What do you want to know?"

"Everything. Refresh my memory."

"We've been over this how many times?"

"Not enough by one. Now start."

He sat silent for a minute, composed his memories, and then unloaded them in order. When he finished, Rachael asked the same questions he'd pondered for the past fifteen years: "Are the photos Dad took of the scroll truly worthless? And if so, why'd they kill him?"

"They're worthless, for the simple reason that scrolls can be authenticated, photos can't." Michael feigned patience he didn't have. "Furthermore, most of Jacob's scroll is nothing new. The Dead Sea Scrolls told us about 'the one who teaches righteousness in the end of days' and the 'Teacher of Righteousness' decades before your father opened Jacob's grave. The Dead Sea Scrolls also told us this Teacher of Righteousness was opposed by a Wicked Priest, who was also identified as The Man of the Lie. Again, things already well-known."

"Can one of the Dead Sea Scrolls be the gospel Jacob hid at Qumran?" she asked. "More importantly, do they still have free refills here?" She turned and looked for the waitress.

"No." He wagged a finger at her. "To both questions. To begin with, the Dead Sea Scrolls were discovered forty years before your dad's death. If that was the secret, it was already out. Furthermore, none of the seals on the Dead Sea Scrolls matches the seal on Jacob's scroll. And lastly, none of the scrolls was a gospel of 'The Teacher.'"

She toyed with her empty cup. "So why was Dad killed?"

"Simple. The photos might be worthless, but Jacob's scroll isn't. Sure, by itself, it has little or no value. *By itself.* But if the Gospel of the Teacher of Righteousness were ever found, Jacob's scroll would be the link. It's like having the key *and* the car. The key's worthless until the car's found. But when the car *is* found, you're still going nowhere without the key. Jacob's scroll would help date the gospel, identify the author and, most important, define the conflict between the Teacher of Righteousness and the Wicked Priest."

"Hold that thought." She jumped up and hurried to the service counter, wallet in one hand, cup in the other. Moments later, she returned balancing a brimming cup. "Sorry. Okay, finish that thought. Why was Dad killed?"

He sighed in frustration. "My guess? He told the wrong person that he knew how to find the Gospel of the Teacher."

She went silent for a moment, head bowed over her coffee, then said, "So what about the ring? Where does that fit in?"

"It's the hard link between Jacob's scroll and the gospel. The end of Jacob's scroll, meaning the part we weren't supposed to see, stated that the two scrolls share the same wax seal and imprint. The imprint of the ring."

"Other than me, who knows about it?"

"Nobody, and keep it that way. If the wrong people knew about the ring, I'd be tops on the endangered species list."

"But if the end of Jacob's scroll is gone—"

"It isn't. I'm sure of that. If the bottom of Jacob's scroll was destroyed, then we've lost Jacob's description of the seal and the Gospel of the Teacher of Righteousness, the link is gone, the ring is worthless, and I'm probably safe."

"Michael, that seems—"

"Unlikely, I know. Whoever stole the bottom of Jacob's scroll probably still has it. It's theological insurance. If the Gospel of the Teacher isn't found, they lose nothing. But if it *is* found, and it's to their liking, they can trot out the lost ending to Jacob's scroll and use it to authenticate the gospel. And should that happen, the ring would become priceless. Interested parties might be willing to ransom it with a fortune. Or kill for it."

Rachael fixed her eyes on his. "But if the Gospel of the Teacher is found and they don't like it?"

"They could destroy the ending to Jacob's scroll at that time, and then set about trying to discredit the gospel. Like I said, theological insurance."

"Michael, how can you be sure nobody knows about the ring? Dad might've told someone."

He held up three fingers, and closed them one by one with his other hand as he spoke. "One, Jacob's scroll mentions the seal, but not the ring. Two, your father's graduate student didn't seem to know about it. If anybody knew, it would've been him. And three, anyone who knew about it could've taken it from Frank after he was killed. But they didn't. Not when he was murdered, and not when he lay in the supply trailer overnight, with the windows wide open."

"Your father took it."

"Because Dad read Frank's excavation notes the night before, so he knew the ring's significance."

"Hmm." Rachael gave her coffee a sip and stole the strawberry garnish from Michael's dessert plate. "So who had access to both my father *and* the artifacts?"

"Everyone. There was virtually no security, other than a locked door. But the lock was flimsy. Could've been picked by anybody with training."

She dug into her purse and tossed an old envelope onto the table. The stamps were colorful, reminiscent of zoo posters. "Remind you of anything?"

"Lions and tigers and bears, oh my. Sure, our picnic at the National Zoo. The fundraiser for the African Plains Proj—"

"Read it."

He turned the envelope over to open, but stopped when he saw the wax seal on its flap: a wax seal that was a perfect imprint of the ring's face. "When did you get this?"

"Mom kept it from me. Only told me about it last week, when I convinced her I was going after Dad's killers. Even then, I practically had to wrestle it out of her. Now read it."

He slipped the letter from the envelope. When he finished reading it, he studied the wax seal more closely, and then handed it back.

"Same as the ring?" she asked.

He nodded. "Identical."

"So you got the ring and I got the seal." Her voice held something he couldn't identify, but it sounded like bitterness.

"Don't be angry," he said. "We couldn't leave the ring with you. If the wrong people learned about it, that ring could've been the death of you *and* your family." He leaned toward her over the table. "Rachael, how did you get this letter? Dad and I were monitored. Your family must've been too."

"We were between houses at the time." She held up the envelope, facing him. "Check out the mailing address."

His eyes narrowed in confusion. "Mrs. Annabelle Wright?"

"Friend of our family."

"Huh." He sat back and drummed the tabletop with his fingers. "So Frank sent us the photos, and your mother this letter. He played it safe, that's for sure. Neither one is good without the other."

"Dad was complex. I never could figure out what he was thinking. But this must have been *his* insurance."

"Hey, it gives us a lead. According to that letter, he saw a photograph of this seal in the office of a colleague, one who'd worked on the Dead Sea Scrolls Project. There are only so many of those."

"What would it have cost him to have given us a name?" The bitterness was back.

He shrugged. "Whoever killed your father, they're professional. The stakes are high, and two more would hardly matter. So we'll have to be careful."

"*Two* more? *We'll* have to be careful?" Rachael shook her head. "No, Mikey. This is *my* baby."

He sighed. "Rachael, even Rambo has a sidekick."

She caught her chin between thumb and forefinger and stroked thoughtfully. "And his sidekick is always a girl. You're right. You *may* come along."

CHAPTER 14

"Okay, we need a plan," Michael said as they left the café and began strolling down the wide sidewalk, past seemingly endless rows of pubs and restaurants. The air heavy with polluted mist, the world colored sad as a death shroud, the gray seemed to wash off the buildings and pool in the heart of the city. Their breath came out in plumes of vapor, and Michael jinked to one side to avoid a slush-filled puddle. "Jacob hid the Gospel of the Teacher of Righteousness in or around the caves at Qumran. In other words, with the Qumran scrolls."

"Dead Sea Scrolls," she said.

"Same thing, okay? Qumran is the place, Dead Sea is the area."

"Testy, testy."

"Now, your father's letter says his 'mystery' colleague had been on the Qumran scrolls project, and—"

"Dead Sea."

"Qumran."

"Dead Sea."

"Qumran."

"Cadbury's."

"Hershey's." He turned and smiled at the impish grin on her face. Both broke out laughing, laughter both desperately needed, but it was too brief.

"And since Jacob's scroll points toward Qumran as well," he said as soon as he recovered, "we have two leads: the mystery colleague, and the Qumran, Qumran, *Qumran* scrolls. So what do you know about Qumran?"

"Let's see, where shall I begin?" Rachael said. *"Khirbet* Qumran, meaning 'ruin of' Qumran, is on a plateau at the top of an irregular border of limestone cliffs. Many of these cliffs contain caves which, given their location, are accessible only with difficulty. To the West lies the Judean Desert, and to the North is a mountain that houses the Qumran caves numbered 1, 2, 3, and 11."

"Showoff."

"Been reading. Okay, that's the layout. Now, check my history. Khirbet Qumran was occupied until 68 CE by the Essenes, who represented one of the major schools of Jewish philosophy at that time. The complex was destroyed in 68 CE. Ashes from the burned reed-rooftops and Roman arrowheads found at the site suggest a battle. The simple fact that nobody returned to recover the scrolls suggests a massacre. The timing fits, because the Jewish rebellion against the Roman Empire put the two at war from 66 to 70 CE."

Michael nodded. "Passable so far. Tell me more."

"Let's cut to recent history. In 1947, a Bedouin shepherd discovered seven scrolls in what's now known as Cave 1. After that, the race was on. Archaeologists tried to excavate the caves scientifically, while Bedouins plundered them for whatever they could sell. In 1952, a French Dominican named Roland de Vaux located Cave 4. That cave contained over 15,000 fragments of 574 manuscripts. A year later, an international team of eight scholars was assembled, with De Vaux as project director. Thirteen years after that, in 1966, De Vaux's team was publicly accused of obstructing release of the scrolls because the content's contrary to Trinitarian Christianity. How am I doing?"

Michael shielded his face from a biting gust of wind and nodded for her to continue.

"Okay, moving on. After the Six-Day War in 1967, Israel expanded its border to the Jordan River. The Qumran complex was in that territory, so became property of Israel. And so did the scrolls. In 1972, a Spanish scholar named José O'Callaghan claimed that papyrus fragments from Cave 7 represent some of the New Testament books. Other scholars disagreed, and claimed the fragments from

Cave 7 are too small to know *what* they represent. But O'Callaghan's assertion excited a lot of imaginations."

"And why is that, Grasshopper?" Michael asked with a grin.

"Like you don't know. Ha!"

"No, I'm enjoying this. And you've clearly done your homework. So tell me."

"Okay, okay! Here's why O'Callaghan's claim got everyone so excited. The Essenes occupied the Qumran complex for over thirty years following Jesus' ministry, and their complex was less than a day's walk from Jerusalem. Yet none of the Dead Sea Scrolls was New Testament material. So questions arose. Did the Essenes store New Testament scrolls in a separate place? And if so, why? They were, after all, orthodox Jews. Unless, of course, some of them were closet Christians."

"In fact," Michael said as he led her around a corner and through a park, "all of the Old Testament books except Esther are represented in the Qumran scrolls and scroll fragments. But to date, nothing's been found that's *provably* New Testament."

Rachael ducked a tree branch and shot him an annoyed look. "Didn't I just say that? Anyway, here's some more excitement: In 1984, one of the scholars suggested that the 'Teacher of Righteousness' described in the Qumran scrolls refers to either Jesus or James, and his opponent, 'the Man of the Lie,' a.k.a. 'the Wicked Priest' is … drumroll, please … Paul! This implies that the Qumran scrolls both validate Jesus as a prophet *and* expose Paul as a corrupter of his teachings."

"The first concept threatens Judaism," Michael said, nodding, "and the second, Trinitarian Christianity."

"Don't understand that, and don't care."

"You should. One of those is where our killers come from. Probably."

Her head whirled so that her eyes met his, but she said nothing. Instead, they walked together in silence as the gloom of the overcast day seeped into their souls. Minutes passed, then Rachael said, "Okay, I'll bite. Explain."

"Think how this might play out. A Jewish gospel that confirms the prophethood of Jesus would threaten Judaism, and therefore Israel's national identity. Similarly, a gospel that exposes Paul as a corrupter of the teachings of Jesus could shake Trinitarian Christianity: Catholic, Orthodox and Protestant churches alike. America was founded—"

"Why?"

"You're kidding."

"Look, I'm atheist, and you're insane. Your mind's gone on God. But tell me anyway. What does Paul, Jesus' second-in-command so to speak, have to do with all this?"

He stopped beside a dimly lit dive of a doorway. "This is it."

She bent and peered through the adjacent window at the crowded cluster of unattended tables. "What, this?"

"Best lobster in town. And we beat the crowd. Come on."

* * *

Over dessert, he watched as she guzzled another cup of coffee. "Sorry, Mikey," she said. "Can't fight a two-pound mollusk and think at the same time. Pick up where you left off."

"Lobsters are crustaceans. And you didn't fight it, you demolished it."

"Actually, Michael, it's neither. In fact, lobsters are giant ocean cockroaches. But good. Great, actually. And this one here, this is the best cockroach I've ever had." She wiped her mouth with her napkin and then tossed it aside. "Now, why would Trinitarians want to suppress a gospel that discredits Paul? What difference would that make? Wouldn't a good Christian want to support the truth?"

"A good Christian, a seeker of the truth, yes. Most Christians, no. Remember, most Christians live for Paul's promise of an effortless salvation. They'll fight anyone who tries to take that away from them, even if it isn't true." He watched in amazement as she beckoned the waiter with her empty coffee cup, and circled her finger over its rim.

Then, he continued. "First of all, Paul wasn't Jesus' 'second-in-command,' as you said. They never even met. After Jesus was gone, Paul claimed to speak in his name, and the people in power took what he said and canonized it. But that doesn't make it true. Every tenet of Trinitarian Christianity is based on the teachings of Paul, even though Jesus never said he was God, partner with God, or even God's son. Nowhere did Jesus teach the doctrines of the Trinity, Crucifixion, Resurrection and Atonement. All of these tenets came from Paul, or from the Pauline theologians who followed in lockstep. The teachings of Paul, in fact, contradict the teachings of Jesus."

"Get outta here." Rachael carved a groove in the icing of her Black Forest cake with her spoon. "The two are complementary."

"Common misconception." Michael snitched a chocolate shaving from her plate. "Jesus taught Old Testament Law. Paul negated it. Jesus declared himself the 'son of man.' Eighty-eight times. Pauline theologians labeled him the 'son of God.' Jesus taught the oneness of God, and prayer to him alone. Paul suggested the Trinity and elevated Jesus to the level of intercessor. Jesus said he was sent, quote, to the lost sheep of the house of Israel. Paul proclaimed him a universal prophet. Jesus—"

"Stop," she commanded, one hand uplifted as the other leveraged a forkful of cake into her mouth. She chewed, then swallowed. "I'm back to not caring. This cake is divine enough for me."

He swallowed a bite of key lime pie, sipped his tea and squared his shoulders. "I'm just telling you why a gospel that calls Paul a liar and a fake would threaten Trinitarian Christianity. Paul taught the tenets of Trinitarian faith. Jesus taught Unitarian. That's why the two schools have been at each others' throats all along."

He pushed his pie away. "Do you know how the Qumran scrolls describe the Wicked Priest who opposes the Teacher of Righteousness?"

She shook her head with her fork still in her mouth.

"The Damascus Document," he explained, "defines the Wicked Priest as an apostate who founded a dissenting group which, and I quote, 'sought smooth things.' In other words, they broke from the strictness of the law and sought an easier path. Some scholars think this apostate was Paul. They say—"

She waved their waiter over again, and he wondered how much she'd heard. "But then again," he said, "you're hell-bent anyway, so none of this matters to you, does it?"

"Michael, you're entering dangerous territory. I've got PMS and I'm not afraid to use it." She chewed her lip as she pointed out her selection to the waiter.

"A second dessert?" he asked, one eyebrow arched in surprise, when the waiter departed.

She tossed back her cup of coffee. "Hm, point one: I don't have a problem keeping weight off, just keeping it on. Point two: diabetes and heart disease are hardly on my list of concerns. Point three ... what's point three? Oh, yeah, can you catch the waiter's eye? I want a milkshake with that."

"A milkshake? In a seafood restaurant?" He faked a shiver of disgust.

"Okay, we'll pick up some Ben and Jerry's later. So ..." She leaned back in her chair and fixed him with a skeptical gaze. "Two thousand years of Christians following the lies of Paul? Hard to believe, Mikey."

"Nah. Paul was the first to call himself a liar. Romans 3:7. Read it in the King James Version. Goes like this: 'For if the truth of God hath more abounded through my lie unto his glory; why yet am I also judged as a sinner?' Weird. Paul thinks it's okay to spread his beliefs through lying, and Trinitarians trust every word he wrote. Figure that out."

Rachael shrugged and leaned back to allow the waiter to place her Linzer torte, then cracked off a wedge. "You go with God. I'll go with the big bang and Darwin. Deal?"

He sat back with a sigh. "Sure. The big bang. Evolution. I believe in those too. Only one difference. I believe in who orchestrated them."

She rolled her eyes and stabbed her dessert, breaking it with a screech as her fork passed through and clawed the porcelain beneath. "Mikey, I—"

No. Don't cut me off. For once, listen. You're telling me that if I keep dropping bombs into a junkyard, someday all the pieces will blast together into a perfect Mercedes. That's what the big bang proposes. That's what evolution teaches. That chaos gave rise to perfection. But we know it works the other way around, don't we?"

He bunched his napkin in his fist and leaned over the table. "Rachael, look around you. Everything you see is *created*. You see a painting, you know there's a painter. You see a statue, you know there's a sculptor. A building? An architect. A car? A factory. Rachael. You see creation, what does that tell you? That there's a *creator*! You think all of this just *evolved*? Then where did ours souls come from? Answer me that!"

She pushed her dessert away. "Michael, shut up, pay, and let's get out of here. Linzer torte wouldn't look good on you."

* * *

He punched through the restaurant door two steps ahead of her and let it swing closed behind him. She hustled to his side, but kept an arm's length between them. After a block he stopped, tilted back his head and blew a cloud of mist skyward. Then he reached out, grabbed the shoulder of her coat and pulled her to his side. "Okay, sorry. Truce?"

"Truce," she said, and playfully swung a punch into his midsection. It bounced off like an orange thrown at a refrigerator. "Whoa," she said, "what've you got in there? A steel undershirt?"

"Eight years of bad memories waking me to my morning exercises."

She held his coat open and looked. "You've changed a lot. What're you wearing now? Hand-me-downs?"

"Banana Republic. Guess all boys grow into their dads."

She brushed his coat closed. "I kinda liked you preppy."

"Hang 'prep' upside down and shake it, and 'dweeb' falls out." He searched the sky through the clouds. "We were guessing your father's killers."

She grunted. "Your conversation is completely bipolar, you know that?"

"So like I was saying," he said to the sky, "the Gospel of the Teacher might threaten Judaism, Trinitarian Christianity, and all concerned interests. That could mean Israel, the Vatican, the Anglican Church in England. Even America, since Trinitarian Christianity's the majority religion and a dominant political force."

He stuffed his hands into his pockets and turned back to the park they'd passed through earlier. "The concept of Paul having corrupted Jesus' message is hotly debated. Ditto Jesus' place in revelation. Was he a man and a prophet, the son of God or God incarnate? Unless we can show that the Qumran scrolls and Jacob spoke of different Teachers of Righteousness, these debates will continue."

She fell in beside him. "What do you mean?"

"What I mean is, we don't know if Jacob and the Qumran scrolls spoke of the same or different Teachers of Righteousness."

"Michael, I hate you."

Laughing, he followed Rachael's gaze to one of the fattest squirrels he'd ever seen. It didn't so much hop as *heave* through the grass. "Look, this is easy. If the gospel Jacob hid at Qumran speaks of the same teacher as the Qumran scrolls, *without naming him*, nothing changes. Jacob's gospel speaks of a teacher, the Qumran scrolls speak of a teacher, but nobody knows who that teacher is. So nothing changes. On the other hand, if Jacob's teacher is identified as someone the religious world *knows and respects*, like John the Baptist, Jesus Christ or one of his disciples, then it's a whole new theological ballgame."

"Which means," she said, "that if the gospel we seek can be found, it could transform the religions of the world."

"And interested parties might kill to keep that from happening." He paused. "For that matter, they already have. So where do we start?"

"To begin with, what's this 'we' stuff?"

He stopped, turned, and leaned against a lamppost. "Thought we'd already decided that. Didn't think I'd let you do this alone, did you?"

She spoke past him, her voice heavy as the gray winter gloom. "Yeah. But I'm rethinking that. Ever hear the joke about the woman whose doctor told her she had only twelve hours left to live? Her husband asked how she wanted to spend the last evening of her life, and she said she wanted to go to the best restaurant in town, see a play and then a late movie, and then dance till she plotzed. When she finished, her husband looked at her irritably and said, 'Sure, that's fine for you … *you* don't have to get up in the morning.'"

A long moment later, she said, "Look, Michael, this is suicide. But I'm on my last dance. Meaning, nothing to lose. You've got to get up in the morning."

For an instant, Michael saw his mother's glowing face as she uttered her dying words, *"I was dead. Now I'm alive."*

"You're looking for who killed your father," he said. "Maybe they killed my father too. But mostly, I'm looking for the God who saved my mother. I'm coming."

Rachael brought her gaze out of the distance and into his eyes. "I know you've spent your career trying to answer the big questions. The … what do you call it? RAG?"

"ROG. The Reality of God."

"ROG. Right. That's the foundation of your work, but it doesn't mean anything to me. And like it or not, I'm more likely to find Dad's killers than you are to find your 'reality.' And why risk your life too?"

He shrugged. "I'm coming anyway."

She shook her head. "When we were together, we nearly killed each other. That's why I asked you to stay away while I was in treatment. Since it didn't work, I don't want to spend my last few months fighting. So, please. Stay behind and record the information I send. You're a world-renowned scholar. If I'm successful, you're the perfect one to tell the story. But you can't do that if you're dead. If I'm successful, we lose nothing. But if I fail, well, if I fail, you can pick up where I leave off."

He said nothing, only pushed off from the lamppost and looked down at his shoes. As he scuffed the pavement she said, "Nothing like the prospect of a slow, wasting death to push a person into a suicide mission, huh?"

"How are you set for money?" He looked the other way and swallowed hard.

"Got more money than time."

"Good. I'm still coming." He took her by the elbow and guided her down the sidewalk. They walked in silence for a block before he said, "Your father's mystery colleague? The one who had a photo of the seal in his office? Well, it was an international team that analyzed the Qumran scrolls, and the membership changed over the years. This has to be done in person. We've got some traveling to do."

"Always wanted to see the world." She stopped, turned to him and ran her finger along the scar on his jaw. "Just so you know, chicks dig scars."

He laughed, she smiled, and for a moment it felt like their first date again. But like their first date, he felt the good mood fade. He realized Rachael felt it too, because she dropped her hand and took a half-step back. He cleared his throat. "Listen," he said, "Frank was murdered fifteen years ago. Maybe my father was as well, four years ago."

"We don't know that."

"I said maybe." His face tightened as his voice took on a hard edge. "And I want the answer to that too. But all I'm saying is, I don't care how much time has passed. These are killers, they don't forget, and the threat's real. *Real.* Got it?"

She scratched where her wig met her scalp, and her smile turned grim. "What a shame it would be if I met an untimely death, huh?"

"We," Michael said. "If *we* met an untimely death."

"Oh. Yeah," she murmured, and looked away. "That's what I meant."

CHAPTER 15

Michael woke the next morning and bolted from bed as if electrocuted, stepped into the shower before the water ran warm, jumped out before it ran hot. Shivering, he wrapped a towel around his waist and tramped foot-puddles through his Cambridge, Massachusetts home while he dried himself with another towel. His housemate drew upon its timber wolf half to sneak up beside him, and upon its Bernese mountain dog half to rub up against his legs in companionable silence.

"Mornin', Arnold," he muttered. "I'm fine, thanks for asking."

Together, they got as far as the kitchen before something Michael had seen but not immediately registered forced him to stop, retreat two steps and look at the front door, lowering the towel from his shower-spiked hair.

He did a slow walk past the brass coatrack that stood sentry at the entrance and picked up the envelope that had been slid under the door.

"'*Michael, dearest'*? Oh, hell."

He tore the letter from the envelope and sat on the hardwood floor. As he read, the freezing draft from beneath the door chilled his naked legs and sent shivers up his spine. Arnold sniffed the cold draft, lay down between Michael's crossed legs and the door, and covered his master's knees with his thick blanket of dog-wool.

After a moment, Michael reached out, rubbed Arnold's head and said, "*My only true friend.* That's what she called me. Her only true friend."

Arnold nuzzled his master's hand appreciatively, then crooned a musical "*Rooooo.*"

"That's 'Ruff, ruff, a-roo,' you stupid mutt," Michael said. He wove his fingers through the thick fur of the animal's massive head and shook it lovingly. "How'd they breed the 'ruff' out of you?"

"*Roooo.*"

Calmly, Michael stood, took a deep breath, and turned from the door. Without warning, his world went black with anger. He killed the coatrack with a flying spin-kick. Then his fists were at the drywall, punching three holes before he hit the short side of a two-by-four. His fist bounced; he reloaded and shattered the stud with the crack of a pistol shot.

Arnold bounded to his feet the instant the coatrack fell—the enemy that dared enrage his master—ready to tear its brass throat out. But then he cocked his head at a quizzical angle and watched the drywall disappear in puffs of white. The pistol shot of the stud shattering was his starting gun, and he launched from the floor.

Michael felt himself blindsided by his Schwarzenegger of a dog and borne to the ground by Arnold's sheer weight. He struggled to free himself, but in a surprisingly maternal gesture, Arnold flopped down and smothered him to the floor. Michael flailed for a moment, pushed, wriggled, and then gave up.

He looked up into Arnold's intelligent eyes and started to laugh, and his laughter turned into bellowed guffaws before he could finally contain it. "Okay, okay. It's over. Now get off."

Arnold didn't move.

"*Oof*, you're trying to save me and your breath's killing me."

Arnold lolled out his tongue in a dog-laugh.

"Oh, God, I believe, I *believe*," Michael said to the heavens, laughing. "Now *save* me!"

Nothing. He turned his eyes to Arnold's lolling tongue inches from his face, wet drops forming on the edges. "I'll give you a Scooby Snack. Or a steak. A rabbit for a chew-toy. Anything. GET OFF!"

With a rusty squeal, the cat-flap on the front door swung open and the real master of the house entered. Panda padded past, cast them a "*You two at it again?*" glance, then the black-and-white tabby scooted into the kitchen. Arnold bounded off Michael and followed.

He sat up, shook his head and looked at the coatrack, and realized he would've broken his foot if the rack hadn't been padded with his jackets. He felt a sudden cold where he shouldn't feel cold, looked down and found his waist towel had come off. Muttering "No surprise there," he stood, picked up the towel, and found Panda and Arnold sitting side by side in the kitchen doorway. Panda stared, but Arnold draped a paw over his snout, closed his eyes and groaned.

"We're all nuts," Michael said, and turned from his pets, naked, towel in hand. As he turned, he looked through his living room windows, realized he'd left the drapes open, and in the same moment saw a gap in the curtained window across the street narrow to a slit. He bolted down the hall, slipped in a foot-puddle as he entered the bedroom, skidded and fell to sitting on the edge of his bed. He righted himself and looked straight ahead at the centerpiece on his dresser. The Gund teddy bear, a childhood gift from his mother, had worn threadbare in spots, as if bald with age.

"She ran off without me, Plump. Now why'd she do a crazy thing like that?"

When it was clear the bear was keeping his opinion to himself, he said, "Between us, how do *you* put up with me?"

* * *

The next two months brought a steady stream of postcards, beginning stateside, then winding through England and Europe, ending in the Middle East. Rachael traveled unpredictably, mailing her postcards as she left whatever city she was in, never mentioning her next destination. It was deliberate, he knew, to prevent him from finding her. He tried not to think about the other reason: she moved quickly from knowing she had little time left. Whatever her reasons, she wanted to be alone, and expressed that wish both in her postcards and in her actions.

For two months, her search for Frank Tones' mystery colleague proved fruitless. Her postcards reported her frustration with oblique wording, and Michael catalogued the list of scholars she'd scratched off her list. Except for the three candidates she missed, two on vacation and one on sabbatical, she seemed at an impasse by the time she arrived in the Middle East. Her last letter was postmarked Amman, Jordan, and wrote that Israel's scholars shared *"depressingly unified opinions, as if selected from a flow chart that doesn't fork."*

Reading that, Michael allowed himself a smile.

Two weeks later, his bedside phone rang at exactly two in the morning. He pounced, but the caller had hung up. Befuddled, he sat on the edge of his bed and shook his head awake. Then he remembered Rachael's code. He snatched the envelope from the bedside table and reread her letter just to be sure.

One o'clock meant the pay phone on the corner, two o'clock the all-night convenience store, three o'clock the Student Union. He sat and waited. Precisely five minutes later the phone rang, a single ring. This time, he didn't answer. Two calls at two o'clock, five minutes apart. He got dressed, set the alarm, and went back to bed fully clothed. At five o'clock, he had to be at the convenience store.

* * *

When the pay phone rang, he ripped the receiver from its cradle. Balancing a large cup of coffee he'd bought for appearances, he said, "Rachael? You okay?"

"Michael, take it easy. I wrote in my letter, no names."

"You just said *my* name."

"You started it."

"Payphone to payphone? I'll take my chances. You all right? I haven't gotten a postcard for a couple of weeks."

There was a long pause. "Michael ... why do you believe in God?"

He stood stock-still a moment, then leaned against the phone booth to make the mental adjustment. "Where can the injustices of life be set straight, if not in an afterlife?"

"Hm. But why?"

"Why what?"

"Why are we here? What's the purpose?"

"Rachael, are you—"

"*Why*, Michael?"

He rested his coffee on top of the payphone and took a deep breath. "Why is *anything* here? Everything we humans make, we make to serve us. Same with God. He made us to serve him. Now, you okay?"

"I ran out of leads."

"Come home."

"Out of gas, Michael."

At last, he recognized the fatigue in her voice, the slurring of her words that hadn't been there in previous calls. A chill ran up his spine and combed the short hairs on the back of his neck straight.

"I sleep like a dead woman, and wake feeling drugged. Takes me an hour to get out of bed. Sometimes my heart pounds, other times I have to force my breathing. So what do I do, Michael? How do I serve Him?"

He conjured a vision of his dead mother beneath his hands, and he stood straight and strangled the phone in his grip. "Don't die on me, Rachael. Don't you die on me!"

"You too," she whispered. "Don't die before you're dead, Mikey. Listen ... after I'm gone, I want you to do something for me."

He swallowed hard. They never planned for this part. "Where are you?" he blurted. "Tell me where you are and I'll—"

"Find a good girl. Stop pushing them away. Settle down and bring some little Mikeys into this world. You keep putting up walls, you'll die a lonely old bachelor with nothing but *books* for family."

He shook his head silently. "You said you're out of leads. You went to the museum in Jerusalem? The Shrine of the Book? Anything?"

"Just the Dead Sea Scrolls. I wrote you. Everybody in Israel repeats the same party line. Depressing."

"Is that where you are now? Israel?"

She paused, and then said, "I visited Qumran, toured the caves, did all the tourist stuff casting about for leads. Nothing. Then I decided to press."

"To ..."

"To press the issue. Look, I don't care. I'm running out of time."

A deep sense of unease pounded on the walls of his chest. "What did you do?"

"I took photos of the seal on Dad's envelope, and sent them to the guys I already visited. Oxford—"

"The new department chairman?"

"No. He's too young to have been involved in something that happened in the '80's. I sent them to Dr. Mardle. Also to Timothy Harper at Cambridge University, Hans Schellenberg at Humboldt University in Berlin, Hiram Bergman, Curator Emeritus at the Shrine of the Book, and Seaton Facet at *École Biblique* in Jerusalem."

Michael mentally ticked off the names. *Good choices.* "Nobody in the States?"

"Mail takes too long. I'll do them last, if I have time."

He shivered. "Uh, look, Rachael ..."

"Time, Michael. Time. It's the one thing I don't have enough of. Just listen. I accused each one of being the colleague Dad referred to in his letter, and threatened to go public if they don't cooperate."

"Which is, basically—"

"A bluff. But hey, what do I have to lose? Talk didn't work, so maybe this will. If I don't hear anything in a week, then I'll mail another batch of letters, and I'll call to tell you their names, too." She coughed with a raspy wheeze that made him cringe.

"Let me meet you. Help you. Where—?"

"Mikey, no. Hang tough for me. I'll be in touch, okay?"

After he hung up, he stood by the payphone, trapped in a turmoil of thoughts. He took an absentminded sip of coffee and reflexively screwed up his face. With a soft sigh, he turned to leave. As he walked past the trash receptacle between the cashier and door, he pushed open the flap and tossed the cup in. Instantly, he wished he hadn't. The ripples of the collapsed plastic liner whooshed as the full cup freefell to the bottom, where the liquid brick landed with a loud thud and slosh. Without looking back, he turned up his collar, shrank into his coat and slipped out the door.

* * *

Three days later she called again, and code-directed him to the payphone in the Student Union. He taught his morning class on automatic pilot, with no memory of it afterward, and arrived at the Student Union well before the appointed hour.

"You'd die if you saw me now," she said when he answered the phone. "Believe it or not, I'm praying."

"Get outta here!"

"Yeah. Here I am in the Holy Land, wearing a headscarf like the mother of Jesus and praying in prostration like Audrey Hepburn in *The Nun's Story*."

"Or, more to the point, like Jesus in the Garden of Gethsemane."

"Either way, you'd laugh your head off."

"You're such a radical."

"TTJ—*True to Jesus*. Picked up your book, and started taking my prayers all the way to the cold, hard floor. Funny, huh? All those years of snickering at people wearing 'TTJ' and 'ROG' bracelets and lapel pins, and it takes this for me to read your work. Heck, if I were a man, I might even do the Jesus thing and grow a beard."

"With all your meds, you might grow one anyway."

That drew an appreciative laugh, as he hoped it would. Then he said, "And it's not just the example of Jesus, but of all the prophets, their disciples and righteous followers. Think of Abraham, Noah, Moses—"

"No lectures, okay, Mikey? Got your book, be happy."

"Rachael, where are you?" A few heads turned, and he realized his voice must have been louder than intended. Lowering it, he asked, "Where can I find you?"

"Hang tough, Mikey."

"I mean it. I want to come. Take care of you, if nothing else." As soon as he said it, he sensed his error. Rachael's silence seemed to confirm it.

But he was wrong.

"Mikey, for the first time in my life, I need help." The crack in her voice was so slight as to be almost imperceptible. "That's why I'm praying."

"Name the place."

"Amman, Jordan. What's your preference? The Sheraton or Hilton?"

"Sheraton."

"Done." Her voice steadied. "The Sheraton, in five days."

"I can be there in three. Maybe two. Dad taught me well. Still got my Hansen Stampeding Pack, ready to go."

"No. Five days. I got two calls from my letters. A fatherly advice call from Trevor Mardle, a second from someone who wouldn't give me his name. Dr. Mardle seemed concerned. Tried to talk me into playing safe and going home. Seems like a nice guy, actually. I can see why Dad liked him. Mr. Anonymous sounds like pay dirt. Wouldn't tell me anything except that he knew Dad, and didn't want to risk a similar fate. His words, not mine. He was clearly frightened."

"Seems sensible." Michael turned the chair around and sat, realizing with a slight shock that he and Rachael had just heard confirmation that others believed Frank Tones was murdered.

"Anyway, Mr. Anonymous is willing to meet me," she said. "In two days, here. Look, I'm running a fever and not thinking clearly. Give me five days. Two to meet him, a couple extra to tie it together."

"Rachael, he might be the enemy."

"Thought of that. If he's the enemy, I think I'd be dead by now. Call you in a couple."

A click, and she was gone.

As he left the Student Union, he made a mental note to buy a couple gift boxes of Cadbury chocolate roses. He crinkled his nose at the thought, but she loved them.

Then he realized what he'd wanted to say. What he should have said: *Rachael, it might not be a meeting. It might be a set-up.*

But no. Fuzzy headed or not, she would've thought of that.

CHAPTER 16

S he bought it," Yogi said as he balled up the empty sandwich wrapper and tossed it onto the sidewalk. "You're such a slick talker."

Yogi and Boo-Boo stood at a sidewalk eatery, watching Rachael enter *Najmun Jamil*, "Beautiful Star," in English. One of hundreds of hole-in-the-wall hostels scattered about Amman, each was characterized by a vain attempt to sweep the squalor of its condition beneath the beauty of its name. It was perfect for the rendezvous.

Boo-Boo turned to walk away. In the same motion, he lobbed the second half of his sandwich over his shoulder, toward the trashcan. Yogi intercepted, rolled back the paper wrap, and followed.

"I told her to check in tonight," Boo-Boo said, "and that we'd meet tomorrow morning. Let's hope she sleeps deep."

"Know what I love about this job?" Yogi bit into his partner's throwaway and spoke around the food in his mouth. "Continuity. That's what I love. Once they stick you on a juicy case, they let you follow it to the end."

Boo-Boo lit up a smoke and examined his partner's face. Fifteen years ago, it had been full but strong. Now it was rounding with fat, with a perpetual four-day growth of stubble topped off with a bleached crew cut. Boo-Boo glanced at his reflection in a store window as he walked past, and realized how little his own face had changed in that same time. "You know why, don't you?" he asked.

"Huh?"

"Why they keep us on the case after all these years."

Yogi covered one nostril with his thumb and blew a wad of mucus from the other. It hit the sidewalk with a splat. Then he took another bite of sandwich.

"For their own protection," Boo-Boo said. "If the operation goes sour, there are fewer agents to either eliminate or transfer the blame to."

Yogi wrinkled his brow in concentration, but only shrugged. "Small price to pay for what they let us do. Our guys see any other teams on this play?"

"Two Americans. Young guys."

"No Italians?"

"Just CIA types." Boo-Boo pulled up to a coffee stand and ordered. He handed a cup to Yogi, who burped, and then took a swig of the bittersweet brew. "Probably running protection again. I called it in and asked permission to eighty-six them."

"And?" Yogi's voice was eager.

He shook his head.

"Ungh."

"But …"

"Don't tease me."

Boo-Boo grinned. "They want us to ortho them before we do the girl. Make it look like a mugging. Bruises and broken bones."

"Hot damn!" Yogi pumped his sandwich hand as if he'd scored a winning goal. "Boo-Boo, this is going to be a night to remember!"

* * *

The bed was a floor mattress, the pillow a solid block of foam rubber of the kind only found in the Middle East. Firm and unyielding at manufacture, it had hardened even further with age. Rachael pounded it with her fist, nearly shredding the cheap, sweat-stained slipcover in the process, but the pillow remained obstinately brick-like. It would take an elephant to make an impression on it.

Yet she slept. Not the deep slumber of the exhausted, but the fitful sleep of the weary. Over the previous ten weeks, she'd scrawled dyslexic doodles on half the globe with her path of travel, retracing fifty years of Dead Sea Scrolls history. Now, she felt her journey nearing an end.

She had taken her medicine, choking down the football-shaped pill with bread and water. She went to bed feeling remarkably better, which was unusual. Lately, her evenings had found her near collapse. So she slept.

And dreamt.

And suffered a nightmare.

The same nightmare she'd dreamt for a month now.

The broad outline never changed. As always, she felt naked and exposed, her body without form or substance. When she looked down, she saw only emptiness, as if she had been erased. But then she was distracted by the *words*, the black masses of text that filled the sky like clouds of locusts.

Just when the words seemed to come into focus, they broke away from their sentences and flew past her, too quickly to read. Sometimes the words flew *through* her. The worst was when the words shot through her eyes or nose. The pain was real, piercing. But the words wouldn't stay, so she couldn't absorb them as she had tried; they always burst out the other side and disappeared, their meaning forever lost.

Tonight was different.

Tonight the print was bold, the design gothic and menacing. As usual, she couldn't read the words, but their meaning was clear. *Get out. Get out, now!*

And this time, the words swirled around her. As they pressed closer, they exploded into dust, filling her lungs and choking her. One single word, she could see at a distance. She wanted to scream when others joined it and composed a sentence that lined up like an arrow aimed at her heart. The leading letters sharpened themselves to a point.

She gasped, but her breath wouldn't come.

She was suffocating.

And then, gaining momentum, the sentence pulled back in its invisible bow and shot forward, stabbing her chest with a searing pain. But unlike earlier versions of the dream, the sentence didn't exit her body through the other side. It backed up and stabbed her again. And again. She felt her consciousness fade, and in the last stage of life, she opened her eyes.

But they were no longer her eyes. She no longer looked out of her body, but rather down upon it, at the huge man who straddled her supine form, one hand clamped over her mouth while the other plunged a bloody knife again and again into the spreading stain on her patterned sleep-shirt. And as she lifted up to watch the scene from the ceiling ... through the roof ... through the clouds ... everything distant but at the same time clear, she realized that this time, it wasn't a dream.

* * *

These'll get crushed. Bank on it, he thought, adding to Arnold at his side, "but it's the thought that counts, right boy?"

He spoke while he carried the boxes of chocolate roses from the kitchen to the bedroom, where his bag lay open on the bed. Michael had arranged for his teaching assistants to cover his undergrad classes, which were only lectures, and for one of the professors who owed him a favor to take over his graduate seminars.

As he passed his study, Arnold at his heels, the phone rang. His unlisted line. The number only his closest friends and associates knew.

He stopped, stepped past, then back, then entered and plopped the boxes on his desk and answered. The voice was Rachael's, but twenty years older.

"Cindy? ... I mean, Mrs. Crawley?" he asked, hesitant.

"It's Mrs. Johnson now, Michael. I've remarried."

He sat at his desk and listened. Arnold sat on the floor and cocked his head, no less intent. Michael hung up wordlessly. His subconscious catalogued the breakables in the room; his cognizant mind fought to contain his anger. But then his mouth went dry and his vision narrowed to a tunnel. The light at the end dimmed to gray; his ears filled with a deep, gut-churning snarl. But somewhere inside, a primordial part of him realized the snarl wasn't his own.

His vision cleared around Arnold, rigid, poised to attack, the razor ridge of his hackles standing erect at the back of his neck, his teeth bared and slavering. Michael felt the temperature in the room drop to freezing and every hair on his body stand on end. He followed the dog's gaze to the telephone, winced, then said softly, "Arnold." And then, "ARNOLD!"

The dog wound down to a growl. His hackles smoothed out like a porcupine dropping its quills. Fighting back tears, Michael stood, scrubbed the beast's head while somberly shaking his own, and started to lead him from the room.

The phone rang again.

Arnold whirled and rocketed across the desk, scattering the pages of an unfinished manuscript and both boxes of chocolates, sweeping the desk clean before he tumbled off the opposite side, phone clenched firmly in his teeth.

In other circumstances Michael might have laughed. But amid the wet growls, gnashes of teeth and pops of cracking plastic, his eyes scanned the field of papers and Cadbury Roses strewn across the carpet. His gaze settled upon Arnold as the big dog demolished what he understood to be the source of his master's anger.

"My only true friend," he said, watching Arnold but thinking of Rachael. Then he fell to the floor, raised his hands to his face, and wept.

* * *

Sixteen hours later and seven time zones distant, Aryeh Leib, the prime minister of Israel, strolled into his office. He worked through a third of the stack of classified briefs on his desk before he paused.

An elimination on an open perpetual? Not so unusual. *But on a father and daughter, separated by fifteen years? Now* that *is curious.*

"The Palestinian Center for Human Rights," he said to his chief advisor, who stood beside his desk. "It lists, what, seventy-seven extrajudicial assassination operations between September 2000 and July 2002?"

"Seventy-eight," the advisor said. "134 Palestinians killed, ninety-three of whom were targeted. The other forty-one were bystanders."

"Children?" Leib asked.

"Eleven."

"Hmm. Seventy-seven operations listed."

"Seventy-eight."

Leib snorted. "If the human rights groups knew the real number, they'd have a stroke."

"They can only count what they know," his advisor said. "I'd bet that number doesn't even cover our operations in Gaza."

Leib sat back and beat a rhythm on his thigh with his palm and fingers. "How many did we have worldwide?"

"Uff." His advisor rolled his eyes. "Only Mossad knows. Maybe even *they've* lost count."

"Prime Minister Benyamin Netanyahu," Leib said. "May he be blessed."

"Sir?"

Leib stopped drumming and looked up. "That botched assassination attempt in Amman, Jordan? Of the Hamas politburo chief, Khaled Misha'al? When was that? September, 1996?"

"1997."

"Whatever." Leib stood, walked over to a wall map and studied it. "Netanyahu had to clear his name in front of the world, so he handpicked an Israeli inquiry team. They exonerated him, of course. Israeli opposition leaders were outraged. Declared the inquiry a whitewash. No matter. The panel's decision pacified the international community, and that was the goal. Five months later, when the panel endorsed the continued use of Mossad to conduct extrajudicial killings of *suspected* terrorists anywhere in the world, nobody noticed."

"Not *known* terrorists?" his advisor asked.

"Ha!" Leib slapped his thigh and turned away from the map. "That was the coup. Since then, we've had a license to kill on the world. We can make anyone a suspect!"

His advisor looked down and shifted his feet, and Leib returned to lean over his desk. "All the same, we have to use discretion. This open perpetual." He tapped the brief in front of him. "What happened on that archeological dig back in ..." He shuffled through the papers in the file. "Back in 1987? What was so important they placed a standing order to kill anyone threatening the find? Research it. And make the kill order conditional upon my approval. I don't want another corpse until I know what this is about."

He sat, skimmed the brief across his desk to his advisor, and reached to the remaining stack of classified documents.

CHAPTER 17

Michael woke in his bed with a familiar weight on his legs. As it had every morning for the last two years, Rachael's list ran through his mind, like a circular Rolodex with five address cards. Trevor Mardle at Oxford … Timothy Harper at Cambridge … Hans Schellenberg at Humboldt University in Berlin … Hiram Bergman and Seaton Facet, both in Jerusalem. Five names. Five professors threatened, one Rachael murdered.

He reached beneath his pillow and wrapped his hand around the reassuring coolness of a checked pistol grip. *More likely to accidentally blow my own head off than an intruder's*, he thought. The same thought as when he purchased it, but he'd handed over the cash anyway.

He swept his hand from beneath the pillow, raised the bedcovers and snapped them taut, blanket-throwing Panda off the bed. She awoke in the air and landed on all fours with an annoyed *"Rrawrgh."*

"Make me breakfast, you useless fur-ball."

He poured himself out of bed and stumbled to the bathroom, Panda doing her morning slalom around his ankles.

Stop pushing them away.

Unbidden, Rachael's words came back to him. He stopped, bent over and scooped the cat into his arms, and then stroked a purr out of her. "You're the only woman I let into my life. Know that?"

Panda fanned her digits, and then skin-tested a claw. He threw her to the floor. He found a pinpoint dimple on his arm, but no blood. Panda was back at his ankles as if nothing had happened, so he lifted her with his foot and gently kick-tossed her toward the bedroom door. "If you were a woman, you'd say I never did anything for you. *Rrawrgh* yourself. Go on, get out of here."

His eyes fell upon his old teddy bear, who still sat on the dresser, but now with a short-barrelled shotgun at its feet. Three banana clips of .223 high-velocity rounds were stacked by its side, the assault rifle stowed in his closet.

He plucked a bunched towel from the corner of the dresser and stepped into the bathroom, then raised his eyes to the mirror. Robinson Crusoe marooned in a reflection of porcelain tiles stared back. "Jesus freak," he muttered. "I'm a Jesus freak."

He ran his fingers from shoulder-length hair to scraggly beard, and then sighed. "A Jesus freak with guns. Lots and lots of guns."

After he threw on corduroy pants and a flannel shirt, he stuffed a 40-caliber Glock into the carryall that doubled as briefcase and gym bag. Then he stepped down the hallway and into his study.

The walls were papered with maps, flow charts and five biographical sketches on butcher-block paper. Each biographical sketch started with the education, fieldwork, job history and publications of one of the five professors on Rachael's list. The findings of the private investigators he'd hired for formal background searches followed.

He stared at each poster, hoping to divine some clue from their words. "Done everything but visit," he said to himself. He turned from the room and switched off the light.

He dropped his bag by the door and dodged a minefield of empty bottles, cans and food containers on his way to the kitchen. His early warning system. Nobody could get past that mess in the dark without being heard.

After he dumped food into his pets' bowls, he tossed the empty cans onto the counter beside an island of a half-dozen others, surrounded by piles of dirty dishes, glasses and assorted eating utensils. He hauled an industrial-sized garbage can from the corner, plucked a couple cans from the pile, sighed, and then swept the counter clean with his arm. The avalanche hit the bin with a cacophony of smashed ceramic and glass. He spun an empty pizza box into the corner, patted off his hands, and then grabbed a cold Hot Pockets from behind the .357 Magnum in the fridge. Then he headed for the door, Arnold padding faithfully at his heels.

* * *

"Use it or lose it."

He looked up from his desk and found the divinity department chairman in the doorway.

"Boston has some truly gifted barbers, Michael, and conveniently located, too. The hedge needs a trim, know what I mean?"

Michael smiled and motioned his boss to a chair.

"You're maxed out," the chairman said as he sat. "Either the university buys back your time, or you're on vacation come summer."

Michael turned and gazed out his window overlooking the Harvard campus grounds.

"You've workaholic'ed the rest of us to shame," the chairman said. "Five books in two years? Unheard of. Nobody can work at this pace and keep up the quality."

"Two were best-sellers," Michael said, still looking out the window.

"*Happy Birthday* is the most oft-sung song in the world. But that doesn't mean it has artistic merit."

Michael turned a blank gaze on his boss, who held up his hands and said, "Okay, okay. They were good. Brilliant, even. So what do you say? End of May?"

"End of May," Michael said, nodding.

"We'll miss you." The chairman stood to leave.

"You're afraid I'm chasing your chair," Michael said with a smirk.

"Dead straight." But then, his boss' smile turned to a frown. "I'm more afraid you're chasing ghosts. We're family here, Michael. We see you tearing yourself apart, and we're all concerned. All of us. Well, not that miserable witch of a departmental secretary. She doesn't care for anyone. But other than her, all of us."

Michael stood and shook his boss' hand. "Thanks. That means a lot to me."

"Enough to keep your eye off my chair?" His boss winked and turned to the door.

CHAPTER 18

In late May, Michael sheared ten years from his head and face, packed his bags, and flew to England with lifted spirits and an executive haircut. He slept during the flight, then spent the express-coach ride to Oxford reviewing his plan.

"First, Dr. Mardle," he said.

"Pardon?"

Jerking in surprise, he turned to the elderly gent sitting next to him. "Oh, sorry. Talking to myself."

"The best company, that. Never an argument."

Michael smiled and gazed out the window at the yellow fleece of flowering mustard. Draped over the rolling hills, the fields gave way to plots of green, but just as abruptly reverted to yellow. From the sky, the countryside would look like a checked ground-cloth.

Mardle first, he thought. *Easiest to cross off the list of suspects. Can't be him. Frank was his friend, Dad was his colleague, and he called Rachael to try to help her. I'll check him out anyway. See what he knows.*

* * *

Michael was startled by how little Trevor Mardle had changed over the years. The same ruddy complexion, the same wispy grey hair. "It's nice to see they still take care of you," he said as he surveyed the man's office. "Stateside, there's little life in a university after sixty-five."

"They don't treasure brilliant minds as they do here," Mardle said with a chuckle. He busied himself with the electric kettle. "Since I gave up the chairmanship, this is what I miss most: a secretary to make tea. But since my wife died, I've learned to do for myself. Now, what brings you to Oxford? Fess up, boy."

Michael accepted a cup of Earl Grey and stirred a sugar cube gone.

"Ah, the strong, silent type, eh?" Mardle said. "Ve haf vays uff mekking you talk, young man! Hans! Bruno! The irons and coals!" he shouted at the open door.

"What brings me here?" Michael said, deciding vagueness was best. "Just trying to figure out the murder."

Mardle pulled up a chair and sat. He sipped his tea tentatively, then put it down. "Sad affair. Poor Rachael was dying anyway, of course. She told me that. But still …"

"I meant her father." Michael fixed him with his gaze. "I'm trying to figure out *his* murder."

He had always felt the expression that a person "didn't even blink" was clichéd. Everybody blinks. It's the natural thing to do. The only people who don't blink are those with something to hide, like in the movies, where the only guy who doesn't flinch when the bomb goes off is the one who planted it.

Mardle blinked, and lowered his eyes to his lap. Then he slowly raised them to meet Michael's gaze. "My dear boy, we couldn't figure that out either."

"We?'"

"Your father and I."

Michael felt his heart jump. "Dad? He never told me he talked to yo—"

A ghostly apparition appeared in the doorway. Not so much ghostly as pasty-faced, Michael thought later, but the rebellious shock of red hair made a striking contrast. "Another job applicant refusing to give references?" the man asked with a smile.

"Ah." Mardle stood. "Dr. Terry Falson. You remember Michael Hansen, no doubt. Seventeen years ago, Rybkoski's dig, the week Frank Tones died?"

"Of course," Falson said with an unctuous smile. "How much we miss your father, as well." He stepped into the room and extended his hand. Michael felt his own smile slip a notch, for Falson's hand slid into his own limp and clammy, almost amphibian to the touch.

He repressed a shudder, and didn't so much release Falson's hand as drop it.

Mardle turned to Michael. "Terry was a graduate student back then. He's come along admirably since, albeit by scooping me on occasion ... and occasion ... and occasion. But competition keeps our work interesting, don't you think?"

"Must dash, sorry. Horribly busy," Falson said, and stepped to the doorway. "When you need that blowtorch and pliers, Trevor, give me a ring. Ta."

Falson disappeared with a wave of his fingers, and Mardle turned back with an apologetic wrinkle on his face. "A prissy twit, if you ask me. But you didn't. Now, where were we?"

"My father," Michael said while he wiped Falson off his hand and onto his pants. "Dad never told me you talked about this."

"He didn't want you to know." Mardle took his seat and gave his tea another sip. "Remember when I visited after his first heart attack? He wanted to talk, but on condition of secrecy."

"What did he say?" Michael asked.

"You know your end of it. As for myself, I always knew Frank was murdered."

"You didn't show it at the time."

"Ah, yes." Mardle cleared his throat. "Initially, I was in shock. Only later did I recognize the incongruities. But by then I was home, and some very odd things were happening."

Michael cocked his head.

"Now, don't pretend surprise. The same happened to the two of you. Certainly you don't imagine you were the only ones worthy of observation."

Michael allowed his expression to drift back to normal. "I see. What happened?"

"You can imagine. This was a safe city back then, and I used to keep odd hours. I guess the lads thought themselves invisible, but after a while I sensed a presence. Once my suspicions were awakened I put them through the paces, doubling back on my walks, bursting out of establishments as soon as I entered them. Those kinds of things. But it *was* odd."

Michael leaned forward in his chair. "Odd how?"

"Toward the end, I think they wanted me to see them. About this time, I noticed my telephone lines made clicking and whirring noises. Not what you'd expect from professionals who wanted to remain clandestine. But exactly what you'd expect from professionals who wanted to instill insecurity and fear."

"Sounds familiar," Michael said with a nod. "And then?"

"Same as you. After a while, Chopper and Cro-Magnon Man, as I'd come to think of them, simply disappeared." Mardle chuckled. "You should have seen these specimens. They looked designed for mayhem and raw meat. Definitely a step back on the evolutionary scale."

Michael drained his cup, then asked, "Can you add anything to what I already know?"

Mardle shook his head. "Gerald and I came to the same conclusions."

"Dad told me about a graduate student working with Dr. Tones."

"Robert Barnett. Mr. White-as-a-Sheet, Don't-Ask-Me-Eyes, as your father described him. Neither Gerald nor I were bold enough to approach him directly. We feared his involvement with Frank Tones was too intimate, if you get my meaning."

"My thought, exactly." Michael leaned back in his chair.

"But you can cross him off your list of suspects. He too recognized Frank's death as murder, found the artifacts tampered with, and was afraid he was next."

Michael had opened his mouth to speak, but Mardle held up a hand. "How do I know? This is how." Mardle raised his cup of tea and winked as he took a sip. "Uck, too cold. Gone gobby, haven't I? Talked too long, that is."

"What, the tea?" Michael said. "What does tea have to do with this?"

"Very little. The one who used to make it? Quite a lot."

Mardle stood and clicked the kettle on. "How I miss that secretary. She was his ex-wife, you know. Absolutely fed up with the man. Of course, that's why I hired her."

It took a minute for this to sink in. Michael watched as Mardle brewed a fresh cup, and then asked, "You hired her because she was Robert's wife?"

"Ex-wife. She had a remarkable working knowledge of anthropological and archaeological terminology, having endured him through all those years of study. She was eminently qualified, and served the department admirably until remarriage and children corrupted her priorities."

Michael waved off the offer of another cup. "So what do you think this is all about?"

Mardle cradled his cup and composed himself, tight-lipped. "Leave it," he said, "just leave it. First Frank, then his daughter."

"My father?"

"Who knows?" Mardle said with a wave of his hand. "Why put yourself at risk, Michael?"

"But what do *you* think this is all about?"

This elicited a long sigh. "Exactly what you do. The Gospel of the Teacher could threaten the major religions of the world, along with their committed concerns. These are formidable opponents, willing to sacrifice nations to preserve their interests."

Michael arched an eyebrow. "You've seen the ending to Jacob's scroll?"

A nod. "Your father shared his photographs. Another thing. Rachael and I spoke shortly before she was murdered. Michael, abandon this. We're completely over our heads."

"What did she say?"

He shut his eyes for a brief moment. "She sent me a shockingly accusatory letter, and I contacted her out of concern. She was murdered a day or two later." He raised his teacup to take a sip.

"So what did she say?"

Mardle froze a moment, and lowered the cup unsipped. "She accused me of hiding the Gospel of the Teacher and threatened to expose me, whatever that meant. Her tone was ugly and I tried to calm her, but she wasn't open to advice."

"Sounds like Rachael." Michael sat back and crossed his arms on his chest. "There's something I don't get. Let's presume there are dozens of interest groups willing to kill to keep this gospel from being found. Fine. But how did they learn about, and then act upon, Frank's find so quickly? It's as if the dig was infiltrated by informants."

"I think the operative word is not 'infiltrated,' but 'staffed.'" Mardle put his cup down, stood, and started to pace the room. "Archaeological digs are routinely monitored by the intelligence community. As the son of an archeologist, you surely knew that, or suspected it."

He nodded. "I've heard the rumors. Always wondered if they were true."

"They are. Site-doping, meaning the planting of fake artifacts, can create major controversies. But this is a relatively minor intelligence issue, because the truth eventually comes out. It always does. Look at the Piltdown hoax." Mardle bounced his eyebrows at Michael, then continued. "An even greater concern is that someone might conceal legitimate artifacts that reveal something alarming about the origin of man. Or about religion. Like the Gospel of the Teacher, perhaps."

"And the greatest concern?" Michael asked.

Mardle stopped pacing and cast his gaze on one corner of the ceiling. "Some say it relates to UFOs, if you believe in such things."

"UFOs?"

Mardle spoke into the corner and gestured with one hand, as if to wave the notion away. "As I said, if you believe in such things."

"And do you?"

The elderly professor leaned against his desk. "Rumor has it, the intelligence community noted similarities between UFO abduction reports and what was being found around the world in archaeological digs. Common symbols. Images resembling alien-like creatures in ancient cave drawings and tomb carvings. That sort of thing. There have been reports of tools unearthed that were too advanced for the period of the digs in which they were found. And then, of course, there's the Roswell incident and, well," he flapped a hand in the air, "and I don't know. It doesn't really matter. What *does* matter is that the intelligence community seems concerned."

"So they're worried about, what? That someone might unearth a two-thousand-year-old laptop or something?"

Mardle gave him a tight smile. "They're afraid of anything that might upset the status quo. A mummified alien buried with his ray gun. A time-traveler entombed with his fourth-millennium *Farmer's Almanac*. Sounds like pure Hollywood today, but who knows what tomorrow might bring? Whether you believe such things are possible or not, the point is that most digs are staffed with members who collect two paychecks. Not among the archaeologists, of course. But administration, clerical staff and such."

"Why not archaeologists?"

Mardle smiled. "I'm surprised at you, Michael. We want to expose the truths *they* seek to hide." He retrieved his teacup, sipped, and disappointment crossed his face. "Cold again," he said, and set it aside. "Michael, I like your company, but you're hurting my tea budget."

* * *

"You don't need a secretary to make your tea, Dr. Mardle," Michael Hansen's voice replied, with an almost audible grin. *"You need someone to drink it for you."*

Two offices away, Terry Falson chuckled, repositioned his headphones and adjusted his receiver for better reception.

CHAPTER 19

Michael spent the next three days expanding the reference section of his mind from the stacks in the Oxford libraries. He spent the most time in the smaller libraries, where a tail would be easier to spot. His plan was simple. He didn't believe Rachael was killed for just asking questions. She'd visited each of the five professors on her letter list, but wasn't killed until she threatened them with exposure. The best way to find her killer was to do the same thing: visit them one by one, making himself a willing decoy. If he didn't pick up a whiff of danger after a few days, he'd move to the next on the list.

After three days he'd seen nothing untoward, and moved to the Old Bodleian Library, Oxford University's main research library. Disappointed to find the 1817 edition of Heinz Zahrnt's *The Historical Jesus* in use, he approached the Religion desk to file a reserve slip. Second in line, he continued flipping pages on the volume in his hand while half-listening to the conversation in front of him.

"Excuse me, but I need this translated," a freshman type asked the librarian behind the counter. "Where can I find a translation office dealing in German?"

"Do you need an official translation, or will an informal read suffice?" the woman responded, with an accent that was unmistakably American.

American? Michael wondered absentmindedly. *What's an American doing working here?*

"I'm verifying a quote," the kid in front of him said. "I need to know if my source got the translation right."

"Here, let me take a look."

"You're joking," the kid said in a voice two octaves higher. "Now that's what I call service!"

Michael reached the end of his book, tucked it under his arm and, finding his view obscured by the freshman's broad back, looked around impatiently for an available librarian.

The woman's voice resumed. "Let's see, this is recorded from Pope Innocent III in 1199—But this isn't German, it's Latin. An understandable mistake, given the authors' names."

Good. My turn. Michael faced forward again.

"In that case, how's your Latin?" the young man joked as he reached for the book.

"Not as good as my German, but I can scrape by."

Michael turned another impatient half-circle to check the other reference counters, but stopped moving when he heard, "Okay, here goes. 'The mysteries of the faith are not to be explained rashly to anyone.' Now, please understand, I'm taking some liberties. This word here is literally translated 'vulgar'—an archaic term for 'commoners.' However, most wouldn't understand that term ..."

Michael took a half step to the side to peer around the young man's shoulder.

"... So perhaps we'd better use 'anyone' in this case. Okay, let's see what's next." Her head was bent to an open book on the counter, her face obscured, her finger on the text. A small brass nametag on her blouse introduced her as June Cody.

Without consciously intending the words to pass his lips, Michael said, "'The mysteries of the faith are not to be explained rashly to anyone. Usually in fact, they cannot be understood by everyone, but only by those who are qualified to understand them with informed intelligence.'" He continued reciting until he finished with, "'The depth of the divine scriptures is such that not only the illiterate and uninitiated have difficulty understanding them, but also the educated and the gifted.'"

The kid turned sideways to face him; the librarian looked up to meet his gaze in astonishment, brushing a stray strand of hair behind her ear. The strand immediately fell free, but she held her gaze a moment too long for comfort before she looked down again and read, "*Enchiridion Symbolorum, Definitionum et Declarationum de Rebus Fidei et Morum*, by Henricus Denzinger and Adolfus Schonmetzer."

"Barcinone: Herder, 1973, if memory serves. Page 246."

June Cody straightened and sighted past the student. "Is there something I can help you with, *show-off?*"

He blinked forcibly, as if to regain his vision, stared into her warm eyes, now cool with critical appraisal, and said, "Uhhh ..."

The young man glanced between the two as their eyes locked in a standoff. He delicately reached to the counter and retrieved his book, muttered "Cheers," to which June responded with a curt smile and nod, and slipped from between them.

* * *

Michael moved to a nearby flat off Holywell Street, and over the next few days, fell into an enjoyable routine: breakfast at home followed by a visit to the library, where he would settle into the serious job of harassing June between newspaper reads and forays into the stacks. They lunched together during her off-hours, after which he would while away the afternoon visiting his professor friends. Frequently, he dropped by to chat with Mardle. In all his conversations with the elderly professor, he never once saw him finish his tea, although the digestive biscuits disappeared at an alarming rate. Sometimes a circle would gather, and on those occasions, the wealth of intelligence in the room could bankrupt lesser institutions.

He spent evenings with June, divided between walks, leisurely dinners and the theater, but at week's end he put their relationship on hold to visit Dr. Timothy Harper at Cambridge University. He returned to Oxford, and to June's annoyance repeated the disappearing act a week later. This time he caught a hop to Berlin, to visit Dr. Hans Schellenberg at Humboldt University.

Both visits were a wash. No useful information, and not even the trace of a shadow appeared on his tail. By this time he was used to disappointments, but still he planned to visit the last of

Rachael's "suspects": Drs. Hiram Bergman and Seaton Facet, both in Jerusalem.

The next morning he lay in bed, frozen in thought. *Time to go again. Next stop, Amman, Jordan. Or maybe Jerusalem.* And in spite of his fast-deepening feelings for June, it was only indecision that delayed him.

He continued to mull over the issue while he watched the mellow rays of the sun invade his bedroom, and was on the verge of conceding to another half hour of sleep when the doorbell rang.

* * *

"So, where are we going?" June asked over her shoulder, gently stirring and folding the eggs she was scrambling.

"Excuse me?" He looked up from the kitchen table. He'd been staring at the cheap plastic tablecloth, wondering if it would be more cost-effective to clean or replace when dirty.

She dusted the eggs with thyme and sesame seeds. "It's time, isn't it?" she said. "Seven days. That's the cycle of your mystery jaunts. Please don't say no. I've already packed a bag and asked for time off."

"What makes you think I'm taking another trip?"

"Women's intuition." She piled toast on a plate. "That, and the travel agent's name and phone number scribbled beside your phone." She turned and smothered him with a "Can't argue with that!" smile.

He looked down. "That note? That was from before."

"Does that mean I'm wrong?"

When met with awkward silence, she turned and gave the eggs a final stir, then slid them onto a plate with pan-fried potatoes for company, sprinkled salt on the eggs and paprika on the potatoes, and bracketed the lot with triangles of toast. She set the plate in front of him and said, "Okay, I'll make it plainer. Can I go with you?"

He didn't know whether to eat breakfast or photograph and frame it. The eggs, scrambled in olive oil on low heat, were a brilliant chick-feather yellow. "I'll only be away a couple days," he said.

"No deal."

He caught her stare and held it. "This is the last trip, but I have to do it alone. I'll tell you about it when I come back."

"*If* you come back."

Her words caught him with a full mouth, and for the first time in his life, he chewed twenty times before swallowing. "June, dear, I'll just be away a few days, and then ..."

He could tell she wasn't buying it. Her eyes had turned to ice, her jaw to stone. It was the "June, dear" that did it, he realized too late.

"It's about the seal, isn't it?"

He didn't just feel thrown; he felt blindfolded, bundled up and hurled into open space. He sat dumbstruck while she pinched a wedge of toast from his plate and nibbled an edge. "I've been working the Religion desk at the library part-time since I started graduate school," she said between crunches. "A couple years ago, Dr. Mardle came in. He wanted help researching the pattern of a seal he thought might have religious significance."

"So?" Michael asked, his heart pounding.

"So he got me."

She reached across the table, dipped her toast into Michael's eggs and swept a potato aboard for company. "Actually, he didn't get me. The seal did. It intrigued me."

"And?"

"And?" She paused with the toast a hair's breadth from her lips. "And nothing." She bit and chewed, pausing to wipe a speck of egg that had caught at the corner of her mouth. "I researched it for days, but couldn't find any parallel in any of the pagan religions of antiquity. But here's the point, Michael. Dr. Mardle made a mistake for which he can hardly be faulted. He's getting on in years, after all."

The kettle whistled. She rose, removed it from the burner, then returned to her chair, sitting sideways, facing him with one arm on the tabletop. "He gave me an envelope containing photographs of the seal he wanted researched. In addition to the photographs, there was a letter written by a woman I later learned was murdered. A woman who was researching the seal when her life was cut short. A woman who, just the other night, you mentioned as having been the only other woman in your life."

Michael tried to find some words of reassurance, but drew a blank.

"The moment you said her name," she said, "I realized why you're here."

He had to try. "How ... How did you know I wasn't working on something else?"

She smiled, triumph radiating from her eyes. "I didn't. But now that you've asked, I do."

He groaned. "I could never play poker, either."

She faced him squarely. "So I can come?"

"No."

"Oh, come on. I'll—"

"No." He met her gaze. "It's too dangerous."

"And for you?"

He pushed his chair back and got up from the table. "I can take care of myself. But I can't take care of someone else."

She bowed her head and dropped her shoulders. "If you go without me, I won't be here for you when you get back."

It was time, he decided, and told himself that he wasn't just saying it to put her off. "When I get back, we'll have a new life to start. Together."

"I won't be here."

He turned and began walking from the room. "That's a chance I'll have to take."

"Don't push me away."

Stop pushing them away. The echo of Rachael's words encircled him like a whip, and spun him around in the kitchen doorway. He found her on her feet, her face flushed with rage. "What we felt when we first met?" she said. "That's once in a lifetime. For three weeks, we've been trying to recapture the magic of those first few days. But every time we get close, you push me away. Why?"

He blinked, and for a moment he looked at her and saw his mother. The tilt to her chin, the angle of her arm propped on her hip, the fire in her eyes. It *was* his mother. He thought back to his father. To Rachael. To Frank Tones. But his memories were overwritten by his mother's face and dying words. *I was dead, and now I'm alive!*

"There's something I've got to finish first," he said.

"Forget the damned seal, Michael. Whatever it means to you … to her … throw it away. But don't throw us away. What's so important about it anyway?"

He leaned against the doorjamb. "It's something I have to do."

"And going with you is something *I* have to do."

He shook his head. "Too risky. It doesn't make sense."

"NOT EVERYTHING MAKES SENSE!" She beat her temples with her fists, and tears spilled from her eyes.

He opened his arms and took a step toward her, saying, "June—," but she turned her back to him, snatched a napkin from the table and wiped tears from her cheeks. Reflexively, he dropped his arms to his sides and took a step back.

She spoke without turning, her words so thick with emotion they almost broke. "You follow your mind, I'll follow my heart. Take me with you. Please."

"I can't."

"Please! I'll—"

"*No.*"

She snatched up the glass so fast, half the orange juice inside it sloshed onto the table. The rest splashed in a bloody-orange streak on the wall as she whirled and side-armed the glass through the kitchen window. The jagged edges of the shattered pane buckled out and then swung back in, spraying a shower of diamond-shaped slivers. Each one caught the morning sun as it fell, and a split-second sparkler of iridescent colors streaked to the floor, where the shards landed with the tingle of tiny bells.

Before he could step forward, she bent and swept the contents of the table in his direction. Then she turned and stormed from the room, leaving him standing in a nightmare of shattered dishes and spilled food.

When the clatter settled down to the hollow whir of a single glass rolling on tile, he heard the apartment's front door slam, reopen and slam again, the second time so hard he could feel the floor shake under his feet.

"Yikes," he whispered. "And she thinks I'm pushing *her* away?"

Another jagged shard fell from the windowpane, embedded itself in the wooden windowsill like a glass knife, and everything but his heart was finally still.

* * *

By evening he lost hope of locating her quickly, and realized he was going through the motions of life, but not living it. And he had no idea how to change that. He'd booked a ticket to Jordan, packed his bag, and confirmed that he could get a visa at the destination airport. He tried to sleep, but eventually gave up and tossed a Crogen Shields disc into his CD player. The music washed over him, but partway through the song "Dying Man's Library," the singer crooned, "*I live in cold comfort, between walls bricked with books.*"

Michael turned his head abruptly, narrowed one eye and fixed the CD player in his gaze, just as the next lines hit him:

The walls, the cursed walls, they tremble and shout,

"No light, or love, will we ever let in.

And as for you ... you, we'll never let out!"

The lyrics that bespoke his own quiet desperation reached out, wrapped their fingers around his heart, and squeezed.

"A life of cold comfort," Michael whispered, as he reached over and thumbed the player silent. "A life bricked with books .... Yep, I've definitely got the books."

The sting of tears came without warning. He fought them back, choked on the knot in his throat, then buried his head in his hands and wept.

* * *

"Michael, I'm sorry."

"No, no, it's my fault."

"No, it isn't."

"Yes, it is, I—"

"No, really, it's—"

"What," he said, "are we going to argue again?"

He expected laughter. He got only a dry cough for a response. "Tell you what," June said, "I'll drive you to the airport and we'll talk about it. When's your flight? Terminal? Heathrow or Gatwick?"

By the time she phoned, he had reconciled himself to life without her. Mentally off balance, he answered as if programmed. Conversation ended on a light note, and he put the phone down as if laying a priceless vase upon its stand. And then he turned to the bed, knowing that now, he definitely wouldn't sleep.

CHAPTER 20

Michael welcomed the empty seat beside him on the airplane. June had dropped him off at Heathrow International Airport, explaining that she hated long good-byes and preferred to part curbside. That way they wouldn't suffer that awful, empty wait until boarding.

Only when he stood from his aisle seat to admit the late arrival to the airplane did he glance up and realize the ruse.

June sat.

He sat.

She buckled her seatbelt.

He buckled his seatbelt.

"How'd you—?"

"Shhh." She held a finger to her lips as the safety instructions started to play on the ceiling monitor. "This is my favorite part."

He plucked the in-flight magazine from the seat pocket in front of him and started to flip pages. "How'd you swing it?"

"What, this little thing?" She motioned around the plane. "Women tools, Michael, women tools."

"Enlighten me."

She mimed a phone to her ear. "'Oh, hello, this is June Cody, Dr. Michael Hansen's secretary. I'm calling to confirm his flight on Royal Jordanian, tomorrow afternoon at three. Oh, yes, well of course I meant three-ten. So that's two tickets, business class … Excuse me? Only one ticket? And economy class? Well, there *must* be a mistake. He never travels without his secretary, and that's me!'"

He shook his head. "And they bought it."

She loosened her seatbelt, rose slightly, swept her ankle-length skirt beneath her and half-turned in her seat. Still she didn't answer.

Instead, she brushed one side of his windbreaker open, ran a finger down his tie and said, "Business-oh-so casual. Why, you could do a cover for *GQ*."

"How'd you arrange the rest?"

"Need you ask?" She gave him a heart-stopping wink. "You gave me the airport, terminal number and approximate flight time last night, when I called to offer a ride to the airport. Enough to find the right airline. Then I booked a ticket through your travel agent. Remember your note by the phone? Had them link our tickets and prearrange seating together. You probably haven't needed to prearrange seating, being a bachelor, but for us personal secretaries, it's reflex."

"Pretty ingenious," he said. "When we arrive, I'll book you on the next flight back to Heathrow."

She reached up and pushed the call button over her head.

"What're you doing?"

"If we're going to argue again, I need an orange juice in my hand."

"It's dangerous. I can't be responsible for you."

"You're not." She looked up as a flight attendant appeared. "Could I have some water, please?" She snatched the magazine from his lap and sat back to read. The flight attendant returned and handed her a plastic glass. She took a sip, shut the magazine and said, "Look, either you include me, or I'll look for the seal myself."

A little girl's hand and face appeared in the slit between the seats in front of them, her eyes inspecting them with open curiosity. Michael reached over and dipped his fingers into June's water glass. Casually, June dug a hard candy out of her purse and placed it in the child's hand before Michael beat her to the punch. With a squeal of delight, the girl disappeared. June arched an eyebrow and glanced between Michael's face and wet fingers.

He diverted his hand, swiped his forehead with his fingers, and repeated the dip and daub, as if to cool his brow.

"On second thought," she said, "forget the cover of *GQ*."

He sighed and lowered his hand. "First sign of danger, you go home. Agreed?"

"First sign of danger, *we* go home. Agreed?"

He cradled his chin in his hand and absent-mindedly stroked the scar on his jaw with his index finger. "Okay, but under one condition. You follow my lead."

"Okay, but under one condition. You pay."

"What?" He dropped his hand. "What does that have to do with anything?"

She lowered her head and spoke to her lap. "You don't think about money. You don't have to. Best-selling author and all. But this plane ticket nearly broke me."

He reached over and lifted the plastic glass from her fist, drained it in one gulp, and tried to hand it back. "And if I tell you to go home, now that I know you don't have enough money?"

She pushed the glass in his hand back to his side of the armrest. "I'll pick pockets until I do."

"This time I *know* you're bluffing."

"Too late."

* * *

The next morning, he stood at a top floor window of the Le Royal Hotel and watched the sun rise over the city. Once again he was reminded of the locals' description of Amman as "the white city." A shaggy carpet of pale buildings rolled over the seven hills upon which the city was built, like waves in an ocean of cream. Jordan's quarries yielded the white rock, considered by many a local treasure. All the same, he hadn't understood why no building was constructed from a more fashionable alternative, until he learned it wasn't a matter of mass architectural hysteria, but of city planning. Building permits stipulated the use of the local rock. Consequently, the blue central mosque, one of few spots of color in the city, stood out like an aquamarine jewel on a sandy beach.

June appeared in the bedroom doorway of their suite, cinching the tie of her hotel bathrobe. She smoothed her tousled hair with her hands while she padded to his side. "No one said you had to sleep on the sofa."

"No one?" He turned from the window with a smile and cast his eyes toward the heavens. "You sure about that?"

"Oh, well, can't argue if you're gonna go Old Testament on me." Giving an annoyed groan, she removed a barrette and shook her hair loose, raked her fingers through it.

"Such a librarian thing," he said. "Letting your hair down, that is."

"Is it working?"

He laughed and, feeling his hands twitch with desire, stuffed them into his pockets. *Keep your distance,* some inner fear whispered, *keep your distance.* Bad memories swept over him like a flood, and he turned away and stepped back into the room. "Come on," he said, "let's order breakfast."

* * *

"So what's the plan?" she asked between bites. The room service cart was adorned with Arabic flatbread, humus, white goat cheese, clotted yogurt *labaneh* and the ubiquitous *ful:* beans stewed with onion, tomato and traditional spices. The basket of croissants and assorted pastries seemed out of place.

Without preamble, he said, "I want to visit where Rachael was murdered."

"In that case, I'm going home."

"Good."

"No, seriously." She pointed the sharp end of a croissant at him. "What's more important, Rachael's murder or the seal?"

He swallowed with a nod, sat back with an empty fold of flatbread in his hand, and stared.

"If you find her murderer," she said, "how will that help? You going to *beat* the seal out of him? You're not the type."

"What type am I?"

"The type who thinks he can handle himself, and then gets killed. Okay, maybe not, but that's what I'm afraid of." She bit into the croissant, catching a shower of crumbs in a cupped hand, and chewed in silence as she thought. "Tell me what this is all about.

Even if I only wait at the hotel while you run around searching, maybe I can think of something you haven't."

Half an hour later, he finished talking and returned to his breakfast. She paced the room, head bowed. "All this time, I thought you were just looking for the seal. In any case, you're not going to find your Teacher's scroll here. The last two contacts on Rachael's letter list are in Jerusalem."

He replied between bites. "Like I said, I wanted to see where Rachael was murdered. Okay, you're right. Forget that. We'll go to Jerusalem."

"No."

"No?" He looked up from his plate.

She sat on the sofa and drew her legs up under her. "Listen, there's a *B.C.* comic strip I like. Two cavemen are walking in the desert. There's nothing around but sand. One asks where they're going, and the other says 'Nowhere.' So the first says, 'Then why are we walking so fast?'"

"Good point."

"Need to be anywhere soon?"

He shook his head and spooned humus into a fold of bread.

"Then let's enjoy ourselves," she said. "Do Holy Land stuff. I've dreamed of coming here. You must feel the same. It's your field, after all. How can we lose?"

* * *

While Michael was finishing breakfast in Amman, Prime Minister Leib sat down at his desk in Tel Aviv and began working through a stack of classified briefs. He pulled the file labeled "Teacher's Gospel" from the top of the pile and opened it in front of him. From his vantage point beside Leib's chair, his chief advisor pointed to the file and said, "The passport flag paid off. Dr. Michael Hansen entered Jordan last night."

"Alone?" Leib asked.

"With a woman. They bought their tickets separately, but the ticketing details show they had prearranged seats together."

Leib closed the file and tapped the cover. "After all that's happened, I can't believe Dr. Hansen would put his life, or that of another girlfriend, at risk. He saw what happened to ..." He flipped the file open and searched the pages.

"Rachael Tones," the advisor murmured.

Leib closed the file again. "Rachael Tones. Whatever. He wouldn't put another girlfriend at risk. He must be on vacation."

"And if not?"

"Then perhaps he will lead us to the Gospel of the Teacher. But there's nothing for him in Jordan. We know that much." He handed the file to his advisor. "If he enters Israel, sound the alarm."

* * *

Benefiting from Michael's fluency in Arabic, they engaged Hamid Ibrahim, a hotel-approved driver, as escort for their week of religious tourism. In late afternoon, after touring the Byzantine ruins of the city, they asked Hamid's recommendation for dinner that night. He took them to Fakhr el-Din, the best restaurant in the old neighborhood of Jabal Amman. But the next evening, when they made the same request, he parked his taxi in front of his own house.

"Michael," June murmured while they followed Hamid inside, "we've been hoodwinked."

He nodded and whispered, "We can't refuse. In this culture, the insult would be unforgivable."

The dinner was the best either could remember. The wonders Hamid's wife wrought with food were heightened by the warm company and simple surroundings. They ate from communal dishes arranged on a cheap plastic tablecloth spread on the floor. From the pureed yellow-lentil soup built on a base of braised onions and roasted garlic to the crème caramel garnished with fresh fruit slices, the meal was the creation of a culinary artist, attended by the most attentive host and their charming children.

A week later, refreshed by rest and Jordanian hospitality, they took their glowing suntans and crossed the border to Israel.

* * *

Prime Minster Leib was leaving his office for a meeting when his chief advisor ran down the hallway, the PM's cordless phone in hand, to catch him by the elevator. "Sir," he said breathlessly, "they've entered Israel. Dr. Michael Hansen and his female companion."

The blank slate of Leib's face took on a tinge of exasperation. "What's with this guy? He's got a death wish, or what?"

His advisor handed him the phone. "The director of Mossad."

Scowling, Leib raised the phone. "I've heard the news. Do we have continuity on this case?"

"We've had a couple agents on it since day one." The voice held the dry rasp of a hardened smoker. "They're on another case at the moment, outside Israel. I've recalled them."

"Good men?"

"Great men. Even I admire them."

The elevator arrived, but Leib turned his back on it. "Then again, you admire Moshe Ya'alon."

His reference to the former head of the Israeli Defense Force, who publicly compared Palestinians to cancer and prescribed either amputation or chemotherapy, elicited a snort of derision from the Mossad director. "Admire him? He's a wuss," came the reply. "He hasn't done enough."

"Don't go rabid on me. I need you under control." Leib motioned his advisor to follow, and strode the hallway back in the direction of his office. "Put other agents on the case immediately until the original pair return."

"Already done."

"And remember, two years ago I recategorized the file as conditional."

"I know, I know," the voice yawned. "No eliminations without your approval."

Leib stopped halfway down the hallway. "I'm serious."

"Got it."

"No exceptions, no excuses."

"Look, if you're referring to those previous incidents, you'd have done the same," the director said. "I couldn't find you, and had to decide."

Leib turned around and headed back toward the bank of elevators, head down. "Couldn't find me, or didn't want to?"

"They had it coming."

"That's not your call. Don't do it again. Got it?"

The director's voice rasped out a laugh that ended in a hacking cough. "You're getting soft, Leib. Since when have *you* cultivated a conscience?"

Leib wagged his head side-to-side and, in a voice pulled straight from an American "Brothers in the 'Hood'" movie, said, "Since the day I offed *yo mama*."

The elevator doors opened and Leib stepped inside, tossed the phone to his advisor, grabbed the lapels of his suit jacket with both hands and shrugged. "What can I say? It's *good* to be the king."

What a wasted opportunity, the advisor thought as the elevator doors closed on the PM's confident gaze, assertive stance and contagious smile. *That was the perfect publicity shot.*

CHAPTER 21

"Qumran." Sitting beside Michael in their taxi, June read the name from a road sign.

"Next stop on the tourist tour," he said. "A residential complex in ruins, the caves where the Dead Sea Scrolls were found, a web of historical intrigue. What more could you ask for in an archaeological site?"

Their Palestinian driver and tour guide showed them the ruins, then led them to each of the caves by number. Most of the cliff caves were inaccessible, but Cave 4 had a second entrance that didn't necessitate navigating the cliff face. All the same, entering was difficult, and exiting harder.

Michael didn't care. He just found it hard to believe he was standing in the cave that had yielded an incredible fifteen thousand fragments of nearly six hundred manuscripts. And the thought wove itself into his mind: *Could this be the cave Jacob described in his scroll? The scroll Frank Tones found in Nubia? The cave in which Jacob hid the Gospel of the Teacher?*

He turned a circle and scanned the limestone walls, recalling descriptions from the scroll. Actually, this *could* be the cave. *Two entrances, the main one overlooking the Dead Sea, situated on a finger of land two hundred paces from the residential complex. Just as the scroll described.*

"This has to be it!" he whispered.

"What's that, sir?"

Michael turned to their taxi driver and guide, Muhammad. "Uh, nothing. I just …"

But Muhammad was already off, leading June out the side entrance. Michael stayed behind, not willing to leave yet.

He remembered that the only intact Dead Sea scrolls, seven in all, were found in Cave 1. But for sheer volume of scroll fragments, Cave 4 dwarfed all the other caves combined.

Yet, that was over fifty years ago. Now the caves were empty, with no hint of secret hiding places or undiscovered caves. *Fully excavated,* his father had said. If the gospel Jacob's scroll described was ever here, it wasn't now.

His expectations deflated, he followed June out the side entrance, in something between a crawl and a low stoop. They emerged to see the limestone cliff's sheer drop below them to the breathtaking expanse of the Dead Sea. June reflexively raised one hand to her bosom and sighed.

A Bedouin child, old enough to talk with sophistication but young enough to be oblivious of social tact, sat nearby. He pointed to June's hand on her bosom and jabbered off a sentence in Arabic, a well-meaning smile on his face.

June turned to Michael. "What did he say?"

"I ... I'm not sure," Michael said, disbelieving his ears. He searched their driver's face.

Muhammad smiled and gestured to the boy. "Don't mind him, he's only a child."

The boy sat and watched, as if seeking a gesture of friendship.

"But what did he *say?*" June repeated.

Muhammad shifted his feet and looked down. "Please understand, it's only Bedouin superstition. He means nothing by it. He only said that tonight, Allah willing, your babies won't go hungry."

"My *babies?*" she asked, a lost look in her eyes.

Michael looked back at the Bedouin child, who gestured once again to June's hand, still held to her chest. Muhammad averted his gaze, but Michael smirked as June looked at him, her face a picture of perplexity.

"Hey, don't look at me," he said. *"I'm* not going to breastfeed them."

* * *

"I still don't get it," June said from the backseat as they drove to their hotel, with Michael sitting up front.

Muhammad spoke over his shoulder. "It's just an old, how do you say, wives' tale? The Bedouins believe visits to that cave cure women who have trouble breastfeeding."

"Mom could've used that," Michael said. He looked out the window and watched the sparse vegetation fly by.

"Your mother is still alive?" Muhammad asked. He followed Michael's solemn shake of his head with, "How did she die?"

Had anyone else asked such a blunt question after less than a day's acquaintance, Michael probably would've ignored it. They'd met just that morning, after Hamid had driven them to the Jordan/Israeli border and hooked them up with Muhammad on the other side. A calm, noble-appearing Palestinian in his late fifties, Michael had liked him right away. Now he found himself trusting him, at a time he knew was foolish to trust anyone.

"She died from a mosquito bite. Nile fever," he answered with less anguish than he expected. "There was an outbreak while we were on a dig in Yemen. She got the fever, went blind in ten hours, and died in the twelfth."

"From Allah do we come and to Allah do we return," Muhammad said quietly. "Did she die a believer?"

Whoa, bounce me spinning off the Titanic's propeller. Where'd that come from? "Uh, if you mean Muslim, no. My parents were both Christian ... kind of."

Muhammad looked at him from the corner of his eyes, then back at the road.

"We lived in the Middle East. She had both Christian and Muslim friends, but kept her religion to herself."

"Uh, guys?" June said from behind. "The milk thing? I'm still waiting to hear where *that* comes from."

Muhammad spoke over his shoulder while keeping his eyes on the road. "Something to do with how the first cave was found. By a shepherd boy—"

175

"But what does this have to do with Cave 1?" Michael asked.

"Nothing. I'm talking about the cave we just left. Cave 4."

"But you just said it had something to do with the first cave found."

"So I did," Muhammad said. "And *that* was Cave 4."

Michael quelled his annoyance. "No, Cave 1. The caves were numbered in the order they were found."

"In the order they were found by the scientists, *not* by the Bedouins. Cave 4."

"Not Cave 1?"

"You guys?" June leaned forward in her seat. "This is beginning to sound like that old 'Who's on first?' routine.'"

Michael turned and shot her such an intense look of annoyance that she recoiled. He looked back at Muhammad. "So, you're saying Cave 4 was found first?"

"Absolutely."

"How can you be sure?"

"Because it's the story of my people. The shepherd boy was a member of my tribe."

* * *

"But what does it *mean?*"

June's voice filtered through Michael's distraction, and he realized he'd nearly finished dessert, but hadn't tasted it. He paused, a forkful of chocolate mousse halfway to his mouth, and inspected it. "What does it mean? Something. Nothing. Everything. I don't know."

He popped the mousse into his mouth. *Too sweet.* He put the fork down and pushed the dessert away. *Why the heck am I eating chocolate mousse with a fork?*

"Look," he said, "I don't know what it means. What I do know is today, I stood in a cave that matches Jacob's description of where he hid the Gospel of the Teacher. Then, Muhammad told us this cave, Cave 4, was discovered by the Bedouins before Cave 1 was discovered by the scientists. That's a major twist to the history of how the Qumran scrolls were found. Not something I've ever run across before, which means the project researchers either never heard the story, or discounted it as just what Muhammad called it: an old wives' tale."

"So what?" she said. "What does it matter which cave was discovered first?"

He raised both hands palms up, then flipped them and lowered them to catch the table edge with his fingers. "No idea. But we've got nothing definite to go on, so we might as well pursue the mysteries. And from what Muhammad told us, we can probably clear this up when he traces the story through his relatives."

* * *

The next day, Muhammad sent his son as substitute while he worked his way through the family tree, which his son reported as being so wide, thick and tangled that it sounded more like a family shrub. To kill some time, Michael and June visited Masada, the mountaintop fortress where Jewish zealots committed mass suicide rather than surrender to the Romans, and Mt. Sodom, where the infamous cities of Sodom and Gomorra were believed to have been destroyed. But he felt he was only going through the motions, his legs walking the sites while his heart and mind wandered through Cave 4, sorting fragments and unwrapping scrolls, recreating in his imagination the first day of its discovery. Not too far from his psyche was the expectation of a call from Muhammad, but his son's cell phone remained silent the entire day. They returned to the hotel hopeful of either a message or Muhammad himself, but found neither. *"Ussboor,"* the son counseled as he departed.

"Patience," Michael translated for June as they left the reception desk and headed to dinner. "Patience. Ha. Ha."

* * *

"Knock you up at eight?"

They were on the way back to their suite after dinner, and at his question, June looked at him with a knowing smile. "Excuse me?"

"Oh, come on, don't tell me you never learned British slang at Oxford. It means 'Shall I knock on your door and wake you at eight?'"

"That's what I thought it meant." She thrust an elbow at his ribs.

Surprised at how much force she'd put behind it, he sidestepped and slipped into the room. She didn't follow right away, and he turned to find out why.

She closed the door quietly, leaned against the wall and eyed him speculatively while he headed for the suite's kitchenette. "Michael, you joke, and then you sleep on the sofa. Why?"

"Tea?" he asked, and sloshed water into the automatic coffeemaker.

"How'd your mother die?"

"Told you. Nile fever."

"No. The circumstances. What were the circumstances of her death?"

He froze, a teabag half-torn from its wrapper.

She tilted her head at him, gauging him. "What is it, Michael? What did I just hit?"

He tore the bag free, dropped it into a water glass and leaned against the counter. "Just memories."

She pushed off from the wall, dropped her purse on the desk and threw her shoulder-scarf over it. "Don't be so obtuse. This is my field, remember? Major in philosophy, minor in psychology."

"Does that equate to lots of argument and little insight? Drop it." *Please.*

She sat on the sofa, tucked her legs beneath her and fanned her ankle-length skirt about her. As she propped her elbow on the armrest and balanced her chin in her hand, a stray strand of hair drifted across her brow.

Good, he thought. *Very good. Seductive, disarming, unthreatening. Typical psychobabble posturing.* He turned away.

"Were you there when sh—?"

Something sank its claws into his guts and twisted, and he turned on her with a face that would have snarled, were he an animal. "Look, there's no mystery here, got it? Everyone who loves me dies. End of story."

"Michael, I—"

"My parents booked a flight out of Yemen to escape the epidemic. But I caught the fever and needed ice baths to keep my temperature down. Nothing else worked. Mom wouldn't leave. She knew that without the ice baths, I would die. The day I recovered, she came down with it."

June straightened in her seat. "It's not your fault."

He slunk to the overstuffed chair between them and braced his arms on the seatback. "Rachael wasn't the only one."

"*What?*"

He leaned over the chair to look into her eyes, but from this angle she was in shadows. As he brought his face level with hers, he lowered his voice to a stage whisper. "Best five months of my life. And it could've been forever. But she made a mistake. She chose me, and I'm cursed."

"You can't possibly belie—"

"*Why not?*" He stood, spun around and stomped across the room, the floor trembling beneath the thin carpet, the ashtray chattering glass teeth against the coffee table. He stopped at the opposite wall, turned and leaned against the dark wood of the TV hutch, his arms folded across his chest. "We were riding our bikes in a park. I made a joke, she laughed, and a *bee* flew down her throat. What are the chances of *that*, huh? I thought she'd cough it up. Didn't realize her throat was swelling shut from the sting until she collapsed and started bucking against the blockage. By the time I got her to the hospital, she was comatose."

She stood and took a step toward him, arms open.

"No!"

She stopped, bewilderment and hurt etched on her face.

"I brought two white roses every day, a single red rose once a week. Her bedside vase was always full. That vase and her face were the only things of beauty in that room."

He stepped away and walked to the window. "Three months later, her parents got a court order to end life support. Never told me. Knew I wouldn't approve. It was her red rose day, and I arrived to find her in the reflex spasms of death. It took three security guards and an orderly to hold me, but by then the room was ripped to shreds. I never told anyone this before. No one."

"Now ..." He turned from the window and looked at her coldly. "I'm in here," he said, then pointed to the bedroom. "You're in there."

"Michael, what we've got—"

A purple rage twisted the muscles of his face into something unrecognizable. "IN THERE!"

* * *

As Michael and June fell into separate, troubled sleeps, the Mossad agents in the room next door were also winding down for the night.

The younger of the two, a sandy blond, finished his report and handed it to his partner, then turned his freckled face to the soccer match on TV.

His superior, stripped to the waist, idly worked the fingers of one hand through the black moss of his chest hairs while he read the report: *Toured Qumran, Masada, Mt. Sodom. Everything tourist so far. Hotel phone quiet. Electronics team promises audio bug in taxi by morning. Lovers' spat before going to bed tonight.*

He tossed the report back to the blond and pointed to the TV. "You didn't mention the score."

"No, sir," came the deadpan reply. "That information's strictly need-to-know."

His superior suppressed a grin. "Send it," he said, and gestured to the portable fax machine beside the phone.

* * *

"I'm downstairs, boss. Ready when you are."

Muhammad rang off before Michael could voice the many questions he was bursting to ask. A glance at his watch compounded his confusion. *Six in the morning? This guy obviously doesn't play for tips.*

He sat up on the sofa and nestled his head in his hands, remembering the way he'd behaved last night. *I'm a monster. She doesn't have to be here. She just wants to help.*

He spent five minutes in apology, followed by ten in dressing and preparation. It went well enough, which is to say neither of them broke anything.

Twenty minutes after he received the call, he ushered June into the backseat of the taxi. Muhammad glanced in the rearview mirror and caught Michael's eye just as he was about to speak. "As you requested, boss, we'll return to Qumran today." Muhammad spoke while he whisked them away from the curb.

As I requested? Michael turned to June and found his *What the ...?* expression reflected in her face.

After another failed attempt at conversation, he not only took the hint, but began to suspect the reason for Muhammad's enforced silence. By the time they arrived at Qumran, the sun glowed orange on the horizon, casting pastel hues on the cirrus wisps that streaked the nearer heaven. Mornings in Boston were never like this.

Once out of the taxi, Muhammad disassembled his cell phone as they walked, explaining, "In your country, you go inside to speak privately. Here, we go outside. Even my taxi, for all I know, is bugged. Some years ago, the CIA was criticized for having illegally tapped roughly one-third of the phones in America. When I saw that in the newspaper, I laughed. Here, they practically monitor our breathing."

"Why the phone autopsy?" Michael asked, and gestured to the pieces in Muhammad's hand.

"Mossad can activate a mobile phone's microphone through the service provider, even when the phone is switched off. The only safeguard is to remove the battery. Neither of you have a mobile, do you?"

Michael shook his head, struck as much by Muhammad's knowledge of intelligence surveillance as by his excellent English. Perhaps his doubts were reflected in his face, but whether that or a lucky guess, Muhammad spoke surprisingly directly: "In the beginning, I didn't trust you either, Dr. Hansen. In this country, we learn to trust no one."

When he didn't reply, Muhammad continued. "Believing and practicing Muslims, and I emphasize the *believing and practicing*, hunger to do something that will give us credit with Allah, something that will distinguish us amongst Muslims. Until I met you, I never had such an opportunity. Yet I became suspicious, as one does when given a gift that seems too good to be true."

"I'm not a Muslim," Michael said. "You know that."

Muhammad stopped walking and turned, his skin bronze in the morning light. "From your writing, it's hard to tell what you are."

"You've read my books?"

"The ones translated into Arabic."

The best-sellers, Michael thought. He kept to Muhammad's side as they turned back to the path. "I clarify the prophets' teachings," he said. "It's not my job to dictate what religion to follow. People have to figure that out for themselves."

"That's the way of the candle," Muhammad replied. "It gives light to others, but as for itself, it only burns. Declare yourself, Dr. Hansen. You say Jesus taught of a final prophet to follow. Tell your readers who you believe that final prophet to be."

"He's right," June said from behind them. "You tear apart peoples' belief systems, but you don't tell them where to find the religion of truth. You write about the reality of God, but you don't say which religion teaches it."

Great. Nothing like a face-to-face with not one, but two literary critic-wannabes. He opened his mouth to respond, and realized he didn't know what to say.

June turned to Muhammad and asked, "You seem so careful. Do you know why we're here?"

The Palestinian rounded the trunk of a palm tree and squeezed through a narrow point in the path. "Dr. Hansen writes about the reality of God, and the true message of Jesus, the Christ. So I'm guessing that you, like many of the disappointed Christians who flood this site, hope to find the gospel of Jesus to support your view."

Pretty good for a taxi driver, Michael thought, and then asked, more for confirmation than clarification, "But why would you, a Muslim, help us find the gospel of Jesus?"

"Because Jesus might name the final prophet, Muhammad."

Michael fell a step behind and muttered to June, "Everyone thinks theirs is the 'religion of truth,' as you put it."

Muhammad laughed. "And most certainly, it's the teachings of the prophets that decide that issue. That's why we hope to find this gospel. That is why your quest is so interesting to me."

CHAPTER 22

Beside the worn path and slightly removed, three Bedouin elders sat on a faded ground cloth, in company with a battered thermos and a bowl of dates. One of the men called out to the approaching group and motioned to Muhammad to join them, in keeping with the custom of their people. Muhammad turned, went through the pretense of extending the invitation to Michael and June, and all three then stepped from the path.

The Arabic coffee was steaming hot, tan in color and spiced with cardamom. The dates were soft and sweet, stuffed with pan-roasted almonds that gave them a crisp bitterness. But it was the conversation for which they had come.

The oldest of the Bedouin elders spoke as his blind eyes wandered, and Muhammad translated for June's benefit.

"I am Abu Ahmed," he said, by which he identified himself not by name but by *kunya*, the parental nickname adopted by Arabs, which in this case meant "the father of Ahmed."

"I am an elder of the Ta'amireh tribe," he continued, "and I speak to you trusting first in Allah and second in my nephew," by which he meant any distant relative, but in this case Muhammad.

The old man sipped coffee from a thumb-sized cup while Muhammad kept up a running translation, reminding Michael of an old Japanese Godzilla movie where the English dubbing was out of sync.

"A year after the big war and another year before Deir Yassin," he said, "my son Ahmed followed a dry goat into an abandoned cave."

Both Abu Ahmed and Muhammad paused, and June asked, "Deir Yassin?"

"Tell you later," Michael said as the old man started up again.

"This was a miracle goat, which entered the cave in the manner of an animal seeking a secluded place in which to die. But it did not die, and instead returned to us prancing like a youth and bursting with milk. After Ahmed saw this, he wondered at the secret to her rejuvenation, and followed her to the cave."

The old man paused while a breeze ruffled his *guttra*, the traditional Palestinian black-and-white headdress. The rising sun had brightened, and Michael foresaw another scorcher of a day. The old man, however, raised his hand as if rubbing the air between thumb and forefinger, and said, "Rain."

Michael turned his eyes to the sky the old man no longer could see, found nothing but scant wisps of cirrus clouds, and wondered if Abu Ahmed was as fully cognizant as he otherwise seemed.

A tug on his sleeve interrupted his thoughts, and Muhammad leaned over and said, "Dr. Hansen, we have lost their knowledge and ways, but believe me, if an elder says rain, it is unlikely to be otherwise."

The old man finished his coffee, was given a refill by one of his companions, and continued. "My son, Ahmed, may Allah be pleased with him, found the goat bedded down in a pile of what we now know to be scroll fragments. He dug through them and discovered a limestone jar unlike anything we had ever seen, finely crafted and the size of a strong man's arm." By way of demonstration, he reached one hand across his chest and stroked from the opposite shoulder to the elbow.

"Ahmed sensed that the secret lay in the jar, and brought it home with him, along with some of the scroll pieces."

He sipped his coffee and reached out a tremulous hand, which flitted about until it landed on the dates as lightly as a butterfly on a blossom. He chewed the fruit carefully, his lips smacking noisily over toothless gums, and discarded the almonds due to their hardness. Observing the man's slow movements, Michael sensed that when he spoke of the old goat seeking solitude in which to die, he spoke with the empathy of one nearing his own demise. He was about to ask the limestone jar's whereabouts when Abu Ahmed continued.

"Ahmed left the jar with me and went to Bethlehem with his younger brother to sell the scroll fragments. I never saw him again. They were ambushed by Zionist terrorists on their return, and only his brother escaped. The ambush of children was not uncommon at the time, being a year before Deir Yassin."

June looked in bewilderment to Michael, who signaled her to be patient.

"Before he left, Ahmed sealed the cave's entrance. His brother returned with good money from the scroll pieces they sold, so other Bedouins went looking for the source. They found other caves and scrolls, and that launched the Dead Sea Scrolls Project. Myself, I lost my first son over those pieces of writing, so I never reopened Ahmed's cave. I could see no good coming from it, but told of it years later, under pressure, when it was soon to be discovered anyway. Some of our tribe looted Ahmed's cave, now known as Cave 4, but the authorities soon discovered it and took over."

"And the limestone jar?" Michael asked.

The old man said, "I hoped to find treasure, but found only a scroll inside. Ahmed's goat died soon after, and the scroll and jar never worked a miracle for the other animals. Yet nothing happens without a purpose, and with time, I came to believe Allah sent my Ahmed and this miracle to bring this scroll to light. So I kept it."

"It's with you now?" Michael blurted, barely able to keep his seat.

The elder paused to savor a gust of wind, and Michael's mind screamed with frustration.

"No," the old man finally said. "Ahmed's cave, Cave 4, was excavated five years after my son found it."

Michael's heart sank, and June's smile sank with it. "In 1952?" he said in Arabic, hoping to speed the process.

"1952," Abu Ahmed agreed, although without conviction. Michael guessed that calendar years meant little to this Bedouin, many of whom dated by historical events rather than by numerical convention.

"After another five Ramadans," the man said, "a foreigner came into camp looking for scrolls or scroll fragments. I was done with it by then; it only reminded me of the price of my beloved son's life. I believed the foreigner was sent by Allah, for no Westerner had ever entered my camp. Furthermore, he sought something known only to me, my dead son, and Allah. So I gave it to him. I didn't want his money."

Over the next few minutes, Michael and June asked questions and received answers. There were, in fact, seals on the jar as well as on the scroll, and the pattern matched that of the ring Michael wore. Abu Ahmed confirmed this by working his tremulous fingers over the ring's face.

"Yes, he gave me his name," the old man said in reply to another question. "But I'm told it wasn't true, for I learned there was no one by that name on the scrolls team." He struggled to recall the name. "Oh, yes, here is how he said it: 'Me Sam Spade.'"

Michael groaned audibly, and asked about the man's accent.

"Accent? Hard to say, since I couldn't understand a word he said. Most everything was by sign language."

Abu Ahmed explained that the man had brought pieces of parchment along with him to give an example of what he was looking for. He described the man as Caucasian, either tanned or of European descent, of medium height and build, and with dark hair.

"Age? Hard to tell," he said when Michael asked. "Maybe twenty-eight, thirty years. Your kind ages differently from our kind."

No distinguishing marks. No wedding ring. Refined manners, and respectful.

"Didn't look at our women. Drank our coffee and ate our food with his hands, as we do." The old man seemed particularly impressed by that last fact.

The sun had risen, and its rays reached out and stoked the fire of the desert day.

"Did you ever see him again?" Michael asked.

When Abu Ahmed simply said no, Muhammad nudged Michael and gestured that they should leave. A Bedouin boy approached to gather the coffee and dates and fold the ground cloth after everybody had stood and stepped away.

"We have to tour the site again," Muhammad said. "Otherwise we'll look like we came only for this meeting, and that could make trouble for these men."

Abu Ahmed spoke, and Muhammad translated. "He wants to show you the cave himself."

Michael wondered how the sightless man could show anybody anything, but noted that his stride was firm despite his age, his direction unwavering despite his blindness.

"This is why we came early," Muhammad said as they followed. He gestured toward the sun. "Any later, and the heat would be unbearable for visitors like yourselves."

The old man skirted the cliff's edge, where a few steps in the wrong direction would mean certain death.

"How does he navigate?" Michael whispered.

"By the angle of the sun on his face and the lay of the land under his feet." Muhammad shook his head. "Believe it or not, blind Bedouins used to lead month-long caravans and arrive within a hundred meters of their intended destination. Like I said, the ways of the elders are lost to us."

June tripped over a rise in the path and the old man stopped, turned, and spoke in her direction.

"He says he tripped in that same spot when he was a child, eighty years ago. He never tripped in the same place twice." Michael translated to June while he watched the old man return to the path, his footfalls as secure as those of the goats he raised.

When they arrived at Cave 4, the old man turned so that the sun filled his face, and then pointed directly at the cave opening. It was the same opening from which Michael and June had emerged to find the Bedouin child just two days before.

"Can he see it?" June whispered in amazement.

An exchange followed and Muhammad answered, "He says he can hear the voice of the wind in the mouth of the cave."

"Goodness," she said. "I barely even *feel* the wind."

Another exchange followed, and Muhammad turned back to them with a broad smile. "He says it's a 'Yoda thing.'" They all laughed, and he added, "Actually, he says 'Give yourself up to The Force' and 'Don't be drawn to the Dark Side.'"

They smiled, but then became somber, for the elder's message had nothing to do with *Star Wars*.

During the walk back the old man retraced his steps, and June tripped and stumbled in the same place. He turned and muttered with a wide, toothless grin, and continued on, leaving Muhammad to translate between chuckles. "He says that's twice in eighty years. He believes you've set a new record in these parts!"

* * *

"They joined some Bedouins for coffee and dates," the older Mossad agent said. "Then the old guy gave them a tour." Using both hands, he steadied his binoculars on the rooftop of their car in the parking lot.

"So?" his freckled partner asked.

"Doesn't feel right. They barely touched the coffee or the dates." He lowered the binoculars from beneath his black, caterpillar eyebrows, and handed them to his partner. The younger man brushed a curtain of blond hair from his eyes and peered through the glasses, catching the procession as it filed along the edge of the cliff. "I'll tell you what doesn't feel right," the younger one said. "Knowing we might be ordered to kill this girl. That's what doesn't feel right."

His superior elbowed him and took the binoculars back, then tossed them through the car's open window onto the rear seat. "You've got to get your emotions under control, kid. She might be a girl, but she's just one of the goys."

* * *

"You asked about Deir Yassin, Miss Cody," Muhammad said while he drove the taxi back to their hotel. "Following World War II, Zionist Jews leveraged world sympathy into a license to invade

Palestine. They displaced Palestinians and confiscated their lands through a campaign of terror, of which Deir Yassin was a prime example. In April of 1948, the Irgun and Stern gangs—Zionist terror squads under the command of future Prime Ministers Menachem Begin and Yitzhak Shamir—entered the town of Deir Yassin while the young men worked the fields."

June glanced at Michael, who sat beside her in the rear seat. He grimaced and nodded, and then turned to stare out the side window while Muhammad continued.

"In the manner of brave, manly men, fearless of unarmed women and children, they massacred every Palestinian they found, whether Christian or Muslim, helpless baby or invalid elder, man or woman, and mutilated the corpses. They raped the women before killing them, and cut open the bellies of those who were pregnant. Then these noble men of war left both mother and baby to die of their wounds, in some cases bayoneting the baby to the chest of its mother."

Muhammad spoke in measured tones, but with the calm of a man fighting for control. "They killed 254 that day. And in such a horrific manner, the whole of Palestine was thrown into shock. The Irgun command sent a message to their men, 'As in Deir Yassin, so everywhere.' Hearing the message, the Palestinians fled in terror, evacuating their ancestral lands to make way for the Zionist Jews. Deir Yassin was absorbed into the expanded boundaries of Jerusalem, and its streets, with typical Zionist sensitivity, were named after the terrorist units that participated in the atrocity."

Nothing was said for a long moment. When June stirred, it was to wipe the tears from her eyes. "They killed *babies*? How do you live with this?" she whispered.

Muhammad gave a rueful laugh. "How do Palestinians live with this? Some run away, like the 700,000 who were scared off. Others endure the hardship of remaining, and pray for the day Allah brings victory to the righteous. And they never, ever allow themselves to forget."

When she regained her voice, June said, "Muhammad, forgive me, but you need to put this behind you."

Muhammad slowed the car, pulled over onto the shoulder of the road and stopped. Silence descended upon them louder than a shout, but then he spoke, his face bent to the steering wheel. "Miss Cody, some of those knives bit deeply when they ripped open the wombs of our mothers, and I sit on my own scar as we speak."

Breaking his code of visual chastity, he turned in his seat and looked her full in the eyes. "Few of us survived, and upon those who did, it is a sacred duty *not* to forget. And I never will."

June tightened a quivering lip and shrank back in her seat, seeing the blood-covered baby that was Muhammad as it lay beside his disemboweled, dying mother, read the eternal struggle for justice and vindication in his eyes, and felt herself wither in his gaze. "I'm so sorry. I … didn't know."

And it was then that raindrops started to pepper the windshield, as if the very heavens shuddered and wept.

* * *

Five miles down the road, Michael glanced through the rain-streaked window and broke the silence. "It was one of hundreds of atrocities," he said. "The headlines were all about the Six Day War in '67, the thirty thousand civilians killed in Beirut in '82, and the Sabra and Chatila Massacre, also in Beirut. But there were hundreds of smaller massacres. Racial elitism's bad enough, but Zionism rendered the concept fanatical because Zionist Jews consider non–Jews *expendable*. That opened the door to all those atrocities."

Muhammad spoke over his shoulder while keeping an eye on the road. "Miss Cody, remember that the Zionists terrorize Palestinian Christians as well as Muslims. No non–Jew is safe, regardless of religion or ideology. Christians and Muslims, on the other hand, don't hate Jews. Our struggle is against those who seek to kill us and throw us off our land. So please remember, the issue is over Zionism, *not* Judaism."

June straightened in her seat and smoothed her ruffled blouse with her hands, then crossed her arms on her chest as if to fight off a chill. "If only we could save the world, Michael."

"Or just this part."

* * *

"Or just this part," the woman's voice repeated, and then, with a languorous sigh, *"Yeah."*

Half a mile behind, as the voices faded from the receiver, the older Mossad agent glanced at his partner in the passenger seat. "Not exactly our greatest ally, is she?"

The younger man shook his head with a frown. "Not our greatest enemy, either."

CHAPTER 23

They arrived at the hotel too early for lunch and too excited to eat anyway. The rain had stopped, so Michael strolled the hotel grounds, partly to ensure privacy, partly to see if the world looked a cleaner place after a good wash.

"So what do we have?" June asked as she joined his side.

"To begin with," he said, "the haystack Rachael was searching seems a bit smaller now. The original scrolls team was an international team of eight scholars, assembled in 1953. Membership didn't change until '58. So in 1957, which, according to Abu Ahmed, was the year he gave the scroll his son found in Cave 4 to one of the team, we still had the original eight."

He sighed heavily. "Assuming that's the gospel Jacob mentioned in *his* scroll, all we have to do is figure out which one of the eight he gave it to five decades ago. Piece of cake."

"How many are still living?" she asked while they skirted the edge of a fountain.

Michael shrugged. "Remember, we're talking 1957. Rule out Roland De Vaux, the project director. John Allegro, too. De Vaux was too old to match the description Abu Ahmed gave, and died in '71 anyway. Allegro's out because of the kind of person he was. He attributed the origins of Christianity to a fertility cult tripping out on—"

"—on hallucinogenic mushrooms," June said between guffaws. "Yeah, yeah, yeah. *The Sacred Mushroom and the Cross.* I read it once. Nearly died laughing."

Nodding, he stopped and leaned against the trunk of a palm tree. "Allegro was agnostic as well. You've got to assume a man like that would've published the Gospel of the Teacher, *if* he'd gotten his hands on it. Anyway, he died in '88."

"That leaves six."

"Yep. Two from America. One each from Poland, England, Germany and France. All Christian, and three are, or were, Catholic priests."

"Throw out Poland, Germany and France," she said, "and what's left?"

"Why Poland, Germany and France?"

"'Me Sam Spade.'"

"Ah." He nodded, recalling how Abu Ahmed's mystery man had introduced himself. "Good thinking. So that narrows it down to just three. Two Americans and one Brit."

June said, "And with that 'Me Tarzan' way of speaking, my money's on one of the Americans."

"So where do we go from here?"

She thought a moment. "We call Dr. Mardle, who probably knows every single one of the team, and a whole lot more."

"I don't want to involve him. This is too dangerous." He shrugged himself off the palm tree, lowered himself onto the grass and stretched his legs. "Dad and I were watched. Dr. Mardle told me he was watched for a while, too. I know it's been years, but how can I be certain he isn't being watched now?"

"Michael, we need help. And you told me that after your conversations, you trust him like your father. And you said it yourself. It's been years. Surely whoever was watching you and Dr. Mardle has given up and moved on to other things by now."

He felt the dampness of the earth seep through his pants, and realized he was only seconds away from looking like a commercial for incontinence briefs. He hoisted himself to his feet. "Let me think about it."

* * *

He purchased a cell phone and a handful of prepaid SIM cards, the fingernail-sized computer chips used to activate the GSM cell phones of Europe and the Middle East. He preferred prepaid to subscription cards, since he could exchange them whenever he wanted to change his phone number. In this way, he'd be more likely to evade a line tap.

He inserted one of the chips into his new phone and made the call. He caught Mardle on the second try and filled him in, whereupon the professor became deadly serious. "I appreciate your concern for my safety, Michael, but at my age, it's hardly an issue. Your father started this, and I hope I can help you finish it."

"You know what's at stake," Michael said. "Talk to no one. And if Chopper and Cro-Magnon man come back, tell me. We'll drop everything and go home."

"I'll look into the names and ring you back at five, your time. But I'm afraid I already know the answer. I know all three, and any one of them can fit your description."

The moment Mardle rang off, the hardwired recorder two offices down clicked back into standby mode, its "message recorded" red light blinking like a warning beacon.

* * *

At five-fifteen, Michael took Mardle's call from beside the hotel's outdoor swimming pool. When he finished, he rang their room and invited June down to dinner.

"Well?" she asked when she joined him at the table.

"Well, we've got to think. And I never think well when I'm hungry."

They ordered. He sat back. She waited. He sucked his teeth, sighed, leaned forward and spread his hands on the table. "I know two of the three professionally, and Mardle knows all three. With what we have to go on, we can't rule out any of them."

"They must be in Dr. Mardle's generation. Late seventies at least," she said. "And they're all living?"

"Yeah," he said with a smirk. "Lucky break, huh? So what do we do now? Drop in on them for tea and an accusation?"

She blew a strand of hair from her face, and it fell back in the same spot. "Were any of them on Rachael's poison-pen-letter list?"

"No. So there shouldn't be any risk in talking with them." In spite of his answer, a nagging concern scurried about in the walls of his mind. *What am I missing?* He racked his brain, but as with an impressionist painting, the closer he got to the picture, the more unfocused it became. He gave up. "So what do you think? Visit them one by one?"

She sighed. "How do you confront an internationally respected academic and tell him to hand over the scroll he misappropriated fifty years ago?"

They spent the entire dinner brainstorming, but couldn't work up so little as a mental breeze. Michael glanced down and found, to his complete surprise, another half-eaten chocolate mousse in front of him, the spoon in his hand muddied with the stuff. "Shall we sleep on it?" he suggested half-heartedly.

"Nah." June spoke as she nibbled her dessert. "Just call them. If you can't get an answer over the phone, *then* we'll pay a visit."

He tasted his dessert. *Too sweet again.* He pushed it away. "Okay, I'll give them a call. But this is going to be tough."

* * *

"Told you it didn't feel right," the older Mossad agent said. The duo was seated on the opposite side of the room, on an elevated terrace partially screened from the main floor by a bank of ferns. "They're on to something."

"I heard." The sandy blond tapped his earphone with a finger.

"Change the bug to another table," the senior agent said. "Before breakfast. And let the waiters know to hold that table for them. They might get suspicious if the waiters always seat them in the same place. Is his mobile covered?"

The blond shook his head and took a sip of coffee. "It's unregistered. A prepaid SIM card. Until we know his number, he's beyond our ears."

"In that case, let's hope he calls from his room phone."

* * *

While making his calls, Michael meandered about the hotel's floodlit grounds. The first call reached an answering machine in England; the second interrupted a sour-voiced housekeeper who seemed to think everyone the world over should be telepathically aware this was Father Kelly's day to go fishing. The third caught Father James Braddot in the Study with the Wrench.

"A leaking steam radiator, I fear," Braddot said. "The bane of an old New Hampshire house."

"In the middle of summer?"

"Never too late to procrastinate. Been meaning to repair it since winter. Hang on."

Michael could hear banging in the background, and then the elderly priest's voice came back on the line. "Okay, I'm all yours."

"Finished?"

"No, but nothing new there. What's it been, Dr. Hansen? Two years, maybe three?"

"Something like that." He reflected on how little he knew of Braddot, having only met him at theological seminars. He told him where he was calling from, and worked his way around to Braddot's involvement in the Dead Sea Scrolls Project.

"It was my privilege," Braddot said.

Michael searched for words, and finally said, "There's, ah, something in the history of the scrolls you might be interested to know."

As he explained, Braddot's breathing became so deep that, on Michael's end of the phone, his exhalations sounded practically obscene. When he related his meeting with the tribal elder, Abu Ahmed, Braddot interrupted.

"I fail to see ... I mean, I left the scrolls team years before the dig you describe in Nubia. So I don't see where this is going. Now, you'll have to excuse me, but this radiator—"

"Where this is going, Father, is right to your backdoor."

The line went quiet. Seconds grew to minutes, but Michael held his silence as tightly as he gripped the phone. At one point, he thought he heard a muttered prayer.

Eventually, Braddot cleared his throat, and then spoke. "Dr. Hansen, I ... I've lived in dread of this call for fifty years. Now that I've received it, well, I don't know what to do. In all honesty? I'm at the end of my life, and I'm surprised at how relieved I feel. That I can clear myself of this matter, and with a colleague and not the authorities. But please understand, I'm terribly afraid."

Michael closed his eyes and took a deep breath. He was about to speak when Braddot said, in a strained attempt at light-heartedness, "You say you're where? Le Meridien in Ein Bokek on the Dead Sea? A land of contrasts, isn't it? Barren and brown on one side, and an aquamarine paradise on the other."

"Perhaps we should meet."

"If you were any good at home repair, I'd invite you here," Braddot said with a chuckle. "But I've always wanted to visit Bethlehem one last time anyway, and it looks as though that's my destiny. And yours, Dr. Hansen, seems to be sorting out this mess. Given your credentials, I can't think of anyone better suited to the task."

"You understand the dangers," Michael said.

"Since I first read the gospel. That's why I never told anyone about it, with the exception of ..." Braddot spoke through a phlegm rattle and cleared his throat. "Are you sure this call is safe?"

Michael spun a circle as he surveyed the near-darkness. Open hotel grounds, a few couples strolling the paths or sitting at the outside tables. But nobody taking an interest in him, at least apparently. "Pretty sure."

"We'll save this discussion for later, in any case. Until then, think about how you can expose this gospel without linking it to me."

"Is that why you didn't bring the gospel to light sooner?"

Once again the silence stretched into minutes. Michael could hear the priest's labored breathing, but then Braddot spoke. "At first? I didn't expose it because of its content, which would've threatened my position in the Church. Years later, when my viewpoint changed and I wanted to publicize the gospel, I couldn't. My reputation would've been ruined, and I would've lived the rest of my life in academic disgrace. As the scholar who stole a Dead Sea Scroll, a gospel that officially belongs to Israel. Surely you can understand."

Michael decided to leave understanding for later, and simply said, "I look forward to meeting with you, Father. And I believe you're making the right decision."

* * *

He entered the hotel not so much walking as floating and found June in a lobby lounge chair, sipping a cup of Turkish coffee.

"Thought I'd give it a t-t-try," she said, set the cup down, and flapped both hands in the air like laundry hung out to dry in a gale.

"Watch out for the last third. It's pure dregs. Shall we walk?"

She shook her head. "I'm afraid if I stand up, I'll bounce through the skylight. So?"

"Got him."

He plunked himself down in the seat opposite and sat back, enjoying the dropped-jaw expression on her face. *Beg,* he thought.

"WHO?"

Good enough. "Braddot. He expects to be here in a day or two. If I understand correctly, he's bringing the scroll with him."

"That's amazing. And exciting. Did you tell Dr. Mardle?"

"Too late in the day. He asked me to keep him informed, so I left a message on his answering machine. As soon as he gets to his office, he'll know."

* * *

That night, he was attacked from all sides. He tossed and turned, kicked off the sheets, woke up in a cold sweat. He drank a glass of water, took a shower, watched a little TV, but nothing broke the spell. Each time he closed his eyes, he found a nightmare with an attitude lying in wait.

"Any messages in the dreams?" June asked the next morning over breakfast.

He shook his head and continued slapping jam onto a wedge of toast. "Messages? It was like a poltergeist screaming at me in a foreign language. I'm missing something. I'm sure of it."

"Don't let your fears get the better of you. We're onto something big, and part of you thinks it's too good to be true."

He dunked his toast into his tea, jam and all, then realized what he'd done. He sighed, laid the soggy mess down and said, "If you're right, we have nothing to worry about. But if *I'm* right, our lives are at stake."

Across the room, the senior Mossad agent winked at his partner. "I'll side with his opinion. What about you?"

CHAPTER 24

At ten in the morning Dead Sea time, Professors Falson and Mardle ran into one another on the way to work at eight, Oxford time. They exchanged pleasantries on the footpath and walked upstairs, where they chatted over tea and a rapidly disappearing sleeve of biscuits. Eventually Falson left for his own office, having bored Mardle to the point of actually finishing his cup of tea.

Ten minutes later a phone call went out. The exchange was local, but switched to a relay. The end line was answered by a digital monotone, intended to convince wrong-number dialers of a fault in the line. But this caller knew the monotone was a demand for a twelve-digit security code followed by a six-digit PIN. Following electronic recognition of the PIN, a beep signaled the caller to file a verbal report. When that was accomplished, the caller hit the pound key and a live voice came on the line.

"Report registered, thank you," was all the speaker said.

"Not good enough. I saw how you took care of business last time. I want to speak to someone in authority."

There was the briefest of pauses. "Report registered, thank you," the anonymous voice repeated.

"You get me someone in authority, do you understand? You get me someone in authority or else!"

"Please hold."

The words *or else* can be a death sentence in certain circles, as the caller was well aware. But his temper was pistol-whipped to the ground when a gruff voice came on the line with, "Or else, what?"

For perhaps the first time in his life, the caller was at a loss for words.

"Listen, Professor," Gruff Voice continued, "you don't have irrevocable tenure with *us*. But for the sake of continued good relations, I'm authorized to tell you that what happened wasn't from us."

"After seventeen *years*? After SEVENTEEN YEARS you tell me this? How am I supposed to believe—?"

"Professor, I'll say this once more, but only once. So pay attention. It wasn't from us. Not in Nubia seventeen years ago, and not in Jordan two years ago. Neither action was from us. Be happy you're off the hook. Now, if you want what's best for all concerned, call if you hear anything new. That's all I'm authorized to say. Cheerio, and call back soon."

The line went dead and the caller in Oxford said "Jerk" while a gruff voice in a distant time zone muttered, "Stupid limey."

* * *

In what would be considered a surprisingly quick turnaround for any intelligence organization other than Mossad, the transcript of the professor's telephone report was under Prime Minister Leib's nose within two hours. The quick turnaround was even more impressive because the call from Oxford hadn't been routed to Israel, but to America. Twenty years prior, the saying was that if you wanted to tell something to the KGB, say it to the CIA. That was the joke. The reality was not the KGB, but Israel. The leaks to Mossad were so numerous as to render the CIA an intelligence sieve, more akin to a junction box than an end-destination on the intelligence circuit.

Leib read the professor's report first, and then the surveillance agents' reports. Then he called the director of Mossad.

"I told you Dr. Hansen might lead us to it," Leib said. "Now, how do you think we should handle this priest? Name's ..." He glanced back at the professor's report. "Braddot."

Ten minutes later, he hung up the phone and tapped the file with his pen while he stared into the distance, and then lowered his eyes to the papers spread on his desk. He hesitated, then drew the three prepared termination orders onto his blotter to sign.

He picked up his pen, put it back down, and then squeezed his eyes shut while he rubbed his temples.

A clerk entered the room and added more folders to the inbox on his desk. Leib glanced at the towering stack, checked his watch, and then looked again at the termination orders in front of him. With a shake of his head, he picked up his pen and signed.

* * *

The same day, Michael took June to the nature reserve at Ein Gedi, both for appearance's sake and to fill their time. He couldn't shake his anxiety, and noticed that Muhammad was similarly edgy, although whether independently or by association he couldn't tell.

He felt a moment of calm settle upon him when they sat for a late lunch; the warmth of the day combined with his fatigue to lull away his cares. Over his second cup of strong tea, June pressed him about his conversation with Father Braddot.

"Father James Braddot is the typical man of the cloth in turmoil," Michael said, rubbing his bloodshot eyes. "He was raised in a religion dominated by the theology of Paul, despite the fact that Braddot's namesake, James, was at odds with Paul from the beginning. When we spoke, he said the conflict between James and Paul always disturbed him, and he hinted that the Gospel of the Teacher has something to say about that conflict."

"So why's he giving the gospel to you, and not to someone else?" she asked.

He sipped his tea, found it cool, and guzzled the cup dry. Sighing, he set the cup back in its saucer with a clink. "Why me? For reasons he claims I'll understand once I've read the gospel. All he said was that he feels I'm the best theologian to take it public. Also, he trusts me to somehow keep him out of it to preserve his reputation."

He shifted in his seat, feeling the fatigue, sun and hot caffeine gang up on him.

"You mentioned something about babies? What was it?"

June's question brought him back. "Oh, yeah. Braddot's no theological parrot, that's for sure. Said every time he baptized a baby, he couldn't believe an unbaptized child would never enjoy the sight of God. Their innocence was beyond question, etched on their faces. Then he quoted Ezekiel 18:19."

"Wait, don't tell me." She scratched her head as she recalled the passage. "'The son shall not bear the guilt of the father, nor the father bear the guilt of the son. The righteousness of the righteous shall be upon himself, and the wickedness of the wicked shall be upon himself.' Okay, that's the scripture, but what's the point?"

The waiter placed their check on the table, and Michael reached for it. "Point? This is Old Testament, but it isn't older than Adam. If there's such a thing as original sin, every prophet since Adam should've taught it. But they didn't. Even Jesus taught the opposite."

She sat back and gathered her black *abaya* about her. Tissue-thin and covering everything from her neck to her wrists and ankles, the local coverall billowed about her and settled in folds in her lap.

"You've gone native on me," he said.

"Most convenient thing I've ever worn," she replied. "I can wear whatever I want underneath. I'm totally mismatched today, but who'd know?"

He laughed, more from fatigue than mirth. "Mom wore one when we were in Yemen. Stick with cotton or linen. You'll sweat to death in polyester."

"Jesus?" she said.

"He'd steer you away from polyester also. He was a wool spokesman, I believe."

"Smart aleck."

"Okay, back to Jesus. Matthew 19:14. Jesus is recorded as having said, 'Let the little children come to me, and do not forbid them, for of such is the kingdom of heaven.' Now, how can 'for of such' be 'the kingdom of heaven,' if the unbaptized bear the stain of original sin and are bound for hell?"

He fished some bills from his wallet and folded them into the check. "Then there's the concept of atonement, which Jesus never taught, and Matthew 7:21-23, in which he taught that *not* everybody who claims belief will be saved and ..." He gave her a sheepish smile. "And, *ha-bee-ba-tee*, I usually put my students to sleep, but today it seems to be working on me."

"'*Ha-bee-ba-tee*'?" she said, as if tasting the word.

"Arabic for 'my love,' when spoken to a lady. '*Ha-bee-bee*,' if spoken to a man. Literally, it means 'my love,' but the Arabs use it for everybody: friends, acquaintances, shop attendants, somebody they've just met. Anybody they like, that is. Don't take it wrong."

"I'll take it the way I like, *Habeebee*. And *Habeebee*, you need to sleep. Let's get you to bed."

"Deal." He stood and pointed a finger at her. "But don't think that just because my defenses are down, you can take advantage of me."

* * *

"Key cards. Ungh. What's wrong with a good, old-fashioned metal key?" Since their arrival, the magnetic reader to their suite had proven temperamental, and Michael had to get the swipe-speed perfect for the door to unlock. He got it right on the third try.

"You take the bed," she said as they stumbled into their room. "I'll sit on the sofa and read."

Without objection, he closed the bedroom door behind him and stripped off his clothes. One eye on the bed, he knocked on the door and asked, "Everything okay?"

"More than. Get some sleep, *Habeebee*."

He rolled his eyes but slipped between the sheets with a smile, sank his head into the pillow and was instantly enveloped in her perfume. He propped himself up on an elbow, ran a hand beneath the pillow and drew out a carefully folded nightgown. The nightgown was practically Victorian in design, but he shook his head nonetheless. "Just a *minor* in psychology?" he muttered to himself, and laughed.

"Everything okay?" Her voice drifted through the door.

"More than. Wake me for dinner."

* * *

Three hours later they went through the motions of dinner, not out of hunger, for the late lunch was still with them, but out of dedication to routine. By the time dessert rolled around, they'd both had enough. He couldn't face another chocolate mousse lacking a bitter bite to it, and she'd lost her appetite after the salad.

The two Mossad agents watched through their curtain of ferns as the pair left the restaurant. The senior agent groaned, for he had personally spiked the entire dessert tray with ricin, a poisonous derivative of the castor bean. It would have induced diarrhea of torrential proportions. Both would have been incapacitated, and ambulance trips to the hospital would've been inevitable. Isolated away from the hotel and each other, they could have been eliminated with ease.

Now, he watched the dessert tray weave past the other tables in the direction of the kitchen. Another diner hailed the waiter, but the waiter pretended not to hear and whisked the tray past. "All those desserts into the rubbish," he muttered. "The guy has chocolate mousse every night, why not tonight?"

"My heart's not in this." His freckled, sandy-haired partner toyed with his water glass. "*Shiksa* or no *shiksa*, what's she done to deserve this?"

"Snap out of it. Remember what Rabbi Dov Lior was quoted as having said?"

"Chairman of the Settler's Rabbinical Council. I know. You told me. Too many times."

"He said 'A thousand non–Jewish lives are not worth a Jew's fingernail.'"

The senior agent wrapped his hairy knuckles around the delicate, hand-painted bud vase between them, picked it up, then stamped it onto the tabletop with a thud. "You know a single rabbi who disagreed with him? Who objected? Anywhere? Anywhere in the *world*?"

The younger agent bowed his head and shook it. "Look, I'm not sure I can ... I mean, what have we become? Monsters?"

The senior man stood and stared down at his freckled partner. "Keep talking like that, and your problem won't be with them, but with me." He jabbed the younger man's shoulder with a stubby finger. "Tonight, you're on trigger. You prove yourself, or you'll see the side of me I keep locked in a cage."

CHAPTER 25

It wasn't a nightmare, but a realization that woke him at two in the morning. For a moment he lay frozen, like a deer paralyzed in the headlights of an onrushing car, uncertain of his senses but knowing he was in mortal danger. The next moment, Michael threw himself from the sofa and grabbed the room's phone.

The line was dead.

He tried to downplay his concerns with denial. It didn't work. The phone service here was surely no more reliable than anywhere else in the Middle East, but vaguely formed horrors crept from the dark recesses of his mind and propelled him to the bedroom door.

June roused at the second knock and called out in a sleep-fogged voice, "Don't come in, I'm not dressed."

In other circumstances, he might have paused to conjure a delightful mental image. But those would have to be other circumstances, for his gut screamed at him that if they didn't move quickly, they'd never live to see them. "June! We've got to get out of here," he yelled in a hoarse whisper. "They're coming for us."

In a heartbeat, the door was open and she stood in front of him. In the dim light filtering in from the hotel floodlights below, he could see the decorative bedspread wrapped around her and trailing behind her toward the bed.

"Get dressed," he said, keeping his voice low. "Quickly. Pants, not a skirt. Pants and sneakers or, or walking shoes. And whatever you do, don't turn on the light."

She disappeared back into the bedroom, the bedspread billowing behind her like a sail filling with wind. He threw on his own clothes and looked up from lacing his shoes when she entered the room, a satchel over her shoulder, in jeans and a dark green t-shirt. He grabbed the shoulder bag that served as his stampeding pack, without stopping to add anything, and together they started for the door.

And that was when they heard it. The light scrape of a keycard in the magnetic reader. A master keycard, no doubt, being surreptitiously swiped. June turned to face him, her pupils dilated as much from fear as from the dim light.

The door was only three steps away. He turned back to the room. *Dead end.*

He looked back at the door. *Enemy.*

And then he heard it again, the scratch of the swipe repeated, quietly. Whoever it was on the other side of the door, he wasn't having any better luck with the magnetic reader than Michael had. This second time, he'd slowed his swipe-speed. *Wrong strategy,* Michael thought, savoring the small triumph. *Gotta speed up. That's the trick.*

He placed his finger on June's lips, pushed her backward into the hallway bathroom, bundled his shoulder bag into her arms and called out, "Just a minute, I'm coming."

The door went silent, and he could only guess what was happening on the other side.

He stepped back into the room and grabbed June's hardcover novel from the coffee table, then sidestepped along the wall until he was at the door. He lifted the book to cover the peephole, saying, "Yes, who is—?"

With the dull thud of a hatchet splitting kindling, the book flew from his hand as three small holes punched through the door at the level of the peephole.

Michael had shot through wood before, and was always disappointed that bullets don't punch out baseball-sized holes like in the movies. Instead, his left tracks smaller than the actual round, in the same way that a nail pulled from a board left a smaller track due to the natural resiliency of the wood fibers. But tonight, he rejoiced. Each of the bullet holes was roughly a quarter-inch in diameter, slightly smaller than the 9-millimeter rounds that made them. Even better, the holes were obstructed with splinters from the blowback. That, combined with the darkness of the room, meant their assailant had zero chance of seeing through the holes.

The bad news was, someone was trying to kill them.

A split second after the bullets passed, he jumped and landed on stiffened legs, hoping to imitate the sound of a body falling. The door erupted inward again, this time at the level of his ankles. He'd expected to see the bullets angled toward the floor, but didn't. This was a pro. Anyone else would've stitched the carpet at different angles, hoping to land a bullet in the right place. This killer crouched to place his shots parallel to the floor, to skim the space where a fallen body couldn't help but catch them. Instead, the wounded book tumbled and flew to pieces.

The instant the shots stopped, Michael pushed off from the wall and threw the door open, expecting a lone assassin. He found two.

The one closest was straightening from a crouch. His head snapped up, his mouth a perfect O, his eyes projecting something between shock and guilt, like a child caught snitching a cookie. He held an empty bullet clip in his fingers, his palm frozen on the base of a second clip inserted halfway into the butt of his silenced automatic. The second man stood with his back to them, watching the corridor, but turned his head when the door opened.

The nearer assassin shoved the magazine home with a click and fumbled with the slide release as he dropped back into a crouch, but Michael landed a brick-shattering kick on his chin. The blow threw the man's head back with a flailing of blond hair and clatter of broken teeth. He felt the man's jaw crunch beneath his foot, and a jagged edge of bone burst from one freckled cheek.

The other assassin followed his head-turn and spun right. By then, Michael was upon him. He brought a crushing high step down on the assassin's forward knee and rode his shin to the ground. At the same time, he grabbed the man's wrist and followed, rather than fought, the assassin's momentum, sweeping the man's arm overhead and turning into his body, knowing the man was benumbed by pain, off balance, and at his mercy. In a fluid motion, Michael swung him over his hip and sent him flying.

The man slammed to the floor with a jingle of ceiling lamps and rattle of nearby doors. Michael straightened the man's arm with a twist of his wrist and broke his elbow over one knee. Then he dropped his knee into the near side of the man's chest, his full weight behind it. There was a muffled, multiple cracking like a handful of knuckles popping, and Michael rebounded to his feet, gun in hand, the depression in the man's chest sucking a gurgle from his throat.

A metallic click was followed by the unmistakable *chink* of a metal slide chambering a round, and he turned to find the blond writhing on the floor like a drunk, but leveling his gun. Behind him, June stood in the doorway, eyes wide, still clutching his bag to her chest. As the gun swung in Michael's direction, she threw a frantic kick from behind and snagged the man's ear with her heel. The assassin twisted and fired, and Michael felt a searing-hot blast lift his hair and blow past his face. He stepped forward, swept the gun aside and drove the ball of his foot into the man's temple. In the crash of unconsciousness, the man's head swung on the tether of his neck, rebounded, then lay still.

Working quickly, Michael slipped the gun in his hand into his waistband, snatched up the second gun, wrested both men's wallets from their pockets and threw all into his shoulder bag. June stood unmoving, her mouth covered with the back of one hand. He grabbed her by the wrist, whisked her over the unconscious youth and kicked away the older assailant's feeble grab at June's ankle. As they ran the hallway toward the stairs, he drew the gun from his waistband, smashed the fire alarm with the butt, and then stuffed that into his bag as well.

They'd nearly reached the exit when instinct compelled him to look back. The second assassin, with chest caved in, dominant arm broken and one knee smashed, had nonetheless curled up, rolled over and pulled a backup gun from his ankle holster with a shaky left hand.

The first bullet blew out the florescent exit sign over their heads. Red plastic fragments scattered onto the carpet with the pitter-patter of rainfall.

Michael pushed June through the door as the second round gouged plaster from the wall and showered his face with a stinging spray. The third flew through the space he'd occupied a split second earlier. But by then he was gone; the bullet killed nothing but the ornamental vase at the end of the hall.

* * *

By the time they neared the lower levels, the fire alarm had sent a dozen hotel guests down the stairwell, but only one couple followed when they exited on the conference room level. Michael and June kept walking, but the other couple apparently realized their error and turned back to go down the additional flight of stairs to the ground floor.

Yet Michael's choice of floor was deliberate. With no idea what might be waiting on the ground floor, he led June into the men's bathroom. From there they climbed up onto the toilet stall walls, through the ceiling tiles, and onto a ledge in the crawlspace above. June spent the first few minutes shaking uncontrollably. Half of him wanted to hug her, the other half held his arms back, fearing he might make her panic worse. In the end he compromised and rubbed her back while she exorcised the demons of her fears and regained control.

"You should've shot him," she blurted.

"You were standing behind him."

She shuddered, but managed to swivel her head around the crawlspace. "Why *here*, of all places?"

He rummaged through his shoulder bag and pulled out the assassins' wallets and guns. "I do some of my best thinking in the bathroom."

"S-seriously. Can't we leave the hotel?"

"It's two in the morning, in the middle of a desert. No taxis, and nowhere to go." He flipped open a wallet and tilted it toward the light that stole through slits in the ceiling tiles beneath them.

"Let's go to the police."

He picked up the second wallet and sorted through the contents, found what he was looking for and held the identification card up for her to see.

"Greek to me," she said.

"Hebrew, actually." He turned the card over and, squinting, she read the other side aloud. "Special Investigator, Israeli Intelligence Agency, Mossad. Good grief."

He put the card back, closed the wallets and tossed them to one side. "Going to the police would've been like one of those cartoons where the mouse runs out of his hole and into the cat's mouth."

A tickle on his nose made him reach up and run his hand over his face. His fingers swept up a smattering of short hairs, as if he'd just stepped out of a barber's chair. *The bullet cut my* hair?

He prodded his scalp, didn't find any dull spot or wetness, and shook his head in wonder.

Another bout of shakes overcame her but as quickly as they came, they were gone. "I ... I would've run straight to the police."

He shrugged. "Assassinations and surveillance operations stretching from Sudan to America, to England, and then back to Jordan and Israel? Over seventeen years? Had to be an intelligence agency. No other interest group could've handled it. But why Mossad?"

She wrapped her arms around herself and shook her head. After a moment she asked, "You still have your cell phone? Can't they use it to locate us?"

He groaned, pulled it from his pocket and removed the battery. For good measure, he replaced the SIM card with a new one from his handful of prepaid cards.

"Typical absentminded professor," she said, then asked, "how'd you know? Back in the room. How'd you know they were coming for us?"

He rapped the knuckles of one hand against the side of his head. "Like you said, absentminded professor. Something was wrong, I just didn't know what. Woke up realizing what it was."

He shifted to a more comfortable position just as the fire alarm cut off. He listened for a long moment, and then continued in a whisper. "I was so excited over having found the gospel's owner, I forgot why we're here. We're goofing off doing tourist stuff, and we got lucky. But we came to Israel to visit the last two professors on Rachael's letter list. We assumed one of them had the gospel, and Rachael was killed because she threatened him. Now we know both of those assumptions are wrong."

The bathroom door swung open, the sound reaching them through the ceiling tiles. Both controlled their breathing and waited. Water ran and stopped. Paper towels were stripped from the dispenser and the metal flap to the trashcan squeaked and slapped shut. The door swung open again, then shut.

Five minutes passed before June whispered, "So?"

He ran a hand over his face. "Sooo, we thought we were safe because we hadn't contacted the professors on Rachael's list. But now we know they don't *have* the gospel. Braddot does. That means Rachael didn't trigger an alarm by threatening the gospel's owner, but some other way."

She shifted her head in surprise. "So Rachael *didn't* contact Braddot?"

"Nope. I kept track of her contacts. When she made her rounds in America, she missed a couple of the Dead Sea Scrolls analysts because they were on vacation. Braddot was one of them. That means we don't know how Rachael triggered the kill-alarm. And since we don't know how *she* tripped the alarm, we might've tripped it ourselves."

He swept a dangling LAN line out of his face and continued. "What that means is that some group—" He snorted. "Yeah, 'some group.' Now we know it's Mossad, don't we? So we now know that Mossad wants to keep the gospel from being discovered, and they're killing anyone who so much as looks for it."

"And here we are," June said, tightening her arms around herself.

"And here we are, not only looking for the gospel, but on the verge of finding it. When I woke up and finally understood what had been bugging me, I picked up the phone and found the line dead. That's when I realized we'd somehow set off the same alarm as Rachael did. And if we didn't get out of there, we'd wake up as dead as the telephone line."

She shuddered again, but it had a finality about it, as if she were shaking off the last of her fears. Slowly, she unwound her arms and asked, "So how do we avoid ending up like Rachael?"

Michael felt his eyes sting and begin to fill with tears, but swallowed hard and forced them back. "*We* don't. June, darling, I never should've gotten you into this. You know those old westerns where the two bandits split up, hoping one of them will evade the posse? Well, right now, those two bandits are us. But you can walk out of here, and they'll probably let you go. It's me they're after. And as long as you're with me, you're in danger."

Her lips seemed to fill out and regain their color as she drew them into a sad smile. "Michael, this isn't a western. It's a spy flick. If they catch me, they'll use me to get to you. We're in this together, *Habeebee*, for better or worse."

He arched an eyebrow. "Till death do us part?"

"Not funny. But speaking of which, I asked how we can get out of this alive."

He cleared his throat. "One of two ways. We either take the gospel public, so there's nothing to be gained from killing us, or ..."

"Or?"

"Or we give it to Mossad to get them off our backs. Unless ..."

She raised her head to look into his eyes.

He grinned with more confidence than he felt. "Unless we can figure out how Rachael and I both tripped the same alarm. If we can figure *that* out, maybe we can turn it to our advantage."

* * *

Thirty minutes later, the bathroom door opened again. June dozed, propped against his shoulder, so he gently nudged her awake.

Stall doors opened and shut, one after the other. There was a scraping sound, two loud clicks, the creak of metal under pressure, and one of the ceiling tiles suddenly lifted up and slid to the side. He did the only thing he could do; he wrapped his left arm around her and drew her close, her face buried sideways in his chest, her eyes watching fearfully as he took aim at the opening with the silenced 9-millimeter.

A head and uniformed shoulders popped through, looking away from them. The policeman swayed for a moment, and then brought a flashlight and semiautomatic pistol up to eye level and started to sweep the crawlspace.

As he turned 180 degrees, the man adjusted his stance on the ladder to complete the sweep. He swung the beam of the flashlight directly across Michael's chest, June's face and eyes, and Michael's outstretched arm. But the flashlight continued its circuit without a pause, and the policeman's face didn't register the slightest change of expression. He simply completed the sweep as if nobody were there, dropped back down, and replaced the ceiling tile.

The sound of the ladder being collapsed wafted up through the tiles, and Michael sat stunned and helpless, expecting the room to erupt with gunfire, the ceiling tiles stitched by bullets, their bodies impacted and ruined. Yet he heard nothing but voices and the door opening again.

"Nothing. What's next?" a voice demanded.

"Ladies' room."

"No problem, so long as there are no pantyhose in the sink."

"Like at home?"

"Like at home." And then a deep, disgruntled sigh, followed by the sound of the door swinging shut.

"What was *that?*" June asked as she reluctantly uncurled from his chest. "He had to have seen us. Had to. Unless ..."

"Unless he's one of the good guys."

"No. Unless it's one of those Daniel-and-the-lions things."

Michael couldn't shake the image of the man's eyes sweeping the crawlspace. Alert, penetrating. If he hadn't seen it, he never would've believed such eyes could miss the tiniest of details, surely not two people and a gun. His own eyes would have stopped, if only for a fraction of a second. Yet the policeman had passed over them as if blind to their presence. "Well, if we're Daniel and they're the lions," he said, "then why don't we get down from here and walk past them and out of the hotel?"

"It's been done before," June said.

"Yes, but by one of far greater faith than us."

"Speak for yourself. As of now, I'm a believer. Big time."

CHAPTER 26

Hours passed, and in a dry darkness made humid only with anxiety and fear, he tried to plan their next move, and failed. With the police looking for them, they not only had to get out of the hotel, but out of Israel. But even then they'd still have to evade Mossad, for the rest of their lives and wherever they went. *The world, after all, is Mossad's playground.* He allowed a deep sigh to escape his lips.

June had curled up on the crawlspace ledge, and rested her head on his thigh as she slept. He looked down in the dim light and thought, *Oh God, please, can't I keep just this one?*

Sure, an inner voice answered. *You want to kill her, keep her.*

The moment the words crossed his mind, he wondered whether he was connected with the devil or the divine. What made him think such things? She was wonderful, everything he needed, and he could've sat next to her without moving for hours. But there was that whisper again, that inner fear telling him, *Keep your distance, Michael, keep your distance. One more lost love will break your heart forever.*

He sighed and jiggled her awake. When she raised her head and looked at him, he muttered "Foot's fallen asleep" while he scooted a head's length away from her. But she hitched herself along the ledge, encircled his knee with both hands and drew herself into a ball beside him. His leg muscles bunched, but she dug her fingers into them and kneaded, as if fluffing a pillow, and then nestled her head back down with a snuggle and a purr.

He blinked forcibly and gritted his teeth, muttered, "So much for keeping my distance." Like a leaf falling from a tree with nowhere to go but down, he allowed his arm to drift through the air and drape along her side. He felt her chest rise slowly, shallowly, and realized she was already asleep. *Just this one? Can't I keep just this one?*

And then, the bathroom door opened.

He shook her awake.

The door closed, and a lock was thrown.

Too many footfalls for one person.

Two seconds of silence, then the words, "They're up there."

He glanced at her, saw eyes widened in terror, forced the second gun into her hand and brought his feet under him in a crouch. *So the policeman saw us after all.*

"Dr. Hansen, Miss Cody, come down from there."

The voice, lowered to a few decibels above a whisper, was unmistakably Muhammad's.

"It's me, Muhammad. Dr. Hansen, come down. We don't have much time. I'm with friends."

Michael took aim, tilted up a ceiling tile and peered through, but saw only a row of porcelain sinks until Muhammad's familiar form backed up into view. Michael turned to give June the good news, and looked straight down the barrel of her gun. Her eyelids were squeezed shut and her face turned away. His heart first skipped a beat, then pumped hammer-blows into his brain. He swung to one side, grasped her wrist and pried the weapon from her hand, half-expecting to find an impression of her fingers in the grip.

Shaking his head, he confirmed that the safety was off, checked the chamber and found it full, clicked the safety on. "How'd you manage *not* to shoot me?" he whispered. When he saw June open her eyes and find his face, he muttered, "Dead men don't buy flowers, *Habeebatee.* Remember that, okay?"

* * *

Muhammad stood beside the same mismatched American couple that had "accidentally" followed them out of the stairwell onto the conference level, but then turned back. The same couple Michael had noticed at dinner, simply because they didn't say a single word to one another.

"Jim Crane," the man said, and extended his hand beyond his generous belly. They shook, and Crane gave Michael his card, which listed his position at the American embassy as Associate Director of Immigration Services.

The look in Michael's eyes must have been sufficient question. "I followed you to this level during the alarm," Crane said. "I waited a few minutes in the stairwell, but when I came back you were gone. I figured you switched stairwells, but then Laura here advised me you didn't come out at ground level."

He pulled a miniature walkie-talkie from his jacket pocket by way of explanation, pointed it toward the woman, and continued. "So I looked around."

"The guy who came in and washed his hands," Michael said, nodding.

"Actually, I was in here before that, only you didn't realize it."

Michael shook his head in bewilderment. The rush of events was beginning to weigh upon him, but June looked positively ready to fold. She was still shaking from nearly having blown a crater in his head.

"The sound of the fire alarm covered me," Crane said. "All the same, I couldn't be sure whether the voices I heard were above the ceiling tiles or from the floor above. But the moment the alarm quit I heard some rustling, and you whispering after that."

"But somebody came in here right after the alarm stopped," Michael said. He looked searchingly between the pair, and then said to the woman, "You?"

"Nah," Crane said, and rolled his jaundiced eyes. "Laura's too ladylike to set foot inside a bathroom. Even the ladies'."

He stretched a broad smile, but the woman remained curiously unmoved. He cleared his throat and continued. "Once I knew you were here, I opened the door as if coming in, did the hand-washing thing and left. Had you fooled?"

Michael nodded, and Crane flabbed a smile. "So I haven't lost all of it, eh? Been a while since I was in the field."

"Why *are* you here?" Michael asked, wondering how much more confusing the night could become.

"Looking out for our own, that's all. We know the history, and have concerns." Crane scanned the bathroom walls, took a sniff, scrunched up his nose and said, "Tell you what, let's catch up on the kids and cookie recipes later, shall we? Right now we've got to get you somewhere safe."

* * *

"Somewhere safe" turned out to be rooms at that very hotel. After the alarm, Crane had requested adjacent rooms on the lowest level, near the stairwell. He'd made it clear to the hotel clerk that he wasn't concerned, but "the little lady" was afraid that next time, the fire alarm might be real.

Crane chuckled, but a quick glance at the "little lady" told Michael she didn't appreciate this jab any more than the first.

So it was one flight up, a few quick steps, and they were in. Using the new keycard Crane handed her, Laura entered through the adjacent room and opened the communicating door.

"Jim, you seem like a great guy and all," June said as she eyed the bed hungrily, "but couldn't you have popped by, oh, say, three hours ago?"

"Aw, now, that would've taken the fun out of it. If the princess doesn't chafe her bottom waiting in the dragon's lair, she's not going to appreciate the shining knight who saves her nearly as much."

"You have to excuse her," Michael said through a tight jaw. "She's new at this princess stuff."

"Yeah," Crane said. "Well, the real reason for the delay, I didn't think you'd trust me without Muhammad here. Took a little while to find him."

Michael nodded, then asked, "How *did* you find him?"

"Car registration. Our guys in America got a report—"

"CIA?" Michael asked.

Crane shrugged. "Let's just say our guys."

"CIA."

Crane turned on a tolerant stare. "We hotfooted it over here, found the two of you out, but caught you coming back in." He opened one of the two grocery bags on the counter, rummaged inside, pulled out a granola bar and peeled it. "Okay, let's talk rules. The two of you stay quiet from here out. Mumbles don't carry as far as whispers, so mumbles only, and in moderation. When you *do* talk, you use our names, not your own, in case the neighbors are listening. The two of you are over there," he gestured to the other room between chomps on his granola bar, "and we're over here. Mmm, good. Want one?"

Michael refused, and he continued. "Leave the phones disconnected. Got a cell?"

Michael showed him the disassembled phone.

"Good, keep it that way. And stay away from the windows. Do Not Disturb signs should work for a couple days. After that, we'll have to shuttle the two of you between rooms while the maid cleans. Hopefully we won't be here that long."

"Why can't we just go to the embassy?" Michael asked.

Laura spoke for the first time, her voice radiating all the emotion of a lobotomized answering machine. "We'd never make it to the embassy. The Israelis have roadblocks, and we have no jurisdiction."

Crane threw the granola wrapper into the trash, leaned into Laura and whispered in her ear. She nodded, then said, "We're here to facilitate. We can bend the rules, but we can't break them. If the situation arises where we confront the law, we comply and you're on your own. If we're all lucky, we'll help you make it to the embassy, but that will take time and good fortune."

Even then, our troubles won't be over, Michael thought. *We've picked a fight with Mossad, and they have agents the world over. Great.*

He headed to the other room and found June very much in the lead. She hit the bed practically at a dive, but then bounced up, eyes wide. "Hey, Mi—" She caught herself in time and grimaced. "My ... My darling Jim," she said. Then she lowered her voice and mumbled, "Muhammad. He must be in danger, too."

Michael about-faced and caught Crane heading to the bathroom as Laura scanned the room service menu. "What about Muhammad? Is he in danger?"

"The police questioned him when he entered the hotel," she said, looking up. "The Israelis don't have to be discreet with him, you know. They 'disappear' Palestinians all the time and nobody can say a thing. So if the police wanted him, they would've taken him when he arrived."

Her steel-blue eyes chilled Michael, but he made his return stare colder. Finally, she broke. "All right. His cover was that he came early, to catch the morning prayer before taking his customers to an early outing. When we left the downstairs bathroom, he went to the lobby to call your room and act out his cover." She glanced at the clock next to the bed. "Five-thirty. Now that they know who his customers are? Probably questioning him as we speak. Unless he screws up his cover, they'll let him go. After all, he's only a driver."

He's way more than a driver. Michael about-faced, and then whirled back, a Ping-Pong ball between paddles. He had forgotten about Father Braddot. "Did the CIA think anyone else might be at risk?"

The ice queen turned her head a fraction of an inch, as if a greater exertion would fracture the rigid crystals of her spine. She stared at him for so long, he thought she was having an absence seizure. But then she blinked. "Your friend Dr. Trevor Mardle, and Father James Braddot. British Secret Service promised to watch over Dr. Mardle, and we've assigned someone to meet Father Braddot at the airport."

"Unless I'm way off my mark," Michael said, "the Israelis will have someone waiting to meet Braddot at the airport as well."

CHAPTER 27

When the passenger flow through customs at Ben Gurion International Airport in Tel Aviv began to thin, the embassy representative felt the edge of a knife-like anxiety at his gut. He tapped the "Fr. James Braddot" placard against one palm, wondering if he'd missed seeing him in the crowd. *How do you miss a priest in a crowd in Tel Aviv?* No, he concluded, no chance. *Unless he's traveling in mufti, like priests often do,* he realized with chagrin.

An airplane crew filed through customs and headed his way, and he stepped into their path. "Excuse me," he said. "Flight 1042?"

"That's right," a flight attendant said with a smile, and then swung around to pass, her carryon in tow.

"Was there a priest on board?" he called after her.

The flight attendant stopped and looked back at the embassy rep, then at the placard in his hand, her smile fading. She exchanged looks with one of her colleagues, then signaled the rep to wait while she dashed back through customs. A minute passed, then the flight attendant reappeared beside a somber-faced flight captain. She nodded toward the embassy rep and the captain stepped forward. "Father Braddot fell ill, I'm afraid. He was taken off by ambulance."

A chill ran up the man's spine. "Was he ... Was he alive?"

The captain tightened his lips and nodded. "He was breathing, but unresponsive. No relation, I take it?"

"American embassy," the man said, and shifted on his feet. "I was to escort him."

"Ah." The captain nodded. "We have limited medical facilities, but he was lucky in one sense. One of his seatmates was a doctor, believe it or not."

Oh, I believe it, the man thought, his heart sinking. *Lucky Braddot. Lucky indeed.*

"He thinks Father Braddot had a stroke while sleeping," the captain said. "I'm sorry to tell you this, but the doctor feels his chance of recovery is pretty slim."

The embassy representative thanked the captain, took out his cell phone and headed for the exits. He tossed the placard into a trashcan on the way, had a sudden thought, turned and sprinted to the unclaimed baggage office.

* * *

Pope Clement VIII would also have been shocked to learn of the death of Father Braddot. He had just heard the man's confession. Indirectly, that is.

He was relating this delicate matter to his closest assistant, Cardinal Giuseppi Venier, while he gazed out his office window onto Vatican grounds. When the intercom buzzed and a voice announced Cardinal McCauley, *again,* line three, he turned from the window and flashed Venier a quizzical look. Pope Clement had just described how Cardinal McCauley had related the confession of one Father James Braddot, in direct violation of the seal of the confessional. Apparently, Braddot had sought absolution prior to travel, but after hearing the priest's confession, the cardinal decided the details were of sufficient importance to compromise the rules of his office and advise the Holy See.

And now, five minutes later, Cardinal McCauley was back on the line.

What can it be this time? the Pope wondered as he lifted the receiver.

"Bless me, Father, for I have sinned," the voice greeted the Pope.

Pope Clement heard McCauley out, assigned him penance and declared absolution, and held his chuckle, if barely, until he clicked off the phone and handed it back to Venier. "I'm recalling the creativity of Pope Alexander IV," he said to Venier. "At the height of the medieval inquisition in 1256, he gave pairs of clergy the right to torture and then mutually absolve one another of the sin."

He looked at Venier, his face still colored with mirth. "The cardinal called me five minutes ago and broke the seal of the confessional, and just now called for absolution. By God, I think he had it all planned! Mark my words, McCauley has the makings of Church leader!"

* * *

"That's it, we're off," Crane said with a final cinch to his tie. He turned his attention to the button-down collar.

"What?" Michael mumbled back, struggling against shock. "You're going out? When will you be back?"

Michael had prodded June awake at eleven o'clock. For the next hour, they'd argued over how to create some form of insurance upon their lives. When a knock came on the communicating door, he opened it to find Crane adjusting his tie.

"Coming back?" Crane said. "No, Slick, I mean we're off. Outta here. It's over, done, finished. And you can stop mumbling. Braddot was murdered. Or, let's just say we don't buy the stroke-on-the-airplane story. His bag was stolen too. The gospel's gone, they've got it, we don't, end of story. Not a happy ending, especially since it means I've got to go back to my desk, but what's a guy to do?"

Michael and June exchanged disbelieving glances and followed Crane on his retreat into his room, where he threw on a sport jacket and grabbed his bag from the bed. Laura was already at the door, dressed to sterile perfection, hand on the knob. June stepped past Michael and blurted, "You're leaving us here by ourselves? You can't do that!"

"Of course I can. What do you expect?"

"You said you were here to help us, to ... to *facilitate*." She interposed herself between Crane and the door.

"And it worked. You believed it. Look, we lied, okay? It's our job. What are you going to do, sue?"

He tried to sidestep around her, but she body-blocked his way out.

"Look," he said, "we wanted that gospel, same as you. Did you really think the American embassy can afford to send its personnel scampering for every American in trouble? We'd never have time for anything else."

"June," Michael said, "we talked about this, remember? The gospel's the only thing worth risking diplomatic relations over."

Crane nodded. "But we lost, so now we all go our separate ways. We simply can't risk an international incident over a couple of loose-cannon tourists, and that's all there is to it. Sorry."

He moved to pass, but June grabbed him by his jacket lapels. "How can you *do* this? They're trying to *kill* us!"

Michael stepped forward and took her arm. "If the Israelis have the gospel, it's over. They'll leave us alone now." *I hope.*

Her grip loosened, and Crane slipped from her grasp as she staggered back a step to let him pass. Laura started to open the door, but Crane straight-armed it shut and turned.

"Look," he said, "what happened last night is an embarrassment to the Israelis, and they're sure to write it off. The police here might not get the news for a couple hours, but after that? You can probably move out like nothing happened. Before you know it you'll be back in the land of milk, honey and Häagen-Dazs."

"But you're not going to wait around and see," Michael said. "Too much risk."

Crane shrugged. "You've got the groceries and the fruit baskets. Watch a little tube, catch a few Z's. Before you know it, you'll be into the next day and safe to go. Tell you what, I'll even give Muhammad a call. It's too risky for him to come, but he might know someone who can help you out."

He started to leave, but then turned back. "We'll leave the Do Not Disturb signs on the doors. We're not checking out. We'll leave through the back, and the room's paid for another three nights. Just be quiet and be cool, and expect the best."

He motioned June away from the door while Laura checked the hallway through the peephole. And then they were gone, their last thoughtfulness being to leave the keycards behind.

* * *

Hours later, June lounged on the bed while Michael repacked his shoulder bag, saving the two silenced automatics for last. A smile came to him, accompanied by the thought, *Bet Dad never imagined I'd ever need my stampeding pack for things like this.* He removed the clip from each automatic, drew back the slide with the slinking whisper of well-oiled metal and ejected the round in the chamber. Then he locked the slides in the open position, picked up the ejected rounds using a hand towel and reloaded them into the clips.

"Fingerprints?" she asked.

He nodded while wiping down the clips with the towel.

"You told me you don't like guns."

"They can save your life, if you know how to use them."

She studied his face. "And do you? Know how to use them, that is."

"I'm no Wyatt Earp, but I've seen all the Dirty Harry movies. Some twice."

"Michael, can I hit you?"

He looked up and smiled, glad to see her mischievousness resurface. She was no doubt buoyed by the prospect of returning home minus the bullet holes and casket. He dropped the gun on the bed and held up both hands in surrender. "Can I stop you?"

"After what I saw this morning, I imagine you could."

She watched as he picked up the gun and lowered the slide on an empty chamber, replaced the clip using the hand towel and applied the safety. Then he wrapped each gun in a pillowcase and returned them to his bag.

"You're playing with me," she said. "You handle those like a pro."

"Had a little training."

"More than a little, I think. Not having a woman in your life has given you time for some things I'm not sure I want to know about."

He closed his bag, swung it to the floor and lay down on the bed beside her, his head propped in his hand. "Just preparing for the final battle, *Habeebatee.*"

"The Day of Judgment?"

"Marriage."

"Unh," she groaned. "What about that Jet Li stuff this morning? What was that? Kung Fu, Kung Pao, Feng Shui, Sushi Rice, what was it?"

"I've been studying 'Uh-Duh.' It's the ancient martial art of panicking under pressure and running straight at leveled spears, bared swords and loaded guns. It's taught in the traditional manner, where the sensei arranges the classroom in lines and then says something like, 'If somebody points a gun at you, give him your wallet,' and the students all slap their foreheads and shout, 'Uh-Duh, Sensei!' Obviously, I need more practice."

She rolled her eyes, but then her face stilled. "I took self-defense classes for a couple of years. Nothing fancy. But this morning, I froze. Or panicked. Or both. First in the fight, then in the bathroom crawlspace. I mean, I totally lost control."

"Not totally," he said. "That kick of yours saved my life. Yours too."

She rolled over, sat up and crossed her legs in the middle of the bed. "That was panic. When you gave me the gun in the crawlspace, I almost shot you. Also panic."

He pushed himself up to a sitting position. "Fear's a killer."

"How do you deal with it?"

He shook his head. "Don't know. You've got to ... swallow it. Recognize the fight that's worth fighting, throw your fear behind you, turn on the war and not turn it off until it's over."

She closed her eyes, took a deep breath, held it, and then exhaled through pursed lips. "I can do that."

"God willing, you'll never have to again." He ran his tongue over his teeth. "Toothbrush. Left it upstairs."

"Hate that feeling."

"Lose anything important?"

"Clothes and teddy bear."

"Teddy bear." He nodded with a contemplative frown. "You have a teddy bear?"

"I have a hug," she said, her eyes sparkling.

"A—?"

"You know, a herd of cattle, a flock of sheep, a hug of teddy bears. A group of teddy bears is called a hug. They drew straws for who would come with me."

"Believe it or not, I understand that," he said. "Miss him?"

"Binky? Oh yeah. Been with me for years."

There didn't seem to be anything more to say, so they sat in silence and surfed their thoughts. She sighed. He sighed. She stood and paced. He watched her pace. She sat down on the bed again. They both sighed, and studied one another as if trying to guess each other's thoughts.

"Braddot," she said.

"Yeah, me too." He shook his head. "Sad. More than sad. Infuriating."

"There's something I don't get. How did he know to look in Abu Ahmed's camp?"

He looked down at his toes. "Braddot's job was to clean and categorize the scroll fragments from Cave 4. Two thousand years of dust, bat guano, rat urine. Miserable work. But one day he found some goat hairs and goat-sized droppings."

"How did goat droppings lead to Abu Ahmed?"

"It got him thinking." He stood and grabbed one of the grocery bags from the dresser, emptied it onto the bed and started pawing through the contents. "The Bedouin beat the scientists to Cave 4. Everybody knew that. But they wouldn't have let their goats in, would they? After all, goats eat *everything*. Furthermore, the story of how the Bedouin discovered Cave 4—and I mean the story Braddot knew, *not* the one Abu Ahmed told us—involves a Bedouin child chasing a *partridge*."

He left a box of crackers and a jar of peanut butter on the bed, shoveled the rest back into the bag. "There was no goat in the story he knew, so he asked around. He was a bit of an explorer, used to tramping around on his own. After he visited a number of the Bedouin camps, he found Abu Ahmed. You know the re—"

A gentle knock at the door cut him off, followed by a rustle of paper. He pointed at June, then the bathroom door. Once she was hidden he eased to the door, gun in hand. Thirty seconds later, he hailed her from the bathroom, and met her with a smile and a sheet of paper. "The cavalry's arrived," he said. "Found this shoved under the door."

The note read, *Don't move. Not safe. Wait for pizza man and be ready to leave quickly. Hamid.*

June looked at him and whispered, "Give me a gun."

"Why?"

"I'd kill for a pizza right now."

* * *

Hamid returned in the evening, his head swaddled in his black-and-white *guttra* in the style of the Palestinian laborers, leaving only the eyes exposed. His red vest said "Pizza Hut," the red soft-sided hotbox said "Pizza Hut," and the mouthwatering vapors he trailed shouted, "Deep Dish Meat-Lover's Special coming through, don't look at my face, just think how much you want to stuff your mouth with Pizza Hut."

The policemen at the hotel entrance stopped him anyway and ordered him to unwrap and rewrap his *guttra*. But they eyed the tantalizing hotbox with more interest than his face, and waved him through. Fifteen minutes later, the swaddled pizza man reappeared, this time headed for the door.

* * *

Michael traversed half the hotel lobby before he realized his stupid mistake. The hotbox was still full, and he carried it flat in front of him, as if making a delivery. But he was on his way out, not in. *Shugar!* he thought. *How do I get out of this one?*

For a split-second he considered retracing his steps, but one glance told him the Israeli policeman at the door had already spotted him and turned in his direction.

There had been little time for planning. Hamid had appeared, handed June a pizza box containing an *abaya*, headscarf and veil. He switched clothes with Michael and wrapped his scarf around Michael's head. Michael, now the pizza man, left first, the swarthy Palestinian and his "wife," covered in head-to-toe black, well behind. In the rush, they forgot to leave the decoy pizzas behind.

Michael kept his stride, even when he felt his legs turn to lead under the policeman's intense gaze.

The second policeman saw his partner's focused interest and also turned as Michael approached their position by the door. Mind blank and moving as if programmed, Michael tried to prepare for whatever came next.

"They stiff you?" the first policeman asked in perfect Arabic.

Michael nodded dumbly. Almost alongside the policeman, he bowed his head and tried to step past. The policeman reached out a hand and caught Michael by the arm. At the other end of the lobby an Arab couple, the lady bearing a satchel and the man a shoulder bag, slowed almost to a stop.

"Tell you what, *I'll* buy one," the policeman offered. "What toppings?"

Suddenly, the mist over Michael's mind cleared and the doughnuts-and-coffee light blinked on. It was evening. These were policemen. And here were pizzas! Tonight, he would get his black belt in Uh-Duh.

"They didn't deserve them," he replied in what he hoped was perfect Arabic. "Here, take both."

He slipped the pizza boxes from the container and into the policeman's hands, collapsed the hotbox and swung it under his arm, and in the same motion turned to the door.

He only got three steps before he heard, "Hey, stop!"

* * *

At the other end of the lobby, Hamid practically yelped. Once, during childbirth, his wife had dug her fingernails into his arm "to let you share the pain." That was nothing compared to what Miss

Cody did to him now. The two had watched events unfold, numbly, but when the policeman yelled for Michael to stop, she laid a hand of steel on his forearm and not just squeezed, but *crushed*.

Aiee, he thought, *if we can bottle that strength, we can get Jerusalem back.*

* * *

Michael froze, but couldn't bring himself to turn around. A couple of quick footsteps approached, then the policeman drew beside him and pressed money into his hand. "No, my friend," he said, and patted him on the back with his free hand, "if we don't pay, then *we're* the ones who don't deserve. Shalom."

Subhan'Allah, Michael thought, mind still in Arabic mode, *glory be to God, he's one of the good guys*. Not until he hit the parking lot did he wonder if the Israeli policeman's noble ethic extended to larger issues, like land.

* * *

PM Leib sat at his desk and rocked his head, cradling it in his hands. "Is there any *good* news?"

The head of Mossad sat facing him, his expression grim. "The original agents have returned and are back on the case. I briefed them personally."

"Great," Leib said. "Meanwhile, you've alerted Dr. Hansen and his lady friend that we're trying to kill them, put guns into their hands, and lost them."

"Mossad doesn't lose people. We only misplace them."

Leib raised his head and glared across the desk. "For your sake, I hope you're right."

"Don't worry." The director stood to leave. "After what he did to my men, we'll find them. And when we do, we'll send them home in pieces."

"Don't take this personally," Leib said. "We're after the gospel, not them."

"*In pieces*," the director repeated, and turned to the door.

CHAPTER 28

Hamid had crossed over from Amman as soon as Muhammad called. Together they assembled their network of friends and relatives, one of whom provided the Pizza Hut connection. The rest formed an expanded caravan of cars that, using cell phones for communication, helped Muhammad evade roadblocks as he shuttled the pair from their hotel in Ein Bokek to his home in Palestinian-controlled Bethlehem.

Once in the safety of Muhammad's home, Michael and June relaxed enough to enjoy dinner. And dessert. And cup after cup of sweet mint tea. But the caffeine wasn't enough to keep Michael's brain going. Stress had a stranglehold on his sleep center, and attempts to reverse the hold proved futile. So in the tradition of their hosts, June joined the daughters of the family while the men slept together in the living room.

The next morning Muhammad and Hamid left early for prayer, and returned with news that Michael and June were still wanted by the police.

"How do you know?" Michael asked over breakfast.

"Some of our families are divided," Muhammad said, "like yours were in the American Civil War. Most Palestinians fight on the side of Intifada, but some collaborate with the Israelis and play both sides of the fence. We know through them."

"Strange," Michael said. "I thought we'd be off the wanted list by now." He felt a vague suspicion gnaw at his gut, but once again couldn't identify it. Just when he felt he was close, Hamid and Muhammad had a rapid exchange in Arabic, then Muhammad asked, "How did the American embassy know you were in danger?"

Michael struggled with his suspicion, but the image was irretrievable, like trying to recapture a reflection in a pond after a stone is thrown in. He shook his head to clear his mind and sighed. "The same way they knew about Braddot and the gospel. The only person we contacted after learning about Braddot was Trevor Mardle, my father's former boss at Oxford. I can't imagine either Braddot or Mardle as an informant, so one of their phones must be bugged."

The ripples in the water of his mind stilled, and the image he sought jumped out at him. In the same instant, he jerked his head to look around the room. "Oh, my God, where's June?"

"In the kitchen," Muhammad said. He sat up straight and rubbed the slight swell of his middle-aged abdomen. "She says she wants to learn my wife's secrets."

Should've known, he thought. Muhammad's wife, Maryam, was every bit the dream-cook Hamid's wife was, so he hadn't been surprised to learn the two were sisters. This, he learned, was the basis of Muhammad and Hamid's friendship. "Can you call her in here?" he asked, his legs twitching with nervous energy.

A minute later June entered, smacking her lips while she wiped her hands on a patterned hand towel. Specks of flour dusted her hair, a spot of olive oil adorned her sleeve. "This better be goo—"

"They don't have it!" Michael blurted.

She stopped and stared at him, her face clouded with confusion.

"The gospel. Mossad doesn't have it!"

Her face transformed. Caught between disappointment and relief, she looked equally inclined to laughter and tears.

"Look," he said, "if Mossad intercepted the gospel, they should've stopped looking for us. But they haven't. Muhammad's contacts found that out."

She sat where she stood, crossed her legs on the floor and dropped the hand towel into her lap. "Is that all you have? Because maybe—"

"Remember what I told you Braddot said? He said he 'always wanted to visit Bethlehem one last time anyway.' What does the 'anyway' mean? When we spoke, you and I were in Ein Bokek. But he didn't say he looked forward to seeing Ein Bokek, Jerusalem or even the Holy Land. He said *Bethlehem*. Specifically."

She swept a stand of hair from her eyes and tucked it behind her ear. "So what're you saying?"

"I'm saying the scroll's here in Bethlehem. I'm saying I talked about the scroll, and he talked about visiting Bethlehem. He called it his 'destiny.' What does that mean to you?"

He leaned forward, pressing his fists into the carpet, and fixed June with his gaze. "Look, there's nothing in the news about you and me. That means the fight at the hotel's being hushed up. Why? And why are the police still looking for us? Only one reason I can see. The same reason they were trying to kill us in the first place."

"But, I—"

"No buts. Why were they trying to kill us in the first place? Because they were afraid we'd find the gospel before them. But if that's the case, once they got the gospel from Braddot, game's over, we're out of it, everybody goes home. But if they *didn't* get the gospel from Braddot, then they're still searching for it, and seeking to eliminate us from the competition."

He looked from face to face, June's hard to read, Muhammad's animated as he translated rapidly to Hamid.

"Okay, so they didn't take it from Braddot," June said, the tiniest hint of surrender in her voice. "So if not Braddot, where is it?"

"We know he didn't have it on him. So put yourself in this picture. Fifty years ago. Catholic priest in Bethlehem. Needed to hide a sacred text. Where would *you* have hidden it?"

"Church of the Nativity," she said without hesitation.

"Church of the Nativity's right. What else *was* there in Bethlehem back then?"

He tugged her to his side, then looked at the two men. "Here's the plan .... Hamid, you return to the hotel and check the security. It has to be you, because they know Muhammad and me. Oh, and find out what your informant friends know about the assault. We need to know whether the police want us for the gospel, or because we beat up a couple of their guys."

"Beat up?" June said, her eyes crinkling. "More like crippled."

"Well, a couple cracked ribs," Michael said.

"A broken elbow, smashed kneecap, splintered jaw, shattered teeth. What's a little collapsed lung and brain contusion between friends?"

Muhammad finished translating Michael's instructions to Hamid, then turned back with a nod. "Okay," Michael continued, "Muhammad, you call Father Braddot's residence. Talk to his wife, kids, whoever, and—"

"Michael?"

"Just a sec, *Habeebatee,* I'm on a roll here. Ask them—"

"Michael, you might be on a roll, but you just hit a speed bump."

He turned to her and arched an eyebrow, saw mirth on her face.

"You told Muhammad to talk to Father Braddot's wife or kids?"

He shrugged a "So what?"

"*Wife and kids,* Michael? *Father* Braddot? I don't think 'Father' means 'father' in this case."

He closed his eyes, exhaled a sigh. "Right. Good catch. Well, maybe he had a housekeeper. Don't all priests have housekeepers?"

Everybody shrugged, including Hamid even though he didn't understand the question, and Michael even though he'd asked it.

"In any case," Michael continued, "if you find someone, tell them you represent, oh, I don't know, the Israeli Antiquities Authority. That Father Braddot had a scroll on loan, which he was expected to return on this trip, and ask if they know anything about it."

Muhammad nodded, then curiosity crossed his features. "Didn't you say Father Braddot's phone might be bugged? Either his or Dr. Mardle's?"

Michael paused, open-mouthed. Stress, lack of sleep, or a combination of the two had made him thickheaded.

"Let me work on that," Muhammad offered. "There's an electrician here who sells detectors for line taps. You connect it between the wall outlet and the telephone like an answering machine. It blinks green if clear, and red if not. He sells a lot of them because of the situation here."

"Okay. But use a line that can't be traced to you. And if it lights up red, hang up and forget it. I don't want you taking any chances."

"What do *I* do?" June asked.

"You bake cookies, and we'll eat them."

She jabbed an elbow in Michael's ribs, he pretended to double over in pain, and the other two doubled over for real, but in laughter.

* * *

Hamid returned late that afternoon, bringing news of a brawl between two drunks who had exchanged shots, but succeeded only in breaking a few bones. All the same, hotel security was still tighter than usual.

"So I was right," Michael said. "Mossad's covering their tracks. But they're still looking for us because they don't have the gospel, and they're afraid we'll find it first."

Muhammad arrived home two hours later, and reported a green light on the black box while calling Braddot's house. And no, according to his housekeeper, there was no scroll.

"And she knew this," Muhammad added, "because she had to pack the dear departed priest's belongings to be shipped to his 'no-good, blaspheming brother.' And what's *that* alcoholic, fornicating, disbelieving heretic going to do with all these old books and sacraments anyway, might she ask? May he choke on them and burn in hell for all the grief he brought Father Braddot over the years, don't you know? But no, there was no scroll in the rectory or in his carryon bag. How did she know? Because she cleans his house and always packs his bags, don't you know? Who else is going to do it for him? Answer me that!"

By the time the normally stern-faced Palestinian finished an amazingly accurate impression of Father Braddot's Irish housekeeper, they were all aching from laughter. Only when the laughter died did Michael recall, with a heart-quivering thump in his chest, that they were stranded in a foreign country, abandoned by their own embassy, *and* hunted by one of the world's most deadly adversaries, in Mossad's own backyard.

June was the innocent here, but he didn't know how he could protect her, much less himself. *Maybe I can trade the gospel's whereabouts for June's life? Or for both of our lives?* The moment he conceived this thought, he realized Mossad might not want to deal. Even worse, the gospel might not be in the Church of the Nativity, as he assumed. *No*, he decided, *first we've got to get our hands on the gospel. Then we can think about buying our lives with it.*

CHAPTER 29

T
he Church of the Nativity," Muhammad explained while he led Michael and June toward it, "was originally constructed in the fourth century, over a grotto that St. Justin Martyr identified as the birthplace of Jesus. The church's grounds contain a graveyard and rectory, and Franciscan, Greek and Armenian Orthodox convents. And the only public access to the church," he said as he accordioned his tall frame and prepared to slip through a short opening, "is this, called the Door of Humility."

Keeping his position, he added, "The door was a new addition in the sixteenth century. Back then, it had a more practical purpose. They built it low to keep out bandits on horseback."

After he'd followed Muhammad through and straightened up again, Michael found himself beside a guardroom containing two policemen. He tensed, but Muhammad clapped him on the shoulder and led him inside the basilica while June crouch-walked through the Door of Humility and joined them. "Relax," Muhammad said, his voice low. "They're ours."

"Palestinian Authority?" Michael asked.

He nodded. "Following the Oslo Accords, Bethlehem was turned over to the control of the PA. You won't find any uniformed Israelis here."

"What about plain-clothed?" June whispered. "Or Mossad?"

Muhammad shrugged. "Unlikely. But even if a Mossad agent spots you here, he can only report it. If he lets himself be known, it could mean his life. We'll watch carefully to be sure we're not followed when we leave."

Michael scanned a mosaic he recognized, one that dated from the twelfth-century Crusades. "You told me some in the Palestinian Authority collaborate with the Israelis."

"I had a friend check these two out. They're okay."

June looked back at the entrance. "What happens if there's a fire? Where's the fire exit?"

Muhammad shook his head. "Disaster. That's what would happen. All other doorways are either bricked over or locked."

Michael made a mental note of that while he and June followed Muhammad through a Gothic doorway and down a flight of stairs into the Cave of the Nativity, located beneath the church altar. There, Muhammad pointed out the three commemorative altars that mark the Nativity, the Manger and the Adoration of the Magi. The actual birth site bore the 14-point silver Star of Bethlehem, inset in the marble floor. Together, they scanned the floor and walls and found everything either cast in stone permanence, or of such insecurity as to offer an unlikely repository.

"The altars?" June suggested.

A cursory inspection ruled them out, too. Michael stood and stared down at the silver Star of Bethlehem, then said, "Don't you suppose Braddot would've had access to areas tourists and pilgrims couldn't approach?"

"Like?" she asked.

He looked around and sighed. "Like nothing I can see here."

* * *

In the end, the gospel found them. The old nun they had passed upon entering, pale as alabaster and stooped from a lifetime of prayer, greeted them as they exited the grotto's stairs and suggested they each light a candle. When Michael extended his arm to touch flame to taper, she reached out and wrapped her shriveled hand around his, her touch light as a breath of air. Delicately, as if handling a bird's wing, she turned his hand and there, glowing in the flickering flame of a score of candles, shone the solid gold face of the ring on his finger. For a moment nobody moved; in the next moment he jerked his hand free and dropped the match, having burnt the tip of his finger.

"How bold we are," Muhammad said, and all eyes turned to him. "We shy from a flame that licks the tip of our finger for a fraction of a second, and from which we are allowed the luxury of escape. But most of humankind flaunt their disobedience in the face of an eternal fire that engulfs all, and from which there is no escape. Ever."

The nun's first words were to Michael. "I've been waiting for you."

He gazed into blue eyes, ringed red and puffy, then noticed her forceful blinking, as if she'd cried her eyes dry.

"Our dear Father Braddot asked me to prepare for your, and his, arrival," she said. "But as you know, he had a more pressing appointment."

"Sister—"

"Sister Sarah, but call me 'E'," she said with a weak smile. "And no, it's not 'E' as in the pill 'Ecstasy.' A couple of our younger pilgrims from the West shocked me with that suggestion."

Her smile twitched, something between whimsical and nervous, but its warmth continued to invade her features. "I finished high school with a circle of four friends. We kept in touch over the years, but my path was so different from any of theirs that, after a while, they started calling me 'E.' They were the A, B, C and D of what they considered normal in our culture, but I was 'E,' as in the multiple-choice question, where 'E' means 'none of the above.' I was none of the above. Get it?"

Michael and June exchanged blank expressions. Sister E tugged her habit with one hand, pointed straight up with the other and repeated, "*Nun* of the Above."

* * *

Sister E was American, but after fifty years in the Holy Land she had lost her ability to do business before tea. Her office in the convent was fully equipped, and she busied herself with the tea service as she spoke.

"I recognized you from the back-cover photo on one of your books," she said to Michael while she prepared their cups.

"Which one?" he asked.

"Oh, they're all the same." She draped teabags into each cup and fumbled with the sugar bowl. "The back cover is the best part of all your books."

He grinned at June and Muhammad. "Ah, another fan."

The warmth left her face, and was slow to return. "Hardly. I tried to get your books removed from the parish library."

"Oh." After a moment, he said, "Just out of curiosity, do you find any fault with my arguments based on the substance of the Bible?"

"It's not a matter of *fact* but of *faith*." She held up a teaspoon. "One or two?"

"Not a matter of fact but of faith." Michael flexed his eyebrows, sighed and shook his head. "One sugar, please. Sweetener might be the only thing we agree upon."

She turned a wizened grimace upon him that he hoped might be a smile, and started handing cups around. He wondered if the gospel she guarded might change her thinking. She had assured him that nobody but Father Braddot ever read it. In fact, only Braddot had the key to the fireproof case in which it was stored. Even now, they would have to pick or drill the lock.

June tactfully drew her away from theology, and whether by instinct or cunning, navigated the conversation to Sister E's connection with Father Braddot.

"We were in love," Sister E explained. "Oh, don't look so shocked. It happens. But in our path, you leave either the Church or one another. So James went back to his home in the States, and I made mine here."

"No regrets?" June asked.

"Oh, I wouldn't say that. Just none enduring enough for me to have booked a ticket home."

After tea, she gave Michael the fireproof case along with a photograph. "How I recognized your ring," she explained, tapping the photograph with one age-gnarled finger.

Michael stared at the photo. "The wax seal. This must be the photograph Frank Tones mentioned in a letter to his daughter,

Rachael. It's the photo he saw in the office of a colleague who worked on the Dead Sea Scrolls Project."

"Father Braddot had copies," she said. "He told me he intended to have them framed."

She wiped a tear from her cheek, and Michael noted dark blots on her habit where others had landed.

"He never read this scroll to me, but before he left America, he told me he wanted you to have it. I was going to fight him over that when he arrived." She leveled hard blue eyes on him. "The very idea of something so precious in the hands of a heretic. But now that he's gone, I'm forced to honor his wish."

* * *

A trip to the locksmith, a short drive back to Muhammad's house, and Michael entered his host's home practically at a run. He ignored lunch, laid the fireproof box out on a floor mat and spread the gospel on the rug. The others gathered around him on their knees.

"Extraordinary," he muttered.

"What? What's extraordinary?" June asked.

"Everything. Remarkably well-preserved. Completely intact. Unusually pliable. And the letters are as clear and vivid as if they'd been scribed yesterday. Simply extraordinary."

He ran his hands over the parchment, and then hefted the scroll jar in one hand. "A scroll jar made from limestone? Fashioned with such precision? I'm no archaeologist, but I grew up with this stuff, and I've never seen anything like it. Maybe Jacob made the jar himself. Like he knew how precious this gospel was."

He tapped the parchment with his finger. "The Qumran scrolls were discolored and brittle, like you'd expect after two thousand years. They had to be steamed before they could be unrolled. Even then, they fell to pieces. This is surely as old, but looks like new."

"A forgery?" Muhammad suggested.

He shook his head. "Nope. No way. Braddot took this gospel from Abu Ahmed in 1957, and it's been with the irascible Sister E ever since. Frank Tones dug up Jacob's scroll and the ring thirty years later." He pointed to the gospel unfurled on the floor at his knees. "This couldn't have been forged, because it was discovered *before* Jacob's scroll. *Before* Jacob's scroll, nobody even knew this gospel existed."

He slipped the ring from his finger, lifted the edge of the gospel and fitted the ring face into the imprint of one of the wax seals. "Perfect match. No, this scroll hasn't been preserved by *man*, it's been preserved by *God*."

June knee-walked closer to the scroll. "What's it say?"

He scanned the text, then placed his finger at the beginning and followed the text right to left, as Aramaic is written. "I'll paraphrase first. Specifics later. Once upon a time, in a land far, far away—"

"Michael ..."

He grinned at her. "Oh, sorry. No, it's 'Greetings, Earthlings, now hear this—'"

"Michael!"

"Dr. Hansen," Muhammad said, his voice low, "what you have in your hands is a sacred scripture. I would suggest that, as such, you should treat it with reverence."

"Right." He kicked his near-giddy elation into a mental corner and turned serious. "Okay, to begin with, this gospel dates to the period of the New Testament. As such, this is the only New Testament-era text to have come out of Qumran. A remarkable find, if only for that reason."

"This isn't a classroom," June said. "Cut to the chase."

"Hush, I'm practicing for how I'll present this to the world on CNN. Now, what was I saying before I was so rudely interrupted?"

She rolled her eyes. "Your arrogance leaves me speechless."

"If only that worked all of the time. In any case, the author identifies himself as ... drum roll please ... James, the brother of Jesus! Oh, *BABY*, where have you *been?*" He threw his arms open as if welcoming a long-lost love, leaned down and kissed the gospel dead center.

"You're going to say *that* on CNN?" she asked while Hamid and Muhammad exchanged confused looks.

"If it'll sell more books, you bet." He continued skimming the text, his finger hovering above the parchment. "Hey, here's something interesting. The New Testament Gospels, the ones we're all familiar with, are written like stories. You know, a sequence of events spread out along a timeline, with many of Jesus' teachings hidden in parables. This one isn't. It's more like a textbook, clearly defining the teachings of Jesus Christ, to whom James refers as 'The Teacher of Righteousness.'"

He stopped speaking, and a moment later whispered, "The Teacher of Righteousness. Yessss." But his whisper was only for himself.

Then he dropped a finger back onto the text. "Okay, here, James wrote that Jesus Christ didn't establish a new law, but rather taught the old, meaning Old Testament law."

"Rabbi Jesus?" June said.

"Hmm. Got a ring to it. Then he lists the Ten Commandments as the foundation of the law Jesus lived and taught. And he clarifies that Jesus was a man and a prophet, but nothing more."

His eyes widened and he didn't speak for several seconds. Finally, he said, "This part's even more amazing. Here, he's saying that the views expressed by the 'Wicked Priest,' whom he also identifies as 'The Man of the Lie,' are heretical. *And*, had they been expressed during the time of Christ's ministry, those teachings would've been condemned. Wow."

"It says 'Wow'?" June asked with a sly smile.

He met her eyes and laughed, more from elation than mirth. "I just mean, wow, this is everything I've been arguing. Wow!"

"So who's the 'Wicked Priest'?"

He patted his head with one hand while he climbed the text with the other. "That's what's so amazing. James identifies the Wicked Priest as Saul of Tarsus, whom we now know as Paul."

"Wow." This one came from Muhammad.

"Yep," Michael said, and turned back to the scroll. "Look here, this is something cool. James mentions the revelation given to Jesus, and, hmm." He scanned the lines once, then a second time. "Shugar!"

"What? What is it?" June asked.

He sighed. "James doesn't say where the revelation is, and it's not in here."

"The *Injeel*," Muhammad said.

"What?" Michael scanned the section a third time.

"The *Injeel*. The gospel of Jesus. That's what it's called. The *Injeel*. Our religion teaches us this."

"Oh, well, James doesn't say. He mentions a book of revelation given to Christ Jesus, but that's all."

"What else?" June asked.

"He speaks of a prophet to follow, who will bear a final law for all mankind. I know, I know," he said, and held up a hand in the direction of his host. "You're going to say the final prophet is Muhammad, the prophet of Islam."

"Actually, they were all prophets of Islam," Muhammad said with a chuckle. "All prophets, Moses and Jesus included, taught submission to the will of God, and that's what 'Islam' means. Just so you know. What was it the sidekick said in the movie *Kangaroo Jack*? 'Here if you need me, Michael.'"

Michael frowned, and June leaned forward and nudged him on the knee. "Anything else?"

"Yeah," he said. "But you might not believe it."

"Try us."

"Oooookay. But I have to give a lead-in here. Remember how Sister E disliked my books?"

"Your books, or you?"

He smiled and eyebrow-shrugged the comment away. "It's because I argue that Trinitarian doctrines don't exist anywhere in the Bible. Rather, Trinitarian beliefs were extracted from *non*–Biblical sources and manipulated into existence centuries later."

"You'll have a hard time selling that to CNN," she said.

"Will I? I'll just refer them to *Harper's Bible Dictionary*, which says, 'The formal doctrine of the Trinity as it was defined by the great church councils of the fourth and fifth centuries is not to be found in the NT.' Even the *New Catholic Encyclopedia* states that it was the product of three centuries of doctrinal development—"

"Please don't give me the—"

"1967 edition, volume 14, page 295."

June sank her head into her hands. "Oh, God, he's citing pages again."

He smiled. "That's not all. Four pages later, this is what they say about the Trinitarian doctrine. 'Among the Apostolic Fathers, there had been nothing even remotely approaching such a mentality or perspective.' When *advocates* of the doctrine write something like that, you'd think people would sit up and listen."

"And then again, maybe not," she muttered between her fingers, then raised her face back up to meet his.

"And then again, maybe not." He stood and walked a circle around the group. "Back to *this* gospel. The point is, during the period it was written and many decades after, Trinitarian Christianity simply didn't exist. What James and Paul differed over was Paul's negation of Old Testament law, and him proposing that Jesus Christ was an intercessor between man and God. The basis of a lot of things, but especially Pauline theology."

June sighed. "What does *that* history have to do with *this* gospel?"

He sat again and lost himself in the text. After a moment, he said, "James ends it by warning, 'This concerns those who were unfaithful together with the Liar, in that they did not listen to the word received by the Teacher of Righteousness from the mouth of God.' ... Oh, *this* is an insult if I've ever seen one. James calls Paul 'the Spouter of the Lie,' 'the Man of Scoffing,' *and* 'the priest who rebelled.' And he cautions not to 'seek smooth things' and to live by the teachings of Jesus, not by—boy, he doesn't pull any punches—not by the lies of Paul."

His finger hovered over the last few lines of text. "He finishes by saying that Jesus Christ never preached Atonement. In other words, he never taught that he would die for the sins of humankind, and he wasn't even crucified in the first place."

"Precisely," Muhammad said.

June sat up straight, her eyes wide. "What? Say that again."

"Precisely," Muhammad repeated.

"No, not you, silly." She nudged him with her elbow but looked at Michael. "Say that again, *Habeebee.*"

Michael glanced between the gospel and Muhammad, who was blushing like an autumn sunset, then looked back down. "He says Jesus Christ wasn't crucified, but was 'raised up' alive. Whew. I've written a lot on this subject, but James' here is the first gospel to confirm it."

He looked up and found that Muhammad had recovered from his blush. "James says that none of the disciples witnessed the crucifixion," he said. "We know this from the Bible, of course. It tells us the disciples deserted Jesus at the Garden of Gethsemane. Christian scholars agree the biblical accounts were based on hearsay, and the four Gospels conflict with one another. Many early Christians even doubted Jesus was crucified. They thought a criminal was crucified in his place."

"I know what my father would say to that," June said.

Michael arched an eyebrow at her, and she postured a defiant face and blustered, "He'd say, 'That's absolutely, totally and completely re-imbecilic-diculous.'"

He grinned at her. "A man of higher education, I take it?"

"Believe it or not. That's why he used 'imbecilic' instead of something more street-worthy."

"Yeah, well, it's *not* ridiculous. The Old Testament was the law of the time, and Deuteronomy teaches that a person who's hanged, which in biblical terms means either crucified or hung by a gibbet, is accursed of God. So a person could be a prophet, or a person could be crucified, but not both. I mean, really, how could a prophet be accursed of God?"

"And without the crucifixion, Pauline theology fails," June mused. "The Resurrection and Atonement depend upon it."

"Precisely. Which means this gospel could create a 9.5 earthquake in the world of Christianity. Which also means every intelligence service in the world would kill to have it, as we have seen."

Muhammad clapped his hands and rubbed them together, nodding toward the food his wife had set out for them. "Which also means," he said, "this could be *our* 'last supper.' Let's eat."

* * *

At roughly the same time Muhammad dripped cucumber-yogurt sauce over Michael's roasted-lamb pita, Sister E returned from her own lunch to her office at the convent. She had gradually reduced her administrative duties over the years, and wasn't accustomed to receiving unannounced visitors, especially male. Both men were seated, but stood with deference as she entered her office.

She sized them up immediately, from their Italian loafers and styled hair to their tailored suits, and wondered what she'd done to deserve a visit from such refined gentlemen. But then she looked from the smooth Mediterranean beauty of the man by her desk into the eyes of the second, the one closest to the door, and felt herself sucked into the feral evil of his soul.

Instinctively she started to withdraw, but he helped her to a chair, insistently, but with a politeness forced upon him by his Church-taught respect for religious elders.

"Sister Sarah?" the first man asked, his voice a melody as he crossed the room to stand over her. "Our letter of introduction."

He handed her an envelope, which she instantly recognized as the official stationery of the Vatican. She read the Pope's request for *fullest cooperation* with these *special sons of the Church*, then glanced into the face of the man beside her. Instantly, as if recoiling from a horror, she turned to the more refined-looking man facing her and sought refuge in his eyes.

"We think you might be able to help us," he said, and fished a tri-fold of papers from the inner pocket of his suit jacket. He unfolded the fax of a computer printout and placed it in one of her withered hands, then pulled a chair close, sat, and took her other hand into his own.

"Dear Sister," he said while he patted the back of her hand, "as you see, the first number Father Braddot telephoned after he received the call from Ein Bokek, or in other words, from Dr. Hansen, was to this office."

He ran a manicured finger along a prominent vein beneath her crinkled rice-paper skin, tracing its tortuous path. "Now we wonder, Sister Sarah, if you would be so kind as to tell us about your conversation with Father Braddot."

CHAPTER 30

Lunch finished, Muhammad served green tea and Michael picked up where he'd left off. "To begin with," he said, "both James and Jesus were 'Teachers of Righteousness.' Jacob's scroll told us this is the gospel of *a* Teacher of Righteousness. Then James, the author of *this* gospel, refers to Jesus Christ as *the* Teacher of Righteousness."

"Those expressions?" Muhammad said. "I've read them before. And everything James called Paul in his gospel? It's all in the Qumran scrolls. The Wicked Priest. The Man of the Lie. The Spouter of the Lie. The Man of Scoffing. The Priest who Rebelled. Those who 'seek smooth things.' It's also in the Qumran scrolls."

Michael spooned sugar into his tea. "Know what else is in there?"

"The passage you quoted," June said. "The one about the unfaithful."

He nodded. "'This concerns those who were unfaithful together with the Liar, in that they did not listen to the word received by the Teacher of Righteousness from the mouth of God.'" He bounced his eyebrows at her. "That passage matches, word for word, a quote from the Qumran scrolls. And *that* proves the Teacher of Righteousness referred to in the Qumran scrolls is actually Jesus Christ, and Paul, the liar and the wicked priest, was his antagonist. And anyone who says otherwise is absolutely, totally and completely re-imbecilic-diculous."

She grinned. "You like that, huh?"

"I only use it out of respect for your father. But the point is, 'the word received by the Teacher of Righteousness from the mouth of God' refers to revelation, and that can only mean Jesus. James didn't receive revelation."

June swept the same stray strand from her eyes, and as always, it fell right back. "So where does this leave us?"

"That's easy. Somehow, we've got to get out of Israel and make the gospel public before Mossad, the CIA, or any *other* interest group kills us for it."

"Why?" Muhammad asked. "This gospel doesn't say anything that hasn't been said before, if not in the Qumran scrolls or by James or Jesus in the Bible, then by scholars like yourself. The true teachings of Jesus, Paul's corruption of his message ... it's all there in other works."

"The *information's* all there," Michael said, "but it's so spread out, it's a trick to piece it together. How many Christians have read the Qumran scrolls? For that matter, how many have read the Bible the whole way through? No, this gospel is priceless. It's written by a true disciple. It's *proof.* It's the keystone that pieces all the scriptural information together, and it makes the teachings of Jesus *prima facie.*"

June nodded. "Latin for 'in your face.' Fitting."

Muhammad waved a hand. "What about denial of the Crucifixion and of the Atonement: of Jesus having died for the sins of humankind? That's new, isn't it?"

Michael scratched his head and sighed. "In a gospel, yes. In history, no. A lot of people sensed something wrong with the story from the beginning. Someone tells them God gave birth to Himself, prayed and fasted to Himself, and then committed suicide on the cross when He was omnipotent and able to save Himself, and they say 'No, don't think so.'"

He threw back his cup of tea, came down wincing when he realized he'd just done this Rachael-style, then stood and paced one end of the room. "People read Pilate's interrogation of Jesus and they find that Matthew records Jesus as having said, 'It is as you say,' and *not one word more.* But John records a detailed conversation between the two. The reader begins to wonder which Gospel to trust. They read Matthew and find the robe Jesus was dressed in was scarlet, but purple according to John. The wine was mixed with gall in Matthew, but myrrh in Mark. And Mark? *He* recorded Jesus being crucified in the third hour. John says it was the sixth. Shall I continue?"

June leaned back on her hands and rolled her eyes. "Knock yourself out."

He narrowed an eye at her and continued pacing. "Suddenly, the biblical account doesn't sound so trustworthy anymore. Keep reading, and the problems get thicker. According to John, Jesus carried the cross. But a Cyrenian named Simon carried it according to Matthew, Mark and Luke. That's why many early Christians believed Simon was crucified in place of Jesus."

With each point he stabbed the air with a finger, as if to poke the audience in its collective chest and back it against a wall. "Luke records the last words of Jesus, something you wouldn't expect a person of piety to mistake, as 'Father, into your hands I commit my spirit.' But John says his last words were 'It is finished.'

"It gets worse *after* the alleged resurrection. Then, any agreement between the Gospels falls apart, like, like ..." He fixed his gaze and jerked his thumb at Hamid, who'd just lifted an over-dunked tea biscuit from his cup. "Like that biscuit."

The sodden biscuit obediently broke off and belly-flopped back into the teacup with a splash.

"You're ranting," June said, and pointed a cocked finger-pistol at Michael. Muhammad hid a smile behind a raised hand. Michael went on undeterred.

"And think about what they say about *who* was at the tomb: Matthew, an angel. John, *two* angels. Mark, a young man. Luke, *two* men. Each Gospel says something different. What the heck's going on here?"

"You're swearing," June said, pointing her finger-pistol at him again.

He brushed her words aside with a sweep of his arm. "Pick up any reference book, and what's the first question you ask: *Who wrote this and can he, or she, be trusted?* So with the differences I just mentioned, shouldn't we wonder which, if *any*, of the Gospels can be trusted? Like, who wrote John, the most famous of the Gospels? Nobody knows. It was written anonymously, twelve years after he died!"

"You're annoying," June said. This time, she pointed both finger-pistols at him and fired. Her hands bucked under the imaginary recoil, then she leveled her index fingers at him again. "Interesting, but annoying."

He swept over to where the gospel lay flattened on the rug and knelt in front of it. "Don't you get it? You find these discrepancies in the Bible, and how do they make you feel? Secure in trusting your salvation to the Bible?"

She lowered both pistols. "Not exactly."

"I rest my case. So, this gospel of James is priceless. It summarizes the scripture, makes sense of Jesus' teachings and his antagonism by Paul, and all in a couple pages anyone can read and understand. Moreover, it's written by an authority we can trust. *That* will put the faithful onto the truth."

"And *that* will lead them to Islam," Muhammad said.

Michael glanced at their host with a furrowed brow and lips parted.

"Both the Bible and this gospel of James record Jesus as having foretold of a final prophet to follow," Muhammad said. "How do you dismiss Muhammad as the fulfillment of that prediction?"

"You're cornered, Michael," June said, leveled both finger-pistols at him again and fired one after the other with a double-cluck from the side of her mouth. She blew the smoke from her finger-barrels, dropped her guns to the floor and shimmied back to lean against a wall. "So we've got a gospel a lot of people want: people with *real* guns. What do we do?"

Michael toyed with a tuft in the rug. "First, we've got to take the gospel out of Israel. If Mossad gets it, it'll give them a stranglehold over the Christian Right in America, the Vatican, and every other Christian church. We've got to keep it from the CIA, too. They'll jump back into the fray as soon as they realize Mossad doesn't have it. Add to them the various Trinitarian Churches." He threw up his hands in frustration. "It could destroy the foundation of their institutions, so some of them might be willing to kill to keep this gospel from going public, as well."

June sighed. "All that, and stay alive at the same time."

Recalling his earlier fears, he stood and shook the cramp from his leg. "Muhammad, I have a plan, but we'll need your help."

"My life, Dr. Hansen, and all the *falafel* you can eat."

"I won't lie. It's dangerous."

Muhammad patted his right flank meaningfully. "Remember, the Israelis have been trying to kill me since before I was born. In this country, sitting and doing nothing can be dangerous."

* * *

Prime Minister Leib leaned forward in the backseat of his limo and spoke into the scrambled cell phone. *"Excuse* me? Would you mind repeating that?"

He had to wait until the director of Mossad finished hacking his smoker's cough. "I said, no trace."

"Then find them."

"One of our CIA moles tells us their embassy personnel had them for a few hours, but abandoned them as soon as they thought we had recovered the scroll. What's more, the CIA still thinks we have the scroll, so they haven't kept tabs on them."

"Find them," Leib repeated.

"We're looking. Sooner or later, we'll get them. We always do."

"And *when* you do, I want that scroll!"

The director coughed again, and gave Leib a rattling chuckle. "I'll send it to you on a platter, like the head of John the Baptist."

* * *

"Fascinating, simply fascinating. Not later than 50 CE, I would say." As the old man spoke, he adjusted a pair of bifocals so ancient, they might qualify for radiocarbon dating themselves.

During a thirty-seven-year career, Dr. Khalid Mumtaz established an international reputation in the science of scriptural authentication. His main fame was in paleography; he could date a script to within fifty years of its radiocarbon-dated age solely on its pattern of writing. Now retired, Mumtaz divided his time between breeding French canaries, freelance consulting and, time permitting, forgery. For the most part his forgeries fooled no one. But then, he didn't intend them to. He produced his replicas rapidly and with minimal care for the thriving tourist trade, and profited nicely. Every once in a while, however, he was called upon to produce something of far more exacting standards. At this, there was no one better in the world.

He sat on a raised stool at a long bench, bent over James' gospel laid out in front of him, his mottled bald pate staring Michael in his face. He ran one hand along the edge of the parchment. "Bovine. Probably calf. Fascinating."

Michael scowled at the man's bald head. "Why's bovine parchment so interesting?"

Mumtaz looked up and studied him, as if suddenly realizing he was speaking to an imbecile. "*Doctor* Michael Hansen, you said? And your father was Gerald Hansen? A fine man, an extraordinary archaeologist. Truly topnotch. You were saying?"

"Excuse my ignorance, Dr. Mumtaz. My expertise is in analyzing scripture, not authenticating it."

"I see." Mumtaz readjusted his bifocals. "Perhaps that's for the best. Theology is, after all, such an undemanding field."

Michael bit his tongue. *Just what I need, a condescending forger.*

"Qumran didn't have cows," Mumtaz said. "It's the wrong terrain for them, and there were no cattle bones in the communal dump. So scrolls written on bovine parchment must have originated outside. Considering the content, my guess is this gospel came from Jerusalem."

He returned to inspecting the scroll, and Michael pulled Muhammad to one side and whispered, "Are you sure it's wise to tell him so much about the gospel?"

"He's completely trustworthy. Don't worry."

"I see," Michael said. "The man forges sacred scriptures, but he's completely trustworthy. Sure, why not?"

June reached over to give him a reassuring pat on the hand. He ignored it and turned back to Mumtaz. "How do you get around radiocarbon dating?"

Mumtaz raised his face, and this time it held pride. "Most of the time, we don't have to. Most of my clients are private collectors who come to me as a respected black-market dealer in antiquities."

"A respected black-market dealer," now there's *an oxymoron,* Michael mused as he gave Muhammad a nervous glance. *And we're trusting this guy with a gospel that can revise the entire canon of Christianity?*

"The collectors cannot carbon date," Mumtaz said, "because of international antiquity laws. If they send a sample for analysis, it puts them at risk of having to explain where it came from. However, to be on the safe side, I laminate a fragment of ancient parchment of known date onto one corner, and then tease it off in the client's presence. If they're bold enough to send this sample for radiocarbon dating, they'll get back the answer they hope for."

Right, Michael thought with an inward groan. *Completely trustworthy. No doubt about it.*

He left Hamid to supervise Mumtaz at his work, but turned at the door. "How long will it take?"

Mumtaz turned on his stool to face him and adjusted his vintage bifocals. "You can't rush perfection, Dr. Hansen. I have to mix pigments, scribe the text, weather the parchment in the clothes dryer and age it in the oven. I need four to five hours to scribe a two-thousand-year-old gospel."

"Think the switch will work?" June asked as they left.

Michael nodded with more certainty than he felt. "It only has to fool Mossad long enough to allow us out of the country."

· * * *

Muhammad returned home with Hamid shortly before midnight. They watched as Michael slipped the signet ring back on his finger, then unrolled the scrolls side-by-side on the floor. "Extraordinary," he said, and shook his head. "If Dr. Mumtaz hadn't changed the spacing of the wax seals, I wouldn't be able to tell the copy from the original."

They took photos of both scrolls, which Muhammad developed the next morning. Michael kept the pictures of the authentic gospel, but threw the photos of the fake into a cheap plastic purse, the kind carried by little girls, and handed it to Hamid.

A few hours later, Muhammad drove him to a local hotel. He needed to make two calls: one from a landline, another from his cell phone, using one of his few remaining prepaid cards.

"We'll make the call from the room first," Muhammad said as he strolled the hallway, key in hand.

Michael glanced over his shoulder at him. "What if the guests come back?"

"No chance. They're on a prearranged bus tour. My uncle is the hotel manager, remember? He sent one of my cousins to keep an eye on them. If they leave the group, he'll call to let me know."

He opened the room door and ushered Michael inside, then connected his black box to the phone line and handed Michael the receiver. "Dial six for room service."

"Very funny. If this call *is* traced, whoever's staying in this room might get some ugly visitors tonight."

"O ye of little faith." Muhammad pulled pliers from his back pocket while he scanned the disheveled room. "How can a family make this much mess in a single night? Disgusting. Okay, you make your call, and I'll disable the toilet. They have three children. With the toilet broken, they'll need a room change when they return."

* * *

Trevor Mardle answered on the second ring, and Michael didn't flinch when he saw the light on the black box switch from green to red. Father Braddot's phone wasn't bugged, so that meant Mardle's had to be.

Acting according to plan, he told Mardle everything that had happened and finished with, "I have to sell James' gospel to the Israelis. It's the only way June and I can get out of this alive."

"When?" Mardle asked.

"As soon as possible. Every moment it's with us, we're at risk. We'll try to arrange the exchange in a public place. Our plan is to meet at the Church of the Nativity in two days, eleven in the morning in the grotto." He gave a bitter chuckle. "I can't imagine them saying no, can you? So stay by your phone during that time, and we'll call when it's over. Wish us well."

And Mardle did.

Michael's next call, this one a cell phone call to Mossad's central office, was of considerably greater sensitivity.

CHAPTER 31

Trevor Mardle sat back, reviewed the phone conversation in his mind, and clasped his hands together. The gospel of James, a treasure upon which the salvation of humankind might depend, hidden for two millennia. *And now it's going to be lost again! The mere thought—*

A couple of footfalls, a knock on the door, a twist of the doorknob, and his colleague and competitor stood framed in the doorway.

"There's a quaint social custom of waiting to hear 'Come in' before opening a door, Terry," Mardle said with undisguised annoyance.

"We need to talk." Falson entered and locked the door behind him, then turned back to meet Mardle's astonished face. "Now."

* * *

Forty minutes later, a lower-level Mossad functionary followed up on Michael's phone call and claimed a child's plastic purse from the lost-and-found at the Church of the Holy Sepulchre in Jerusalem.

Twenty minutes later, the purse cleared security. Immediately after, the photos of the forged gospel were forwarded for translation.

Three hours more, and the director of Mossad personally carried the file to Prime Minister Leib's office.

"Lunch?" he said as he entered.

Leib looked up from beneath heavy eyebrows and froze, his pen halfway through his signature. "You've got something."

"Yeah. An appetite."

Leib finished his signature, threw down the pen, then sat back and swiveled in his chair. He nodded at the folder the director still held. "Whatcha got?"

"They want to sell us the scroll. Day after tomorrow. They'll call to say where." He dropped the folder on Leib's desk and sat down.

"Their price?"

The director hacked his smoker's cough and motioned to the folder. Leib leaned forward, flipped it open and read. Five minutes later he closed the folder, still holding the translation of the gospel in his hands. "Idiots. The gospel of Jesus' brother? It's worth a hundred times their asking price. Still …"

He placed the translation on top of the folder and reclined back in his chair. "Still, ten million dollars is ten million dollars."

"Plus the diamond he's demanding," the director said. "That could be worth another ten mil."

Leib grunted, and the director fished a pack of cigarettes from his jacket pocket, jiggled two steps of butts out and plucked the longest with his lips. He produced a lighter from his pocket, and the cigarette danced on his lips as he spoke.

"Hey," Leib said, "stink up your own office."

"Why, when I can stink up yours?"

"Don't you—"

He lit up, inhaled and blew a mushroom cloud toward the ceiling.

"Awww," Leib said, "I'm going to enjoy firing you."

"Can't. I'm too good. You need me."

Too cocky, and quickly becoming a liability, Leib calculated, but said nothing.

"We captured the SIM code from his mobile when Hansen made the call. If we find them before the exchange, we'll take them out clean and snag the scroll, free of charge. If we can't whack them until *after* the exchange, we can target his SIM card with rockets."

Leib sat up straight. "Make sure you don't damage the scroll."

"I already gave instructions." He tapped ash into an ashtray beside the chair. "If you don't like smoking, what's the ashtray for?"

"People more important than you."

"They exist?" He nodded a smirk at Leib. "The rocket order will be activated immediately following the exchange. As I said, the first call he makes, we'll send him home in pieces."

You made a rocket order without my approval? Leib filed the thought away and said, "Don't forget a cover story. Bundle him and the girl off to the morgue with a Palestinian. Do we have any Palestinians on ice who were killed in explosions?"

"Several." The director took another puff and smiled. He'd introduced Leib to the idea, and it had served them well over the years. The body of a "disappeared" Palestinian activist, one of many preserved in a freezer for the occasion, would be warmed and placed in the ambulance before picking up the targets' corpses. By the time they arrived at the morgue, one big unhappy dead family, nobody would doubt the government's claim to a Hamas connection. In this case, two Western academics went too far with their sensitivities and, tragically, were caught in a crossfire. It would take the heat off Mossad while warning any others who harbored obstructionist ideology.

* * *

The pair in Muhammad's living room shattered Michael's expectations. One was old enough to be a grandfather, the other in his late teens, yet they worked together as if of one mind. He was stunned by the speed with which they labored, and that one of them had actually grown old in this line of work.

He drew himself over to where Muhammad sat on the floor and muttered, "Do they always work in peoples' homes, the wives cooking in the kitchen, kids playing in the other room?"

"I don't know," he answered. "It's my first time too."

"What's the problem?" Rasheed, the teenager, asked in perfect English. He didn't look up, and his hands never stopped dancing over his project, spread out on the floor in front of him.

267

"Well, the kids, for one," Michael said.

"Children learn by seeing, then by doing," Rasheed said as he worked. "The Zionists teach their children to shoot from the age they can hold a gun."

Michael glanced at Muhammad's face and read concern, which Rasheed saw but ignored as he continued. "We're called terrorists, but Israeli rockets and bombs are equally indiscriminate. Do you think that because our children are maimed or killed by a smart bomb, that in any way lessens the horror?"

Michael said nothing, so Rasheed stilled his hands and turned from his work, kneeling on one knee. "When the Israelis kill our women and children, they call it 'collateral damage' and hush it up. But when theirs die, they call it terrorism, saturate the news and make movies about it. Tell me, when was the last time you saw a Palestinian in the occupied territories who was *not* terrorized? They've all buried someone in their family, and live with the Zionists' daily humiliation and terrorism. But the Palestinians don't control the media, so nobody knows."

Michael swallowed hard in the face of the youth's intensity, and said, "Rasheed, it's all wrong." As he spoke, he sensed Muhammad's vigorous nod of agreement beside him. "Whether by Israelis or Palestinians, terrorism is wrong. If it were open warfare, unconventional tactics might be accepted. But as it is—"

"You speak the Western, Zionist-controlled media lines," Rasheed snapped back. "'*If* it were open warfare'? What do you call this, if not open warfare? They invade our country, drive us out of our homes and off our land, restrict our livelihood, kill our women and children, impose sanctions and curfews—"

"Rasheed," Michael interrupted gently, "I know the argument. I'm just saying terrorism is wrong. By *both* sides."

Muhammad leaned forward and tapped Michael on the knee. "Even Muslim scholars debate this issue, and like Rasheed and me, they don't agree. There are a few extremists, but most moderates teach that terrorism is contrary to both humanity and Islam."

"So what do you want us to do?" Rasheed said. "Sit back and let them kill us?"

Muhammad met the youth's angry gaze with mournful eyes. "I expect honorable conflict. And if not that, then yes, better to suffer and die, without having transgressed the laws of our Creator, than to live in disobedience and earn his wrath."

Rasheed turned angrily away from them. After a moment he said, "Okay, gather around. Briefcase Bombs 101."

Michael and Muhammad huddled close on the floor as the older bomb expert moved to one side. Rasheed ran his hands over a maze of wires, electrical components and junction boxes. "This nest? Don't touch. We've lined the briefcase walls with glass, taped with the same alarm foil used on windows in home security systems. If anybody fractures the glass while trying to disarm the mechanism, the foil tears, the circuit is cut, and you can guess the rest. So whatever you do, don't drop the case."

He pointed to two self-retracting cords that he'd harvested from talking dolls. "Attach these to the opposite lid before closing. Activate the device with this switch here, close the lid *slowly*, and allow the cords to retract. After that, whatever you do, *don't reopen it.*"

"Or the briefcase talks," Michael said somberly.

"And that would be bad."

Michael nodded as he scanned the briefcase's crowded interior.

Rasheed pointed to an external digital display beside the handle. "Once activated, this clock will start its countdown. This here? This is where you place your documents."

Michael followed the youth's finger to the capped section of PVC tubing centered between two oily bricks wrapped in grease-paper and smelling of almonds and fuel oil. He smiled. The PVC tube was secure, watertight and, most important, scroll-sized.

* * *

"You'll call Sister E?" Muhammad asked when he returned to the room after showing the bomb experts out.

"You might get further with her," Michael said. He closed the briefcase and stood it in a corner. "She's not exactly a charter member of my fan club."

Muhammad took out his cell phone and made the call. Minutes later, he hung up and said, "Nice lady. She said she looks forward to seeing us again, and invites us to stay for tea."

They spent the next day in preparations. The morning of their scheduled meeting, Michael assembled his cell phone and called Mossad. The moment the line opened, he gave his name and overspoke the switchboard operator's greeting. He knew the message would be recorded, and Muhammad had cautioned against allowing them to stall him. "Church of the Nativity," he said. "11:00 AM, one man only, no wires. Money in two suitcases, stand them upright on the car's roof in the parking lot." He clicked off and immediately disassembled his phone.

Muhammad lowered his wristwatch. "Eleven seconds. No way could they trace that call."

* * *

Seven minutes later, the transcript of the call was on the Mossad director's desk. He immediately checked the phone record. The line hadn't been open long enough to allow satellite location of the source, but the SIM card was the same.

"Ha!" he said to no one in particular. "Almost got 'em."

CHAPTER 32

Muhammad arrived at the Church of the Nativity with a tour group an hour early, and Michael and June followed in the next busload.

June looked around the church. "I don't see any Americans, do you?"

Michael and Muhammad preceded her down the steps and into the grotto. They didn't see any Westerners there, either. "Something's wrong," Michael said. "When I telephoned Dr. Mardle to tell him Father Braddot had the gospel, both the CIA and Mossad knew about it within hours. Then I called him two days ago to tell him about this meeting, but it's like no one was listening to that call."

He shrugged and scanned the room again. "I leaked our intention to sell the gospel, thinking it would eliminate suspicion from Mossad, and cue the CIA to show up and provide security. So where *are* they?"

"The Palestinian police we passed on the way in are on our side," Muhammad said. "I told them to play along. But if there's a problem, they'll back us up."

"Hopefully, they won't have to." Michael turned to the stairs and froze, his mouth agape. His mouth was still open when Dr. Mardle stepped into the grotto, Terry Falson at his heels. Muhammad stepped to the side and immediately assumed the role of a tourist viewing the antique wall hangings.

Mardle smiled at Michael. "Couldn't miss the show, now could we, dear boy."

June blanched and exchanged looks with Michael, her eyes wide.

"You've got to get out of here," Michael said as he shook first Mardle's hand, then Falson's. "We can't guarantee your safety."

Mardle refused to leave, and they argued until a mismatched pair entered the grotto and introduced themselves as Yogi and Boo-Boo. Michael immediately noticed the tasteless skull and crossbones that dangled from one of Yogi's earlobes.

"I specified one man. *Only* one." Michael focused on Yogi, but saw Mardle and Falson step back to the wall in his peripheral vision.

The bigger of the two Mossad agents drew his fat lips into something between a smile and a snarl. "You got two."

"You're early."

"Look who's talking," Yogi said.

Michael's nerves took a turn around the mental winch. The Church of the Nativity was sacrosanct, inviolable. Even when Palestinian fighters took refuge in the church two years earlier, the Israelis had waited them out rather than mount an assault. Which was exactly why he'd picked the spot to begin with.

Michael's cell phone rang, and Hamid reported he had received the suitcases, transferred the money to garbage bags and swept over them with a handheld metal detector. He had found and removed two tracking devices, after which the money swept clean.

Two minutes later, he called again from his vehicle. He was being followed.

Michael turned to Yogi. "Call them off."

With the air of a man with all the time in the world, Yogi pulled a phone from beneath his Bermuda shirt and made a call.

A mile away, Hamid changed SIM cards. Five minutes later, he called and signaled all clear, but to wait. Another five minutes and another SIM card, and he reported he was safely on his own.

* * *

Five miles away, in the heart of Jerusalem, the director of Mossad slammed his fist to the table. The audio monitor and everybody in the room jumped.

"Nothing. We have *nothing*!"

Each call received by Michael's cell phone had been traced to the bagman. If the bagman had used the same SIM card twice, they'd have his location. As it was ...

"We have the make, model and license number of the car."

The director spun around and locked eyes with the dark, gangly rookie who had spoken. The room fell silent as he stalked across the room, clerks easing away from their positions beside the doomed employee, who stood and straightened to attention.

The director brought his face within an inch of the rookie's, and barked from one corner of his mouth, "David!"

A young clerk behind him sat bolt upright, hurriedly tapped his keyboard while scanning his computer screen, shouted "Stolen!" over his shoulder, and then lowered his gaze to the floor.

"Borrowed, more likely." The director flashed a cold smile. "But we'll never know. We'll find it abandoned. No fingerprints. Locals are Palestinians, so even if they know everything, they'll tell us nothing. I can't even place a roadblock or notify police, because the Palestinian Authority controls Bethlehem, not me."

"We might get lucky with one of our informants, sir."

The director lifted a lit cigarette to his lips, took a strong pull, and then blew a cloud of smoke in the rookie's face. "Who's going to think twice about a Palestinian humping garbage bags, face wrapped in his *guttra* like half the laborers in the city? Any more strokes of genius, Einstein?" He turned to the room and shouted, "Any more strokes of genius, *anybody?*"

Behind him, the rookie slumped back into his chair with a creak. The director cursed, flipped his smoldering cigarette over his shoulder and stomped across the room as the rookie bolted from his chair, brushing red-hot ash from his lap.

* * *

At the same instant the Mossad director said a silent prayer for Michael's SIM card to remain in use, Michael fiddled with the cell phone in his pocket, dangerously distracted by the unexpected turn of events. Mardle and Falson being here meant two more souls might get caught in the crossfire.

"You've got what you want, now it's our turn." Yogi gestured to the briefcase in Michael's hand.

While waiting for Hamid's calls, Michael had quickly assessed both men. Yogi was the bigger of the two, powerfully built but turning to fat. Definitely not smarter than the average bear. Boo-Boo, on the other hand, had a disconcertingly familiar face, though he couldn't place it no matter how hard he'd tried. Short and wiry, this man looked lightning-quick. If the top blew off the blender, he'd have to take Boo-Boo out first. If he could. He just didn't think Uh-Duh would work with these two.

June opened her capacious handbag and removed the scroll, and the two agents' eyes swung from the briefcase to her, then back at the briefcase. The unasked question hovered in their eyes: *Sooo ... what's the briefcase for?*

The grotto filled as a new busload of pilgrims filed through.

"We're not from the farm," Yogi said. "Before anybody goes anywhere, this gets authenticated."

Michael noted that Boo-Boo not only kept silent while his partner spoke, but eased two steps back. Michael flicked his eyes to June's, then back to Yogi's. He had expected the Mossad agent to match the plastic-purse photos with the gospel and assume the best. He'd told Dr. Mardle of his plans to sell the gospel to Mossad, and had expected that message to get through and be believed. But if the suspicion in the air was anything to judge by, the record of his phone call *hadn't* gotten through. If the agents found the gospel to be fake now ...

He glanced again at June, noticed a sheen of sweat on her forehead, and knew her thoughts were similar.

Yogi lowered his phone and flipped it shut with a slap of plastic. "He's on his way."

Michael gave June another nervous glance, then scanned the faces of Dr. Mardle and his colleague, and felt relief at their clueless expressions. Of all the surprises, they were the most worrisome. Never had he considered that Mardle might jump a plane and crash this meeting. He suddenly felt his heart pound, and realized his grip on the briefcase was wet. As he knew from the movies, the best-laid plans always crumbled to pieces. But that was for the drama and plot. He'd thought himself smart enough to have figured out all the angles, yet now realized he'd reckoned wrong.

At that instant, one of the angles he'd failed to consider stumbled down the stairs and into the grotto.

"Ah, Dr. Michael Hansen. I heard so much about you from your father," the old man said. He straightened from his stumble and adjusted his vintage bifocals. "How amusing that we should meet for the first time under such circumstances."

Five minutes later, the man muttered, "Fascinating, just fascinating. Bovine, I believe. Most likely calfskin."

"Could be pigskin for all I care," Yogi said. "Just tell us if it's authentic, old man."

Lips pursed, Dr. Mumtaz lifted his eyes from the scroll, which lay open on the Altar of the Manger. "Only the most precious of scrolls were written on calfskin, my dear boy. Don't they teach you anything in your line of work?"

Yogi snorted. "They teach us to kill old Palestinian professors who annoy us."

Boo-Boo spoke from behind him, eyes twinkling. "Actually, they also teach us to kill old Palestinian professors who *don't* annoy us."

Where have I seen him before? Michael wondered, his mind grating on the question. He wished just this once that his exceptional memory for words also applied to faces.

Yogi glanced over his shoulder at his partner and then faced Michael, causing the skull-and-crossbones earring to flash from the ceiling lights. A fat, lazy smile draped across his fat, lazy face. "They just teach us to kill Palestinians, okay? Now, Professor, you do your job, or we'll do ours."

But Mumtaz was already at work. With scalpel and forceps, he teased a triangle of parchment from one corner, then dropped the fragment into a plastic sleeve, placed it in a self-sealing envelope and passed it across. Yogi applied an adhesive foil seal that displayed a security hologram, signed across the seal and passed it back. Mumtaz slid the envelope into the inner pocket of his well-worn blazer and adjusted his bifocals. "You'll have the radiocarbon results tomorrow," he said dryly. "From a visual, I'd say it's definitely original, dated to approximately 50 CE." He rolled up the scroll while he spoke and then, to Michael's surprise, handed it to him, not Yogi.

"Hey," Yogi said, but then closed his mouth when he looked down the single black eye of the silenced 9-millimeter in Michael's hand.

"Take it easy," Michael said. "Back up. And no stupid stuff, like covering your buddy as you go. Boo-Boo, to the side, please. Slowly."

The pilgrims in the chamber stilled, and the two tourists closest to the stairwell quietly slipped out. Boo-Boo's hands drifted to his jacket opening. Muhammad saw and slipped up behind him. Boo-Boo's eyes bugged, and Michael knew Muhammad had tapped him in the back with something cold, hard, and .45-caliber.

Muhammad stepped back quickly, leaving Boo-Boo with no way to know where he was standing. Boo-Boo couldn't do anything but say, "Yogi, don't. We're covered."

Yogi drooped his eyelids to half-mast, slouched his shoulders and pasted a bored look on his face.

June took the briefcase from Michael and placed it on the altar. The moment she lifted the lid, the aroma of almonds and petrochemicals wafted into the chamber. Taking the gospel, she placed it in the briefcase. Then she attached the self-retracting cords to the opposite lid, flicked the activation switch, and closed the case to the sound of dolls' voices jabbering requests for their mommies, their bottles, their potties. The external digital clock began its countdown.

"If you open it again, you don't want to hear what it has to say," Michael said with a wink.

June locked the briefcase and retrieved a tube of Insta-Glue from her purse. Then she squirted it into the locks and along the seam, placed the briefcase on the floor and stepped back.

The drama over, Michael put the gun down on the altar and pointed to the briefcase. "Take it easy. This is our insurance until we get out of here."

"Pretty stupid insurance," Yogi said, and picked up the case. "I could've dropped you for that stunt."

But Michael noted that Boo-Boo had shifted edgily in the background. Muhammad stepped to one side and stowed his weapon. Michael allowed himself his first deep breath in what seemed like hours.

At the rush of footfalls, Yogi turned to the stairs and yelled in Arabic, "Hold! Stand down! There's no problem down here."

The footfalls slowed and a Palestinian policeman appeared, gun extended in a double-handed grip. He worked his way down in a crouch, back braced against the stairwell's wall.

Yogi reassured him, again in Arabic, but the policeman didn't retreat until he got a nod from Muhammad.

"You've got plenty of time," Michael said as he handed Yogi a map and instructions. "But not if you take a detour to the bomb squad. If you attempt to disarm it, get there too late or fail to make the call, well …"

Most of the tourists, Dr. Mumtaz included, slipped from the chamber, but a few remained as if rooted. Yogi turned on them threateningly. "Why don't you folks clear out of here?"

"What, you kidding?" one said in a thick Italian accent. "This is better than a movie!"

"Your phones," Michael demanded, and extended his left hand.

Yogi nestled the briefcase between his feet, then straightened and stared Michael in the eyes, hands on hips tucked threateningly beneath his Bermuda shirt. "Why?"

Suddenly, Michael understood Yogi for the sadistic, mindless psychopath he was; a man who could only survive in a job that legalized violence. Yogi was the kind of thug who understood force, and nothing but.

"Why give me your phones?" he said. "Because you want to go home tonight in one clean piece, not in a bloody box of a hundred when that bomb blows, that's why."

"Huh, the man has a way with words, doesn't he Boo-Boo?" Yogi muttered over his shoulder, his eyes fixed upon Michael.

But then he blinked. He stood momentarily frozen, and then slowly lifted a hand to his earlobe, where the only thing he found dangling was a severed wire.

Michael had snatched the gun from the altar and fired before he realized what he was doing, as though the gun leapt from the altar into his hand and exploded in the same motion. Yogi didn't even have time to flinch.

"Next time, I'll shoot out your fillings. Got that?" Michael had never before felt such a surge of hatred. And he realized he was on the brink of killing this man.

But it was Yogi who saved himself. The man actually laughed.

"Hoo-kay, two phones coming right up," he said, with a you-got-me-this-time smile and a nod to the gun in Michael's hand.

Michael pocketed Boo-Boo's phone but returned Yogi's with the words, "Call and tell them the gospel is authenticated and you're on your way, but that's all. If you say anything else, I won't send the signal to deactivate the bomb. You can bet on it."

While Yogi made the call, June rummaged in her purse and handed the battery and body of a doctored cell phone to Michael. He drew a SIM card from his pocket, inserted it, assembled the pieces, input a number and exchanged phones with Yogi when he finished his call. The screen of the one he'd handed over was smashed, the display crystallized.

"You got the better deal," Yogi said when he saw the destroyed screen.

Michael had to admire the big man's calm, and borrowed from it while he pocketed Yogi's phone. "Don't worry, it's still under warranty. Now pay attention. Push the green button once to retrieve the number, and a second time to dial. But don't call until you're there. If you aren't within fifty feet of the deactivator, your luck runs out. You'll get an answering machine with my voice. Wait for the beep, leave the message. Oh, and do it with feeling, or I'll think twice about sending the deactivation signal. When the clock hits zero without a boom, you'll be good to go."

The two agents stood for a moment, as if considering their options.

"Clock's ticking, fellas," Michael said, and pointed his gun at the briefcase between Yogi's feet.

Yogi picked it up and turned slowly, looking back as if to snap a mental picture of Michael's face, then took the chamber stairs two steps at a time. Boo-Boo angled after him, turned his back to them, sidestepped the wall of the stairwell, and was gone.

For an instant, Michael's mind replayed an image of a slight man in a lab coat, the man who'd sidestepped the corner of the hospital corridor right before his father died. Even as he thought, *No, it can't be him,* his feet were moving toward the stairwell.

Dr. Mardle pushed off from where he'd flattened himself against the wall and grabbed him by the arm. "Michael," he said in a breathless rush, "you just gave away the greatest scriptural treasure of this age. You—"

Michael glanced at the stairs, Mardle's face, and back at the stairs. He tried to pull away but the elderly professor's grip was firm, despite his age. Giving up, he patted Mardle's hand on his arm and winked. "No, don't worry. It's just that—"

As if awakening from a stupor, his mind cleared of the image of the hospital and he recalled his senses. He took June by the arm and guided her and the two professors out of the grotto and up the stairs, hoping nobody but Mardle heard his final words.

CHAPTER 33

"They've got it!"

Yogi's message was relayed through the Mossad command center in Jerusalem, and the rocket order was activated. If Michael's SIM card didn't locate him, their people would.

Meanwhile, in the grotto, the lone Italian tourist spoke into his sleeve as he emerged from the shadow of one of the wall hangings. "Team one: something's up. Meet me in the parking lot. Team two: follow the Mossad guys, but don't move on them. They don't have the gospel. And everybody, pay attention. This Hansen guy, he's kill-him-or-he'll-kill-you quick. If he goes for a gun, your mother is going to miss you."

* * *

In the parking lot, two burly characters in athletic suits casually started to kick tires and act exceedingly disinterested. Anybody who happened to notice them might have been suspicious, but nobody did. All eyes were on the Door of Humility as Yogi and Boo-Boo drove off.

Just then, two busloads of Palestinian pilgrims drew up and filled the church with a crowd that obscured everything but the exit. They squeezed the Mossad agent still inside the church against one wall as Michael and June ducked behind the pulpit. She threw a black *abaya* over her yellow pantsuit while Michael tore off his red polo, leaving himself in jeans and a black T-shirt. Together, they led Mardle and Falson out the restricted side door, thoughtfully left unlocked by Sister E. Their leaving went unnoticed amidst the busloads of Muhammad's tribe; as prearranged, the women were all dressed in yellow and the men in red shirts. By the time the

Mossad agent worked through the crowd and found Michael's red shirt behind the pulpit, the agents outside wondered why the marks were taking so long to exit the Door of Humility.

* * *

As they ushered Mardle and Falson into the convent next door, June asked, "What if those agents find out the bomb's a fake, and there *is* no deactivator?"

Michael shrugged. "They won't know until the timer hits zero and nothing happens. By then, they'll be on the other side of town. What I want to see is if they try anything dirty. If they do, it'll come back to bite them."

* * *

Ten minutes after Michael led his troupe through the restricted side door of the church, Yogi and Boo-Boo pulled up beside the specified road marker on a desolate stretch of road. Yogi checked the digital timer on the briefcase. "Made it here with time to spare."

Following Michael's instructions, he pushed the green button twice to retrieve the number and dial. He turned to Boo-Boo and said, "Give you a hundred to do this."

"Nope, he said it had to be you." Boo-Boo reached across and patted the flab of Yogi's ample belly. "Anyway, you look more the part."

Yogi grimaced. "I feel like a fool, but here goes."

After four rings, an answering machine picked up and Michael's voice called out from America, inviting callers to leave a message. At the beep, Yogi began singing, "I love you, you love me, we're a happy family ..."

When he finished the Barney song, he thumbed the red button and blew a raspberry at the phone. "You know," he said to Boo-Boo, "when I killed his girlfriend, I didn't even work up a sweat. But after what he did back there, I'm going to kill him slow and painful. Not like that wimpy injection you gave his father. Too easy—"

Michael's answering machine gave an end-of-recording-time

beep. Startled, Yogi's eyes jumped back to the cell phone Michael had given him, still inches in front of his face. "That second beep …" He thumbed the red button again while holding the phone to his ear. "It didn't disconnect. Son of a—"

The helicopter's rockets struck the car before they knew it was there. The force of the explosions killed the pair instantly, the shrapnel killed them a second time, and the ignited gas tank transformed the car's interior into a roiling inferno.

* * *

When notified of the rocket strike, the Mossad command post exploded with applause and backslaps. The director ordered all agents withdrawn and the preloaded ambulance dispatched to the scene.

"Case closed," he said as he stood to leave. "Call me as soon as Yogi and Boo-Boo get back with the scroll."

* * *

As planned, Michael and his entourage headed for Sister E's office to wait until evening, when they'd have the best chance of leaving undetected. The only hitch: they now had their two uninvited guests to keep alive as well.

As they settled in, Sister E jiggled cups in their saucers and strewed more sugar from the spoon than made it into the tea. Michael glanced at June, then rose from his seat, intending to assist with the tea and reassure the nun.

With the whisper of low wood on high rug, the door opened and two brutes in tracksuits entered sporting big guns and soulless ice-pick eyes. "Nobody a'move," the first man said.

Sister E dropped to her knees and her face paled. Falson, standing behind Michael with Dr. Mardle, placed a hand on Mardle's shoulder, as if to tether them together.

A deep, violaceous scar ran across the first intruder's right cheek, running from his ear to the corner of his mouth, drawing his lips into a permanent snarl and slurring his words. Nonetheless, the man's Italian accent was thick enough to override his speech impediment. He kept his gun on Michael while his partner, his jet-black hair streaked with silver at the temples, lifted Muhammad's shirt and removed the gun holstered in the small of his back. Silver Streak pushed first Muhammad, then Michael back into chairs. As he sat, Michael felt the metallic chill of a pistol behind his ear.

The first intruder tapped Michael's temple, and then trained his pistol on June, who had risen from her chair and stood facing them. "You move," he said to Michael, "I kill'a her quick." He stepped forward, drew her purse from her shoulder, removed Michael's automatic and threw the purse onto Sister E's desk.

The thug's disfigured expression was strangely immobile, as if he were brain-damaged. *One too many whacks to the noggin in the boxing ring?* Michael wondered, taking note of the man's cauliflower ear. His thoughts were interrupted when a third Italian sauntered through the doorway in the manner of a famous trial lawyer entering a courtroom, with one dissonant note: he waved a 9-millimeter Heckler & Koch in Michael's direction. "Dr. Hansen," he said, "you're too fast. One move, even a small one, and the woman dies and we shoot your legs out from under you."

Though clearly Italian too, this man's English was almost flawless. Nobody moved except for Sister E, whose skeletal hands shook from fright.

"Good," Trial Lawyer said, as though he had commanded the jury's attention and would now launch into his closing statement. "I'll give you one option, and one only. The gospel, or the woman in pieces."

Brain Damage slipped behind June, snaked an arm around her waist and pulled her close, keeping his gun on Michael. "But do'n worry," he said, and then sniffed her hair. "If we got to, we'll use'a her good before we ice her."

June slumped in his grasp and began to shake, and Brain Damage bent under her weight and nuzzled her hair. "Aw," he said with a leer, "do'n waste you energy. You need it for later."

Michael crouched, and Silver Streak leveled his gun upon him, blew a two-note whistle to get his attention, and then slowly shook his head while clucking a soft tsk-tsk-tsk. Dr. Mardle grabbed a handful of Michael's shirt from the back, roping himself and Terry Falson together with Michael like mountain climbers on a line.

Staring into Silver Streak's predatory eyes, Michael instantly understood the elderly professor's fear; he faced a man more accustomed to delivering death than merely threatening it. And from where Silver Streak stood, resting one hand on Muhammad's shoulder from behind, pinning him to his chair, he had everybody in the room covered.

With every muscle in Michael's body tight as cords, he glanced back at June and saw her clench her eyes and swallow, her head bobbing with the effort. The image of her terror-stricken face in the crawlspace came to him, and he feared she was on the verge of crumbling.

In the next second, her lids flew open as she twisted and slammed an elbow into Brain Damage's right eye. Michael let out a shout, but June was beyond hearing. The thug straightened in time for her to spin opposite and elbow-smash the other side of his face. His skin split and his head rebounded, but he dropped his gun to the rug and clamped both arms around her waist.

Michael stared as she reached over her shoulder, found Brain Damage's cauliflower ear, and tore. It ripped to a bloody flap, but Brain Damage only growled and tightened his grip, as if he'd grown up wrestling Tasmanian devils.

His body overriding his good sense, Michael tensed again, but so did Mardle's pull on his shirt. Silver Streak leveled his gun beside Muhammad's ear, trained the barrel at the center of Michael's chest, and thumbed back the hammer with a click. Michael's whole body started to shake, the weaker part of his brain commanding him to fight, the stronger part forbidding him.

Trial Lawyer stepped in front of June, braced his legs and backhanded her. She sprayed a bloody mist as her hair whipped around and encircled her face. Smiling, he looked down at Sister E from where he straddled the rug in front of June. "Spare the rod and spoil the child, eh, Sister?"

Brain Damage hoisted the slumped June in his arms, but the moment her head swung to center, Michael saw fire leap from her eyes. Straightening, she kicked a foot into Trial Lawyer's crotch, so hard it sounded like a fastball smacking a catcher's mitt. He buckled and turned left, his right hand pressed into his crotch, his face contorted in pain so great that he gagged.

When Brain Damage raised one hand to grasp at her flailing arms, she reached down to his lone arm encircling her waist. Grabbing two of his fingers in each of her fists, she tore them apart, splitting the webbing between them and popping knuckles from their sockets.

Brain Damage screamed and lost his grip as she spun an about-face, stabbed two long-nailed fingers up his nostrils and twisted.

Trial Lawyer quarter-turned away from her and bent over, tossed his gun butt-first into his other hand and coiled his arm backwards to strike. As he unwound and swung at June's head, Sister E jumped from the floor and screamed, "NO!"

The gun butt clipped the nun behind the ear and she pitched face-forward onto her office floor. A trickle of blood ran down the parchment-thin skin of her pale neck.

When Sister E yelled, June spun around, but Brain Damage wrapped both arms around her from behind and pinned her to him.

"Sister," Trial Lawyer moaned, "forgive me." Bent over and shuffling from his own injury, he helped the nun to a chair.

"Out," she said to him. *"Get. Out. Now."*

June looked into Michael's eyes, and he shook his head at her. "Turn it off."

"Out!" Sister E repeated, but Trial Lawyer gathered tissues from the box on her desk and held it to her scalp, then turned to Michael.

"The gospel," he said. "Or else. You have two hours to bring it back here. Now go. Your lady friend and the sister will stay with us."

Silver Streak nudged Muhammad's head with his gun, and he stood from his chair, Silver Streak's gun at his back.

Michael passed June, still vise-gripped in Brain Damage's arms, as he angled toward the door. Brain Damage stepped on the gun he'd dropped to the rug, and Michael noticed that both Silver Streak and Trial Lawyer followed him with their pistols. Brain Damage held on bravely, the bent rake of one hand horribly mangled, his face battered and bleeding from both nostrils, his torn ear hanging from his cheek on a tongue of bloody flesh.

To Trial Lawyer, Michael said, "Hit her again, and your guns won't be enough to keep me from killing you." Then, to June, "Turn it off. Turn it off and wait. I'll be back for you."

She nodded, but as he neared the door, he turned for one last look. June, still nodding, snapped her head back, directly into Brain Damage's face. His nose flattened with an explosion of clots and blood and he hurled June from him, snarling. Silver Streak caught her by one arm, spun her into a chair, pinned her down by both shoulders and leaned close, an understanding smile softening his features. "Signora, please. It serves no pur—"

Muhammad grabbed Michael by both shoulders of his T-shirt and pulled him out the door to the tune of June hawking and spitting in Silver Streak's face. Mardle and Falson followed as if leashed together, and when Michael turned and read their faces, he couldn't tell whether they hovered closer to strokes or heart attacks. For a moment, he considered turning back, but Sister E's office door slammed shut and he heard the click of a lock.

Muhammad threw his right arm over Michael's shoulder and led him off to the stairwell. "Did you see *that?*" he said. "That's no woman back there, that's an avenging angel. A one-woman army."

They halted in the stairwell, and Michael followed Muhammad's insistent nudge and sat down while the Palestinian stood over him. "Give me the mobile phones."

Michael looked up at him, mentally disconnected. "It's useless, Muhammad. I transferred my SIM card to—"

"Not yours. Theirs."

He gave him a blank stare.

"The cartoon bears. Yogi and Poo-Poo. Their phones, remember?"

He fished them from his pocket. "Forgot, sorry."

Muhammad disassembled both phones and threw the pieces down the stairwell with a clatter, saying, "Those could've killed us, if Mossad thought to trace them." Then he gave Mardle and Falson instructions, and they split up and left the convent in pairs.

Muhammad's precaution wasn't needed, although neither of them knew it at that moment. Mossad's surveillance curtain had already been withdrawn.

* * *

The foursome regrouped at a nearby café, and arrived back at Muhammad's house three labyrinthine taxi trades later. Michael ran inside, yanked the second gun from his stampeding pack, grabbed the scroll jar and contents and turned for the door.

"Stop," Muhammad said. "We need a minute here."

But Michael's passions were driving frenzied at the controls, and Muhammad had to bury a fist in his gut to slow him. He doubled over and slid down the wall to the floor, clutching his stomach, while Falson and Mardle cowered in a corner of the room.

"Michael, go to the bathroom," he said.

"Muhammad, I—"

"Go to the bathroom."

He looked up and blinked at Muhammad, trying to figure what type of metal or rock the man's fist was made of. Past the half-century mark at minimum, and the Palestinian had belted him with a punch he hadn't even seen coming.

"Look," Muhammad said, "you want to run back, blasting away, with the odds three against one? Now, go to the bathroom."

"I ... don't understand—"

"An old soldier's trick. It forces you to calm down. You can only rush things so much in a bathroom. In addition to which, you might get into the thick of things and suddenly, oh my, you need to go. Don't embarrass me, okay?"

Michael went to the bathroom to satisfy Muhammad, but found himself stopping to check his face in the mirror and talk sense into himself.

He walked out a different man ... and into a different room. The sight that confronted him made so little sense he felt suddenly dizzy. Terry Falson stood blocking the room's doorway, scroll jar under one arm, gun in his free hand, covering Mardle and Muhammad where Michael had left them, only both were now sitting on the floor. The incongruous tittering of women's laughter came from the kitchen, behind the wall that separated the rooms.

"Join your buddies," Falson said, and motioned with the gun. "Sit."

Michael's felt his temples tighten as he stared at his gun in Falson's hand, June's ransom cradled in his other arm like an elongated football. "Dr. Falson," he heard himself say as if from a distance, "what are you doing?"

"I'm sorry about this." And Falson did, indeed, look sorry. Yet determined. "When I saw the gospel slip through our fingers, I couldn't take it. I can't lose it a second time."

With a strenuous grunt, Mardle got up from the floor, looking for the first time every bit his eighty years.

"Sit down," Falson commanded, but Mardle ratcheted himself upright.

"My back hurts," Mardle said with annoyance, stretching himself to his full height. "And don't be an idiot, my boy. What do you think you're going to do, kill us all?"

"If I have to."

Michael looked into Falson's eyes, and believed him.

"This is bigger than one person," Falson said. "Bigger than a million people. This is about the salvation of humankind!"

"You're right," Mardle said, and took a feeble step forward. "This *is* bigger than one person. But the fact is, all you've ever cared about is one person, and that person is *you*. You bugged my office to steal my research, and now you're threatening murder for a gospel that commands 'Thou shalt not kill'?"

Falson's face grew bitter. "Don't lecture me on ethics, *Trevor*. You're the one selling secrets to the CIA. If it weren't for your tattle-telling, Frank Tones and his daughter might still be alive."

Michael's head jerked as if he'd been slapped, but Mardle kept his gaze on Falson. "Frank and Rachael meant more to me than anybody ever meant to you, Terry. You think you can kill us and just … what? Go back and hand over the scroll to whomever you deem worthy? There will be questions. Like why we left the country together, but you came back alone. How I was killed. How the gospel came to be in your possession. What dig will you say you were on when you found *this* scroll, Terry?"

Mardle took another step forward. Falson's only response was to retreat into the doorway. But the old man ran out of luck when he lunged for the jar. Falson's pistol coughed a pencil tip of flame and whispered a metallic *cha-chink* as the slide chambered another round.

Mardle collapsed in a heap on the floor at the same instant Muhammad jumped up in a crouch and leapt forward in what Michael could only reckon as a suicide bid. Falson swung the gun in the Palestinian's direction, but instead of the silencer's cough, the air hummed with a vibrant clang.

Falson pitched forward, his unruly red hair framed in a black circle as all expression slid from his face. Jellyfish-limp, he fell unconscious into Muhammad's arms. The black circle, at the end of a slender arm, disappeared back into the adjoining room as quickly as it had appeared.

Muhammad dropped Falson to the ground none too gently and turned. "You see," he said, arms spread wide and face beaming, "I told you my wife works wonders with a frying pan!"

CHAPTER 34

Michael knelt beside Mardle and ripped the fallen man's shirt open, buttons popping in all directions, grabbed the bloody T-shirt at the neck and tore it down the middle. Muhammad broke a tissue box in half and pressed its contents on the dime-sized wound in the center of Mardle's chest, but blood filled the stack of tissues and ran down the gutters between his naked ribs. Michael didn't want to think about what the exit wound must look like, didn't want to consider what a bullet could do to an eighty-year-old's heart and lungs. He forced himself to meet the elderly professor's gaze and said, "Not pulsing. That's a good sign. We'll get you to a hospital."

He tried to stand, but Mardle grabbed his sleeve and yanked him back down.

"No." His eyes were clear and his grip strong, but bloody spittle ran from his lips as he spoke. "No time. You know it."

Michael raised his eyes from Mardle's face. "Muhammad, call an ambul—"

"No." Mardle reached for Muhammad with his other hand. "Please. Help me die better than I lived. Hear me out."

Michael started to get up from the floor. "There's still a chance if we get you—"

"Listen." Mardle tightened his grip on his sleeve. "It was me. I'm sorry, but … it was me. The CIA wanted informants. I needed money. Couldn't imagine any harm. But then Frank was killed."

Unbidden, Michael's legs dropped him back to the floor. "You? I thought your office was bugged."

"It was, but … that was later." Mardle turned his head and nodded to Falson's still form in the doorway. "He did it. To advance his career. Scooped some of my research." When Mardle turned to face Michael again, his eyes held tears, but desperation to get his story out had strengthened his voice. "Forgive me. I was trapped. When Frank was killed, I thought the CIA did it. And that made me an accessory to murder. How could I have known he'd be killed over his find?"

"You were friends, Dr. Mardle."

"*Best* friends." He heaved and coughed, a liquid rattle. Blood spurted from beneath Muhammad's hands on the pressure patch, and Michael looked up and locked eyes with his host. They both looked down when Mardle continued.

"When Frank found Jacob's scroll, his graduate student told me on the sly. Remember dinner that night? When you arrived at the dig? Frank's tantrum?"

Michael managed a nod. "I thought it was something personal. An insult, perhaps."

Mardle shook his head, placed his hand over Muhammad's on his chest and winced. "When your father arrived, I realized Frank intended to partner with him. On his find. But I wanted it … for myself. So I told Frank I knew about the scroll. That he had to partner with *me*."

Michael, his voice a near-whisper, said, "When we came back to the table, you said … you said 'Check,' and he exploded."

Calm came over Mardle's face, and his grip on Michael's sleeve relaxed. "Chess-speak. I had him cornered. If he didn't partner with me, I could've … *would've* gone to the press. Checkmate." A weak smile. "Frank never did take losing well."

Michael grabbed a floor cushion and tore the stuffing out of it, then handed the stuffing to Muhammad, who replaced the blood-soaked tissues. As he worked, he said, "So you blackmailed Frank Tones into partnering with you. But someone killed him and stole the ending to Jacob's scroll, instead."

Mardle nodded, and seemed to gain strength. "The CIA let me believe they'd killed Frank. Used it as a threat. Told me they … they would *expose my involvement* if I didn't continue working for them.

When Rachael came along, they promised to leave her alone—I *made* them promise. But after I kept tabs on her for them ... she was killed just the same. When they told me they had nothing to do with her murder ... then, I knew there was a leak somewhere ... in their organization. *That* leak led to the murders. And to me being followed when I left Rybkoski's dig."

"Falson," Michael said, his voice gentle. "Where does he fit into this?"

Mardle smiled. "Michael, my boy ... strange ... I don't feel a thing. I feel ... warm."

Michael glanced from Mardle to Muhammad, who clenched his jaw and leaned harder into the pressure patch.

"Don't," Mardle gasped, and raised his hand. "Can't breathe."

Muhammad leaned back, and Mardle's chest rose as he dropped his hand back down to his side.

"Falson?" Mardle said through pale lips streaked with blood. "Terry didn't learn about my work ... about the CIA ... until years later. When he bugged my office, heard me talking with Rachael, then the CIA. When she was killed, he ... connected things. That my informing had led to her father's murder ... and then hers."

And maybe my father's as well. "And then, two years later," Michael said, "Falson overheard my conversations with you—"

"And was torn between exposing my ... duplicity, and seeing the project fulfilled."

Mardle's lips bleached from pale to white, and his breathing quickened. "After your last call, he ... he stopped me from informing the CIA. He was afraid history might repeat itself, with you ... as the victim."

Michael groaned. *"That's* why the CIA didn't show up at the Church of the Nativity." *And why Mossad demanded authentication of the gospel. The message that I was going to sell it to them never got through.*

Mardle's eyes flickered in Falson's direction as he took a tortured breath. "His conscience won the day in England, but ... he threw his morals out the window, didn't he? When he saw a chance to have the gospel for himself. To get all the credit ..."

"Stuffing," Muhammad murmured.

Michael ripped more stuffing from the cushion and asked, "How did Frank Tones keep the ring secret?"

Muhammad changed the pressure patch and Mardle heaved, a sucking sound escaping from his wound. "Don't know," he said between gasps. "Perhaps ... his assistant never knew. Frank had ... palmed jewelry before. Remember? The pharaoh's necklace?"

Mardle raised one arm and craned his neck forward. For a moment, he stared at the web of blood trails on his chest. A look of profound sadness washed over his face, then his head dropped to the floor with a thump, his arm fell to the swamp of bloody rug by his side with a wet slap, and he lay still.

Minutes passed, yet neither of them moved. Eventually, Michael nodded sideways to where Falson lay. "What'll we do with him?"

Muhammad opened his mouth, but closed it and studied Falson for a moment. "He's not breathing."

"That's a bad thing?"

Muhammad shuffled over to Falson's side and placed a hand on his chest. "I'm serious."

"And what makes you think I'm not?"

"Do you know CPR?"

Michael stood, strode over, and knelt down. "Even if I did," he sighed, "my heart's not in it."

Muhammad felt Falson's wrist and sighed. "Neither is his." He prodded the back of Falson's skull, and then guided Michael's hand to a depression in the bone, which crackled like dry leaves when pressed. "They say cast-iron cookware is good for the health. I'm not so sure."

Michael sat back and leaned against a wall, one knee bent. "What do we do now?"

Muhammad stood slowly and took out his phone. "One of my friends might know someone who can clean this up."

"Do you have film? Or a digital camera?"

Muhammad paused, cell phone in hand, and raised his eyebrows. "Both."

Michael pushed himself from the wall and stood. "Got an idea."

The doorbell rang, and both of them jumped. Michael followed Muhammad to the front door, feeling as though his entire body was coiled like the proverbial spring.

* * *

Hamid had taken a circuitous route after ditching the car and now, much to the consternation of the women of the family, took the garbage in, rather than out.

As the two Palestinians huddled over plans, Michael searched Mardle and Falson for their passports and, holding them in the folds of a tissue, dipped them in the pool of blood on Mardle's chest. Then he wiped his photographs clean of fingerprints, and methodically bloodied each one's back before placing it on the counter to dry. He started with Frank Tones' pictures of Jacob's intact scroll, and ended with the photos he'd taken of the gospel of James two days before. Lastly, he snapped digital and plain-film photos while Muhammad and Hamid held the gospel of James spread open beside Mardle's dead body. As an afterthought, he wiped down the gun and returned it to Falson's side.

He waited in the house while Muhammad went out to make arrangements. Fifteen minutes later, a pair of Palestinians arrived with a furniture truck, but not Muhammad. Within minutes they'd rolled up the carpet, gun, bodies and all inside it, and bundled it off with such routine proficiency, they appeared bored.

After another five minutes of pacing the bare concrete floor, Michael felt ready to explode. "Where's Muhammad?" he asked in Arabic.

Hamid waved at the door. "He can move inside Bethlehem, you can't."

Michael stopped pacing and faced him. "What?"

The Palestinian rose from scrubbing the bloodstained floor and stepped between Michael and the door. "He's getting Ms. Cody. He said if you try to do it yourself, either Mossad will identify you and take you out, or maybe you'll do something stupid and get *everybody* killed."

Michael glanced into the corner, saw the empty space where the scroll jar had stood, and took a step toward the door. Hamid stopped him with a hand on his chest. "See?" he said. "You're thinking Rambo-crazy. How will you get there and back without being spotted? With your American face? Just stepping out the door is a risk."

Thirty minutes later Muhammad returned, minus the gospel but with a second "wife," covered head-to-toe in black. June tore the veil from her face, flew into Michael's arms, and just as quickly flew back out.

"Did you see that? Did you *see*?" she said, and stirred the air with a gleeful flurry of fists, her feet dancing in place. A smile the size of a half-moon on her face, she raised one hand and jiggled the broken tip of a fingernail in front of his eyes, her excitement lifting her to the tips of her toes. "A month from now, that goon'll blow my fingernail out his nose and curse my memory!"

Muhammad exploded in laughter, bent at the waist, and had to lean against the doorframe for support. "You," he gasped between laughs. "Michael, you ... you should have seen it." He broke into another guffaw and had to sink to a squat. "They ... they practically *threw* her at me. Another five minutes ... another five minutes, and maybe they would've *paid* me to take her. Tough guys? Ha!"

June beamed at him as if he'd paid her the highest praise, and turned back to Michael as if expecting a prize.

He put his hands on her shoulders, his arms straight, and realized the psychologist inside her could read volumes from that gesture. On one hand, he held her at arms' length; on the other, he never wanted to let go. Her lip was split and her cheek bruised from Trial Lawyer's blow, but she was the most beautiful thing he'd ever seen. He blinked, and the shutters of his eyes captured her elation in a mental photograph. *The woman who took a blow that would have felled most men, and yet bounced back to terrorize a roomful of brutes.* He hated the words that would destroy the moment, but had to say them.

"Mardle and Falson ... they're dead."

She stilled and searched his face, turned and found Muhammad suddenly quiet, and glanced around the room. Her eyes settled on the faint bloodstain at Hamid's feet, the bristle brush in his hand dripping pink suds into the bucket.

"What ... What happened?"

"It was their time," Muhammad said as he straightened and stood. "Their sins caught up with them."

CHAPTER 35

Prime Minister Leib rubbed his eyes with his fists. Ten million dollars and the diamond gone, the scroll and two of Mossad's best agents up in smoke, and now he had the murder of two other Western academics, internationally respected archaeologists no less, to explain. Make it four, and someone, somewhere, would yell "Foul!"

And the workday had barely started.

Leib closed the file and handed it to his aide. "Cancel all standing orders, deactivate the case, and get my morning coffee." He pulled the next brief from the stack and threw the cover open. He was into his second cup when the director of Mossad strolled in. Leib motioned him to sit, and the first thing the man did was light up a cigarette.

Leib gritted his teeth and stared at his desktop. "The radiocarbon result from the parchment fragment submitted by Dr. Mumtaz read '35–55 CE.' Which means the scroll was authentic. Priceless to us. Our two agents were killed and the scroll destroyed because of your rocket order."

The director bent his head to his lap. "Nobody will miss them more than me."

Leib raised his eyes from his desk. "You made a rocket order without my approval."

The director snapped his head back, lowered his cigarette hand to the chair's armrest. "I told you about—"

"You made a rocket order *after* I specified that any termination order was conditional upon my approval."

"You already approved termination. I only—"

"No exceptions, no excuses."

The director's face stilled, the furrows on his brow leveled out and disappeared. He leaned back in his chair. "Let me guess. You aren't man enough to share the blame, so you're throwing it all on me."

Leib lifted a pen and drummed his desktop. "Why haven't you cancelled the termination orders and deactivated the case, as per my instructions twenty minutes ago?"

The director waved his hand. "I wasn't in my office."

"I heard differently. That you walked out the moment my instructions hit your desk. You're stalling."

The director stood and pointed his cigarette at Leib. "Two of our best men are dead because of *them*, another two in the hospital. You're damn right I'm stalling. I'll stall until I see their bloody corpses gutted on an autopsy table."

"Or until you're relieved of your position."

The director straightened, quarter-turned his head and looked at Leib through narrowed eyelids. "You wouldn't dare."

"I already have. Effective five minutes ago."

Two guards entered the room, and Leib pointed at them. "These gentlemen will escort you to your car. We'll send your belongings to your home. Like I said, I need you under control. You're not. Give me a resignation letter and I'll accept it. For old time's sake."

Leib pushed himself from his chair and strode to the door, stepped through the doorway and disappeared.

The director stood for a moment and then let out a sigh. He raised his cigarette to his lips, and the only sound in the room was the sizzle as his long drag stoked the tip orange. He reached to stub it out in the chair-side ashtray, but stopped, took another strong pull, and then flicked the butt to the rug. Smiling at the guards, he ground it into the carpet with his foot, then sauntered past them and out the door.

* * *

Michael was eating breakfast when Muhammad dropped the morning newspaper on the living room floor beside him. He unfolded it and read while Muhammad lowered himself to the floor and dug in, scooping humus into a fold of bread.

"Hey, here's some news," Michael said, and began reading. "'Three Hamas operatives were killed yesterday in a helicopter attack of surgical precision. This closes the books on Walid Hussain, the object of a nationwide manhunt for the past four months. His two compatriots were burned beyond recognition, but identity will be sought through DNA and dental records,' blah, blah, blah." Michael looked up. "That explains Yogi and Boo-Boo. But who's Walid?"

Muhammad signaled pause while he finished chewing his mouthful. "He was killed six weeks ago in a rocket attack in Gaza. Sometimes the Israelis save the bodies for later, to distort events to the media. Read page three."

Michael turned a page, and his face darkened. "'The bodies of two prominent, internationally respected archaeologists were discovered last night beside a deserted section of road outside Bethlehem, apparent victims of a brutal double murder. Evidence suggests they were robbed and ...'" He read the rest in silence, then folded the paper and threw it aside. "Why are the Israelis still looking for June and me?"

"Don't know. Neither do my contacts. Maybe ..." His mobile phone rang. A few minutes of conversation, and he clicked off and said, "Good news. The heat is off. The Israelis want their money back, but the police have orders not to detain you beyond a body-and-bag search." He gave a bitter smile. "Perhaps someone is concerned about Israel's image if another Western professor is hassled or harmed."

Michael considered the news. "So we can leave?"

Muhammad jerked a thumb at his phone on the floor beside him, and spoke around a mouthful of egg and white cheese. "According to him, no problem. Just expect to be searched."

A moment later, he swallowed and sat back. "How about if you and Miss Cody fly to Egypt? First class, of course. Just to, how do you say? Just to pick your noses at Mossad?"

Michael winced. "*Thumb* our noses. Just to *thumb* our noses at Mossad."

"In any case, first class, on their money. I'll send the rest to you across the border through one of the tunnels at Rafah."

"The smuggler's tunnels? The ones Israel's always trying to close?"

A shrug. "That's the only way you'll get your money out of Israel."

"Half the money. We want you and Hamid to split the other half."

Muhammad paused only briefly, then motioned to the floor-spread. "Eat up. This is the most expensive meal of your life."

"One other thing." Michael held up the digital camera. "You know a hacker who can put these photos online? Untraceable?"

He nodded slowly. "Not here. In Jordan."

Michael nudged a manila envelope toward him with the edge of his hand. "First, send this. Overnight express. Make sure it's untraceable, and don't get any fingerprints on it."

Muhammad bent his neck and read the address line. "Grace … Sickarney?"

"One of England's most celebrated journalists. The envelope contains the photos and passports, including the roll of film we took of the scroll next to Mardle's body. Not to mention an anonymous letter explaining everything." He held up the digital camera and said. "After Ms. Sickarney breaks the story, put these photos on the Internet."

"Two days?"

Michael shrugged. "Watch the news. If the pictures of Mardle's body don't convince her to publish immediately, that means she's taking time to DNA-match the blood on the photos. That's why you've got to send this by express mail. I need her to receive it before Mardle's body is shipped back and buried. Whether through Grace Sickarney or pictures on the Internet, I want the whole world to have James' gospel."

CHAPTER 36

"D aniel and the lions," June said when they exited the customs area at Boston's Logan International Airport two days later, dragging their carryon bags. "First the policeman in the hotel men's room, then the baggage x-ray in Egypt, now customs in America. What's going on? Is *everyone* blind to us? Because if they are, we can have some serious fun with this."

Michael stopped walking. "News broke."

She followed him to a television in the waiting area. The screen was filled with a photograph of the scroll that proclaimed the gospel of James, Jesus' brother. Trevor Mardle's body was in a background frame, but heavily pixilated. The anchor's face took over the screen while he summarized the anonymous letter received. That was followed by photographs of Jacob's scroll, the gospel again, and the identical seals of the two scrolls transposed side by side. A crawl at the bottom announced a weekend documentary titled *Facts of Faith*, then the screen switched to a riot in France.

"So much for being unable to authenticate photographs," June muttered.

"They're authenticated, all right. By Mardle's blood." Michael turned from the television and they headed for the terminal exit. "As for the gospel? It's like the parables in the Bible. Those whom God intends to guide will believe. As for the rest?" He shrugged, an empty hand in the air.

Half an hour later, they entered his house in Cambridge and parked their cash-stuffed carryons by the living room sofa.

"The kid next door said he'd check on these two before we got back," Michael said, motioning to his pets. "Guess he forgot."

June stepped to the middle of the room to survey the damage.

Arnold circled her with an appreciative "Woof," then cocked his head at Michael as if to ask, *She joining our pack?*

"I'm not sure a dog and a cat could have, uh, accomplished all of this," June said. She dragged a finger along the top of the television, flicked the dust-dunes off her fingertip, and then scanned the misaligned furniture, empty soda cans, plastic shells of microwave dinners, old pizza boxes and crumpled takeout bags. "Now I know how Jane Powell felt in *Seven Brides for Seven Brothers*."

"I don't have any brothers," Michael said.

"And you won't have any bride, either, if you keep this up."

"Well, like I told you, when I left, I wasn't expecting a *House Beautiful* photo shoot when I got back."

He marched to the answering machine and punched playback.

"You're not going to check messages now, are you?"

"*Habeebatee,* I've just *got* to hear that Barney song."

"Michael, it's the voice of a dead man." She squatted to Arnold's level and grasped his massive head in her hands. "Who's taking care of you, beautiful?"

"Like I said, the kid next door. When he remembers, that is. Name's Arnold."

"The kid?"

Michael pointed. Arnold closed his eyes and growled an ecstatic dog-moan as she scratched behind both his ears. "Arnold. The furry blob that just gave you his heart."

It took four skipped messages to find it, but when he did, they listened in silence while the message played, "... won't you say you love me too?"

Michael's grin vanished. "And they would've killed us, if they'd gotten the chance."

He reached to shut off the machine, but stopped when Yogi's voice continued. The recording finished, the machine beeped, and his world went first gray, then black. As he went rigid, so did Arnold. But the warning rumble in the beast's chest faded from Michael's ears as rage overcame him.

And then ... nothing.

A blanket wrapped its arms around him from behind, its warmth filling his back and climbing his spine until the flush invaded his neck and face.

"It's all right, it's over," her voice whispered. "It's over. Wherever you've gone, come back. Michael, darling, come back."

Her arms tightened, his muscles uncoiled, and he hung his head in her embrace.

"So I was right," he muttered, "I did recognize that guy. And Dad was murdered after all." When he could bear to, he gently pulled away from her and turned around, saying, "I have something for you."

He grabbed his stampeding pack from the sofa and dug through bundles of hundred-dollar bills until he found a walnut-sized chunk of crystal, the shape and color of rock candy.

"Michael?" she said as he dropped it into her hand.

"Courtesy of Mossad. A bit heavy for a ring, but if we get you a trainer, start you on some barbell curls ..."

"You have *got* to be kidding!" she cried, and held the diamond up to the light. "Quick, where's some glass I can cut?"

"Uh, kitchen. In there."

She flew out of the room and left him spinning in her vapor trail. Chuckling, he reached to close his bag. A shriek from the kitchen wiped the smile from his face and his bag hit the floor with him running.

June stood next to a cabinet, a glass in one hand and the diamond in the other, eyes focused beyond both with an ecstatic expression on her face.

"Wh ... What is it?"

When she didn't reply, he stepped to her side and followed her gaze up the ladder of shelves, to the two-year-old gift boxes of Cadbury chocolates.

"Oh, Michael, I knew we had chemistry but ... Cadbury *Roses*. Don't you just love them?"

He swallowed hard. "Well, you know. I mean, who doesn't love

Cadbury's." Then he glanced around the room, as if searching to see how much more ridiculousness he could find. "Umm, June, darling, you're holding a rough diamond a smidgen smaller than a golf ball, and you're screaming over a box of chocolates. Sorry, but something has to be said."

She laughed, gave a girly toss of her head that grabbed his heart by both ends and wrung it dry, and then lifted the glass and ran her finger down the fresh gouge on its side. "Don'tcha think a *cut* diamond would've been more practical?"

"Cut diamonds can be traced. Yeesh, didn't you see *Reservoir Dogs?*"

Their eyes met, and his mind spun into a tight power-dive. "Um, look, June, you know my history. You die, you take me with you. Deal?"

She tilted her head Arnold-like, but kept her eyes on him. "Is that your way of asking me to marry you? Because that's not how it usually goes. Heroes usually jump from one conquest to another, and leave a grieving throng of discarded bimbos in their wake."

"Yeah, well. There's only one bimbo I'm interested in. Now, what ... oh, ouch. See, you *can* hit me. Now, what are we going to do about a priest?"

She leaned against the counter and rolled the diamond from one palm to the other. "Beats me. Where will we find a priest who represents our beliefs?"

Her eyes traveled over his shoulder, and she nodded. "On the other hand, have you ever read *that*, or is it just for display?"

He half turned, knowing what his eyes would find: the second of the two gifts from the Sudanese driver, Mahmood, seventeen years earlier. The one he'd given Michael to remember him by. The one that had sparked his first interest in comparative religion. The one he now kept on display in a bookholder, high and centered in the bookcase opposite. He gazed at the antique copy of the Holy Qur'an, handwritten in the highest calligraphy, a jumble of memories playing through his mind. His mother's voice echoed faintly in his head. *I was dead and now I'm alive. Michael, dearest, come to life.*

With a blink, he was back, seeing more clearly than ever before.

The telephone started to ring. He ignored it. "June, darling, we've got to talk."

He led her back to the living room, ignoring the telephone's cries for attention.

The answering machine picked up on the fourth ring and a drill sergeant's voice said, "Dr. Michael Hansen? Grace Sickarney, BBC Foreign Affairs Desk, calling from London."

He went rigid. *How could she possibly have—?*

June swept an errant stand of hair from widened eyes and moved to his side.

"I'm following up on a story about a newly discovered scroll, purported to be the gospel of James, that supports the, quote, Reality of God and True to Jesus theology you've popularized through your books."

He leaned against the wall, rolled his eyes at June, wiped his forehead with the back of his hand and shook imaginary sweat from his fingertips. "Whew. Thought I'd been found out."

"Dr. Hansen," the voice continued, "please get back to me ASAP. This new gospel could blow the top off time-honored Jewish and Christian beliefs, and at the same time change the way the world views Islam. With your expertise, you're the perfect person to spearhead a team of experts in a roundtable discussion. But this is breaking news, and we're talking first available flight to London, limo to our studios, and piece-to-camera before you hear the first strike from Big Ben."

She left her contact details and hung up, and before Michael could pick up the phone to return the call, it rang again, this time from CNN. After the fourth call from a major news agency, the doorbell rang. June followed him to the window, and together, they parted the drapes on a mob of cameramen and journalists flooding the front lawn.

"Gee," June said as she yanked the drapes closed, "you *sure* you don't have a throng of grieving bimbos out there somewhere?"

* * *

"Read the report to me, if you don't mind." It was late evening and the Pope had taken to his bedchamber. His request bore the nasal twang of a head cold.

Cardinal Giuseppi Venier pulled his gaze from the document in his hands and looked toward where the Pope sat at an antique writing desk, his nose nestled in a linen kerchief. "You've had a long day and you're not well, Your Holiness. Perhaps you should rest."

"After this. Please, read."

Venier hesitated, then obeyed. "Analysis of scroll received in the diplomatic pouch from the Italian embassy in Tel Aviv. Specimen is an unusually well-preserved parchment scroll bearing text in Aramaic, with dimensions measuring—"

"Have mercy on me, Giuseppi. Just the summary. I'm fading here."

"Right. The summary." Venier flipped pages and read, "'Document deemed authentic, dated to 40–60 CE and authored by the disciple James. Contents are consistent with the teachings of Jesus and the views of the Apostolic Fathers, but contrary to those of Paul, who is condemned in the strongest of terms and identified as a liar and a corrupter of the Jesus' teachings …. Jesus is identified as …'"

Venier's voice faded to silence. He looked up from the document and mumbled, "Your Holiness, I—"

"Continue, please."

The cardinal cleared his throat. "'Jesus is identified as a man and a prophet but … nothing more.'"

The Pope groaned and shifted in his seat, muttering under his breath.

Venier glanced between the document and the Pope. "Are you certain you're all right?"

The Pope waved the concern away and motioned to continue. Venier resumed reading, flicking a nervous glance at the pontiff every few seconds.

"'Emphasis is placed upon Jesus Christ having taught the unity of God, and having predicted a final prophet to follow. The crucifixion is denied outright. Hence the content, authored by a true disciple and the most reliable witness yet discovered, is contrary to Trinitarian theology and ... and negates the canon of the Roman Catholic Church.'"

The Pope rose unsteadily from his chair and shuffled toward his bed. "Yes, well, nothing new then, is there?"

Venier nodded. "Nothing we don't already know."

The Pope gestured to a small wall-mounted safe, its door ajar and waiting: the most secure of repositories in the most private of bedchambers. "Put it with the others."

Venier swung the fireproof door open, glanced at the three scrolls within, two labeled "James" and the third labeled "Injeel of Jesus." He paused, choosing his words, then said, "Excuse me, Your Holiness, but you've seen the news reports. How will we handle the accusations?"

The Pope sat on the edge of his bed and tapped his forehead. "Denial, my friend. Denial. It's worked for two thousand years, it'll work for a few thousand more."

Venier placed the new gospel among the others, then asked, "These scrolls ... if the truth ever gets out, they could bring ruin to the Church. Shouldn't we ... destroy them?"

The Pope slipped between clean white sheets and let his head sink into the pillow. "Destroy them? That, my son, would be sacrilege. Put out the lights as you go."

And with that, and a sniffle, he drew the covers over his head.

LOOK FOR THESE CAPTIVATING WORKS OF NON-FICTION
BY DR. LAURENCE B. BROWN

MisGod'ed: A Roadmap of Guidance and Misguidance Within the Abrahamic Religions

God'ed?

Bearing True Witness

Made in the USA
Lexington, KY
02 November 2011